D0712777

The Spiral Code

The Spiral Code

JAMES EDWARD KAUNE

To Jo Ellen and John
May your journey on the
Path of life be successful
and happy

James E. Kaune

VANTAGE PRESS

New York

Cover design by Victor Mingovits

Cover design by Victor Mingovits

Vantage Press and the Vantage Press colophon
are registered trademarks of Vantage Press, Inc.

FIRST EDITION

Copyright © 2012 by James Edward Kaune
Published by Vantage Press, Inc.
419 Park Ave. South, New York, NY 10016
Manufactured in the United States of America
ISBN: 978-0533-164899
Library of Congress Catalog Card No: 2011909427
0 9 8 7 6 5 4 3 2 1

Dedication

This book is dedicated to my wife for her patience, support and understanding, and to my family who all encouraged me to continue my work.

CONTENTS

Prologue   ix
Introduction   xi

Chapter 1
The Rugged, Blood-Covered Mountain   1

Chapter 2
Welcome to Atlantis   25

Chapter 3
Life with Ashley Anne   88

Chapter 4
Closing the Circle   169

Chapter 5
The Counterattack   237

Chapter 6
Storm Clouds: Dark Side Attacks   292

Chapter 7
The Final Battle: Birth of Mythology   343

PROLOGUE

Life is a precious gift that has been given to each one of us. Our living pathway is defined by a three-dimensional spiral with one end so small it is called zero and the other end so vast it is called infinity. All of us are on a journey through this pathway.

Our location on this spiral is determined by our past and present experiences, the people, past and present that have influenced us, and our reactions to our abilities to achieve fulfillment of purpose through the process of cause and effect. This is commonly called karma. Our future will be determined by our reactions to all of these experiences.

I feel that I should tell the following stories that filled my mind as I saw death and experienced the laws of nature at work while I was fighting, as a warrior, with many others, in a very nasty war.

I saw clearly that cause and effect prevail in our lives as each one of us creates karma, so to speak, with every thought and action we make.

INTRODUCTION

This book will clarify the fact that one's daily actions determine the direction, upward or downward, that he or she travels that day in the 3D Spiral Code of Life that surrounds all of us.

Destiny and fate are things that each of us will experience. Do we have any control over either one of them? Yes. We do by the decisions we make. These two parts of our life become intertwined with one another as we make our individual judgments and resolutions day by day.

We were all given birth under different circumstances and therefore we face different environments and different problems. Our reaction to these problems shapes our path of life.

We did not create ourselves. We were procreated. Who did create us? Surrounding us everywhere is creation in action. All living things, the active Earth itself, our sun, the galaxy and the universes are available for our view by our own observation and by observations and publications provided to us by our fellow human beings.

Therefore, it is obvious that there is a dynamic universal creation in progress. Who is in charge of it? We are not. There is a power that is. To simplify our communication let us call this power The Creator.

Since all processes have rules we must find these Laws of Nature and use them to survive.

We have clues to help us. First, we must think about the instincts and senses that are built into the human brain. For simplicity, let us call this part of the brain the source for human survival.

The survival instinct is vital for human beings to stay extant. It was given to us by the creative process. Our first communication with the outside world was to cry.

Sometimes we were slapped by the birth doctor to be sure we would learn to breathe. We cried because of pain. This was simple. We cried after birth to be fed because the stomach indicated that the feeding tube was gone! If we were not fed after birth by others around us we would not have survived.

Therefore, very early in our lives we learn that interaction and communication with our surroundings is a vital part of our growth and they remain so as long as we live.

Obviously, we tend to make alliances with others of our own kind for survival and most life-forms do.

What else does survival require? It requires an ability to reason, react and communicate with nature. This is often called a connective ability. This ability separates us from all other life. The unanswered question is when was mankind given this unique ability?

We should think about that significant question. If we were not important to the Creator why would He bother to create us and give us our instincts and uniqueness?

The answer is that each one of us is important to Him. He wants each one of us to survive and it seems that each one of us is placed in our particular situation to see how we will react. It should be noted that each one of our reactions has an impact on those around us as well as impacting our own life.

Our Creator wants us to communicate with Him as well as others. How do we communicate with Him if we do not know the rules? Some think that answers come from connecting with Him by using the brain's left parietal lobe through meditation.

Others say that our connection processes with Him have been written down for us by our elders, philosophers, teachers, religions, true thinkers and our compatriots. All of these sources have given us their views.

Maybe we need all of these outside and inside communications to help us relate with nature. As we consider what we see and meditate about it we react. Our resulting actions frame our life's path.

Let us think about another survival instinct. We do not want others to hurt us. Basically this requires that our actions do not involve harming others. The ones we harm or the ones who depend on those we damaged will eventually cripple us. We have violated a basic law and we must expect retribution one way or another.

Is this a basic rule? It could well be. Do not do evil things to other people!

Our senses tell us what is happening around us. There are many reactive instincts built into our brain. Each one in combination with thought and deliberation gives us a clue about how to deal with the occurrences we are having.

All contacts and our reaction to them have given us a learning bank that will shape our interpretations about life.

The bank consists of voice advice, written suggestions as well as instincts to help us do the right thing. We must evaluate each situation and its meaning before we react to it.

Our reaction to a circumstance is based mostly upon the reasoning, pondering and meditating that we have already done and stored in our minds. These stored concepts are very important. Why?

Sometimes our reaction to a situation must be made very, very quickly. We do not have time for deep thought. We have already stored in our minds those things that make sense to us, that have survived the test of time and are available!

We use this knowledge storehouse to make our decision. If we stored well the resolution will be the right one. It is not hard to conclude that all of our stored data is shaping our judgments and forming our basic code of living.

Successful results of our reaction to our inner thoughts seem to indicate that a soul resides within our brain that understands the difference between good, the right thing, and evil, the wrong thing. Some choose to ignore their inner feelings of right and wrong. They will follow a dark and disabling path.

Our Creator does not destroy this soul that is within the body. He has given each one of our souls a significant meaning and several unique personal talents. We can nourish our souls by using these natural gifts to support and benefit others or we can use them to injure others. Either way leaves its indelible mark within us and identifies who we are.

Therefore, by our own actions, we can move our soul upward on the three-dimensional spiral of life toward light or we can also move the soul downward if we do not. Logic would pick life and light.

If we choose the illogical and deceitful self-serving path of darkness often enough it will lead us to a second and final death.

A good analogy is that each day we make decisions. Each action taken is like throwing a stone into a pond at our feet. The stones make waves. These waves affect the entire pond.

Good pond waves help the light in this pond to shine and this will help those around the pond to see their path better. A bad wave diminishes the light and sight of others. Sometimes merely giving a smile and giving encouragement to others will uplift them and help them have a better day. A scowl is discouraging.

We must understand the point clearly that each decision we make during our daily life activities always has a direct impact upon those around us and affects our ability to accept the light energy that surrounds us.

The following stories were sent to my mind during my combat with the enemy and are woven into a cloth of life with vivid figures for us to view as we consider the above postulation.

The story figures become real and surreal in my mind as I was swept into combat during this manmade madness called the Korean War.

The Biblical symbol of war in the Book of Revelations is the Red Horseman, who is the second of the Apocalyptical Horsemen. He will eventually be replaced by two other horsemen. Apparently, in the future, all of these horsemen will and must be defeated by the forces that follow the code of life during a horrendous battle.

Obviously, we on Earth have yet to defeat the Red Horseman.

The following account covers two of the three stories that I feel that I must tell. I saw all of them during my periods of exceptionally high stress, feeling death nearby and feeling that my chance of survival was slim at best. I prayed. I lived.

This chronicle includes life experiences to this point as well as a story that begins after a colonization mission from another civilization has landed on Earth. The aim of this alien mission was to help the denizens of Earth progress and prosper.

This mission landed before a mighty flood covered the Earth and comes to its end shortly after the flood subsides.

The Spiral Code

CHAPTER 1

The Rugged, Blood-Covered Mountain

By peering over our ridge, I can see the Chinese and Korean soldiers regrouping to resume their methodical ascent toward us. We watch the enemy persistently and effectively advance up our mountainside. They leave their dead comrades behind them. Battlefields have a stench that one can never forget. A battlefield is truly Hell's inferno in microcosm.

We had just guided the gunfire of our off-shore ships and naval aircraft effectively. We had obliterated a host of soldiers in a North Korean and Chinese division. We also have disrupted their movement down the Korean Peninsula. We are proud of our work beyond the front lines of battle.

We have directed the gunfire of the USS Floyd B. Parks (DD 884), my ship, as well as others including our battleship's huge guns. The shells were all on target! A battleship round sounds like a freight train overhead and when it strikes it cuts a huge swath of destruction ahead of it.

Battleships are an extremely effective destroyer of enemy men and equipment.

Our high ground has served us well as a spotting location of the enemy troops and has also allowed us, by naval gunfire, to repulse several attacks of those trying to silence us. Communists benefit from limitless manpower and they will eventually succeed and overrun us. We simply cannot kill all of them.

I have been told that most soldiers think about their life experiences before facing this type of enemy onrush. If this is true I am no exception. I am thinking about bitter life lessons I learned before I left my home for boot camp in San Diego in hopes of helping us win World War II. I now find myself in another war. I do not know why I am remembering the past as the enemy rushes toward us but what I do know is that they will overrun us.

I had been a damn good boy scout and I was about to be awarded the distinctive award of Eagle Scout. All of the paperwork for my promotion had been submitted by my scoutmaster. It included a strong recommendation from the Indian Chief from the Pueblo. We used their land for training purposes and he called me White Scout. I was proud of that title!

After I received permission to use Indian land for our outings the Chief always told me to leave our campsite as if we never camped there. We always thought that we did but the Chief always reported back to the scoutmaster telling him exactly where we had camped. I do not know how he did it. My Dad would say, "The Chief was in our store today and he said that White Scout left his trail." He would then smile and say, "Never underestimate the inherent wisdom of people and never equate education with wisdom."

One day I was called into my scoutmaster's office. He was a stickler for the moral codes that scouts are bound to follow. He said, "Ed, I am asking that headquarters hold your promotion papers to Eagle Scout at this time." I was stunned.

He continued, "You have two problems. You do not have a swimming merit badge and even though you have more than enough merit badges you do need this one. You are frightened of the water and you have let fear rule you. You must turn this fear into faith and action."

He continued, "You have volunteered to serve in the Navy and in a few weeks you will be at boot camp. Sailors swim! I want to see how you do at boot camp before I reconsider your name for promotion."

He added, "However, there is another difficulty. This will be a tougher problem for you to overcome. You have not admitted to your father nor to the authorities in Santa Fe that you ran a group known as the Gang of Seven. I know it was done for self-preservation."

He continued, "Some very ugly things happened to you and nobody seemed to care or do anything about it. When you were attacked while going to a scout meeting at the Presbyterian church you overreacted and roughened up your opponents more than you should have and you and Al, your number two, severely defeated a gang of pick-up truck attackers. The latter has become legend."

He then admonished, "Your gang then proceeded to intimidate other gang leaders. Intimidation is not the mark of a good scout. By the way, your Dad knows and agrees with my decision."

His lecture continued, "Think about this while you are away and see if you have learned some very important life lesson by your gang idea of how to assure your personal and gang group safety. You might have eventually been arrested because of your actions."

He said, "Ed, calling on anger, the dark side, for strength is very dangerous and can become out of control. Your pride is another problem. Your group was formed for protection purposes only and we all know that to be true. No charges have ever been made against you. However, you must personally realize the danger and the negative influence from using dark side tactics. Gang attacks on society and gang dictatorial rule through fear is dangerous and it is not what scouting is about!"

He continues, "When you return and can convince me that you understand the danger of gang rule I will remove the hold."

His decision was one of the bitterest moments of my life but that was not the end of my problem.

The Boot Trainer in charge of my section solved one problem quickly for me. I had told him about my fear. He looked at me and said, "Sailor, I understand that you are having some problems swimming. I want you to go to the swim training area tomorrow. I want you to see Petty Officer Jones. He is the swimming champion of our Navy Team. He will give you special attention."

I saw Petty Officer Jones. He said, "I understand that you have a problem." I said, "Yes, Sir." He said, "I want you to go to that door (hatch) and go up the ladder (no navy person calls any series of steps anything but a ladder) and see Petty Officer Anderson." I did. There were a lot of steps to climb. When I got to the top Petty Officer Anderson said, "Sailor, step over to that spot and turn around. I will be right behind you." In seconds there was nothing but me, thin air and water below. I was in the area where they trained sailors to abandon a sinking ship. I survived sputtering but alive. I learned to swim.

My Navy Chief Petty Officer at boot camp, who was in charge of making men out of boys, was good. We learned to dislike him but we learned to respect him. I was selected to be a squad leader even though he made me feel like I knew very little about anything.

One day during our training period he called me into his office and said, "Sailor, do you remember telling me after you saw me saluting the 'guys with the gold stripes' that you wanted to be one of them so you could be a leader in the navy and make a difference while serving?" I said, "Yes, Sir!"

He added, "Do you remember what I said?" I replied, "Yes, Sir, you laughed so hard that tears came to your eyes and you said, 'You are so damn dumb you do not know that you are asking for a tremendous responsibility! Giving orders can save or lose the lives of many others. You must understand this quickly, Sailor, or I have not done my job. Now, I am really going to find out how dumb you are by recommending that you take a Fleet test so I can see if you have any brain in your head at all!'"

I took the test and time had passed. I still did not think that I knew much. Now, it was getting time for us to graduate from boot camp and get our orders.

I was called to the Chief's Office. I wondered what ship I would be ordered to board. He smiled. This was rare. He said, "That is correct, Sailor. The Fleet must be desperate. You passed the test and you will be getting orders to the Naval Academy Preparatory School Training Camp at Bainbridge, Maryland. Do you know where that is?" I replied, "No, Sir." He replied, "You damn well better find out! Now get out of here and don't get lost on your way out." I looked at him and said, "Chief, I will never forget you or the lessons you taught us. Thank God for leaders like you."

He smiled and said, "Get the hell out of here! Remember the rules of behavior and think of others. Your life and those around you will depend upon your actions."

That admonition hit me heavily after I discovered later that if I had just seen my scoutmaster during my brief navy leave periods he would have forwarded the papers.

I had let down my Indian Chief, my parents, my girl (who assumed that I had lost interest) and my group that fell apart when I left.

Pride, anger and the dark path had scored a victory. All who had worked with me during my boy scouting adventure would have felt pleasure and enjoyment, as I would have, instead of feeling disappointed, regretful and sad.

This incident also kindled the fact that fear is has not necessarily been a friend. In my mind I reviewed my actions. I had made excuses. I really had time to see my scoutmaster but I was never sure that I wanted to face him. Why not! I had made an egregious error! His lessons and my poor reactions burned into my mind.

The naval preparatory school was tough but thorough. I was selected to be a Fleet Appointed Plebe at the U.S. Naval Academy. I knew about the Academy Honor Code and I vowed that I would not violate it or my country.

I am now a raw Ensign in the Gunnery Department on the USS Floyd B. Parks with hull number DD 884 and the Skipper has given me this critical forward observer mission assignment on a one-time basis. CIA agents will be in the boat that takes us to the Korean shore. Because Spooks (CIA) are on our ship and involved in gaining intelligence data our work is considered to be Top Secret. No one was ever to know about their involvement. I still do not know what they really did during this forward observer mission.

The Parks, a destroyer, is part of an American armada operating off the Korean coast. We are one ship and a very small part of the destroyer forces that has surrounded the Korean peninsula during the whole campaign. The destroyers supported General MacArthur's breakout at Inchon Harbor and his return up the peninsula.

General MacArthur and his troops had reached the Chinese border but suffered a disastrous rout in late 1951. While he was driven down the peninsula he was determined to keep at least the southern portion of that battered country free. While being driven southward the Parks has been assigned to fight at Wonsan Harbor. Among other things, our job is to interdict hostile troops along the eastern coast and to pick up navy aircraft pilots who make emergency landings in our waters.

I am now viewing a death scene below me. I truly hate the smell of death in the air but I vow to take my fear and turn it into action! I do not know why but I began to wonder if an Eagle Scout has ever been awarded this honor posthumously. I feel sad about dying. I wonder how my Mom and Dad will take it. I hope that they are proud of me despite my shortcomings.

In moments, we will be in hand-to-hand combat. We could use some help. A little napalm behind their line of attack could obliterate enough Korean and Chinese to deter more attacks, but all aircraft had departed for their bases. Our mission plans did not anticipate this scenario.

Forward observers do not fight the enemy one-on-one. Our job is to check out the situation, direct gunfire, call for aircraft attacks, destroy targeted enemy positions and quickly depart. The basic plan of survival is to melt away into the hills. We cannot accomplish this feat while being surrounded by a ring of angry enemy soldiers! This is a cockamamie situation!

The official report of this incident will probably say that this navy bombardment action successfully achieved its mission.

How did a Bull Ensign ever get himself into this mess? Nothing I studied at the Naval Academy can answer this basic question. The tactical and strategic writings of Sun Tzu did not. We who fight and die here must refer to this as a U.N. police action. Why this euphemism? Soldiers and their families must bear the horrendous pain of war. I can only hope that the people of our country appreciate what we do.

I suspect that soldiers in other eras have wondered about this same sort of thing. I am sure that the great Roman warriors did. I don't know why I have such a fascination about the Roman Empire.

I can remember daydreaming about valiant centurions during a high school ancient history class. Our teacher was so very boring. She could put the most fervent student to sleep. She droned on and on, with a deep and sometimes cracking monotone voice, with no verve or panache.

Though well-educated and informed, her presentation failed to penetrate the mind or light the imagination unless, of course, one chose to take the path of daydreaming to escape. The hypnotic hum of words and dates were a perfect mantra for me. My mind would wander and I would imagine what it would be like to be a Roman soldier.

I pictured myself as a bold centurion facing impossible odds and conquering all-powerful foes. But I was not educated enough to realize that battle begets a scene so horrific that a participant never forgets watching death happening. There is an inexplicable atmosphere surrounding the dead and there is a basic shock that those who see it and are still alive feel. How could I really know? How can anybody who has not faced it?

Now that I realize that I am on a real field of death on this desolate mountain and I am feeling a temporary silence before being overrun the pain is unbearable. What will I be able to call myself after this attack? I can't call myself a dead hero because I am not. What is life after death like? What will I say to my Creator? Does He love me?

Has this basic navy mission, successfully completed, ended my life? I can clearly understand why forward observers do not live long.

The Skipper selected me because I am an assistant Gunnery Officer and I will be replaced by a senior reserve officer who is already on his way to the ship. In short, I am expendable.

I earned ribbons from my Academy days to prove my mettle as a marksman. I did not renew these medals that are about the only ones I know of that must be renewed and I will never enjoy shooting people.

As the enemy climbs the slopes toward our isolated outpost, I aim, fire and kill. There are too many of them for me to have any real effect.

Suddenly, a grenade explodes with deafening force. My buddy's body absorbs the shrapnel produced by the blast. His blood covers me as it splatters from his now lifeless corpse. My friend becomes an ally of another sort; he becomes a shield to hide me from the enemy. I am suffering from shock.

Semi-conscious and unable to move, I lay underneath him. The voices of the enemy, no longer a distant echo, surround me. I can hear their orders and utterances and the intensity of their frenzied conversation sounds familiar. Automatic rifle fire rips into the already mangled bodies of my comrades. They will be left to rot on this desolate mountain. I probably will join them as a grim MIA statistic, published in my hometown newspaper.

I discover that I have been overlooked among the carnage and the foreign voices gradually fade away. I think that I can wiggle my toe. Is this toe movement caused by imagination? I manage to shift my position slightly. I am alive! All is silent, and I am alone.

I frantically search for and find our small field radio. I can use it to send a coded distress message to my ship. I enter the key code sequence into the battered but hopefully serviceable unit. Our CIA agents (Spooks) assigned to the Parks gave me the code before we left to do our work. This signal could have been my undoing. The enemy is alert to these signals!

The Spooks, too, will require rescue. The beep tells me that the message got through; the rescue rubber boat will stealthily arrive on the beach at Wonsan Harbor exactly twenty-four hours from now. The standard protocol calls for a four-minute window at the rendezvous point.

By using a discarded carbine as a crutch, I lift my body and stumble along starting the long and tortuous journey to the rescue area.

It is said that being close to death and under stress can lift memory blocks that our soul has retained. It allows us to probe into a mysterious (psychic and akashic) knowledge that is locked into our souls. The Creator has stored the knowledge about human experience, history and cosmos history within us. Our individual souls have access to our history and experience. These thoughts often feed our inner thoughts and help shape our present thinking. I can feel this effect happening.

Fear of failure dominated much of my childhood because my parents' reaction to a mistake was remarkably sharp. My father, reared by German stock, sternly demanded perfection in all tasks. My mother, a southern lady, de-manded that I strive to be a flawless gentleman and a suc-cessful scholar. She was happy that I wanted to become a doctor. Few accomplishments, if any, merited praise. When I left Santa Fe for the navy I imagined I would do things that would earn their respect. Through that respect I felt that I would find my own self-respect!

Whoosh. The sound of a metal bayonet hitting the rock covering my hiding crevice obliterates my vision and brings me back to the reality of Korea. Someone is standing over me and I pray that I have not been discovered. Am I doomed to die now, just when I have almost completed my descent from the mountain?

The probing bayonet continues to scrape the rocks be-hind me. Despite my fear, I do not move. I lay limp in my partially covered position. I lay motionless underneath rub-ble and debris, praying that he will not see me. My crude camouflage is apparently effective. Eventually, the soldier moves on and so do my recollections.

I begin to think about my hometown, Santa Fe, NM. It was built to conform to a simple European plaza con-cept but without walls. Each corner of the central square (plaza) contained a point of authority. These points were a church, a school, police center and a governor's man-sion and headquarters center. Other inhabitants of the square were businesses of all kinds. Hotels were nearby the plaza.

A well-known trading route tying Mexico and the Mid-western United States together ended at Santa Fe so they called the trail the Santa Fe Trail. Strangely enough the Santa Fe Railroad bypassed Santa Fe. Politics, as usual, was at work.

Fort Marcy was on a hill north of town and housed the U.S. Army. There was a pueblo, Tesuque, nearby, an art colony on the outskirts of town as well as housing developments surrounding the Plaza area. Dramatic changes were hap-pening during my lifetime. New Mexico became a territory in 1848 and the 47th state in 1912 and this history was the deciding factor that made Santa Fe its capital city.

As my mind continues to drift back to Santa Fe I recall many exploits I had as an enthusiastic boy scout.

Older Indians no longer display much hostility toward the white man. Instead, they had resigned themselves to coexistence with the invaders who had conquered them.

Our scout troop respected nature and would not violate local tribal rules when we camped on reservation grounds. The Chief Medicine Man and spiritual pundit had taken me under his wing. One day he invited me into the kiva. It is a gathering place for the local native Indians. He liked to talk philosophy. I liked to listen.

To the outsider a kiva may only be a big hole in the ground or structure partially above ground. In reality, it is a carefully constructed cavern or structure covered by a dome or roof made of adobe. It is basically built with blocks of tightly packed and thoroughly dried mud with straw interspersed. It includes a fireplace, altar space and the sipapu (a hole in the ground for communication with the underworld). It has an entrance and lighting usually from the roof. For the tribes of the Southwest, this is sacred ground.

The services held in the kiva fascinated me. Honed by years of tradition and custom, the Chief Medicine Man led mysterious chants on topics from sickness to the harvest. The mood ranged from a somber to a festive one. During this service I watched and wondered about the significance of these chants. This ritual was much different than the cowboy films depicted each Saturday at the movie house.

After one service the Chief asked me if I had dreams. I hesitated. He said, "Of course you do. We all do." I then admitted that I had both kinds, night and day. He smiled and said, "Tell me about them."

I told him about the Roman centurion. He smiled, squinted and looked at me for a long time in silence. It was as if he was trying to see this lanky scout as a great warrior. He finally said, "White Scout, dreams are part of your communication with the spirit of Creation. Truth is shared during these periods and sometimes you are viewing pieces of your past lives and deeds that you did a long time ago. Your akashic record is being fed to you."

I nodded and said, "Chief (Morning Sky), I see you going to mass with my Uncle when you are in Santa Fe. You are Catholic. Therefore, you cannot believe in past lives."

His reply was direct. He said, "White Scout, I am Catholic to please your Governor who does favors for my people. Your Bible does not talk of past lives. But it does not tell you that you did not have one."

He continues, "You were created a long time before this life. My religion speaks more freely about the travels of the soul. All true religions blend and complement one another so that, when viewed together, the whole is seen. Someday we will learn to share our souls with one another. You White Men try to restrict God. But He is everywhere. He is in the sky. He is in the heavens. He is here on Earth and in all parts of the Earth. The ego of the whole human race restricts us too much. Life is about living. It is not about power and control."

He then looked up into the sky and uttered a chant. Soon a white dove landed on my shoulder and I had goose flesh. He said, "You are a rebel and a warrior. You have many scars on your soul. You must find and spread peace. That is our mission on Earth. You will not rest until you do so." That ended the conversation, but I never forgot it.

After the outing was over, I returned home and related the story to my Dad. He grinned and said, "Son, Morning Sky has been training birds for years. He controls his people through religion just like our priests control us. Now get back and complete the work I told you to do." I persisted, "Dad, I don't think so." His reply was brief. "Think what you want to think, son, but beware and always observe before you form an opinion."

I continued, "Dad you fought in the First World War and saw death. My Uncle Dick was in the Lost Battalion. Do you believe in life after death?" He paused before replying: "Yes, I do." I pursued my thought. "Previous lives?" He looked at me with a smile and said, "Maybe we are to live the best life we can without delving too much into the unknown."

I remembered Morning Sky told me that we all have a mission to accomplish. We must do it in order to progress. Our fate was written in the stars. If we fight our karma, we will lose our guiding light. We will literally find ourselves in the dark, finding no peace, until we fix our attention on our assigned tasks. We must learn to live with one another. If we refuse in this lifetime, we could be sent back to try again to follow the path of life and we better follow it or regress to oblivion.

I jolt to reality. Darkness is all about. But it may not be my ally. The Koreans are equipped with Soviet infrared sensors. I have a small compass to guide me in the dark. But I must fend off panic and think clearly. Panic will lead me to sure death.

I am returning to my recollections. I am recalling my relationship with Janice, my girlfriend and I begin to feel better.

What a thrill her words evoked: "Yes, Edward, I will go with you." Finally, I had a date with the elusive Janice. She is tall, with auburn hair, an hourglass figure, and perfectly shaped legs. Janice also captivates the boys with her deep brown eyes. Her simple, oval face accentuated her beautiful eyes and she had a habit of looking deep into the eyes of anyone who was talking with her.

This habit often unnerved people but still, at the same time, attracted them to her. We all knew that someday she would be a model. She was neither too skinny nor too fat. She wears her hair pageboy style and it hangs casually on her shoulder. Her warm smile reveals she has both compassion and intelligence. This makes her intriguing. All of the boys want to be with her and date her. She has the pick of the class. But she has agreed to come with me to the Santa Fe High School Thanksgiving Party. She said that I was the first to look at her in the eye and ask.

Her last date had been with my proud cousin Richard. Richard was endowed with the strength and dexterity that made him a good football player on the SFH team. After my fiasco during the final fall season game, I realized that I could not compete with him or my companions in the sports arena. I have intelligence and stamina but not a natural ability on the playing field.

Despite this I had won a date with Janice, perhaps just for this single evening. I would make the most of it. I knew that she liked to talk philosophy, which did not interest my football buddies one bit. They had other things on their minds. But I like to philosophize. I want to know what is inside the minds of people. I want to know what drives them to act the way they do.

My teammates said that I thought too much. I was caught up in the details and theory that caused me to miss cultivating the gut instinct needed for success on the playing field. Our coach thought so too. I spent a lot of time on the bench. A fiasco during the game that season validated their feeling. I was playing end as SFH faced its rival at the annual homecoming game. We had lost several key players during our fierce bout and were losing by three points.

The clock ticked toward the final seconds. The coach looked at me in desperation. He must have died inside as he sent me out to the field. I was the last available whole man.

The call was for a pass. We were gambling on a long bomb as the clock showed ten seconds remaining. I ran like the wind toward the goal posts. Over my shoulder came a perfectly thrown pass. So many thoughts rushed through my head. Would I prove myself? Was I moving fast enough? How far away was I from the line? The ball passed through my flailing arms but, miraculously, it bounced off my foot and went straight up in the air. I scooped the flying object into my arms and crossed the goal line! Was I considered a hero? I was not! Although we won the game, the coach did not see my performance as an act of triumph. As I looked at him for approval I saw instead that he was shaking his head, which lay buried in his clasped hands. He was sitting on the bench.

The stands erupted with joy and relief. Fans and teammates carried the quarterback off the field. I walked to the locker room and changed. I never returned to the football field nor did I talk to anybody. I realize now that I was foolish to do that! I should have stuck with my teammates and made light of the situation. All of us would have benefited from it. Pride, the Dark Side, won again!

Yet, despite it all, I had a date with Janice. My father gave me rare approval to use his car. So the night started very well. I made dinner reservations at the swank downtown hotel, La Fonda. The choice would cost me three months' wages as stock boy in my father's store. It did not matter to me what I spent. The evening would be worth every cent.

We went to the La Fonda hotel, had dinner and danced to their band. It was a great date!

We had many more dates and enjoyed each date more than the previous one. During one of our many dates I told Janice about the football fiasco and my foolish reaction to it. She, of course, knew. I told her, "My Dad told me that I had made a serious mistake. I realized it and that is why I had apologized to all concerned."

I said, "Janice, we all make mistakes and this was a big one! My Dad told me how very disappointed in me he was and so was the coach. I should have gone into the locker room and told them that they should remember that through the grace of God I caught the ball and it just might happen again! Have faith! Then I should have laughed and congratulated the quarterback for throwing a great pass! Everybody would have laughed and felt good! My stupid pride had adversely affected others!"

I told Janice that Dad had further pointed out, "You allowed the sin of pride to spoil the night for all. The vibrations you sent were very self-oriented. You must correct this type of reaction!" She noticed that I had tears in my eyes. She replied, "I wondered why you apologized to everybody and I knew that it took much courage for you to do so. I wanted to date you because you had a heart and guts."

One and a half years of dating Janice had passed and I felt very comfortable with Janice. I wanted to tell her how I felt.

One night we went to Bishops Lodge for dinner and danced to their band. She snuggled deeper into my shoulder. The band played a waltz, then a fox trot. Janice moved very close to me and put her head on my shoulder. Infatuated and aroused, I decided to take a risk. After all, risk taking had gotten me this far. I whispered, "I think that I am falling in love with you." Then I kissed her ear. I do not know how I ever got the courage to say such a thing. But I knew that it was a wonderful event. I felt giddy inside. She let me kiss her when I took her home. It was the first love that most of us have experienced.

I remember when Richard and I agreed to double date for the Valentine Dance at the school gymnasium. This time we went to La Fonda but after dinner we went to the dance. My visions of Janice and I kissing on the way home were not to become a reality.

Several of us had planned in advance to go to El Nido, the local juke box bar, after the party so that we could enjoy talking together before heading home.

We danced and enjoyed the music, until some unwanted troublemakers interfered. They were resident Spanish-Americans and a mixed crowd at El Nido was not uncommon. Some Hispanics and whites did not mix well in Santa Fe and this is not unique but sad. Cooperation is the key to world success, not ethnic cleansing.

America, despite its racial troubles, has been the beacon to the world that shows this to be true. This ethnic separation is not harmony. We must have respect for all people and work together. I had always tried to do this and had some Latino friends.

However, some Hispanics had formed gangs, Pachucas, and they were determined to stir up trouble. One of the gang approached us on the dance floor. He wanted to dance with Janice. I knew things were going to get ugly. Looking at Richard I motioned toward a rear exit through the kitchen. "Take the girls home," I said with my eyes.

I stepped forward to confront the intruders. Before I said a word, they began striking me from several directions. During the ruckus, Richard successfully slipped out the back with his date and Janice. Meanwhile, I fell to the ground as the kicks and the blows continued. I had to block pain and conserve my strength. A knife penetrated my thigh. That did it! My temper was now in control and so was I.

I grasped the legs of the nearest chair. My blood-curdling scream must have shocked the attackers. I smashed the chair into the back of the bastard who had just stabbed me. Before the others could react I had another chair in my hands and swung it over my head. I could have killed someone had not the gang decided to flee from my madness. I became known as the screaming gringo.

It took me hours to fully recover my sanity. Even the doctor seemed uneasy because I felt no pain as he sewed stitches in the emergency room at St. Vincent's Hospital.

Convinced that I had initiated the hostility, the police called it a case of white kids taunting Hispanics but they did not press charges. My parents, furious at my indiscretion and lack of self-control, grounded me.

I was seething inside and I vowed to right the problem. I would form my own gang! I will protect my people and see to it that my people are not intimidated or attacked by a Hispanic gang. I want every adversary gang leader in Santa Fe to know who we are. Al, my closest friend, joined me in forming the Gang of Seven.

My strategy was to completely defeat any gang and leader that attacked any one of my seven! I received instructions about how to use this method of battle from the Indian Chief who said, "Do not waste your strength trying to negotiate with implacable and uncooperative enemies. Conquer them by more effective means." I always paid close attention to what he said.

I would tap into the strength of anger as each attack happened. Our first encounter proved remarkably successful. After each incident we left a message reading "Beware!" followed by the number seven. We felt the closeness and camaraderie of a mutual mission accomplished. I loved the feeling of being a warrior. My father commented that gang wars were on the increase. This upset him very much. I said nothing.

Our future encounters were even more successful. We became very accomplished at our trade.

Once, three tough rival gang members sideswiped Al and me while we rode our bicycles on the outskirts of town. They jumped out of the pickup and one swung a baseball bat-sized stick that caught me on the shoulder. The searing pain was awful but I recovered from my fall and immediately went berserk.

This was getting easy for me to do. Before long, the two attackers lay on the ground with their broken stick. I jerked the head of the loud-mouthed one upward so he could see my eyes and said, "If you or anybody does not want your face permanently smashed to a pulp, you will be very careful what you do around me and my gang."

My Gang of Seven was never bothered again. I could go anywhere in Santa Fe without trouble. My mission had been completed! However, as explained earlier, this program of vengeance had an enormous cost!

I remember, very sadly, when Janice said, "Ed, you have changed. You have become like a don and you seem to relish your new reputation more than you do me. We don't talk about life and philosophy anymore. It seems that your ambition to be a great surgeon and save lives has been replaced by something sinister. I do not like it. It frightens me."

She continued, "I will always be your friend but I can no longer be your girl." She hesitated, kissed me on the mouth, and said, "I really did love you and I wanted to have your children because you were sensitive and caring about other human beings."

I was stunned but nothing that I could say would change her mind. I had lost her. I had succumbed to the lust for power and lost love.

Again, the Chief's words came into my mind, "When a leader exercises unbridled antagonism he creates jealousy and hatred. This may well persuade those who were once friends to cease to be his friends." I had used dark side tactics for my mission and as a result I received the dark side rewards. The Laws of Nature are immutable.

I jolt to reality again and back to the unvarnished truth of Korea. Why am I having these vivid memories? I must really concentrate on ways to meet the rescue boat on time!

Suddenly a very clear voice tells me that I will have more memories of my present life and of past lives I had experienced. I will accept them and record them! This got my immediate attention!

I sense that my reaction to these memories will determine my fate. Will I choose life or will I choose to ignore the truth and die here?

I was the Chief Acolyte at the Santa Fe Episcopal Church and enjoyed the lesson readings each Sunday. I am remembering the story of Moses. Moses asked his people to choose freedom. They cheered when they were freed from Egypt. Some did not like the subsequent desert life and did not show gratitude to God for the freedom that was given to them so what happened when Moses was on Mount Sinai gathering the Ten Commandments as a code for his people to follow? They built an idol, a Golden Calf, and worshiped it!

Because of this act they spent 40 years in the desert until the stiff-necked non-believers died away. Their souls did not advance. Not worshipping our Creator and Him alone with gratefulness has its consequences!

My watch indicates that sixteen hours remain before the rendezvous deadline. I must establish my bearings and figure out a strategy. I will need to travel away from the mountain, through an adjacent valley, up the other side and then down to the boat. This should take me about sixteen hours. Considering that I have to hide from the enemy as I weave my way along the path line I better correctly recall the topographical map we had studied onboard the Parks.

After two hours of limping along, I stop to rest behind a clump of rocks. I am out of breath and need a rest! My mind starts to recall my life again!

My mother did not follow the family's Catholic base. She used to say that the Earth is filled with old souls who have been here before and new souls who have not.

The old souls have a karma to help the new souls avoid pitfalls and to develop and reshape themselves because they have not yet evolved fully. Old souls must be sensitive so that they can appreciate the value of sharing love and knowledge with the new souls who are innocent and do not really understand the consequences of eating the forbidden fruit.

New souls are extremely vulnerable to simple temptations and it is up to the older to help the younger evade them. I always wondered where Mom got all of this philosophy. It did not come from our church.

Charlie, my roommate on the Parks, graduated from Northwestern University. I think that he was a new soul. Why am I now remembering him?

I am in peril and I need help. That is why! I did not give help to him when he needed it so do I rate help? I cannot clear my mind of this memory! I am tired, hurting and confused.

I remember the day that Charlie and I were on the bridge when a land-based gun blasted at us and the shells barely missed our ship. Their round of firing did very little damage.

Charlie was the Assistant Watch Officer and his duty was to sound General Quarters. He seemed to be a bit upset. He aimlessly ran from one side of the bridge to the other so I sounded the general alarm. The Captain stepped onto the bridge the precise moment that poor Charlie was passing the hatchway. He stomped on the toe section of the skipper's shoe with his heel and all 250 pounds of his weight tore into the captain's foot as he spun around to change his course. The awkward scene resulted in our first battle casualty of the day. It took about two months for the skipper to recover. His temper never did.

I remember another incident near Wonsan Bay. Since our ship was a haven for downed pilots, who were lucky enough to ditch their damaged planes near us, we rescued these fellow warriors. At times we needed two sittings in our wardroom. I can remember one particular day when a crippled plane that had been hit by enemy fire splashed down near us. The sea was rough. A fast recovery by boat was essential. I was the Watch Officer and had the "Con."

Sailors were lowering the rescue boat into the choppy sea as I steered the ship to put them in the leeward side. They stopped midway down the side to wait for Charlie who was the boat captain and, as usual, arriving late.

As the boat hovered over the water, he leaped for the lifeline. Like a plump pendulum, his ample bulk arched far away from the hull. He hung onto the line and, as was inevitable, he slammed back into the steel skin of the ship. "Damn," the Captain muttered, "now there are two naval officers in the water."

All ended well enough, with two very wet naval officers rescued and on board. We all had a good laugh, including Charlie. But the rest of us never recognized his hurt. We never extended our help or tried to understand him. His compulsive eating was an obvious sign of his feelings of inadequacy.

He was almost killed in a cold, miserable storm off the coast of North Korea. I was the conning officer. After refueling, the Parks was trying to break away from our fueling ship that was alongside. The wind and rain had become worse and it was almost impossible to sail parallel with the tanker.

The fuel hose-securing lines had become fouled and Charlie, against all safety rules, was attempting to free the lines by brute force. He was in a panic and obviously not thinking clearly. He should have used an ax to chop the lines free. The lines began to break under the force caused by our ship's pulling-away movements. I could not instantly change course without endangering both ships.

A remnant of the tanker's rig caught his leg and pulled him overboard as well as several broken pieces of the rig. The tanker crew picked him up with the shattered rig and flew him to the carrier. They transferred him to Japan and subsequently to the U.S. Naval Hospital in Bethesda, Maryland.

He recovered but later resigned his commission. He did not ever answer our inquiries about his health. I never saw him again. I will always regret not talking to him and giving him some encouragement when I could have done so.

Maybe he would not have panicked if someone had given him some feeling of self-worth. None of us ever did. Why?

I look at the sky and say, "I am truly sorry that I did not act right!" A voice that I cannot explain said, "Are you truly sorry?" I reply, "Yes, I am truly sorry! This memory haunts me and I cannot shake it!" The voice says, "This is a life lesson. Use it wisely!"

The voice continues, "You are forgiven but the hard thing for you to do now is to forgive yourself. This is also part of living."

I feel my life and memories fading away. Suddenly I burst free from this scene. I look down and I see my own body below me. I am hovering over the land and I notice that a silver cord seems to tie me to my temporal body. I am fascinated and I wonder why I feel no pain. Is this how we feel as we die?

A voice from a bright light speaks to me. "You are not living your life as you should. You have violated many of the basic principles of cooperation and the Laws of Nature. You must face some of your past lives so that you can alter your present spiral pathway."

It continues, "Mankind has advanced remarkably, achieving great technological triumphs, but he uses this knowledge to destroy his fellow human beings and his surrounding environment through avarice, deception, power, lust and war. These characteristics, if not changed, will destroy many souls.

"As you remember your past I want you to tell me what you will have learned from it."

I am frightened and think, "This must be a hallucination. Remembering my past in this way is bizarre!" I return to my body. I am getting damn tired of this! I must slither away from this rocky resting spot and move out from underneath the underbrush.

I smell smoke. It hangs over me like a pall. The Koreans have set a fire to flush out possible survivors from the mountain. They are really mad at us! That damn radio message! This is what makes them think that there are survivors!

I will use the smoke as cover and crawl into one of the deep crevices that are cut into the earth. These furrows will allow me to stay below the flames. But now I fear that burns may be a major injury. I hurt enough already.

Filled with brush, the crevices could be my funeral pyre. Fortunately, the growth is minimal. I slide into a narrow opening and cover myself with dirt and rocks and debris. I silently pray that it will not ignite while I wait for the fierce crackling to subside.

The Koreans are close. I can hear them talking in clipped, excited voices.

I freeze into my position, but realize that I had been spotted by a scouting team. No time to think. I slide my 45 from its resting place in my belt and instinctively shoot.

My predator obviously caught off guard, collapses before getting off a shot. While fighting for my life I use the falling body as cover, I obliterate the other four soldiers. I grab some of the firepower from the dead and with no sense of direction, I run as swiftly as I can. I notice that I do not feel leg pains anymore. It is amazing what one can do when survival is at stake!

I keep my pace until I am again safe in a ridge closer to the seashore. I check the watch. Eleven hours to go. I must keep hidden and moving! My body needs to stop and rest but I am now afraid to rest even though my body demands it. I feel dizzy.

Now what is happening to me? I must be losing reality! I must be dreaming! Unknown guides are leading me away from Korea but I can see my live body below me! I rise above the Earth. I am over ancient lands. I must be about to face a past life and learn from it. If I do, I wonder if I will maintain any sanity at all and even if I do remain sane will anybody ever believe what I tell them?

CHAPTER 2

Welcome to Atlantis

The topography of Korea is changing before my eyes. The Earth is not the same as the Earth is today but I recognize it as the Earth. I recognize the footprint of the Pacific Rim below and I can see the Rim of Fire, the Philippines, New Guinea, Indonesia, and Malaysia. I see a myriad of ancient civilizations with their kingdoms and slaves as we flew over them.

We travel onward over the location of the Tuamotu Archipelago but I do not recognize it. Tahiti ought to be there but instead there is a large and lush island. Tahiti as a large island does not exist. I suspected that the now scattered islands we see in the Pacific Ocean today were at one time harboring a very large island in the Pacific Ocean.

I see it very clearly below. The guides are still silent as we approach it. There is no mention of an island like this in any ancient history books that I have read. I see a strange, well-advanced society, below me. I see no churches, synagogues or mosques but I do see towering pyramids, more like ziggurats. They are not relics nor ruins, but active hubs of a very advanced civilization. These are religious and commercial centers.

This area is a stark difference to the myriad of ancient civilizations around that are not advanced. They have kingdoms and slaves. The guides are still silent as we approach a large island. If these large structures have religious centers, the Holy Scriptures concerning life and post life for people on Earth must be kept here. My guess is that scriptures must tell people how to live in this planetary school called Earth.

I begin to muse, "If these structures are religious life learning centers why is it that in Egypt, for instance, they became tombs where only the elite could enter to receive eternal life? Did the high priests hide the truth of the scriptures from the public? Did they feed the people only what they wanted to feed them so they could have power over the masses?"

I think, "If this is so then obviously, this cabalistic action resulted in the deterioration of the true meaning of these magnificent temples. Was the fruit of power eaten and digested so well by the pyramid dwellers that the leaders would turn the places of worship into preservation centers reserved only for the salvation of their ilk?

"Truly, all of us were given a life and a mission to accomplish. Secrecy from truth is not a true mission. We will all be judged on our actions and not by the height of our position in life! Were these leaders practicing dark side people?"

How sad it is that a lust for power is so consuming! I ask my guides. They say, "All that are given life have the choice to fulfill their karmas or ignore them. They are responsible for their actions."

Their answer sparks a memory in my head. I recall a story about vessels that came from the heavens and brought gods and goddesses to Earth. Some of these gods and goddesses were foolish.

The people that lived in the City of Paradise built by the Heavenly People lived a lavish life surrounded by lush gardens, produce and vegetation. They knew about the Creator and His rules of living but they ignored the Laws of Nature.

They begin to fight over who was going to rule! They ignored the Heavenly forces that had brought them and as a result there was a great war in the skies. The Heavenly forces cut all ties with the rebel gods and goddesses and banished them to live here on Earth by the sweat of their brow and on their own.

Before the Heavenly warriors left they destroyed the City of Paradise. This story has a familiar ring to it! The Bible recounts this story and calls the City of Paradise the Garden of Eden.

The surviving renegades from this group of people that were forced to leave their old surroundings and settle elsewhere formed three Tribes. One went to the Pacific Ocean, one went to the Atlantic Ocean and the third Tribe settled on a site near the now thoroughly destroyed Paradise City. This Tribe believes that there is one God and He has given us the Rules of Life. The obvious conclusion is that we are expected to follow the criterions of life.

We fly over South America and then northward to the Azores. I recognize the topographical footprint of the Mediterranean Sea, Spain and the Atlantic Ocean but not this strange large island with huge pyramids on it. This once high technology and bustling island must be marked by the Azores and that is all that is left to show where it was. The people and the ultra-modern flying machines that are darting around the island and the pyramids are long gone! This large island must be what is left of the once large island that housed the legendary Atlantis!

I ask my guides about this. They say, "You will see, Achilles, son of Peleus." I say, "That is no answer!" They continue, "Remember, James Edward alias Achilles, that Zeus consorted with Thetis, your mother. Deftly, the theologians named their issue, your father Avatar (Hindu), as a descendent of the Deity on Earth."

I respond by saying, "I have read about Avatar and the mythology about Achilles, the hero of the Trojan War and the unprotected tendon attached to his heel. When am I going to learn about the Achilles of this era?" The lead guide smiles and speaks, "You are an avid reader of mythology. Remember its lessons. I remember that my teachers in high school always mentioned the legendary Atlantis during our brief covering of mythology."

The Guides continue, "You were almost immortal except for an exposed tendon that was cut by your enemy." I ask, "What did I do wrong?" The expected answer is, "You must tell us about the battles and the wars as you lived them. You will then give us your interpretation." That ended the conversation.

The buildings I see keep reminding me about the relics of the ancient Egyptian, Aztec, Mayan, Teotihuacán, Toltec and Totemic structures that we can see today. These relics must also have been religious buildings built for study and contemplation. Perhaps governing and maybe commercial transactions were done there. Whatever they were they were abandoned a long time ago.

I wonder, "If these structures were once alive with bustling activity why are they not alive and active today?" I know that the Free and Accepted Masons have used the lessons of integrity and honesty from the builders of the pyramids as their base for morality for centuries. Construction required knowledge and three basic construction considerations: pillars, strength and beauty. The Masons knew how to build many beautiful structures using these as a base. Who gave them the knowledge?

Somehow I am concluding that the high priests took this knowledge but revealed only what they wanted to tell the people. Again, this action taken to enhance their power, resulted in the loss of many magnificent principals of life. The knowledge they hid must have been truly powerful!

I ask my guides to confirm my thoughts. They say, "You will see, Achilles. Remember that the world is made up of two kinds of people. There are those that believe and have self-control and those that do not believe and practice self-indulgence."

I ask, "Please explain this thought!" The Guide answers, "Self-control is love, joy, peace, patience, kindness, goodness, faithfulness, and gentleness. Self-indulgence is fornication, impurity, licentiousness, idolatry, sorcery, enmity, strife, jealousy, anger, selfishness, debauchery, party spirit, envy, drunkenness, and carousing. Is that clear enough? Do you need more explanation?" I reply, "No, I think that you made your point very clearly!" They continue, "You must tell us, very clearly, about the kind of person you were, Achilles."

I am swept into the heart of this strange city in the Atlantic Ocean. The island country's name is Magogania and its capital city is called Atlantis. The Guides are now filling my brain with memories of my past.

I now know that there are two Titan Nations busy lusting and battling for power. Maybe the denizens ought to talk to one another about cooperation!

I hear people talking about politics and the leaders of these two great island powers. It is obvious that there is a struggle for control of the world. Yet, at the same time, these powers are talking to one another about a joint space program called the Space Command and unity. Is there really a spark of hope here or does unity really mean a unified world command with one ruler! So far in history, all single rulers of nations have become despots and destructors of civilizations and people. A world leader concept sends chills down my spine!

Both countries that I will be dealing with have similar problems and passions, yet they speak with different accents and have many opposing concepts.

This reminds me of our Biblical ancestors who followed different sons of Abraham, Isaac and Ishmael. Each spawned different philosophies.

Are these two countries so busy lusting for power that they have forgotten their original mission in the City of Paradise? Is it designed to help the indigenous people?

Suddenly, I am no longer free and floating around in the atmosphere, but I am locked into a mortal body. I look at myself and see the figure of a tall, blond, and very muscular man. My patrician features and face bears the scars from battles fought some time ago.

I have strong blue eyes that, I know, must fascinate people around me. The scars that I bear actually add character to my noble countenance. I am alone. I must be Achilles! This ought to be very interesting!

What is next? I suspect that very soon I will know more about him, what he is doing and, perhaps, know why.

My mind continues to fill in answers to my numerous questions. I am an expert in physics and understand the technology of communication devices. I know how to create nano-technology manufacturing plants and I am an expert weapons designer. I am also a superb hacker. I can break into any system. I am a denizen of Gogania, the Pacific power in this bi-polar world.

I am well respected but have no control or power to influence the political decisions being made. Since I do not like most of the political decisions being made, I want to improve my ability to have an effective role in these matters.

My present passion is to make a difference in this world! Obviously, to accomplish this great goal I need to be part of the political arena. We technical, engineering and scientific people are the workhorses of societies but we seem to have very little influence over the direction that societies take.

There are two avenues that I can take to penetrate the political part of the system. I can become a member of the Space Command or become part of the families that do rule. Maybe, I can be both!

I cannot do this without help so I am forming a Group of Seven that is dedicated to this cause. Cautiously, I am assembling this loyal team of co-conspirators who share my desire to make a difference and leave the world a better place than it is now. Seven seems to tie into the Laws of Nature.

I am assembling a team with each member being an expert in their field of endeavor. I will be the common bond that will make them effective.

We can advance together with the common goal of helping our world become an integrated society with individual governors who respect each individual person and give each person the right to forge out his own destiny with freedom and dignity. This will not be easy and this will work only if our governing body truly respects each person.

Servitude to the almighty government is the alternative and that will have the disaster of total disintegration of the planet.

I know that if I exude charm and make people comfortable around me it will make my daunting task easier. Society grants unusual opportunities to people with drive, eloquence of speech and charisma.

The gift of a successful leader is to advance oneself while working for the greater cause of creating a government that fosters freedom and reward for successful work done. The challenge is for one not to become corrupted by power.

I must forego many of life's pleasures and indulgences with a single-minded discipline of improving my skills of persuasion and appeal.

I have hatched a plot that might work. It will make me a public hero and being one will provide the exposure necessary to become a household word.

I plan to do this by saving the life of the daughter of the Minister of Defense. His position is third in the line of succession. The Chairman is first. The Minister of State follows him. None of the other two ministers have an eligible daughter.

I must meet this woman, but how? I am thinking of a charade that will place the daughter in great peril and then execute a heroic rescue. This is wonderful! However, one small detail remains! I must figure out how to do this!

I know that a rescue plan will be successful and I do not allow the thought of failure to enter my mind! Okay. There remains another small problem!

I am now successful! I ask myself one small and simple question, "Do you really believe that people will follow this nonsensical logic and really think that you are a hero?"

The Minister of Defense's daughter is a striking blonde named Ashley Anne with an hourglass figure, blue eyes that mesmerize people, a rounded oval face and full lips. She is a private person and does not like publicity and attention.

I have learned that she will soon leave her parents' home and move to a private apartment. I must move quickly if my act of heroism is to have a maximum impact!

After she moves, her pattern of rhythm will change completely and the timing of this plan will be all wrong.

My colleagues and I have discussed this hero concept for weeks. During these sessions, we have covered various options including mishaps, falling objects and vehicle accidents.

Each of these schemes causes a dangerous incident and is fraught with problems but that is part of the intrigue. We have finally agreed on all of the details of a plot and it is time to act.

Training a dog and obtaining the proper pedigree papers for him is essential to the plan. Karl is a dog trainer and is one of us. The canine we have chosen possesses enough physical strength to accomplish the feat we have in mind for him yet will cause little concern when on leash in public. Why is it that people love dogs?

Karl turned to animal training after tragedy struck his household. He is an excellent candidate because his loss has turned him into a cold, vengeful person seemingly devoid of any feeling except hatred toward the ruling society that allowed his family to be slaughtered.

His household had been mistakenly identified as the dwelling of renegade terrorists and the enforcement officer's orders were to exterminate all inside. They did except for Karl. The State admitted its terrible error and apologized to Karl but all of this came too late! I know that I can depend upon him. His rage will keep him in focus.

Choosing an owner for this fine beast proved to be more difficult than choosing the trainer. We settled on Sharon, the young wife of a mid-level representative in the Ministry of State. Her husband, Peter, is part of the Seven. She is an extremely attractive woman with a perfectly shaped 120-pound body. Her sharp features are framed by her dark hair and olive skin. More importantly, she has an analytical mind and a willingness to apply her insight to our cause. She considers herself a rebel and a severe critic of the system.

She and Elaine, my late wife, were close friends and shared mind expansion exercises and hallucinogens together.

They had delved into the mind expansion cult. It was a loose group of cynical malcontents who showed their disdain for reality by escaping through mind-altering processes. Drugs were involved. "Mind expansion" eventually killed Elaine and shattered my life.

Her untimely death cured Sharon of the habit but, nonetheless, she as well as her husband Peter are restless, ambitious and in need of a purpose. I am providing this for them.

One more player In our dangerous plan to "save" the Minister's daughter is Isaac. He is a proven expert courier and intelligence agent. He has delivered secret messages when it seemed impossible to do so. He has accomplished his tasks even if they required violence. I have come to know him as a wily operator, who occasionally does favors for diplomats by intimidating their opponents.

His job includes intelligence gathering, interpretation, and analysis. He is the one who uncovered the fact that Ashley Anne arranges to have lunch with her father Roland, the Minister of Defense, occasionally, and he is the one that suggested the appropriate day to execute our plan.

Ashley always uses the shuttle train because she likes to shop at the underground mall near the Defense building.

On the designated day of the "accident" all seven of us must be in Magogania. Sharon will be visiting her friends at a seaside resort. I have arranged to have a weapons progress meeting at the Ministry of Defense. Isaac has discovered some very sensitive technology information that must not be leaked to the general public for the ministers to analyze and act upon.

He is used by all Ministries because of his expertise at intelligence interpretation. He is also a superb hacker. He is to deliver his information to the Ministry of Defense by using a prescribed route and a precise schedule.

My mind fills with the "what if" syndrome, playing all alternatives over and over again. The plan we have selected will be executed no matter what the outcome might be.

None of us can communicate with the others prior to the day of the incident because that could tip our hand and lead to exposure during any ensuing investigations.

Sharon must convince her friend to visit the lower stores in the Defense Building. A shuttle connects all of the Capitol Building Complex together. The trip to Atlantis from the resort is a very short one but this trip is an essential piece of the plan.

Isaac's timing must, indeed, be precise or we will all be doomed. I hate complicated schemes. Simple is always better.

I dimly remember my father, Avatar, preaching, in the inner sanctum of the pyramid that self-glorification leads to the death of a soul. I never paid much attention to him. Why?

My affluent friends have stopped worshiping at the pyramids and they do not believe in the tenets of the pyramid religion.

My father blames me for not pulling Elaine away from hallucinations. He does not approve of my lifestyle. Our conversations have become very heated. Despite all of this, I do love him. He has a warm soul. He does love me and deep inside I know it.

Finally, the day of action has arrived. I have eaten an early breakfast, applied a proper dose of after-shave and have dressed properly as a senior government scientist.

Although I am a Goganian I work with both governments concerning space technology as it relates to the Space Command. I have attained this position despite my relative young age.

I feel nervous despite the extensive planning and detailed analysis that we have made. My palms feel cold and clammy but I am perspiring. I have never understood how both can happen at the same time. An extra splash of cologne helps. "Get control," I command myself. I look at my wristwatch. It is time to move.

I leave the room with my usual confident swagger and tuck the official documents that I am to deliver to the Defense Building into my briefcase. It is a short walk to the transportation vehicle which airlifts me to the government complex. Once inside the craft I realize that I cannot turn back.

The plan is being executed. This curtain on this stage of life has risen! This plan will unfold and the results will be good, bad or tragic. In any case, I know that the results will truly affect many people. What have I done?

The ride seems interminable even though I will arrive at the station on time.

Delayed by a routine security check, Isaac almost misses his rendezvous but he manages to convince security that he is on an urgent mission and walks briskly to the meeting point.

I know that we are all wondering if Ashley Anne will arrive as we had calculated. I do not immediately see her. I look around. A twinge of panic ripples up my spine.

Suddenly she is there! Isaac walks past her and presses a button on his case which releases a scent, undetectable to humans, onto her skirt. The colorless essence identifies the target for our canine co-conspirator who has been taught to lunge at the person with the identifying scent and knock them down.

The shuttle tube has a monorail slot at the top and a stabilizing centerboard at the bottom that rides in a closely machined slot. The boarding platform rises four and a half feet above the bottom bed and the shuttle fills most of the entire ten foot tubular liner that was made by using ceramic-metallic powdered metallurgy techniques.

A bystander talks to Ashley Anne as she stands on the ramp. In my mind I yell out to her, "Please! Stop talking!" She looks up, reacting to the whoosh of air from the tube. She runs toward the platform. I start to breathe again!

The dog breaks free from Sharon and races toward the scent. Perfect! He slams into Ashley Anne. Unprepared for the impact, she loses her balance. The lights of the shuttle bounce off of the wall opposite from the entry point as both lady and dog tumble into the tunnel.

Mustering the necessary strength and courage, I leap into the pit and, with one mighty thrust, I heave Ashley to the opposite side of the platform. My briefcase is still locked to my belt. The speeding shuttle covers my peripheral view as I vault out of its path. I am not quite fast enough and I feel pain as the bullet nose of the machine hits me. I can see that my leg is now at an awkward angle.

The impact propels me onto the platform alongside Ashley Anne and our eyes meet. I must be close to losing my consciousness because I can see into her soul.

I can see a wonderful blue light surrounding her and I feel the ethereal energy that dwells within her. This insight sends a tingling sensation throughout my body. I know that somewhere long ago we have met. This thought and my feelings frighten me. I immediately try to squash them but I cannot. What have I done?

The episode has obviously frightened Ashley Anne and I sense that a bit of humor might break the spell. I say with a wry smile, "You know the least you could do after breaking my leg is to have dinner with me." She smiles and replies but shock has taken its toll and is draining me of the ability to hear or speak.

In my mind I hear her say, "Accept God's energy now!" I think, "What energy?"

There is surge of energy within me as I hear her voice. I try to do what she asks even though I do not consciously know how. I relax and give my soul to our Creator. I don't know what is happening but I can feel a flood of energy entering my body. I slip into total unconsciousness.

I should not have recovered at all. My heart had stopped. I remembered dreaming about wondrous beings in a land that was always filled with light. The doctors say that my recovery was miraculous. I am a badly battered fellow. Even though bruises cover my body and every muscle I have aches, I am determined to get out of the hospital as soon as possible. I have things to do!

Sharon and Pete pay a courtesy call and, while others are present and can listen, Sharon tells me that her dog, Chipper, had been acting strangely for the past few weeks. She states, "I can't imagine why he bolted." She cries as she tells me that the shuttle had killed Chipper instantly. They had really become close friends. I mean it when I say, "I am sorry, Sharon. I understand why you are so very upset. We lost a loyal friend."

She looks at me straight in the eye and states, "Chipper was a fine and loyal animal. I hope that he did not die needlessly."

I muse, "I have hurt an ally. Where am I leading her?" The phrase "Quo vadis (where go you)?" seems appropriate. She says, "I see a tear in your eye!" I nod.

Ashley Anne comes to visit me and expresses her appreciation for my bravery that saved her life. She says, "I delivered the briefcase you had locked to your belt as you requested to the Ministry and I accept your invitation to dinner." I do not remember asking her to deliver the briefcase.

I thank her and say, "Fate could not be so cruel as to extinguish the life of such a beautiful person as you are. I am merely the instrument of fate." She replies, "More than you might think, Achilles!" What did she mean?

Next, the Minister of Defense, Roland, drops by to extend his appreciation. He is a gruff man, born into a privileged family but obviously very shrewd. He is a six-foot-three tall man and built like a rectangular box with a very short neck. Despite his heavy build he is handsome.

He was a ruthless athlete in his prime and was inducted into the most coveted Society of Olympic Excellence. He graduated from the University with honors. His booming voice projects easily and he speaks with command and authority. I can tell he is not impressed with my heroism. I do not blame him. He, obviously, is wondering about this whole episode.

It is obvious that he has done a thorough background check on me and he is impressed with my academic achievements but not terribly pleased about this incident or me.

There is something in his tone that leads me to believe that he has doubts about my authenticity and this makes me uncomfortable as well it should. I can only hope that my story will hold together. I do not like the alternative.

I fall asleep thinking about my forthcoming evening with Ashley Anne but also think, "What a hell of a way to get a date! I damn near got myself killed!"

I know from pictures of her that Ashley is a striking blonde with a well-proportioned body but the portrayal of her belies the fact that she is an incredibly beautiful woman with a patrician aura, an oval face and piercing blue eyes.

Her figure is classic. She does have an hourglass-shaped body and her long legs are perfectly formed but it is her radiance and quick smile more than her appearance that draws me to her.

When she entered my hospital room I could see the blue light shining within her. When she is talking to others I can tell that they feel her warmth. She has a way of commanding attention when she enters a room. It isn't anything in particular that she does. It just happens. My aches and pains subside as I think of her.

However, I now feel a bit of sadness because I am losing my ability to see her light. I realize that it was a brief gift. What is happening to me? I have never felt like this before!

My evening with Ashley Anne must run smoothly. I like her. There is something about her that makes me want to be with her. I must coax her into believing in me, convince her to follow me, and charm her. The chemistry must be right.

As I guide the official air car to her apartment, I feel the same cold sweaty palms and nervousness I always feel prior to a critical assignment. When she appears at the door I find myself just looking at her. I am speechless. How stupid can I be? I fear disaster.

She returns my gaze with an amused grin. Finally, I utter sheepishly: "Ashley Anne, my palms are cold and I am perspiring at the same time. I want to tell you that you are the most beautiful person that I have ever been blessed to behold. I want to tell you in a suave and debonair way but I can't. All I can say is that you are the most beautiful person inside and outside that I have ever seen!"

She laughs and says, "That is a good line and I have never heard it before, Achilles; how do you know what I am inside?" I say, "I saw the light within you when I thought I might die." She replies, "Really! That is remarkable. I was saying a prayer that you would live."

I offer my hand to her and she takes it as I lead her to the waiting car. Our discussion soon leaves the trivial. We talk of childhood and goals in life. I learn that Ashley Anne has been deeply hurt by two men that she had trusted. She was sexually attacked by a companion who was in the ballet school with her. She wanted to be friends and he wanted more. He took her without permission.

Her father, instead of understanding, seemed to blame her. She was deeply hurt and no longer fully confides in him. I tell her that I have a feeling of inadequacy because my parents never found anything positive to say about me. I needed their love and, even though I must have been a difficult kid to rear, I wanted it desperately. I did not get it.

My eyes drop as I say, "It would have been a blessing if either parent would have made me feel that I was worthy of their love! I still have confidence problems." She listens very intently to my story. I could almost detect a tear in her eye. She obviously believed that my emotions were real and they are.

She gave me genuine empathy. It is comfortable being with a person that can share pain and understanding. Yet, I wanted her to know how I felt inside. I told her the truth. She sees what is in my soul. She can destroy me with this insight. I think that she knows that fact.

I told her that I want to make a difference in the world and make it safer and better. I told her that I fear that I have lost my way and wonder if I am really walking along the right path. I told her that I see decay in our government. I want to correct this decay and have our leaders believe in a moral code. Does she believe me? What will she do with this knowledge?

We must rush dinner because we are attending the theater. I say, "There is so much more to say and there is no time left!" She agrees. The theater is superb. She lets me hold her hand during the performance and I can feel an energy exchange between us. I love it. What am I going to do now?

We stop for a nightcap and continue our earlier conversation. Every time she looks at me, I melt inside. She is compelling. She has me talking more about myself than I had intended. She does really listen. I can only hope that I am not a bore.

She asks about my father and his philosophies. Obviously, he is a well-known and respected High Priest in the Pyramid ministry. She asks if I often visit him. I reply, "No, because we always quarrel when I do."

She says, "Tell me more about your father's beliefs." I reply, "My father believes that the first requirement of attending a Pyramid is to pray before entering the Pyramid. One must enter in peace and with patience. He says that an angry soul with impatience will anger the Creator."

I continue, "We must glorify Him by coming in with love in our hearts and to cleanse ourselves of the desire to seek self-glorification, hoard silver, indulge in sex without love and practice sloth." She replies, "I think that he is right."

I nod and say, "It's not the real world." She replies, "What is the real world?" I reply, "The world is a place of fierce competition and ruthlessness." She says, "How do you propose to change this?" I say, "I want to be the leader that will show integrity, confidence, courage and calmness by example. I want people to change our government philosophies because they want them to change and want me to lead them to this goal."

I continue, "If I am this leader I must be willing to accept responsibility, accept the challenges, draw the plans, carry them out and do what it takes to accomplish the dream. The foundation for all of this is faith, conquering of fear and belief in this mission. I want to be the example to my followers and I want them to believe in me."

She looks at me for a long time and then asks, "What is your weakest quality?" I reply, "The lack of patience." She smiles and says, "That does not surprise me. Is that why you lost Elaine?" I looked her in the eye then I looked at the ground and said in a very low voice, "I did not give Elaine the understanding and love she needed, Ashley Anne. I will bear this burden forever."

I continue, "I had not been a very good husband. At first, as a young married couple, Elaine and I had looked to each other for strength and approval. However, I became obsessed with my advancement and I spent more and more time in the world of science and influence. As you know, I have been asked to become the Dean of Science at the University."

I proceed to explain, "Fortunately, unlike most scientists and engineers, God gave me an ability to speak. I want to be able to influence people by talking with them. Elaine was more of a private person. She was shy and did not like to socialize but she would mingle with people and become gregarious to help me."

I know that I have said too much but I say more, "My mind had focused on other things and I almost ignored my family without realizing what I was doing. I see now that I loved my career and ambitions more than I loved them. This was a dark side path and has caused me untold grief and still does. It always will."

I continue. "I always told Elaine, 'You will be queen of the planets.' She replied that she did not desire power and wealth. She wanted a family based on moral standards, with more children to rear and to nurture. Soon hallucinations instead of me became the foundation of her emotional life."

I pontificate. "Mind expansion stimulated her imagination and generated the illusion that she was in paradise. Unfortunately, drugs shut down the inflow of universal energy into a person and this allows the dark forces to take command."

I talk more, "This path inevitably stimulates the destructive forces that will lead all participating souls to move to the Dark Side. If this is unchecked it leads to eventual soul death."

I explain, "She created another world for herself but it turned out to be a living hell. I could no longer take her to functions. She eventually decided to engage fully in illusions. I found her late one night, after I returned from a diplomatic soirée, lying on the floor and quivering. I was heartbroken and powerless to help her. She died without uttering a word."

I admit, "Our son Orion was five when Elaine died and he has never recovered from the loss of his mother. He has suffered far more than a boy his age should. I tried to make amends and become close to him. I wanted to become a good father and tried to be but I could never replace Elaine."

After a long, long pause she replies, "One can never replace a lost parent but you can share the grief with your close family and grow stronger together. You did that. What else did you learn?" I know Ashley wants to see deep into my soul. I reply, "I learned that a misdeed is a fierce burden. I feel responsible that she died as she did. I will try to be patient and understanding in the future. I cannot change the past but I can plan a better future."

She persists, "Is your father really wrong?" I look her in the eye then look into space. I have tears in my eyes and say, "No, he is correct." She gives me a wondering look saying, "Do not condemn yourself forever, Achilles. God has let you live and has forgiven you. You have a destiny to accomplish. Forgive yourself!"

I say, "You believe in the scriptures and you do attend the Pyramid rituals." She says, "Yes, but the High Priest seems to emphasize fear and sacrifice and his liturgy tries to dominate rather than teach. Competition is not what we are all about. Love is. I wish that your father was our priest because I feel very uncomfortable with my priest's philosophy."

She continues, "Your dad seems to have the right concepts about the universe. The power and position of our most high priests has become their main concern and your father is not like that."

I say, "How do you know?" She replies, "I have studied his works." I nod.

She continues, "The priests keep the masses in check while the government plans world domination. This is not right!" I look deep into her eyes and say, "You are a very perceptive and caring woman. Never change. Maybe, somehow, we together can influence and change the direction of both our churches and our governments."

She looks at me with a wistful smile. What did that mean?

She says, "It is getting late and I have an early appointment tomorrow." I take her home. At the door I kiss her firmly on the lips and she responds.

I look her in the eye and say, "Please come to the Ambassador's Ball with me. I will be a totally lost soul if you do not." She hesitates. I add emphatically, "I really want to be with you and need you!"

She looks at me quizzically and finally says, "I will go with you but I don't know why because I have already made a solid commitment. I never break obligations." I reply, "I am looking forward to sharing more time with you."

I realize that I may be interfering with a competing suitor and I wonder when he will become my bête noire.

I am beginning to wonder if we are really in total control of our fate. I can remember what my mother told me, "We all have karma and woe will be to those who do not complete it because they chose not to do so."

I want to be with Ashley Anne and I think that she wants to be with me. Before she closes the door she says, "Achilles, you are not at all like the reports say you are. I will go to the ball with you, but you will find that it will cost you dearly. Are you willing to pay the price?" I reply, "I will willingly pay any price."

She smiles and closes the door. I wonder what Ashley Anne meant. I know that it will take every iota of energy and planning to win this beauty. Ostensibly, I have saved her life but have I won her heart? She is one smart woman!

It does not take long for me to find out one of the repercussions of convincing Ashley to pick me for her escort to the Ball and it soon becomes obvious to me that Eric is my competitor for her hand.

He is a powerfully built and competent athlete who also has an insatiable thirst for power. He has red curly hair, a round face, green eyes, and a pixie grin that charms all women. He keeps his body in great shape with all muscles tuned. His confidence attracts people to him. He is a superb car racer. Damn! He is good at what he does! He also has the ear and the respect of those in power.

Within three days after my date with Ashley Anne he confronts me and is obviously furious that I caused Ashley Anne to break her date with him. He says, "I challenge you to race against me in the Olympic Car Race. You will not live to see the results." It takes me a microsecond to figure out what is happening but I immediately accept!

The Minister has decided how to deal with the upstart Achilles. He is going to get me killed! This Olympic event pits the finest drivers in Magogania and Gogania to race each other every eight years. It is well known that the Minister of Defense enthusiastically endorses Eric. He likes him. I suspect that he has already picked him to be his son-in-law.

Immediately after the challenge the Minister must have contacted his counterpart in Gogania. I suddenly have received the Olympic Committee's sponsorships for the race.

During the next meeting of our group we discuss our situation. I say, "We have had a good stroke of fortune! The gods are with us and Ashley Anne already believes in our cause! This is our first step to make us part of the Space Command! This is our first goal and we are on our way!"

I add, "Remember, one of our goals is to get people to know me better. One way was to get me a state sponsorship for the races. This has been achieved! My petition, once rejected, has suddenly been approved. Eric and the Minister are behind this change of heart. Obviously, I am moving in on Eric's girl, Ashley. I suspect that the Minister wants to get rid of me and a good and fatal car wreck would do the trick."

Pete says, "That is just great! What do you know about car racing except to dabble with it?" My whole team is staring at me. I say, "What is there to know? Never fear. Victory is near!" Isaac says, "Good God help us!" Pete says, "Remember, you were the one who convinced us to follow this madman!" Isaac is smiling.

My team has decided to split themselves into tasks: Pete, Chief of Staff; Karl, Chief of Interior Information; Isaac, Chief of Judicial Information; Theudas, Chief of Commercial Information; Judas, Chief of Educational and Theological Information; Hector, Chief of Transportation Information. I am Chief. All of us agree to these tasks. I wonder what they are really thinking now. Are they wavering?

Isaac queries me, "So you think that after you win the race you will be inducted into the Space Command and that this is the first step toward our taking command." I reply, "That is right. Let us make it so!"

I say, "I understand that over half of the participants in this Olympic and grueling race are killed or seriously maimed, but the prize is substantial! The victor is always assured an appointment to the elite Space Control Command. They hold the power that will help us meet our goal. The rewards are commensurate with the pain and risk. These two keys, pain and risk, are the universal axioms of competition and I am willing to endure them for our cause."

Isaac, with a broad grin, says, "Achilles, we all are wondering how you convinced us to join and follow you in the first place. You really are some piece of work and this scheme is really 'off the chart' in madness. Even so, we will follow you." I see broad smiles and that is good.

I continue, "I know that I am the fish and the Minister has the bait. The hook has caught me and I am being reeled into the boat. Fish have been known to break the reeling line and so will we. I will win this race!"

Pete adds, "You better not play with Ashley's heart. Sharon and she have become very close. Do you like Ashley?" I say, "I want this entire group to know that I do not like her." I stop and see my group's faces change their demeanor. Then I say, "I honestly and truly love her! I would die before hurting Ashley! She is one of us at heart. I want her to be part of our hearts. I am going to marry her if she will have me and I will love her forever!"

There is total silence. It seems like eternity until Isaac says, "Damn, that statement is totally sane. I think that I speak for the group. We want government change and we believe that we will be successful in our quest to have it. Lead us onward!"

I say, "Isaac, thank you! We will win and we will win change! An acceptable governing body is one that follows the Spiral Code of living. The basic truth of this code is to treat others as you want to be treated and to treat others as you treat yourself!"

I continue, "We are bound together with cause and love. If this is madness then all I can say is 'Hail to the madness!' Watch out world for you are going to have one great experience." There is genuine laughter. The tension that I had felt has disappeared. Our group is now truly together.

The Olympic Race course is set by bilateral agreement. This one starts in Atlantis and runs from the point of departure over Greenland to the North Magnetic Pole and hence into space.

The participants must fly to the South Pole where re-entry takes place. This year we fly from Antarctica northward on longitude 15 to Africa where a preplanned race cluster of caves and a forest is located.

There are three caves. Long ago the ends of caves had been blasted out, just for this purpose. The forest that follows contains trees grown so close together that tipping the racing car to squeeze in between is required. The final run is in Magogania where a mandatory obstacle course is located near a stadium that is built for the sole purpose of viewing this long and grueling race.

This race is scheduled to run every eight years. I reflect that if I did not fall in love with Ashley and Ashley in love with me Eric would not, with Minister Roland's help, have arranged to get me killed by having my application to this race approved.

It is also interesting that this year all participating race cars are configured in a delta shape. Eric's favorite race craft is a Delta. The only variation is the nose section. All are ovals but some can be blunter than others. In effect, we are going to be a bunch of blunt oval-nosed, three-sided flying pyramids with blunted canopies at the top and a flat bottom containing the landing wheels.

I have made a complete study of the records and the video library of previous races. There are always clues to show why winners won and losers lost but it is very difficult to spot the real reasons. I am determined that I will.

I focus my study on Eric's strategy during his recent successful races. He has become unbeatable. Why? The more I study the more convinced I am that he has inserted an extra fuel cell into his craft because this is the only explanation for the added endurance of this cocky bastard's machine.

The racing rules restrict all air cars to five fuel cells. Eric uses his jets and his superconductor much more effectively than all other contestants because he is not worried about fuel consumption. No wonder he can afford to be so aggressive!

How does he get this extra cell inserted? How can the insertion of an illegal fuel cell occur if the official inspectors look at the machine just prior to racing? Each machine must be inspected three times. The final team, supervised by the Minister of Defense, gives the clearance for each car to race! I have answered my own question.

Further study convinces me that not only will Eric's craft have an extra fuel cell but there will also be sabotage done to my machine during the final inspection. What can the rascals do?

I study the casualties of past races to find the answer. Inspections of wrecks that happen during each race are mandatory. Rarely can anything definite be determined after an "accident" but during my study I discover two instances of car destruction caused by a breach in the fuel line. This type of break will assure that any machine will stall, have a fire or explode sometime during the race.

Although the designs of the racing cars must follow parameters set by the Racing Commission there is latitude in certain features. I study the nose design of each contestant. I decide that a needle tip could disrupt the air flow and leave a partial vacuum just in front of the machine that, at times, might be helpful. It must be retractable but the control equipment will have to be extremely light. This is a dilemma. I finally decide to use a screw to extend the needle and to retract it.

During all of these studies I wonder about Ashley Anne. Will she really let me take her to the Ball? I am worried because there is something in her voice that tells me that all is not right. I should have known it. I have the feeling that she might make an excuse at the last moment and not attend with me. Was I that bad? Was Ashley viewing me as a game player? So far there have been no excuses forthcoming and tonight is the night! Maybe giving a little personal gift to her is appropriate. I buy her an Angel pin.

I approach the door with trepidation and knock. As she opens the door, my mouth opens but again words will not come out. I just stare because I am still awed by her beauty. Finally, I say, "Your beauty is beyond real, you are an Angel and the brightest beautiful star in the universe!" I give her the pin and she puts it on but there is something bothering her. What scheme has been cooked by Eric and Minister Roland? Are they poisoning her feelings for me?

She remains quiet during our ride to the Ambassador's house. Our conversation is polite but the zing is not there. I have to do something quickly or this relationship is gone! The evening starts with cocktails and Ashley Anne pays more attention to the other guests than to me. Finally, it is dinner time. We talk and I try to be animated. But the conversation is cold and detached. It is time for me to make some kind of move and do it damn quickly!

I take her hand and tell her that I want to talk privately on the balcony. She is reluctant but she yields to my leading her by her hand. A spectacular view sets the scene with stars lighting the sky. I turn to her and look straight into her eyes as I say, "Ashley Anne, I have never felt the feelings that I have for you in my entire life. When I sleep I dream of you. When I eat I think of you. You have consumed my soul and I want to be with you forever. I love you so very much and I don't know how to tell this to you any other way! I want us to be married so we can love one another forever! I feel that a great wall has suddenly come between us and I don't understand why." In reaction, she stares at me without expression. I have lost her or did I ever have a chance in the first place?

I continue, "I do not know what has come between us but I hurt and cannot stand the thought of losing you to the unknown. Tell me what is wrong. I wanted to tell you after our first date that I loved you, but was sure that you would dismiss it because love at first sight is unbelievable."

I kiss her, frightened that she will return my affection with a slap. She does not, so I kiss her again and again, very gently at first. She responds. The kissing becomes deeper, passionate and exploring. I tell her that I am hopelessly and deeply in love with her!

She is wearing a gown with a slit that beckons me. I want to open it. She is fighting her feelings for me. I have to know why so I ask again, "Why are you angry with me?"

She replies, "I have learned all that I can about you. Maybe Father is right. I am beginning to think that you are using me. If that is what you are doing, I won't tolerate it and I am hurt! I do not intend to be used. I am a human being and not a thing."

I am now confused. What is going on? I reply, "I love you. I need you and I want to be with you always. I will never hurt you nor use you. A man does not hurt a woman that he loves. He cherishes her! I cherish you and I want to be your protector and lover forevermore!"

I want to say more but our host knows how to end a party so that people will not linger. He had arranged a champagne toast for the heads of each of our governments. This will be followed by the playing of the National Anthems. The assembly chimes ring.

Ashley Anne and I do not speak much during our return home but she lets me hold her hand and she puts her head on my shoulder. For me, the impact of what I have done has slowly and wonderfully become apparent. As of this moment the course of my life has changed forever. I begin to detect that her aura is returning.

When we arrive, I open the air car door and she steps out. I lead her to her door and as she opens it I pick her up and carry her into the house. Although surprised at my audacious move, she buries her head in my shoulder. We close the door and begin to kiss more and more deeply. I unfasten her gown.

She tells me that I am the first man to visit her new apartment. She then looks at me quizzically and says, "There is a tear in your eye. I didn't expect that!" I say, "I am in love and these are happy tears."

She says, "Please don't race your car." She knows something that she is trying to tell me but cannot. I do not reply because it does not compute. My eyes do not fix on the flowing curtains, exquisite furnishing or plush carpeting. As her gown falls to the ground, my eyes focus only on her. I gasp as I gaze at her perfect body. There is one exception. I notice a scar above her vagina.

I sweep her into my arms and continue to kiss her deeply. I then move my hands to draw her closer to me. I lift her gently and take her to the bedroom.

The following weeks are pure joy. Ashley Anne does date Eric and sees her other suitors to please her father but she will allow only me to sleep with her. I am confused.

The best thing that I can do is to take each day as it comes. All suitors, with one exception, understand that they have lost Ashley Anne. Eric persists in his pursuit and suggests that after the air car race, she will return to him. It is no wonder that the car race seems to upset her.

All former suitors tell me that Ashley Anne is frigid and will never let any man touch her. I believe them. I suspected that her ugly encounter had turned her frigid to others. I tell Ashley Anne that I want to be in her heart forever.

We discuss everything. Tears come to her eyes as she says, "Sweetheart, I can't tell you everything about the ugly rape incident yet because I can't bear the pain of resurrecting this horrible memory. It has cursed me for years.

Give me some time." I immediately put my arms around her, cuddle her, kiss her and say, "I will wait until you are ready. I love you." She rocks in my arms for a long time and then falls asleep. I put her to bed, kiss her and return to my apartment.

Ashley Anne and I now have dinner together very often. I have never known such pure joy. I gain energy from each experience. Nonetheless, I am beginning to feel uncomfortable because I know that I am spending too much time with her and not enough on preparing the car for the race.

If I do not spend more time with my machine I will fall behind schedule and will not be ready. Winning the race will bring me public acclaim and place me in the perfect position to gain influence with those guiding our future. I am seriously considering forgetting the whole thing but it has occurred to me that if I do not race I will fail everybody including Ashley Anne, even though she is the one who is telling me to drop out of the race for her sake.

I plan to tell her of my decision this very evening even though I know that it will bring me grief. I open the door and say, "Honey, I am here!" She comes into the room emerging from her shower. Her fragrance proves an irresistible aphrodisiac. She says, "Have you ever danced with a naked woman?" My sexual reaction is instant. I am crazy with desire.

She takes me by the hand and leads me to her room, where the lights are low and dreamy. We dance closely. We give up and go to bed. We both woke up hours later and we kiss thoroughly. She says, "I can tell that the race is bothering you, Sweetheart. I thought that it was out of your system." I tell her that I must race for her good and for mine.

She appears stunned and there is a good reason. She knows that I can well be killed during the race. She obviously does love me and things have changed in her family. The ensuing chill is awful. She throws me out of her apartment. I am saddened beyond belief and feel that I cannot go on without my lover.

A huge war rages within me but I decide to press onward and devote all of my efforts to the car race. Ashley Anne would not respect a coward and I know it. She has placed a terrible test burden upon me. I know that there will be more.

As the day of the air car race approaches, I study the routes and the details of the race with care. All seven of us, the group that could shape the future of Magogania and Gogania if I am successful, inspect the air car. I had just flown it to Gogania for their final inspection and approval.

The Chairman had beamed as I explained the details of the machine to him. He told me that he might make a huge wager on my winning car but there was something about his manner that bothered me. I take Karl to the side and say, "The Chairman is not on our side. Something is wrong but I cannot put my finger on it." He says, "I feel it also, Achilles. I will work on trying to ferret out what is wrong."

The pressure mounts and I make last minute alterations. We are all raw. Karl is the steady force that keeps us from falling apart. We go over every inch of the machine to assure that all changes fall into the confines of the rules. We then take video pictures so that we can see if any untoward changes have been made by the Chairman's people.

I tell Peter of my problems with Ashley Anne. He replies, "As I told you, Sharon and Ashley have become very good friends. They act like sisters. Give Ashley some space. Sharon says that she really understands why you must race but she fears that she will lose you."

He continues, "Your enemies are planning to kill you and they might succeed!" I say, "If that is so, why am I racing, Peter?" He smiles. Suddenly, it occurs to me that Ashley Anne had to solve the problem of preparation time for me. I was not capable.

Peter says, "Because you must. It is your destiny!" I muse and realize that destiny and fate are interesting companions.

Setting the exact course in the computers so that I will remain within the assigned race corridors is almost as important as the actual piloting. It is vital that several alternative plans be installed so that any unknown problem can be handled quickly. Wind shears and other phenomenon have to be built into the guidance system's automatic responses.

For example, because of magnetic fluctuations at the pole, the superconductor is very sensitive to magnetic variations. The craft can lose some efficiency. More power will be needed to help lift the craft.

Eric with his illegal extra power cell will not be affected. I choose in my flight plan to fly low while over the ice pack and use the surface effect principle (capturing air between my craft and the surface of the earth to increase pressure and give me a little added lift that I might well need). Even though I will have to fight extra drag the overall results may be favorable.

I will use the concentrated magnetic effect at the pole to achieve orbit. Because of this tactic I figure that I will trail Eric as we enter the following cave and forest areas, but not by far. Since I will be lighter than he I can conserve more fuel over the flat areas than he does.

Looking at the visual records of the course triggers something in my mind. Many of Eric's competitors have mysteriously lost control just before reaching the final speed tube at the Stadium. What caused this repeated phenomenon? Could it be a laser beam? It might be done with a hidden beam that temporarily blinds the pilot. We use such tricks during our war games. It is very effective. We place a shield in my helmet to counteract this possibility.

During my final flight tests we continue our search to see what they might have done to my machine. We find a spurious circuit attached to an explosive device that would trigger in the ionosphere. It would destroy the computer guidance module.

I report this to my Chairman, Nebo. He says, "I'm glad that you found it. Keep up the good work." His reply was exactly what I expected. He didn't offer to investigate nor submit a report to the Committee. Why?

It is time to test my machine on the track since we have done all that we can except that part. I call Peter away from his testing and say, "Peter, it is time for me to try once more to get Ashley Anne to speak to me. Do you think that Sharon can persuade her to watch my final run of the Labyrinth? We can all go to dinner after the practice."

He shakes his head and says, "Achilles, the things that we have to do for you to keep you stable is astounding. You are supposed to be our leader! Remember? You are supposed to be fearless, filled with successful ideas, the man with the plan and the strong stoic undefeatable symbol of authority! Try to remember that! You now look like a bowl of jelly!" I smile and so does he.

Two interminable days later Sharon comes over while I am making fine adjustments to the computer, and says, "Achilles, I have invited Ashley Anne to come, watch the preliminary runs and go to dinner. She will come only if you promise not to touch her!" I reply, "What the hell kind of date is that?"

She replies, "Achilles, you just do not get the picture. Ashley refused your proposal to marry her because you two talked about having children together. Remember that she was told that she could not conceive! That fact seemed to pass right over your head like so much wind! Men, ugh! She wanted to prove to you that she could conceive before she accepted your proposal. Well, she is pregnant!"

She continues, "There are tons of hormones running around her body. Expect some strange reactions from her. She is terrified that you will be killed and, frankly, I don't blame her!"

She lectures, "You better have an engagement ring and a matching wedding ring in your pocket during the race to remind you that you have family responsibilities as well as being responsible for each one of us!"

She continues, "Ashley went to Dr. Abaris who is a friend of Vera and Roland and, as you know, is the best in the business of fixing broken bodies. Ashley told him that she would lose you because you in your discussions said that you wanted to have children with her. She wants to have children very much also but because of the damages from the rape other doctors told her that she could not have children of her own. Abaris told her that basically her ovaries were in good shape and by using the new medical nano-technology he could clean out the scar tissues and repair the nerve damages."

She says, "He was obviously successful! She took the gamble, proved that she could bear children by ruining her reputation and ruining her future life just for you. What do you do in return? Get into a stupid race that will probably kill you!"

She admonishes me, "What kind of gratitude is that? You must remember that she told you that she could not conceive. You apparently paid no attention. Do not ever, ever reveal the confidential information I just gave to you. I gave it to you so that you would see what is going on around you! Now go and do your man thing and do not dare to get killed or we will do it ourselves. Do not ever violate my trust in you." I was thinking that the sentence before the last was a non sequitur.

Pete comes over and says, "Commander, we want you to think with your head! You need sleep and you better get it." I reply, "I'm not a Commander!" He says, "You damn well better be one and damn soon!"

I continue, "I promise not to touch Ashley but it will kill me." He smiles and says, "Do not change the subject! I am not talking about Ashley. She is seventh in line." I say, "To kill me?" He smiles. I say, "Like a cat, I have nine lives." He smiles. He replies, "You better prove it!"

The remaining bench and static testing goes well and all bench testing is complete. All of the rest of the testing must be done while I fly the machine. My mind is now focused on the forthcoming dinner. What could I say to her? I want to kiss her but I will keep my promise. I get into the craft and take off for the preliminary tests. I fly it unbelievably well. I pat the machine. It purrs. I think, "I better grab hold of myself. This cannot be so!"

Before the Labyrinth test, I look for Ashley Anne but I cannot see her. My heart sinks but I power my machine and she purrs like a satisfied cat. She responds better than I expected. I check the computer and hit the throttle. Just as I roar past the starting point I see Ashley. She did come after all! My heart jumps and I give the car an extra shot of fuel. I show off my skills by flying a little too fast but with panache to prove to Ashley that I was a worthy pilot. This is what lovers do while trying to prove their worth.

I remember reading the scriptures that tell us that all of creation will respond to love. If we have faith and love that we can move mountains simply by requesting them to do so. I remember that my reaction was, "What idiot wrote this stuff?" Maybe, just maybe, I was the idiot. Maybe if my craft and I can become one and I can figuratively move the mountain, take my fear away and win the race!

The run is perfect. I feel strangely serene and say, "Thank you magnificent machine and all of your parts. I love you." It purrs! Maybe I really have lost my mind. I begin to wonder.

I fly back to the hangar and I am surprised that the whole ground crew cheers as I get out of the cockpit. I turn and there is Ashley Anne looking directly into my eyes.

I say, "I love you, Sweetheart, and I want to kiss you but I have promised not to touch you. My heart jumped with joy when I saw you here." She looks at me and says, "I am still angry with you and I am still hurt." I say, "But you love me." She replies, "Don't you dare touch me!" I repeat, "But you do love me." She repeats, "Don't you dare touch me!" I say, "Hold hands at least?" This was a last-ditch effort on my part. She replies emphatically, "No!"

We go to dinner, nonetheless. I keep my promise and do not touch her all evening. When I bring her home she opens the door and steps inside. I look at her forlornly and say, "Do not close the door, please!" She holds out her hand. I take it gently and I pull her to me. We kiss. We sleep soundly together. The following morning I agree that I will spend the remaining time before the race testing and practicing.

Time has become very precious and I sleep fitfully. My group is worried because I am very nervous and jumpy. They must have consulted with one another. Ashley Anne calls me and suggests that we picnic in one of the parks high in the mountains located in the underdeveloped world. She says, "You need rest and it has come time that I become acquainted with your son Orion. A school break provides the perfect opportunity for all three of us to have a relaxing day together."

We fly to the school and pick up our pass from the Dean of Students' office. Orion is ready but, I can tell, nervous about being with Ashley Anne. An instant rapport forms between them. Could it be that their souls have met before? I cannot decipher all the insight that Ashley Anne has given to me. It has profoundly altered my view of the meaning of life.

Somehow, I am delegated to do the job of packing our gear into the air car while they chat. After we arrive I am designated to be the unpacking man. This has got to cease!

When I look up, they are racing each other up an incline. Orion triumphs, but not by much. I lose sight of the two of them and after they are gone for an hour I begin to worry. However, my worry is for naught because they return side by side. We then enjoy a relaxing picnic among nature's mountainous beauty. When we are ready to leave Orion holds the car door for Ashley Anne and just before she enters, she pecks him on the forehead. I can tell that he likes her and accepts her.

During the trip back we all talk, hardly letting each other get a word in edgewise. We let Orion out in front of school and then we continue our journey to Ashley Anne's apartment for dinner. After dinner we lie in front of the fireplace, look into the flames and embrace. She says, "I like your son. You have done a good job of rearing him." I kiss her as the firelight dances delightfully over our bodies. We move together and become one.

As we sip tea later, Ashley asks, "Tell me about your name, Achilles." I explain that my father had given me that name because he felt that someday I could well be a leader. Ancient writers said that it was the name of a great leader who fell because he was corrupted by power, defied the will of God and defied the Code of Living. God's shield was withdrawn from him. He was then vulnerable. His enemies were then able to sever the tendon that was connecting him to God and then they were able to kill him. My father wanted my name to remind me that power worship is dangerous.

I ask rhetorically, "What did he know that would prompt him to give me that name?" She says simply, "He wanted you to always be reminded that lust for power is the forbidden fruit. Why do you want to change it?" I reply, "I do not know!" She says, "Then keep it, Achilles, and remember the scriptural admonition that reminds you that your body while on Earth is mortal. It is your soul that is immortal as long as you love God with all of your heart and live by His rules. One rule is doing onto others as you would have them do unto you." Again, I realize that Ashley is a very insightful woman.

I return to work and I almost feel that my Paraclete is talking to me so that I can visually see the minor modifications that I have to make to my machine. I make them and then run the central obstacle course several times to assure myself that they are effective. All of the practice runs made by the various participants are videotaped by the race surveillance teams. I review them.

Savvy competitors replay these records over and over. My team does. They are invaluable. A careful study reveals how each pilot will most probably react to various situations. With this insight I can decide on potential counter moves.

Hours of practicing consumes all of my spare time and then some. Sometimes, the desire to come to Ashley's apartment is overwhelming and I go to her. However, I literally fall into her arms and fall into a very restful sleep.

Sometimes she shows her frustration by saying, "Since you love your damn machine more than you do me why don't you go sleep with her!" My reply is always the same, "I love you with all of my heart." She usually says, "I wonder."

Today I had a particularly good set of practice runs and I also receive an invitation to a dinner party at the home of the Minister, Roland. "A Celebration of Alliance," was the theme of the announcement. I have bad vibrations so I asked Isaac to check with our allies to find out what was happening. He reports, "Roland knows of your problems with Ashley and think that they are serious. He is delighted! Beware Achilles, he is plotting to set you up for a fatal re-lationship rift with her."

I reply, "If Roland plans to upset the balance of my finely tuned program of preparation he has already succeeded. He is a bastard." Isaac replies, "That may well be but you must not get rattled. He knows that you are tired and he will try to get you to say or do something stupid. Do not! We will help you if you need it. Take care!"

Peter returns with the news that Ashley plans to stay with her parents for the evening of the party and the day after. This means that I cannot take her as my companion and must go stag. I do not like the predicament. But I am curious about Ashley's room and resolve to see where she slept as a child and as a young adult. She has often told me that she always feels safe and secure there.

A valet greets guests at the entrance and gives each one of them a champagne cocktail. I can use a drink. Inside the foyer awaits a carefully prepared seating plan. I should have expected that Roland would have Ashley seated next to Eric. Damn that man!

At another table next to Roland's wife, Vera, is where my assigned seat is located. Next to me is a vivacious and bodacious woman named Jessica Serra.

She is an actress with a reputation of being a man killer. She has long, sparkling auburn hair, an oval-shaped face with a pug nose and a long slender body with perfectly shaped legs and an ample bustline. Her décolletage was a tip-off to me that I am in trouble. Under these conditions I expect the meal to be nothing short of dyspeptic.

I manage to talk with Ashley before the meal, but a swirl of introductions, nods and handshakes constantly interrupts us. Many guests want to chat with me and by their questions I can tell that I am the subject of much gossip. This is not surprising since I have been the target of much gossip before this event.

I greet Jessica as I settle into my seat. Her conversation is honey dipped and complimentary but I can see that it is totally insincere. The more she gushes the more nervous I become. The glares Ashley gives me from the next table are awful! What a mess I am in!

The meal begins with oysters, which I despise. I slip the morsels to Jessica, not conscious of the message I am sending. Ashley does not miss it. Ashley engages in animated conversation with Eric. I feel nauseous, a condition inversely proportional to the pleasure and obvious exhilaration experienced by Roland.

I find some refuge in my conversation with Vera. She says, "Achilles, I feel that I know you and the source of your unpredictability." I reply, "Tell me more, please." Vera continues, "I know your father very well. This may surprise you but we, who keep the faith of the pyramid, communicate with one another." Vera is about to tell me more when Roland breaks into the conversation by interrupting with a toast. He raises his glass and says, "To peace and cooperation." We all reply.

After the toast, Jessica places her hand on my arm, then on my leg under the table. "Take me to bed," she whispers into my ear. I instantly know that I am in trouble. I feel tense. I am about to be drawn into the Minister's trap and I better do something about it and fast.

Ashley's eyes tell me that she can read Jessica's mind, if not her lips. If her eyes could project daggers I would be a dead man. I manage to struggle through two more courses. Roland continues to interrupt my conversation with Vera. She knows something that he will not let her tell me.

Jessica drops her napkin and we both reach down to retrieve it. Her hand brushes against my thigh. Ashley witnesses the episode. By this time she is probably dreaming of my demise. My mind races through scenarios of what might happen next and I don't like any of them.

Roland signals a nearby security guard. Why? Jessica casually strokes my arm, attempting more intimate conversations. She says, "So, my sweet Achilles, I understand that you have quelled several uprisings in the undeveloped lands and single-handedly fought and defeated a horde of attackers with their own weapons! You are so brave. Weren't you frightened?" I reply, "Not as frightened as I am now." She smiles and says, "Am I making you nervous?" I reply, "Yes."

How can she know about an incident in my past unless she was briefed concerning my exploits? My trial by fire is coming damn quickly and I better be able to parry the blow by doing the unexpected.

We adjourn to the drawing room so that the guests can gaze at the gorgeous gardens. Jessica says that she feels dizzy and asks if I will accompany her to the balcony. Again, Roland seems to observe my every move and nods at the security guard.

Jessica and I stand together on the balcony. This is not good. As she turns toward me, a look in her eye gives me the clue about what is about to happen! In a flash, I put an acupuncture needle into the back of her neck. I always carry one. In my world it is a necessity.

She cannot move and I can see that it terrifies her. I speak to her in low tones so that anyone who attempts to overhear will catch only mumbles. I say, "One peep and you're dead." I allow her to see my countenance and my eyes are riveted to hers. At this moment Ashley strolls to the balcony and sees me whispering to Jessica. From her vantage, we are too close. Ashley flees to her room, leaving me one last glare of disbelief. Meanwhile, I keep to my task, giving the needle a push which gives her a jolt of pain. I say to her, "I'm not bluffing."

I frisk her and find what I suspected. Underneath her fake fingernails are tiny vials of fake blood. I direct her to take the nail repair kit from her purse and to very carefully and very quickly remove her fingernails. I take the removed nails and put them into my handkerchief. I direct, "I am going to pull out the needle, but one false move on your part and I'll jam it back in. You'll be permanently paralyzed."

Terrified, Jessica realizes that I have uncovered her plan to smear herself with the fake blood, rip her dress and accuse me of rape! I look at the security camera and say, "Inform whoever hired you that I understand the game and that I will never forget this ugly misdeed."

Roland is clearly perturbed because the security guard shrugged his shoulders and spread his hands indicating that nothing happened. All observe our return to the hall. Jessica's hair was not even mussed.

Something still bothers me. Perhaps those bastards had made a false video showing violence that never occurred with Jessica. She is a good actress! The occurrence never happened. I ask Jessica if this is true. She replies, "Yes." I know that I must retrieve it! How?

We all return to our seats. She is now very quiet which gives me time to talk with Vera. I ask, "I notice that Ashley is not here. Is she coming back to the party?" She replies, "No." I ask more questions and learn that Vera and the Minister met during their University days and that Ashley is the center of their lives.

I also discover that Ashley is an extremely jealous person. What is hers is not to be taken away. She expects those that she loves will love her always and protect her at all times. Fits of pouting are not uncommon when these principles are violated.

Vera then asks, "I understand that you are not fond of your name, Achilles. A person who experiences many deep internal conflicts often does not like his or her name.

"I also know about your persistence. It never allows you to be defeated or deflected from your chosen path. I know about your tenderness. You have reared your son, Orion, from your heart." I wonder, "Why bring this up at this time?" She continues, "Many people are bothered by their given name!" I do not see a meaningful connection of the sentences.

She continues, "You are charming and magnetic but you can be ruthless. You have brought sadness into Ashley Anne's life. You must stop hurting her. She has had enough of that!"

We are interrupted before I can complete my thoughts or ask any more questions and Vera has made it plain that I have some serious fence mending to do with Ashley. I had better do it quickly. Ashley is hurt and brooding. The more she thinks about the situation the worse the situation will be.

Jessica, meanwhile, wants to talk. No wonder! I look into her eyes and say, "Why did you try to frame me?" Her eyes are moist as she replies, "I was forced into it and now that I have failed, my life is in grave danger. I am now a great liability and I must be eliminated before I can tell my story."

She tells me that certain guests and other politicians who wanted me out of the way had conspired to support the story of my ripping off Jessica's dress and raping her on the balcony.

Even though the incident did not occur, the ploy already damaged my relationship with Ashley. It could have also disqualified me from running in the air car race and ruined my reputation. I must get Jessica to a safe place.

Pete and Sharon are seated at the next table so I excuse myself to confer with them. I say, "Pete, don't ask questions. Just listen!" I tell him what has happened. I say "Take Jessica to the Pyramid where my father is now staying until the car race is over. He will look after her. Tell him that she is in mortal danger. Give him some of these fake fingernails as proof of the plot that was hatched." I slip him the fake fingernails, except one, and tell him to save them for evidence.

I continue, "I need a pilot's escape pack. I'm going to do some flying with it." I can tell Pete is about to ask where he is supposed to find one but I preempt him by saying, "Don't ask. Just deliver! Put the pack behind the corner bush at the front of the house. You have half of an hour to do all of this and no more!"

The two of them leave the house with Jessica before Roland realizes what is happening. Meanwhile, I linger with my after-dinner drink in hand and ask Vera, "How do you know that I am a man with internal conflicts? Am I that transparent?"

She smiles and tells me things about myself that I have not allowed myself to remember. She continues, "Self-delusion is a very dangerous thing." I reply, "I admit that I have faults. We all do but one of them is not my total love for Ashley Anne. She is the best thing that has ever happened to me. I love her completely and without reservation." Vera is about to say something but Roland whisks her away to another group.

Out the front window I notice a commotion. Apparently one of the guests has lost a diamond broach. Everybody begins to search for it. Interestingly enough it is Isaac that finds the missing broach. I know that it must have been Sharon who hid the broach!

Meanwhile, I see that Karl has put my safety pack behind the bush. They have concocted an effective ruse to divert attention. I slip around the rear of the house to the spot where the safety pack is hidden.

It is now time for me to bridge the Ashley gap. I have threatened Ashley's world. I have a very short time window because a full security team will make a final check of the grounds once all guests leave. I had better not be on the grounds when they do their thing.

I fly to the window that I think is Ashley's but it is not! I panic with sweaty palms. I go to two more rooms before I find hers. My heart leaps when I see her. She has slipped into her nightgown and is preparing for bed. I use my tool kit to open the window and I step into the room. She is about to scream, but I say softly, "Please, look into my eyes and see torment." This stops her, at least temporarily. "Don't you dare touch me," she states defiantly. "Ashley you," I stammer but before I can continue, she cuts in and says, "Don't you dare call me Ashley."

Cautiously, I continue, "Ashley Anne, you said that you would always listen no matter what the situation might be. You have never gone back on your word. Please listen now for there is little time." She tentatively puts down the vase that I presume was destined for a collision with my head.

I tell her about the scheme and do not permit her to interrupt. I show her the fingernail vial and tell her that there is a fake video in her house that will be used to frame me. I tell her about Jessica and tell her she can confirm my story. I lean over to kiss her but at that moment, Vera taps at the door. I heard a cough that told me that Roland is with her. I leap out the window and fly to the safety pack hiding spot where I stash the gear and make my way back to the party.

Roland is coming down the stairs to see if I am there. He sees me and curtly says that he is happy that I have enjoyed myself. I wonder what makes him think that I had enjoyed his caper! "Vera has retired early" he observes, "and I will relay your farewell to her."

During the commotion while the valet service men are retrieving cars I walk over to the bush, pick up the pack and put it into the back seat as I enter the driver's seat. A tip is expected and I tip well. Nobody seems to note or care about my package.

The next few days at the Ministry are hectic and work piles onto my desk at an alarming rate. None of it seems very meaningful but I have no choice but to do it. I call Ashley but find that she has embarked on a several-day vacation with her mother in a posh resort on the seashore. I wonder if Ashley still loves me.

I bury myself in work and into the task of testing the air car. I work like a demon. Hour after hour I fly and attempt all maneuvers that I think will be required. My crew is delighted at the performance and makes the minor modifications that I think will help the car to conserve fuel.

I still talk to the machine and tell her that I love her. I wonder if nature can feel the transfer of energy! Can faith be that powerful? I fly to the edge of the machine's endurance and my own. Although I am exhausting myself, each push improves the performance.

I am now completely fatigued and drained. I need Ashley. I go to her apartment in vain hope of finding her so I can put my head on her breasts and feel comforted. She is not there but I decide to sleep in her bed anyway.

In the midst of my slumber, I awake to see Ashley over me, holding a hand-powered laser. She orders me to get out of bed and strip. I do but my mind considers my predicament. If that laser were to discharge, I am a dead man. If I attempt a quick judo-type attack, the laser might go off! Maybe I can talk her out of this madness. Being naked in her room, I figured, will hardly support any kind of rational story of self-defense.

I am about to spring into action when she warns, "Don't even think about it." I decide to let the play continue. "Lie down!" I do as she demands. She unloads the power section of the laser which turns out to be the hiding place for the spurious video. She giggles and slides down beside me. Soon we embrace and my fatigue is forgotten.

I say, "You are a foxy bitch." I kiss her on the forehead. We indulge in foreplay and have the best sex that I can ever remember. She then falls asleep. It is early in the morning when I awaken. I kiss her and she mumbles something unintelligible. I leave her apartment and go into the cool dawn air. I take the holographs to Isaac who knows what to do with them.

The next few weeks are critical and I can only see Ashley briefly, albeit almost every day. With final training under way, I make sure to sleep well and maintain a special diet. I spend several hours at the physical fitness gym either playing a contact sport, lifting weights or running and walking. This is a tough regimen but absolutely essential.

Finally, the time for the race is at hand. The night before the race is tearful and tense. Ashley does not want me to race and she tells me so over and over. She has scores of excuses that would allow me to gracefully back out, but it is too late. The fateful game has already started.

She becomes very angry with me again and says, "Sleep with that damn machine that you love so much! You love her more than you do me!" I reply, "I love you more than anything else in the world, Sweetheart." She replies, "You have a strange way of showing it!" She throws me out of her apartment again. I'm beginning to feel like a bloody rubber ball!

I have obviously threatened her world. She also knew that I would not get the proper sleep if I stayed with her. I went to sleep on the cot next to the racing car. I patted my machine on its nose very affectionately before falling into a deep sleep. I think that the damn thing purred again! Oh my! Stress does strange things to people.

I know that I will see Ashley at the starting line and I am wearing her scarf.

THE RACE

The announcer can be heard by all participants and fans. He says, *"The competitors are approaching. They are the forty finest air car racers in all of Magogania and Gogania. If history holds true, ten will finish and eight will reap rewards. The rest will meet their final fate or fade out of the race."*

My starting position is the worst possible and Eric's is the best. Wonderful! I wonder how our impartial judges managed this stunt! In the final moments before the race Isaac calmly gave me my safety pack which was not a safety pack at all. We had designed a plastic seal material that is activated by kneading the cylindrical raw material and placing it over the crack. Simple! How do we stop the high-pressure fuel spurting out?

We designed a nitrogen freezing system with a patch and two flexible hoses constructed with tips of composite. We would insulate the pipeline from the cold temperatures. We would use water with the liquid nitrogen to repair the crack area with an ice pack and would temporarily seal it. I would then rapidly cover the area with the plastic patch material. We cannot allow the fuel flow to be slowed at all! We are prepared if my fuel line were weakened or damaged by a booby trap.

Isaac also tells me that there will be two suicides in the race. The one who eliminates me will have his family taken care of for life. The other will simply die during the race. He tells me that both had been caught in a government sting operation. The crime had not been made public or they would have been disqualified, driven from the race and forced to live in total disgrace.

I would have been if Jessica had been successful! My antagonists are ruthless, clever and frankly bastards! These assassins are motivated to do their job well. My job is to prevent them from doing so. This race is going to be bloody.

Pete will take over the leadership of the Group if something should happen to me. He pats me on the helmet and says, "Good luck, Achilles. I have no intention of taking over your job. It is your bag. I do not want your damn job so you better win or I will kill you!" I reply, "'Kill me? Remember that I have nine lives. That is a bunch of deaths!'"

We laugh! We both needed that relief as nonsensical as it was.

I am smiling, but sweat covers my palms and my gut churns. I say, "I will be fine. Say a prayer." He smiles and says, "If I pray the Pyramid will collapse." I say, "Try it. You might like it." I can tell that Pete's guts are churning also. I learn later that he did pray.

The announcer continues: *"There's the signal! With a mighty roar this race begins. Don't be fooled by the cars immediately pulling out in front. A slow start may be deliberate to save power. Low fuel is the most common reason for cars not completing the course."*

It does not take long before my first adversary makes an overt move. A black car with the number 999 deliberately moves into my corridor and is ahead of me. Each race participant can pick his own number, as long as it is not longer than three digits and no one else has selected it first. Eric, being first seed, picked his number first. He has chosen the number one and already heads the pack. I was the last to pick a number. Number 333 was available so I picked it for Ashley, Orion and me.

The announcer observes 999's move and says, *"Black, 999, has forced Achilles to slow his pace and alter his approach to the obstacles. Car 333 appears rattled."*

Black 999 glides just underneath me, hugging the path of my machine just under the exhaust, making it difficult to see. He will try to flip me over. I gun the throttle, risking loss of fuel, in order to get a visible fix on him.

The announcer describes what lies ahead: *"The first of the obstacles is a formidable feat of nature: It is a huge natural arch. The arch has a stalagmite jutting upward from the floor almost to the top. It is dangerous at best to fly by or over it."*

Most drivers will choose to fly just under the arch and over the top of the stalagmite to reduce the hazard, but I plan on saving fuel by going alongside it. There is very little room. If I can keep Black 999 concentrating on me, perhaps he will get too close to the obstacle by forgetting how little room there is between the thick base and wall. That is all it will take to wreck his ship.

I race toward the arch and gun the engines. He follows, keeping his attack position. He guns his craft with the intent of flipping me onto the side of the arch just as we move through it. I fly as low as I dare and put my car on its side, missing the stalagmite by inches. A tremendous explosion occurs just below and behind me.

I tilt the craft so that I can ride the shock wave like a surf board and gain a boost in speed without expending much fuel. My heat-resistant coating, which all cars have for reentry from orbit, will protect my craft from the heat. What a ride!

The announcer declares, "*This is unreal. The first casualties of the race have occurred already. Some fancy flying through an arch ended in a tragedy for Black 999 and number 333. It ended in a disaster for both of them and many behind that could not see because of the smoke and fire!*"

The boost of the explosion propels me to the front runners. Eric's number 1 remains ahead and I fall into a respectable fourth place as we skim along the course. At the obelisk we turn due west for the continent. We will turn northward at the next obelisk. Eric makes liberal use of his fuel. Right behind me in the sixth position is car 666.

The commentator continues: "*Miraculous! Number 333 has reappeared in the fourth spot, having somehow escaped the explosion. He must have used a tremendous amount of fuel in the process. His life may be saved, but his prospects of finishing the race are dim!*"

We approach the glacial areas, where several narrow frozen passages lead to the magnetic pole. My plan is to make maximum use of the high banks to avoid the fierce cross winds that rip across the Polar Regions this time of year. The trick is to come out of the banks at the appropriate time, lift using the magnetic field to help, fly over the geographic pole at the prescribed height and then lift into orbit.

My plan is reasonable, but car 666 is not. His pursuit is fierce, causing many close encounters. I try to evade him by flying close to jutting peaks but he will have none of that. He is a talented pilot and he anticipates my moves. He is not fooled by my evasion tactics. My palms are wet and cold. The situation is tense. I try more evasive tricks but to no avail. I enter the crevasses as planned.

A split passageway lies ahead. If I can fake my intentions to travel up one of them and at the last moment shift to the other one I intend to follow I might be able to evade him. We approach rapidly. I head for the middle of the right passage. Suddenly, I shift to the left passage, averting the split point by a hair. It was too close. This could well have ended my life.

Car 666 takes the right passage. With my nemesis having been detoured for the moment, this allows me to concentrate on the magnetic pole. I must adjust the superconductor in time to help lift me out of the passage. A cliff barrier blocks the end of this run. I will fly low for surface effect.

Before my mind can refocus, car 666 comes barreling down over the banks, straight at me. He must have expended a huge amount of his fuel to accomplish this feat, but, of course, he does not care about his ability to finish the race. He aims to finish me.

I have only a split second to react. If I go up, he has me. If I go down, he has me. If I stay my course, he has me. Now what do I do?

At the last possible moment I flip so that my car is perpendicular to the bottom. At this altitude, I have questionable lift but 666 roars by under me. I flip back, hit full throttle and skim the bottom which, fortunately, did not have any boulders for me to hit. I zoom by and under him. One projection in my way would have proven fatal.

Car 666 is very close behind me and is more determined than ever to pin me down. In the melee, I have approached my lift point. I can see that 666 plans to force me into the cliff wall before I can break free. My only hope is to surge free in the last possible second. I adjust the superconductor to maximum which places a tremendous strain on the machine. I point the nose straight up, activate the belly thrusters to keep me away from the wall of ice, and activate the tail thrusters at full throttle. All I can see is the cliff wall, lots of dust and small debris at each side and the sky above me.

Helplessly, I close my eyes, waiting for the end. I feel a jolt underneath me as 666 hits the cliff and explodes. I also feel myself riding a tremendous shock wave which is propelling me at an enormous speed. Once again, misfortune has been turned into an advantage.

"*Phenomenal!*" The announcer shouts. "*Once again, Car 333 narrowly averts a disaster! Car 666 exploded underneath him and propelled him upward with incredible speed. He is now in first place!*"

I ride over the pole as required and am lifted to the ionosphere. Eric is not far behind. Traveling across the back side of the globe in orbit will allow conservation of fuel and a respite. Maybe I can get my shattered nerves under control.

Achieving the right orbit is vital during this stage. If I lift too high, the reentry will be difficult. If I stay too low, the drag of the atmosphere will slow the machine and the friction will cause heat buildup. My calculated orbit will balance all effects. Eric, with his extra fuel, does not need to worry about such impediments and takes advantage of his higher orbital speed. Soon we are neck and neck.

I delicately adjust my sensors that could be adversely affected by a rough reentry. Since there will not be time for me to recalibrate, I check to ensure that all protective covers are intact. In my mind, I replayed the twists and turns that are ahead.

The announcer explains the course: "*After reentry the cars will once again hug the earth and traverse a land-based obstacle course. The caves require pinpoint driving. The first has a wide mouth and rough walls with jagged edges, but few stalactites or stalagmites. It is the most basic of the three that make up this phase of the race. It is a warm-up for the more treacherous caves to come. It requires lots of sideways flying but it does not have many surprises. A long tunnel precedes an opening at the other side of the tunnel. Only one car will fit at a time. This trap has wiped out many participants in the past.*

"The second cave lies almost parallel to the first. Drivers must backtrack through a thick forest to enter it. They'll have to avoid some pinnacles, trees and rocks in order to reach the mouth. Expect some action. The cave is literally littered with giant stalactites and stalagmites. Our monitors will check the speed and position of each car as it traverses the course."

"The third cave is far ahead of the second cave and has a long labyrinth of branches that must be negotiated during passage. At each fork, only one direction connects to another through passage. The others have dead ends. It's do or die. Making the wrong turn not only assures a pilot of failure but tempts others to follow to their doom. The resulting chain reaction can be deadly. If the first in line attempts to reverse his move, he will collide with those who followed him."

A warning signal indicates imminent reentry. Pete, Isaac and I have altered the usual reentry programs to make the descent more efficient and effective. It will take me closer to the cave's mouth. There is a risk of high heat and the possibility of sensor damage using this flight plan but I think it is worth the risk. I figure that since the heat tiles had withstood two close encounter blasts without triggering the heat alarm they can withstand the extra reentry heat. Is this true if they have been undamaged?

I activate the modified entry program but I do not expect the jolting and jarring that follows. The heat indicator reveals that the bottom of my ship is just above the safe limits. I can tolerate the present reading but no increase. Escape is impossible, because I have no safety pack. There is nothing to do but ride the machine and pray.

The announcer observes: *"It looks like trouble again for Car 333 even before he reaches the caves. His reckless descent may mean his disintegration in the atmosphere."*

The needle wavers at the point of disintegration. I wait. It seems to be an eternity and then slowly the temperature drops. Our newly designed tiles have done their job!

Suddenly, I am at the mouth of the first cave with no other cars in sight. I enter at a modest speed. Eric's Car 1 shocks me as it roars past. He must have had more fuel in his extra pod than we had calculated! He suddenly slows his speed! The bastard knows that any avoiding maneuver will cost me precious fuel. Since Car 666 has honed my ability to stand the craft on end, I flip onto my side and pass him without costing me fuel. Car 1, obviously angry, used a tremendous burst of fuel and passes over me.

We are so close that I can see him in his craft. He had gambled that his excessive use of fuel would leave me hopelessly behind. He enters the small exit tube ahead of me but he must be enraged that we are still so close. I let up on the power just a bit and ride close behind him benefiting from the vacuum he has created.

He does not decelerate as we enter the second cave and I allow him to maintain a slight lead.

Eric seems suicidal as he maneuvers the cave. His craft is heavier than mine, and so more cumbersome, because of the extra pod. This should work against him, but Eric is a wily flier. We thread the stalactite and stalagmite barriers together but I stay within my prescribed route, determined not to press my luck.

The edgewise flying I have mastered again proves useful. Eric and I come so close to some obstacles that pieces fall from these majestic structures and crash down. They litter the floor of the cave and slightly alter the pathway for those following us.

Eric and I trade positions while traveling through this cave. As we come out, we are even. Eric must start conserving fuel now or he might not finish the race. He has squandered his advantage but even so I know that he remains relaxed because he knows that my fuel pod had been sabotaged. I wish that I knew where but that knowledge will come soon enough.

I approach the third cave ahead of Eric and I plunge into the darkness.

The announcer explains the situation: *"Fans may wonder how drivers can negotiate the dark paths. They depend on fine-tuned, predetermined flight plans and sensors. But that is not all. There is the human factor consisting of memory, instinct and wit that makes the difference between success and failure. Each pilot must know when and how to adjust his course to fit the circumstances."*

My palms are again clammy and wet. Fortunately, my helmet has a headband that absorbs the droplets of perspiration before they can cloud my eyes. The motion of the craft is jerky and I do not have the time to smooth the rough edges. My head thrusts from side to side.

My sensors tell me that Eric is directly behind me. I can see electronic jamming signals attempting to interfere with my sensor signals.

When did that bastard install this illegal equipment? Fortunately, I know how to handle that problem because I loaded a piece of software into the computer that will, on receipt of an interference signal, analyze the frequency and instantly change my sensor signal frequency. I can tell that Eric has become frustrated. He vainly runs his frequencies up and down in an attempt to thwart my defense. It does not work.

He makes a move to pass me. Good! He uses fuel uselessly. His craft occasionally lurches, like mine, telling me that his preplanned path also has some rough calculations. His attempt to overtake me costs him dearly. It takes time to settle back into a prescribed course. We careen through the remainder of labyrinth and the end comes into sight.

The announcer traces our steps: *"Practice has made perfect fliers in Cars 333 and 1. Both are charging through the caves as if they had been running this course for years. The next phase, the forest, will be very interesting to watch."*

I roar through the cave exit with Eric immediately behind me. I set the guidance program to get me to the forest and activate a helmet light shield to prevent blindness as we rush into the bright sun. Eric moves his craft forward and speeds past me.

This bravado continues to cost him fuel. I calculate his speed as he roars into the high, clear air. He is a formidable enemy. I cannot match his speed. Eric levels out into a low orbit course. I place myself into a ballistic trajectory just as if I were a missile. I shut the power as I approach the apex. I know that this is a risky maneuver and that my heat of reentry will be fierce. During my climb in the atmosphere I used the nose needle for the last time. Hopefully, it saved me some fuel.

The forest is hundreds of miles northward, toward the colder climates. The trees are massive. I check the fuel. Prayerfully I ask that I will not have to shift to my final fuel cell until I emerge from the ordeal of the forest. I have come to the conclusion that it is this final fuel cell feed line that has been sabotaged. If so, I will run out before the race is completed.

If the heat shields have been damaged during my last reentry I am a dead man but I am committed to this course because of my fuel problem. If the program for reentry is off by just a minuscule amount all is over. I wonder what Ashley will do if burning to death in a fiery cinder is my fate! I love that girl! I simply cannot allow this to happen! Whatever happens, I know that Orion will have a loving person to take care of him.

The heat indicator again hovers at its limit. The warning light glows. One more jump in the temperature and my composite, metallic body will disintegrate. What am I doing in this damned race anyway? I am smelly, sweaty and racing into oblivion.

This may be an adventurous but it is hardly a noble end. The indicator touches the red danger zone and stays there for what seems to be an eternity. I can't activate my thrusters. I must do this at the precise moment the computer tells me to or I am in real trouble. I look out of the cockpit and see a shining object! "Oh, shit," I mumble. Eric is approaching my entry path and collision is imminent unless he takes evasive action. The bastard plans on playing chicken not realizing that I am committed to a fixed trajectory and I cannot alter it unless I want to break apart.

I am transfixed as I stare at him. At the last second, he tips his craft on its edge, allowing me to roar past, with bits of flaming tile trailing behind. At this moment, he must be assuming that I am a madman. Until the very end of his days I am sure that he will believe this to be so.

Finally, the signal is given and I am still alive to execute the activation of the thrusters. The forest is ahead! There are three routes through the forest. As a pilot faces the forest he can take the one to his left, take the center or take the right route. The left route is filled with obstructions such as boulders and requires a medium use of fuel. The center route is longer but is a much safer route and requires the most fuel. The right route requires the least fuel but is the most dangerous because the trees are very close together and hard to evade.

Not wanting Eric to follow my route, I head toward the center and veer into the right path at the last possible moment. It was too late for him to change even if he was tempted to do so. He stays on the central course.

Maneuvering in and around the trees becomes tedious and I experience one near miss after another. My detector tells me that another craft has followed me into this right course and the signature indicates that he is a Magogania craft. Behind him is a car from Gogania. Where on Earth did they come from? Until reaching the forest, they had apparently followed Eric. Now they have locked onto my path and I have become their preferred guide.

As the four of us enter an open grove, I notice that one of the trees that should be to one side has fallen into my path. My space is gone. If I steer to miss it, I will lose fuel and time. I can't afford to lose either one of them. I notice that the tree has collapsed onto one of its neighboring trees. I can barely see light through the foliage but I note that the fallen tree trunk has not crashed fully to the ground. I head for this new and smaller passage slanting the craft to match the angle of the trunk. Leaves and small branches are flying by but I manage to traverse through by only breaking small branches.

A muffled explosion sounds behind me. Someone had not made it through nature's roadblock. The other pilot probably altered his course. This cost him time. The rock formations lie ahead with trees growing out of their crevasses. Because of the altitude restrictions, only three paths can be followed. If I clip just one of the plethora of jagged edges of the rock in any one of the ravines, my craft will disintegrate. Two routes require level flying. One route, the shortest, requires sideways flying. I decide on the latter. I have become an expert on sideways flying but I must not become overconfident!

My choice of options proves the best. I hear from the announcer that other cars using the other routes are plagued by rock slides and felled trees. I feel good but the forest trip has taxed me and drained me of energy.

As I emerge, I see that no one is ahead of me. Eric has fallen behind again. I fly up to the bottom of the ionosphere for the trip to the obstacle course.

The announcer observes, "Car 333 has lucked out and is ahead. But Car 1 is catching up. Eric will pass the more aggressive Achilles in this last stretch. In all, ten craft remain, five from each country. The approaching obstacle course will be a brutal test of endurance and risk. The object is to come as close as possible to the obelisk that is the centerpiece of this labyrinth. Twelve obstacles stand in the way. This uneven pattern is full of strange twists and

*turns. Blocks just wide enough to accommodate one craft
are around the obelisks."*

I am using my final fuel cell as we enter this final portion
and nothing has happened so far but, suddenly, I detect a
puff of smoke coming from the rear thrusters.

This tells me that there is a crack in the fuel line. I immediately activate the backpack. Now I must locate the
problem. If my analysis is correct the crack will be at the
manifold next to the cockpit. Not only will I have a loss of
fuel but the fumes will contaminate the control area and
I will have trouble breathing. The crack is exactly where I
thought it might be.

I would have put it there if I were sabotaging a craft.
The ice patch seems to work and I hope that I have not
frozen the fuel flow. The leak subsides. I use another plastic patch! Fuel consumption returns to normal after a brief
fluctuation but there is a flutter in the line! That caused a
trail of smoke to appear behind me! I have a feeling that
I had better use one more overall plastic patch now! If
the reinforcement patch does not hold I am finished in all
ways!

Eric passes me as my attention focuses on activating
the ice patch. We plunge into the obelisks. I will not use
my energy to pass him on this portion of the course, but
I will make him think so. He concentrates on blocking my
way, attempting to block any effort to pass. Good! This just
causes him to use more energy and zigzagging more than
necessary.

As we round the twelfth obelisk, Eric again zigzags to
prevent my passing him. but I suddenly switch to the far
side of the course using another path and, before he could
prevent it, we are neck and neck!

I see the car as I think about that cheating bastard and
being angry gives me extra strength. The time for action has
come. I resolve to use a burst of speed and power at this
very moment. It might well crack the ice/plastic pack, but
it must be done. We were in the arches when I pass Eric. I

use every ounce of energy and concentration I possess and increase my advantage and pray that the plastic patch will hold a little longer.

The announcer's next observation is a jolt: *"Car 333 is in trouble. He is done. He is defeated! He is in a smoking coffin!"*

Vapor spews from my exhaust which indicates that I have not solved all of the problems in the fuel system. The cockpit is filling with fumes. I activate the air mask system but I know that I have precious little oxygen left. My craft may soon explode.

I know that everyone in the crowd expects to see me escape with my safety pack. Only my colleagues know that I cannot do that. The ice patch is at its limit. I find a chunk of plastic patch. I knead it onto the ruptured area. Will this patch work be successful? I do not know.

"At any moment, Achilles' machine will blow to pieces and Car 1 will win the race!" the announcer proclaims.

Eric steers away from my machine, so as not to be affected by my demise. I must stay ahead or lose the race. The rules of the course allow me to rely almost exclusively on the computer preprogrammed pattern. If that chunk of plastic fails my car will go to pieces. What a hell of a way to end my life!

The last pillar looms ahead. I prepare to take control of my machine. I must engage this tremendous pillar hurdle. It is placed closer to the previous pillar than the rest, so a sharp turn is required. The arch before the pillar is low, so that I will fly near the ground on the approach. I did it!

This final hurdle is not a solid structure. Balloons positioned three miles above the obstacle course project beams of light to mark the boundaries. I zoom upward so that I can arch over the beam of light and then plunge toward the ground. I have to pull out with the speed of 1.5 Mach and stay parallel to the ground, alongside the rock wall which measures our movements. Inside the wall sensors placed by the Committee examine all moves.

Unknown to me, Isaac, Pete and Hector are sitting in the front Committee boxes, which provide a perfect view for this part of the race. They can see the craft whizzing along the course that leads to the finish line. A large screen allows them to observe the cars as they traverse the tunnel.

Isaac, Pete and Hector have detected both cutting and blinding lasers embedded in the wall. They will concentrate on the cutting lasers. It will be difficult to disable them because the guards ensure that no one enters the viewing stands with anything resembling a weapon.

Hector has studied the underdeveloped people and their habits very well. Fascinated by the blowgun, a favored weapon of some of the underdeveloped people, he has even tried the technique himself. He has become rather proficient and is able to nail us with paper wads from tremendous distances. Pete and Hector decide that the only hope for disabling the trap is through this technique. Paper wads cannot accomplish this goal, but the candy that Hector liked to roll around in his mouth might be the right projectile.

Hector needs a blowgun long enough to be accurate but not so long that the friction will interfere with the distance required to hit the wall. The guards continue to eye the crowd for foul play. Hector discretely rolls a program into a hollow tube with a diameter that will just fit the sticky but slimy spheres that he will propel to the wall. The blowgun is ready.

Hector loads his mouth. He decides that he will fire five spheres at each opening and calculates that he can fire one shot every second. With this timing, a quick mental calculation confirms, the final shot will be fired just seconds before my passing the laser ports.

Pete and Hector can see the vapor trail issuing forth from my craft. This has diverted the attention of the guards temporarily. The first projectile misses its mark. The second misses. The third is a partial hit. The fourth misses. The fifth is right on.

0

Hector begins the second series. The first misses but the second hits dead center just as my car passes the ports. One of the guards notices the unusual activity in the stands. He yanks the tube from Hector's hand and says, "What the hell do you think you are doing?" Hector's answer is swift. "I was thinking of firing a spit ball at the announcer. That son of a bitch is prejudiced." The guard smiles, takes the tube, smashes it and says, "You better not have arms. If you are armed consider yourself under arrest!" He checks both of them and says, "You ought to be ashamed of yourselves. This is a very serious race and you can only think about childish pranks?"

Meanwhile, ignoring all warning lights, I roar over the finish line. The winner's light illuminates my cockpit! I have won! I have not violated the tube dimensions. I can hardly believe it!

There is no time to celebrate, though. I remember the marshland at the end of the end runway. I cut all power after pointing my air car toward the muddy surface. I can't figure out why I cut the power since I have just run out of fuel. Reflex is a wonderful thing. I point the nose up so I can douse my machine in the muck without burrowing under the surface. I create an unbelievable mass of flying water, shrubbery and wet dirt. The craft skids to a stop.

I hit the escape button and am ejected into the muddy marsh. Just as I exit, flames envelope my car. Why? There is no fuel base! Vapor would have just flashed. I am puzzled. There was one more booby trap! Fortunately, it fired too late.

At first there is silence, except for my burning craft. Rescue equipment arrives at the scene and the flames are quickly extinguished. Pete and Isaac arrive on the third rescue aircraft and we hug. I tell them to open the air car and examine it for evidence so that we can prove who did the sabotage. I am certain they will find what they need to find. It will lead them to Roland and his henchmen.

Only six aircraft finally finish. Eric is second. My Gogania colleagues who followed my paths are third and fourth. The Magogania pilots cover the fifth and sixth spots.

The Minister and his aide arrive on the scene. Hector has already slipped over to Eric's machine and is discretely taking holographs of Roland's men removing the extra fuel cell. This will disqualify Eric.

Hector broadcasts the holographs of the removal by instantly transmitting them to our headquarters and directly to Admiral Zadoc as well as to Roland. The Race Committee meets in private. They are about to decide that I am to be arrested and jailed for having an illegal fuel tank, with sabotage and with intent to murder. Why? Because of fake holographs that had been furnished by Roland's people to them.

However, at that moment Admiral Zadoc burst into the room and shows them the correct videos instead of the fake videos that were sent to the Race Committee to describe what has happened.

He reveals that Roland's hackers are under arrest and that the extra fuel tank was followed but not destroyed. He shows them the confessions from the people who were hired to take the extra fuel cell from Eric's machine and destroy it. They were threatened with death if they failed.

Roland came back in time to hear the whole presentation by Zadoc. I was told that his face turned ashen. Zadoc told the Race Committee that the smartest thing to do to keep the Race Committee's reputation intact was to say nothing about this at present but announce that all of the data concerning this race must be evaluated and be thoroughly analyzed before a final decision is made.

Pending this analysis all aircraft will be cleared and the ceremonies will continue. Agreements are signed and notarized that Eric will be stripped from his position, charged with attempted murder, face a long, long prison term and face disgrace.

My craft's booby traps were added to the mix of illegal actions and infractions.

Eric and his cohorts failed to defeat my craft and they will face charges of sabotaging of my fuel line and adding the extra fuel tank to Eric's craft.

These infractions will be confirmed by the Race Committee. The papers are signed by Odysseus, Nebo and the Race Committee Chairman, Roland, who knows he has deep trouble ahead of him.

These arrangements will delay the publishing to the public of the rightful race positions to all other craft completing the race and their commensurate rewards.

All people in the decision room agree and are satisfied. Pete, Isaac and Hector will meet with Roland to assure that he will carry out his duties. He will do so because he and all in charge do not want to expose this whole tawdry affair! Also, he and all of the others involved do not want to go to jail! Politics, as usual, is at work.

Eric, not yet aware of what has happened, is furious and has blood in his eye. He stalks over to me and lunges at me with a star knife in his hand. I step aside and he misses but twirls around and is attacking me again. This damn star knife is a brutal hand-to-hand weapon. Ashley, who has just arrived on the scene, screams out a warning.

This is not helpful to me. She watches in horror. Fortunately, I found some tapes of Eric in battle style as I was searching for race tapes. I noticed how he cripples his opponents with this awesome weapon. He always attacks with a downward thrust. This causes his opponent to raise his hand and arm to ward off the attack. Eric then suddenly changes his attack to a low and upward motion, tearing the stomach and rib cage of his opponent to pieces. I suspect that he would follow this pattern in his rage.

Sure enough, his right hand is up. I feign a parry and his reversal starts. He understands my countermove too late. I break his arm using a hand chop. I follow this by another two blows to his knee with my foot. He first looks at me blankly as his leg collapses under him and then he screams in pain.

The medics that had assembled to take care of me have another unexpected patient instead. Eric will receive his short-lived honors with a bound arm and a wounded knee.

I now have another attacker, Ashley. Her legs are caked in mud and her eyes are lit with fire as she begins a one-way conversation. My mouth opens several times to say something but it never has a chance! She says, "You Macho Bastard, you are incorrigible and an ignoramus." Those are the kindest things she says as I stand in the marshlands, being transfixed by the piercing language coming from such a beautiful mouth. I could not believe such things could come forth from such a beautiful woman!

She continues, "I am not happy being your personal harlot. You are the most inconsiderate human being ever born. You are rotten to the core. I am pregnant, but I don't suppose that you or that damn machine care!" I muse, "This machine gave her life for us!"

She begins to sob and tears flood from her eyes. I still stare at her and am transfixed but I now say, "Can I now say something?" She continues to sob and pounds my chest with her fists. I gently hold her hands, take her body to mine and look her in the eyes and say, "I love you Ashley, with all my heart." She replies, "You scared me to death you idiot!" I took out the ring that Sharon told me to carry and put it on her finger. She looks at it in silence.

It seems to calm her a bit so I ask, "Marry me right now!" and I show her the wedding ring. She looks at me but does not speak. I continue, "How about tomorrow? Do you think you could be ready?"

She just looks at me and then she says, "Tomorrow! You are truly a nut case!" I reply firmly, "Tomorrow!" I kiss her gently. She answers, very quietly, as she buries her head on my shoulder. "This is insane. I can't understand why I love you. You are a real piece of work! There is not a single rational cell in your entire brain. Yes, I will marry you."

A crowd of onlookers witnesses our embrace. I turn to them and exclaim, "She is going to marry me!" One woman says, "I don't know why. You are dirty, smelly and crass. If I were she I would send you home to clean up and become presentable before you got your answer."

That woman is correct and I really don't feel much like a hero but this wonderful, beautiful woman is in my arms and it makes me very happy!

I pick her up and carry her out of the marsh. The Race Committee Representative, Chairman Nebo, approaches and I say to him, "She has just consented to marry me." He smiles and says, "Some people have all the luck. Congratulations."

He then turns to Ashley Anne and adds, "You do realize that controlling this irrational man will be a very difficult thing to do?" She smiles and responds by saying, "Mr. Chairman, I know this all too well!" He smiles.

This vision fades away and I am in the land of outer darkness. The Guides ask me, "What have you learned, Edward?"

I reply, "There are two basic forces in the Universe. Love is one of them and the other is fear. Follow love for it will lead you to abundant and everlasting life. Follow fear and it will lead you to hate, total destruction and everlasting nothingness."

They say, "Where are you on this spiral of life?" I reply, "I don't know but I know that I love Ashley and she is on the way upward!"

They smile, nod their heads and command, "You may continue and you still hold God's shield."

CHAPTER 3

Life with Ashley Anne

Nebo, Chairman of Gogania, is a tall, dark-haired, muscular man with piercing brown eyes. He loves power and will do anything to keep it. He leads the group with an iron fist. He asks that Ashley and I follow him as he approaches the waiting room where results of the race will be read.

He says, "This is the best damn race ever run. There will never be another like it. Achilles, you made it a hell of a show! I made some very heavy first place bets on you yesterday." As we looked at each other squarely in the eyes I say, "Mr. Chairman, what took you so long?" He looks at me sternly and then laughs. He then looks at Ashley and says, "You are really going to marry this madman? He does not know the word defeat and his actions are totally unpredictable!"

Ashley answers, "Yes, Mr. Chairman, I am going to marry him." He smiles at me and says, "You have nerves of steel, Achilles, and you are pretty damn smart. You will be a great asset to me and to the Space Command. Isn't that right,

Admiral?" Admiral Zadoc smiles and I know why. Nebo continues, "You will be tested sooner than you might think." I look at him and wonder what he is really trying to tell me.

The announcer states that at this time the race results will stand even though there are cubes of data still to be studied. He says, "The Race Committee hereby declares that the ceremonies are authorized to continue. Pending interpretation of the analyzed material that we now have in hand the results that have been broadcasted will stand! All seem to agree that this was the best race in the history of the Race of Honor!"

There is a great cheer from the crowd! He continues, "All pilots who completed the course are asked to assemble immediately." I grab Ashley's hand and move toward the stands. Even though I am smelly and messy people crowd around me and ask for my autograph. A cute blonde kisses me. I liked that. Ashley does not.

Sensing her ire, I kiss her thoroughly and say, "You are the only girl in my life." She looks at me and says, "Keep it that way! I am your only woman! You better totally understand that fact! You really do need a shower!" I smile and say, "I clearly understand all four statements."

I see Orion making his way toward us. He is smiling. I say, "Orion, meet your mother." He kisses her on the cheek, hugs her and says, "I love you, Mom." Tears roll down Ashley's face. There is nothing in this world or the next world that will ever change the power of love.

We approach the award arena. The winners take their positions. The tentative award medals are given in reverse order. Each will receive a substantial prize and a position in the Defense Department. Eric, now bandaged and assisted by a walking fixture, receives his medal and glares at me. My name comes last as the First Place Winner. There is a thunderous applause and the Goganian national anthem is played.

I step to the podium. The crowd is silent. I am to speak. It occurs to me that I should have thought about what I would say. I look at Ashley Anne. She looks back at me.

Now what do I do? My father always told me that when things get tough pray and get on with the task. I do.

I look at the people who are now quizzically looking at me and obviously are waiting for me to say something! All that can be heard are the chirping of the birds outside the arena.

I look down and then at the crowd again and say firmly, "Let us bow our heads and pray for the souls of those proud and brave pilots that were killed in their quest for glory and recognition. They fought for honor, glory for their country and to make their families proud of them. They are true heroes!

"We will miss them and our hearts are with the loved ones left behind. Let us, who survived this race, ask God for the wisdom we need to make our lives full and meaningful. We must realize the preciousness of life and realize that we can enrich the lives of others by our actions. Only by doing our best with the talents we have will we realize peace within our souls."

I admonish, "By doing our best work and always respecting others as we travel on our path of life will we find the true meaning of the Code of Living."

I wait in silence. I note the total look of surprise in the faces of many of my colleagues who have heard me scoff at religion.

I explain, "The greatest achievements of mankind have always been achieved by cooperation with and the respect for the abilities and aspirations of those surrounding us.

"This ingredient is the essential. It brings trust, confidence and love. I would not be standing here as victor today if I did not have my faithful crew and future wife behind me all of the way. They believed in me! We formed a cohesive and dedicated unit that overcame my frailties and produced a perfect blend of machine and man. I am grateful."

I declare my gratitude by saying, "I thank the Race Committee for their tireless efforts to arrange all the myriad of details that were necessary to make this race possible. Let us applaud them." The crowd joins me in enthusiastic clapping.

I pause until there is complete silence and while I silently muse, *The struggle between Eric, the Serpentines and me and my group is not over yet. It has just begun!*

The secret society, called the Serpentines, were founded by the Professors at Atlantis University, now called the University. They enlisted other professors in all colleges from Magogania and Gogania and eventually invited senior students from these Universities to join them.

Their aim is to rule and control the people of Earth. The plan is to organize the leaders of the tribes inhabiting our Earth into a world government. The goal was to have a world government that would share the fruits of the Earth's to all people according to their needs. This sounds great but someone must do the labor required and must direct it.

Obviously this requires intelligent supervision. The Serpentines decided that it would be them, the government, that would do the directing.

They found that the tribal chiefs were not too keen about someone else taking their job and sending the fruits of their labor to others. They stopped cooperating. The Serpentines then decided that these rebels must be conquered and controlled because only the Serpentines were smart enough to control the World Government! They forced the rebels into submission!

Magogania defeated the Serpentines but they went underground and started to infiltrate into both Magogania and Gogania. They pose a grave problem to our nations.

I continue my speech, "Love between people is the key to life. My greatest love, Ashley Anne, has given me her love and agreed to marry me. I did not earn it. She gave it to me. She is my life, my love and my treasure. I cannot imagine life without her." The crowd then gives me an applause that sounded like thunder!

I continue, "I now ask that our two great nations, Gogania and Magogania, continue to hone and improve their great joint venture called the Space Command. It was founded to secure peace for this generation and all generations to come. It is our mission to nurture it. It is our greatest challenge. Let us move boldly to accomplish its charter."

There is silence and then suddenly I hear an explosion of clapping and cheering. I smile. Orion comes over and hugs me and Ashley gives me a passionate kiss. I look at both of them and say, "God has blessed us this day."

The Space Commanders' orderly comes over and gives me a freshly tailored and pressed space uniform without rank. He says, "The Admiral expects you and your fiancée to be at the Headquarters Reception Room at seven o'clock sharp."

I look up and see Vera. Ashley's mother is one powerful woman and she is coming toward us with fire in her eye. She says, "Achilles, you are a unique piece of work. There isn't a rational cell in your entire head!" I say, "This is the second time today I have been given this great news!"

She continues, "Smart Ass, are you getting the idea? You think that you are to be married Friday! Think again! How is this going to happen? A Magic Wand for instance?"

She looks at her daughter and says, "You are no better than he is! This disease may be contagious! I ought to have you both quarantined before it spreads!"

She continues her admonishment, "Bring this oversexed maniac home with you and clean him up. Try not to mess up the house too much! He really belongs in the loony bin! Put this gruesome groom-to-be in the guestroom and throw away the key. Maybe he will disappear!"

She looks at me and says, "Achilles, your uniform will be delivered to our house." Continuing my great affinity to put my foot in my mouth I say, "It seems like a very good idea." Vera gave me a look that would melt the Universe. She says, "You have turned my sane, sensible and rational daughter into maniac number two. Congratulations!" She leaves.

Pete approaches and says, "Sharon will see to it that the Pyramid will be ready for your wedding. Your father will perform the ceremony. Vera is sending electronic invitations as we speak." I say, "Vera is one sharp woman. I must never underestimate her ability but she has a sharp tongue! How did she know about a wedding Friday? Am I missing something?"

Pete smiles and says, "You have no idea what you have missed, do you? Sharon says that you are oblivious of what is going on around you. Keep it that way! Stay cool and enjoy it. You deserve it. We are dedicated to taking care of you but we want you to understand that this task is not easy, in fact, it is damn difficult!" We laugh.

Odysseus, Chairman of Magogania, comes over, shakes my hand and says, "Achilles, you have surprised me at every juncture and you have convinced me that you will make a superb space warrior. Others may consider you foolhardy. I don't. My question to you is simple. What god do you serve? He is obviously protecting you." I answer, "The God, our Creator."

He replies, "Really!" I say, "Sir, who is your god?" He is surprised and taken off guard. He answers, "Achilles, I pray to the God of our Pyramid, the God of our forefathers and the God our Creator." I say, "Seems to me that we pray to the same God."

He gives me a wondering smile, looks at me and says, "Let us keep it that way."

Vera returns and springs another of her edicts upon me, "Achilles, after the state dinner, you will not see Ashley Anne alone until after the wedding. Maybe she will regain her senses. I doubt it! Nonetheless, tomorrow you will meet me in the Great Hall dining room for an early morning breakfast! Be there!"

Roland's limousine arrives. We enter. I am extremely tired and I put my head on Ashley's shoulder as we travel to Roland's home. As she kisses me and as I fall asleep I mutter, "Honey, I wonder what Vera has in mind for breakfast tomorrow? She will probably have poached Achilles." Ashley laughs. She is radiant. We arrive. In less than one hour, I am to be cleaned, dressed and ready for the reception.

Our rooms are ready and complete with accessories for grooming and becoming ready for a formal affair. I head for the shower. As I step out there is a knock at the door. I am told that the tailor is waiting to perform a final fitting. My uniform with its dark blue pants are form fitting. My top is a white cotton turtle neck. The blue, Gogania's color, pants blend with the hunter green jacket, Magogania's color. The tailor said that Ashley gave him my measurements. They were amazingly accurate. Very little adjustment is necessary. How does she know my measurements?

Meanwhile, Ashley has dressed. She is ready before I am. I gasp as I see her. She is dressed in a full-length solid white flowing gown. Her diamond necklace supports the rising sun pendant with a bow below making it look like a cross. It is the symbol of Magogania. Her flowing golden hair tops the perfect vision of the goddess of grace. She is glowing and beautiful. We are ushered into the waiting car. Roland is in his uniform and Vera has a form-fitting, solid dark blue gown. Ashley Anne looks at me, pulls my head over and kisses me thoroughly. She says, "This is all you will get tonight." She smiles. I frown.

We arrive at the Space Command's Reception Room. The assembled group is gracious, extremely perceptive, and each is competent in his field of expertise.

Ashley knows each one of them and the entire background of each. I know them because I have worked with many of them. She knows them because she is interested in people and what motivates them. The reception is relaxed and friendly. The bell sounds and alerts us that the State Dinner Reception is about to start. The special reception is over. It seemed to me that we had just arrived.

We are all taken to the Great Reception Hall where I find myself meeting with leaders that are inaccessible to most of our citizens. The dinner chime rings and we are ushered to our seats in the main dining room. Ashley Anne and I sit at the head table.

After dinner the speeches begin and they are all political but mercifully this time they are short and to the point. This is followed by my formal induction into the Space Command as Commander Fourth Class. The proper insignia is now attached to my uniform. I shake hands with Admiral Zadoc, Admiral of the Fleet of Magogania, and approach the podium.

Again, I am caught short and without a prepared speech. I rise and look at all in the room. There is total silence.

I commence, "We are privileged to reside on a planet that is one of the infinite planets in a universe that is surrounded by an infinite number of universes that fill infinite space."

I continue my professorial observation. "We are a small speck in an unbelievable and thriving creation! Grasp this astounding fact about the massive creation and its massive size then turn your thoughts to the fact that the Creator loves life, each one of us equally and wants us to love Him!"

I continue my commentary. "He has allowed us to break the light barrier. We have confirmed that matter can be converted to definable waves of energy. As matter approaches the subatomic stage it starts to vibrate like a violin string and can travel as a membrane of coordinated matter called Quantum. We sent a vessel into outer space and it left the Earth, went into space and was returned to us intact! Galaxies are formed by the coming together of quantum membranes. You might imagine that navigation in deep space is rather difficult but God does this routinely. Soon, if we follow the code of nature and accomplish our karmas we will be able to travel to far away stars and planets."

I say, "Our Creator wants us to and expects us to behave ourselves and follow His code of living so we can be at peace with Him. Each soul is important to God. He wants each one of us to help Him run the Universe."

I repeat, "The question we must ask ourselves is simple. If each soul is important to Him should we ever dare to reject Him? Let us vow to follow His code before we act!"

I say, "We must understand that despite living in an infinite system we, individually, are loved by our Creator and we were brought here for a reason. Each one of us is important."

I continue, "Our forefathers gave us a great storehouse of knowledge to enjoy. We are expected to expand their wisdom and use it wisely. Our ancestors made mistakes. We now have two countries as a result and each has been struggling for power. This has not been healthy for any of us."

I say, "Now we are trying to unite in peace. The material things we have are meant to be a means and not an end. I think that our forefathers created the Olympic Race to teach us the cardinal rules of sportsmanship and life."

I explain, "These are rigid standards including mutual consideration, respect, cooperation, hard work, discipline and training and were meant to be a learning experience."

I say, "They are all necessary if we are to live success-fully together in the peace that we seek. Competition, to sharpen our skills and cooperation, for the good of others are the keys that will lock our nations together as a proud people. The end is to achieve a better life for all of us as well as for the aborigines of the Earth."

I continue, "The games also serve as a useful diplomatic tool to promote goodwill and a sense of comradeship. The Race is an example and yet a warning. It is held once every eight years but has become progressively more bloody and difficult.

"Making the course more difficult is not our problem but making it safer is. Killing is not the object but competition is. Let us make the games a source of competition but not a source of slaughter. Let us drink to peace and coopera-tion and make the lessons of the games be our guide of life."

I hold my glass high. Everybody stands, drinks from their glasses and applauds.

Dancing follows the formal ceremonies and would end at one in the morning by the playing of both national anthems. This has been fun! The night is over. I am sad because I know that this is the end of an era for me. I am tired because I have been running on reserve energy for a long time. My body is demanding a rest.

I fall asleep in the limousine as we travel home. Ashley kisses me and disappears. I am guided to the guestroom and I make no protest. I have never been so tired! I go directly to bed.

I am awakened at 8:00 a.m. and I am reminded that I must meet Vera in an hour. I do not recall taking off my uniform or slipping into guest pajamas. Because of God's grace and shield I am alive!

Nonetheless, I am very apprehensive about the forthcoming meeting. There was something in Vera's eyes that told me that this talk might be one of those deep and serious conversations. I am not sure that I am up to the challenge.

When I reach the dining room Vera is waiting. She looks refreshed. I still feel tired. I say, "It is good to see you looking so well." Vera says, "You look terrible! Relax! The damn race is over! Now sit down, close your eyes and relax all of your uptight muscles. Enjoy some well-prepared breakfast!"

Vera looks straight into my eyes and I know right away where Ashley learned to do this. She seems to pierce through all seven veils we human beings try to hide behind. She says, "Your father and I have had several long talks about you and your rebellious spirit. We think that you are in pursuit of power." I say, "Power is a matter of perception. If it is used for self-service it is corrupting. The holder of power must be the servant of all."

Vera says, "Really! Your actions belie your tongue!" I look into her eyes and do not answer. I know there is more to come. She continues, "How do you interpret the Five-S Rule?" I answer, "One must serve God and Him alone. Do not serve self-pride. Do not serve the god of silver. Do not serve the god of sex and immorality for sex is a symbol of love and requires commitment. Do not serve at the throne of sloth."

She says, "Very good, Achilles! You learned your catechism well. Whom do you worship?" I say, "God, the Creator of all things." I muse, "Why does everybody ask me who I worship?" She says, "I suppose you are going to tell me that you and Ashley did not have illicit sex. Her fairy godfather gave her the child that is within her body. Is that statement correct?"

I reply, "Ashley and I love one another. We are committed! We did not serve the god of sex and immorality. We serve the God you do. I love her with all of my heart."

Vera replies, "You evade beautifully. Ashley loves you with all of her heart and will refuse you nothing. You have asked her for too much already! What will you ask of her now?" I answer, "To be with me forever." She looks at me and says, "Make it so, Achilles! Make it so."

Vera abruptly shifts the topic and says, "How far have you penetrated into the secrets of the Inner Sanctum?" I look at her for a few moments. She smiles at me and says, "Achilles, you are transparent even though you are damn smart. You know more about the communications and weapons systems of the world than anybody and you are a hell of a technician."

She continues, "This is a moment of trust. Either you trust me or you don't." I answer, "I trust you." There is another moment of silence. I say, "I have detected that there is a Powerful Force that is watching us. I don't know how to contact it but I am working on it." She smiles and asks, "What have you found?"

I reply, "Eden is a true story. One dedicated remnant of the ejected group from that era gave up all material things and joined the undeveloped. They carried with them the

Adam and Eve story. They have been blessed with exceptionally long lives and I do not know why. Perhaps because they have chosen to worship the God of all Creation and are the chosen race. They are the tribes that surround Noah. Most have drifted from faith but not Noah who talks with God."

She asks, "What do you know about this sect?" I reply, "Once their leaders could communicate with the Federation Force in their Inner Sanctum. Perhaps, they knew how to use their parietal gland to connect with God but they cannot do this anymore. The ancient remnant must have neglected to teach it to their progeny. This does not help."

I continue, "However, there is something very interesting about Noah. He seems to be able to communicate directly with God and tap into the energy that is the source of all Creation. He has learned to interconnect. Noah believes and understands what life is all about. I am still struggling with these concepts."

Vera nods, looks at me and says, "There are many remnant priests whose children have become corrupted by lust. They are spawning mythology and misrepresenting the Pyramid teachings. They are preaching Baal which is a religion that believes fertility is god. It does not have the love of God as its centerpiece nor harmony and peace as its base. Lucifer has his grip on them."

I reply, "I know. Lucifer's Lieutenant, Arkite, is the leader and he is a brilliant son-of-a-bitch. Arkite has served in the Most High Temple in Gogania. He has a medium build, is medium boned but is a strong man with a square face and piercing eyes. He seldom smiles. He was given the gift of articulation."

I continue, "Arkite is known as an excellent participator in the martial arts of self-defense. He has lust for power. He wanted the job of Chief Priest. This position was awarded to my father, Avatar."

"He was awarded the position of the Most Excellent Chief Prince and as such is responsible for truth, preservation, protection of the Pyramid Temple, our religious beliefs and our nation's civil rights."

I say, "Over his altar, supported by nine columns, is a chandelier holding nine lights. They stand for belief in God by focusing on God with agape, integrity, courage, confidence, calmness, dedication, enthusiasm, patience, and optimism."

I say, "Arkite is bitter at being shunned for the Chief Priest job and is focusing on revenge for being slighted. He has listened to Lucifer and is on the dark side. He has forgotten all about his duties. He has become a turncoat and he has convinced other priests to follow him."

I express an opinion, "Judas is one of my seven followers and a priest. I hope that he is not one of the turncoats. I will be careful and I will eventually uncover the truth about his faithfulness."

She smiles and continues, "Your Father and I think that at one time eons ago you were Lucifer's First Lieutenant. You rebelled against him. You paid the price but you are a viable soul because you did. You have had a long journey. The key to keeping true faith alive on Earth is contained in the scriptures that are in our Inner Sanctum. Using these insights will show one how to live and grow together in harmony."

She explains, "The scriptures are split into twelve sections. Your karma is to deliver these to the Holy Place in Tibet just before the great flood occurs but power may corrupt you. Your soul life and Earth's future depends upon your accomplishing this karma."

I reply, "I will resist temptations." She looks straight into my eyes. She says, "Perhaps! In any case, you will need God's Force to be with you at all times. You need His Shield. Do not resist His help. You have been asked to deliver the scriptures. Do it!"

There is a long silence. Vera finally says, "Do you know about Ashley Anne's unfortunate experience?" I am silent. She continues, "After the violent rape the doctor said that she could never conceive. You must be aware of this so that you will realize the miracle of her baby. Don't you ever, ever violate her complete trust and love for you."

I am silent as she adds, "By the way, this meeting is over and I still think you are incorrigible!"

Vera leaves me sitting and pondering, "How did that beautiful and powerful woman ever get so much out of me? I acted like a human sieve. Indeed, Vera is not an ordinary woman."

I report for duty at the Space Command Headquarters. Zadoc welcomes me. My desk is small but adequate and my duties are explained to me by Zadoc himself.

One of my duties is to find Arkite. Zadoc asks, "Where is Arkite? You gave me some information about his spreading Baal in South America and the building of the pyramids. What is his game?" I reply, "I don't know where he is now but his game is revolution. I have spent many hours following leads. I don't like what I see and I believe that he has breached our security."

Two days pass and many subjects have been discussed. Suddenly, it dawns on me that I have not seen Ashley since the Ball. Zadoc and I have talked for hours after each workday. We eat dinner at the office. I then go to Roland's house and am greeted by the butler who guides me directly to my room! Vera has gotten her way. I will not see Ashley until the wedding! Vera truly is really not a woman one can ever ignore. Is Zadoc part of the picture? Of course!

Suddenly, it is our wedding day. The wedding is upon me. With sweaty palms, I attempt to dress. Fasteners will not fasten. The trousers will not come on. I am a human wreck. Miraculously, I hear a tap at the door and a voice saying, "Sir, could I be of some help?" My answer is immediate and simple, "Yes." Vera's valet enters and says, "Sir there are times when all of us need help." I reply, "It seems that I need help all of the time!"

He laughs and says, "Sir, to realize that fact is the start of true wisdom." He takes immediate control and I know that without him I have no chance whatsoever of arriving at the wedding on time. He smiles and deftly gets me in shape to leave. I say, "Thank you. You have my deepest gratitude!"

He smiles and says, "Ms. Vera has told me all about you." I say, "Anything good?" He smiles and says, "Yes, and it has been my pleasure to assist you. Ms. Vera is a very unusual woman with great insight and wisdom. Listen to what she tells you. It will be good advice."

He adds, "She really likes you but she says that she really does not understand why. She says that our future is in your hands. Do well for us." I say, "Thank you. I will do well for all of us with your help, the help of others and especially with God's help." I head for the car port and note that all limousines except mine have left.

I look at my watch and know that I am going to be late if the driver does not break some speed laws. He breaks them. We arrive precisely on time, to the very second.

I proceed to the proper spot in the Pyramid. The crowd is silent. I try to hide my nervousness. Pete looks at me, smiles and says, "So this confused man beside me is my leader? Achilles, you are a damn wreck!" He gives me the wedding ring. I nod with approval. Avatar, my father, looks me in the eye, nods his head and smiles. I grin back at him and my nervousness ameliorates.

The choir begins to sing. The music is tranquil, soothing, and has the energy of the Universe within it. I can see a glow around the choir and feel the flow of energy pouring into us from the sanctuary. Fascinating! We really can draw energy from the creative force that surrounds us.

I suspect that we can also lose energy if surrounded by cacophony. I note that the musical selections are taken from the works of a cluster of composers who had lived in our society before Adam's Revolution.

The Bridal March! We, at the altar, all turn to see the attendants walk down the aisle. I have never paid much attention to the pageantry of the wedding ceremony before.

I wish I had. It is magnificent. The women attendants are gorgeous and dressed alike in pale green gowns. Green signifies that marriage is the combination of two souls and that life abundant will spring from this union.

Ashley is a goddess. Her white gown was outlined in detailed pearls with pearl accessories. Her necklace is solid gold with the sign of the sun in the middle. A bow cross is above the sun and a red equilateral metal triangle is pointing downward inside the sun meaning God has created the sun and the sun has created the planets and showered life to the Earth. It is unbelievable. She had chosen this gown because it is a replica of the gown Vera had worn at her wedding.

As Ashley glides down the aisle with her father the crowd stands. She looks at the guests with a warm smile that makes all feel very comfortable.

Ashley and Roland approach me and he reluctantly gives me her hand. Holding hands, Ashley Anne and I approach the altar and exchange vows and rings. We are declared man and wife. Her veil is lifted. She surely is a true angel.

Avatar looks at me, realizes that I am in a daze, smiles and says, "Son, stop staring at Ashley and kiss her! She is your bride!" There is a chuckle from the crowd. I kiss my bride firmly on the lips. I then kiss her on the cheek. Then I kiss the other cheek. Then I kiss her again firmly on the lips.

My father says, "May you always be this ardent when you greet your wife." The crowd laughs and claps. We walk down the aisle together and we enter the limousine.

After we are seated, I kiss her gently, look at her eyes and say simply, "I love you sweetheart with all of my soul." She beams and says, "I know. May this always be so!"

Two receptions have been arranged. One reception to be held is a huge affair. The other reception to be held is a smaller dinner reception in the tower. Our ride seems to be incredibly short.

The first reception for the entire guest list is being held in the Great Hall. It is a mob scene. What amazes me is how this whole affair could have been organized in a few days. Ashley and I managed one dance together before we are ushered into the tower room for the more intimate gathering with immediate family, friends and dignitaries.

I speak with Dad. He is somber as he says, "Achilles, you have married an angel. She has her job to do and you have yours. You are bound by love. There is nothing stronger except the love that God gives to each one of us. The Force is watching you. Be Alert!"

"You will need God's energy tonight! There will be an assassination attempt. You must assure that it is not successful." I reply, "Dad! This is a hell of a conversation! What am I supposed to do?"

He says, "You have been warned! It is now your problem. You are purported to be the smart one. Be one and use your head! Whatever decisions you execute will affect the fate of the people on Earth. You are not alone! Ask God for help because whatever decisions you will make or any one of us will make has an impact on the fate of others!"

He adds, "Right now, I suggest you pray and be guided by your inner voice." The meeting is over. I pray silently for guidance. Vera comes over and she and my father are instantly engaged in a deep discussion.

I remember the long line of limousines that are waiting for their riders outside. I take a leap of faith and approach my helpful limousine chauffeur, Mercury.

I say, "There is something not right concerning tonight's events. Is there something that you have noticed that would be helpful to me? You know more than our secret service ever will." He tells me that he had overheard conversations between the chauffeurs to the effect that Eric was up to mischief. He is planning something. I told him to tell Pete all that he knew. He smiles and says, "You honor me by your faith. That took guts, Commander. I will do as you ask."

Because of his new status in the Defense Department Eric is invited to the reception. He is talking to Roland who looks pale. Why? I am sure that Eric is probably reminding him of his promises of an assured race result.

Pete makes a toast of good will to Ashley and me, and so does Avatar who is especially eloquent.

Odysseus and Nebo are especially attentive to Ashley. She has them charmed. I am equally successful with their wives. They seem to be very down to earth in their conversations and attitudes. They are quite aware of the world situation and are especially interested in the Space Command venture.

Evelyn, Nebo's wife, knew that I had graduated with a Doctor of Philosophy in Particle Physics. She knows that I am part of the probe program that was created to study deep space. My group has researched the barrier that separates the energy world from the material world and resolved it. Quantum mechanics is at work!

We built several membrane type probes and launched them. One has recently returned. It was obviously captured by intelligent beings on its journey. They changed the program so that the probe could indeed get back home. By so doing we would have proof that intelligent life exists throughout the infinity of space.

Evelyn smiles at me and says, "I know about this top-secret project, but I do not have a clue about the science behind it. You must realize that we simple mortals have not spent our lives wrapped up in science!"

I say, "Evelyn, I am sorry! I often get into didactics when I become passionate about a subject!" She replies, "I understand and I do not want to deflate your passion. We need it!"

I begin to wonder about why she knew about this project. Why was she so interested in asking me questions about it? I know that Nebo wants me to answer her questions so I answer her questions. What was Nebo trying to learn? Did I fall into a trap!

I finish by saying, "The results so far had been spectacular. We do not know how fast the probes traveled. What we do know is our velocity indicator was pegged at a billion times the speed of light. Space is infinite. There are clusters of galaxies, clusters of universes, billions of inhabited planets and each second more are being created. Each second universes die and new ones are created."

I continue, "In my opinion this is the pattern of creation and everlasting life. People are born and people die. Their souls will travel in one of two directions. One is down the vortex toward the voids of hell, The Dark City, and the other is to ride the zephyrs upwards to the heavens and enriching other souls depending what they learned and did on Earth."

Evelyn asks that I continue. I do. "Some souls are repeaters in this school of Earth. I think that I am one of those. I now realize that, indeed, God is able to travel anywhere at any time. Because He is and identifies Himself as 'I Am' we are part of Him. He made us!"

Evelyn queries, "What does he expect of us?" I say, "He always gives His children, and we are indeed His children, the same basic rules to guide us. One is to love our Lord God with your entire mind, strength, being and soul."

I continue, "He will always answer our prayers, maybe not as we expect, but if we follow His advice it will always be for our own good. A second rule is to love your neighbor as yourself (He expects that you will love yourself because He loves you and He wants you to live in His house forever). A third rule is to do unto others as you would like for them to do unto you and you will receive His forgiveness for sins because of His Grace."

I add, "Evelyn, how do you like that for a heady conclusion?" I stop. Evelyn asks, "Why is it that you are not a priest?" Every eye in the place is looking at me. I do not know what they are thinking. There is dead silence.

I say, "There are two basic life choices, the philosophers who think about life and its meaning and spawn the arts. They present their theories through the arts and works to represent how they interpret life. They are in, the broad sense, the priesthood. There are the scientists who observe the facts about what is happening around us, interpret what they see by experimentation and present their theories about how and why things happen. They are the builders of human abilities. I am one of the people in the latter identification."

I continue, "Both have their false prophets. When a pet theory is proven to be wrong pride and power takes over and they both lie and try to force others to swallow untruths. This is a dark karma-less path. It leads to misery, poverty and unhappiness to all! I chose science and engineering as my life's path. Both ways lead to the conclusion that the Creator exists and rules of nature must be followed or we will all wallow in darkness."

Silence remains. All eyes are on me and I know that they are thinking, "What is up with this brash warrior and who does he think that he is? What was Ashley thinking when she chose him for a mate! He is not part of the ruling class and he is part of the armed forces!"

Vera breaks this eternal silence, as only she can, by suggesting that perhaps some souls are joined together in clusters for a particular mission. The whole room becomes involved in discussions about theology. The whole room becomes animated. Some do not believe. Their souls have been dimmed by the selfishness of self-love.

I see that I have started some discussion! I suppose that is why philosophy, religion, and politics are not smart dinner conversations. Human ego gets involved and good communication ceases. However, I never like humdrum and dull dinners. This has not been one.

Ashley is obviously having fun. Suddenly, I am asked about the details about the space program. I say, "I cannot answer those questions because I am only a piece of the puzzle. This program is huge. It is top secret for a reason. We are dealing with unimaginable power."

Meanwhile, Mercury told Pete that the assassination attempt will occur after dinner and after the final toasts are given. It will be timed to occur as the guests are departing.

Pete has given me a sign so I leave an animated and interesting conversation at the table for just a few moments.
Pete has notified the resort security so that an under-jacket
laser deflector is waiting for me. They will have two waiting. Two of us are to be eliminated and a good assumption
is that I am one target. Who is the other?

The security will be shifting because the Chairmen and
other very important people will be departing for their
quarters.

Our plans are set, such as they are, and I return to the
table just in time to finish the discussions that the groups
of artisans, composers, artists, scientists, playwrights, etc.
could be clusters of souls whose time had come to combine
their talents to help educate the Earth's souls and make
their lives richer and more meaningful.

The signal sounds for drinks and final toasts before the
evening ends. I pray that this will not be my last toast. I
wonder how Ashley will react. I do not want to think about
it. The Rebellion is starting now. Will I taste the bitterness
of the dark vortex in the end or will I instead smell the
sweetness of the zephyr?

Eloquent toasts interrupt my musings. Both chairmen
approach Ashley and me. Nebo says, "Your loyalty is to
both countries and to peace. Cooperation, progress and
the welfare of all people on Earth is the goal." Nebo smiles
at me. I lift my glass and say, "To peace, loyalty and prosperity." We all drink.

Tension grows. Evelyn bids her farewell with the comment, "After your honeymoon and upon your return to
Atlantis, Achilles, you will be invited over to dinner to continue our dinner table conversation in more depth." I say,
"Your gracious invitation is accepted with pleasure." She
departs. The crowd is still heavy around us.

Somehow, I know that the assassination will occur at
the lift! An idea came to me in a flash. One man from each
side could aim at us as we enter the lift that would take us
to the upper floors and our rooms. Vera and Roland had

decided to stay on a level just below ours and leave early the next morning.

Vera wanted to transfer to Ashley a present that her mother had given to her on her wedding night. It was to be passed from mother to oldest daughter.

Ashley and I walk over to Vera. I order, "Vera, take Ashley to your quarters now! Use the service lift." Vera looks at me. She knows something is wrong. She replies, "That is in the kitchen work lift!" I say, "I know it! Go!" Vera confirms in her mind that something is brewing.

Ashley starts to object but, instead, looks at me and accompanies Vera to the lift. I kiss her. The kitchen doors close. They are on their way.

Roland and I approach the main lift; I hear an expected yell from Hector and Pete simultaneously. I dive straight at Roland and as we fall I shield his body. I can feel the laser beams burning my protective vest and back protector. Singe one! Singe two! Singe three! One more and I am a dead man. The shield cannot withstand another hit but before they can shoot again Pete's laser hits the assassins. They die instantly before they can activate the suicide bomb they carry on their backs. Hector disarms the bombs before they can explode automatically. I am singed and the shield is smoldering.

The bombs are taken to the security vault to be taken apart later. Both dead men have tattoos of serpents on their upper arm. I know that this Serpentine symbol is for the hit men for Satan and is a mark of the beast. Mankind will see that symbol again during the reign of the Blue Turban who will be defeated but at a tremendous cost in lives of the faithful. Peace will follow this awful war. I wonder if I must be at that terrible war. I would rather not be!

The security guards help me take off my smoldering jacket and shield so they can have them for evidence. So much for my wedding suit!

We will have a difficult but not impossible task of finding out who hired the assassins. Isaac killed the driver of the get-away air car and deactivated the self-destruct bomb before it exploded. Good! Pete is in control and knows what to do. My job for the day is over. How quickly all of this has happened! Roland is a mess! We are assisted as we get into the lift.

I look at Roland and say "Eric, the son-of-a-bitch you love tried to kill you! Why? Simple! You have failed to eliminate me and the Serpentines are punishing you! This is the way the Dark Side does business! Why do you follow the Dark Side?"

I add, "We may never see the birth of your granddaughter if you don't wake up and see what is happening!" He looks at me in total disbelief. He is stunned. He stammers, "Thank you, Achilles, my son."

As we walk into Roland's suite, Vera exclaims, "You and Roland look terrible. Have you two been fighting?" I answer, "No, we were protecting one another during a Serpentine attack." Roland needs me and he knows it! Will he ever love and respect me?

Ashley looks at the soot all over me. She knows. She says nothing but puts her arms around me and won't let go. She finally says, "It is Eric, isn't it?" I nod. Roland kisses Ashley and Vera. He looks at me and hugs me as he says, "Thank you, son. I will not forget. I am upset and very, very tired." He goes to bed. This has been a total shock to him. He looks terrible. He is in need of rest and reflection.

Vera gives Ashley a huge diamond ring. This precious heirloom was given by her mother to her upon her marriage. They embrace. As we leave, I kiss Vera. She strokes my cheek with her hand. There is a tear in her eye. I kiss her. It is not necessary for her to say anything. I grasp Ashley's hand and take her to the lift. I still have the special key to the penthouse in my singed trouser pocket.

After the lift doors close we embrace, and kiss deeply. The doors open and in the hallway there is a beautiful dessert table on wheels. The champagne is properly chilled in the ice bucket.

I look Ashley in the eyes and tell her that I love her with my whole heart. I tell her that I would like to be with her for eternity. She tells me the same. We toast. She puts her head on my shoulder and a flood of tears comes to her eyes.

She says, "Darling, why must I love a warrior? Those laser burns on your back tell me that you were almost killed. Must I live each day thinking that it will be the last time that I will ever see you? Why can't you take the job at the University as the head of the Science and Engineering Department?"

I answer, "Sweetheart, have faith. We should not separate ourselves from our karmas. We are expected to accomplish them. We are facing the vortex of Arkite. We must not be drawn into his maelstrom." I lift her up and into the big easy chair. I kiss her gently. Our bodies are fused into one. Soft music plays in the background.

Finally, I pick her up gently and carry her to the bedroom. The bed is ready. After our lovemaking she looks up at me and simply says, "I love you. I'm exhausted. Hug me." She cuddles alongside me; lays her beautiful golden head on my shoulder and falls into a deep sleep.

She has awakened earlier than I and has ordered us breakfast. She says, "Honey, on the way to the resort let us go to that great beach in the undeveloped lands where the waters are warm and we can sunbathe on the sand. I have made us a picnic basket including wine."

I reply, "It sounds like a perfect way to start our honeymoon. Make it so!" She replies, "You really ought to dress first." We laugh. I hold her gently and kiss her. I ask, "How are you feeling?" She replies, "Relieved. I am fine. I'm trying to figure out what I am going to do with a new husband. We really cannot spend all day, every day, in bed." I say, "It sounds like fun!" She looks at me and sees that I am ready for sex. She says, "I'm sore, Achilles. Give me a break!" We laugh and I hug her.

We contact Mercury, dress in beach clothing and race off to the undeveloped lands. I have Mercury armed with infrared people detectors and lasers just in case some local denizens wanted to attack the beach.

He stays with the limousine just over a sand dune so that we could have privacy. He had brought some paperwork with him and was using the backseat as an office. We stay in touch with the communicator.

Ashley strips completely naked. I will never, ever be able to contain my excitement whenever she does that. She is looking at me smiling and says, "Darling, you certainly are a passionate man. I can see that we are going to spend a lot of time relieving your problem."

The noon sun is hot and we are tanning all over. Ashley points out that she can wear any style of clothing without showing any part of her body that has not been sun-tanned. This sounded fine to me. We finally dress so that we wouldn't get too sunburned and eat our lunch.

Ashley is lying so her head is on my shoulder and I am blissfully looking into the sky contemplating what eternity and space is all about. Suddenly, I note two specks in the sky. They shouldn't be there.

I tense and Ashley immediately feels it. She asks, "What is it?" I tell her to run like the wind with me to the car. We grab the picnic basket as I communicate with Mercury and tell him to get the car ready to leave . . . Now!

The limousine is ready. I put Ashley in the back seat and tell Mercury to strap her and himself in with the double strap. I get into the driver's seat and say, "Mercury, what model pods do we have, what is the model number of the frame, what is the type and make of the superconductor?" He answers all questions immediately. I study the instrument panel.

I tell them that we are in for a rough ride. I strap the laser onto my belt and put the detector into its holder. As we roar away, a laser cannon beam obliterates the spot that we just vacated.

Who are our attackers and how do they know where we are? I know that I cannot outrun those bastards. I will head for the archways that lead to the forest and marshes. I had trained for the air car race there. It will be our best chance of escape. Heaven must have been with us, for if I hadn't spotted them early they would have obliterated us on the spot.

Fortunately, I am in one of the most powerful limousines made and Mercury has it in top condition. I push the red communication button. There is no response.

I tell Mercury to get the magnetic communicator out of the picnic basket and give him the code word for Pete. I tell Mercury to forget what is about to happen and concentrate on the magnetic communicator.

I say, "Continuously give our location to headquarters." We head, just above the ocean surface, toward the archways. As I suspected, one craft follows me and the other stays high overhead. The first two laser shots are accurate and deadly. I have just entered the archways as the high craft's beam hit the top of the arch and the following craft hit one of the columns. Our chances of survival are almost zero.

My mind is racing. The crafts fire for effect several times in a row. Good! I am dealing with poorly trained adversaries. They have to wait for recharging. This allows me time to get to the forest. As the first few trees brushed against the limousine Ashley screams. The poor girl is terrified. What an awful thing to do to her! Mercury is shaking like a leaf in the wind.

I remember the huge tree in the center of the forest. It is almost impossible to see unless you expected it. The craft following me is intent on getting me into his sights again. I head straight to the big tree. In the last possible second I flip the limousine on its side. I miss the tree by centimeters. I hear the welcomed explosion behind me. Three laser shots hit the tops of the trees above me. The second craft is above the trees. I slam the crossover shut so that a huge ball of exhaust issues forth. It looks like I was hit. At least I hope so.

I skim along the surface to the marshlands. It seems that I am spending a lot of time in the marshes. I wonder if the Creator is telling me something. As we land, muck flies all around us. We just miss the rocks. We have to get to the boulder formation quickly so that the rocks will shield us from the deadly lasers.

I am going to use Ashley and Mercury as decoys. I am gambling that the crew of the remaining craft will be so intent on killing us that they will land to assure that we are dead. They do!

I tell Ashley and Mercury to run to the rocks and hide. The enemy, whoever they are, will use infrared detectors to locate us. I dive into the muck and bury myself in it. I break off several reeds and jam them in my mouth to use them as air passages. The infrared detectors will not detect me under the slimy cold muck if I make no movement.

It works! They are detecting Ashley and Mercury. Two men come running by me. I rise up and hit them in the back of the neck with my laser. They drop. I lean over to look at them just as a laser shot goes where my head was. A third man! Oh, shit! I fall to the ground, roll over avoiding a second shot and hit him in the head with my laser. I call out for Ashley and Mercury. They came out from the boulders.

I am furious. We have a damn Mole at the Space Command! He knows where I am. Mercury and I examine the bodies. I strip them of their armor and note the mark of the serpent and scorpion. It finally dawns on me. These people are soldiers! They are not assassins. They are part of an advanced scouting group from an invasion fleet! They want us dead so that we could not sound an alarm. It is obvious that our red alert communicator did not work. Our satellites have been neutralized.

Mercury heads toward the scout ship. I shout, "Fall down quickly!" I grab Ashley and we fall into the dirty marsh waters. The explosion is deafening. A detector activated the self-destruct feature. We were not carrying the code.

I thought this might happen and warned Mercury just in time.

We will get no information from the machine. I rip the insignia off of the leader and we run to the limousine. Of course, it is in poor shape!

Mercury says, "My beautiful machine is a wreck!" We open the fuel compartment. I free the jammed crossover. The car will work again. We have to get back to headquarters fast!

We were about to have a surprise attack. Where in the hell are our intelligence people! Are they asleep?

As we roar into the sky I say, "I have never chauffeured a smellier, dirty group in my life. Don't you people ever bathe?" This seemed to make them feel better, although not much. I can only detect a wan smile.

I land the torn up and smoking limousine right in front of the security guard at the Defense Building, jump out and demand that he contact Admiral Zadoc immediately. His reply is, "Who are you?"

I don't have time to argue. I say, "Contact him now, damn it, now!" I grab the communicator and hit the red alert button and yell into the communicator, "Get Roland and the Admiral into control central. We are in an emergency condition. This is Achilles speaking." The head of security grabs the three of us and escorts us to the hand analyzer. He takes us straight to the control center.

The Admiral arrives just as we do. He is furious. All the Space Commanders, except those on watch, come rushing into the room. I ask, "Who is on watch?" The Executive Officer and the Satellite Officer report that they are.

The Executive Officer says to me, "Commander, you are under arrest!" I look at the screens and all look calm and well. I go over to the Admiral and say, "Look closely at screen #1, very closely! Have you ever seen a flying bird that doesn't move?"

He looks startled but looks at the screen. Sure enough we have a stationary bird. I say, "Admiral, we are being fed a false signal. Someone in this room knows it. When I go over to fix this problem cover me. I must work quickly so we can see how bad the problem really is." Then Zadoc says, "You better be right or you will be shot as a traitor!"

I move over to the main cable panel and open the cover. I ask the technician for a pair of cutting shears, well insulated. I ground the end. Suddenly, the Executive Officer pulls out his laser to shoot me. The Admiral drops him. The Satellite Officer lunges at me with a knife, I parry his lunge and hit him in the throat with my hand bent so that the fist knuckles hit his throat near his Adam's apple. He chokes to death in his own blood. I shout, "No one is to leave this room or touch a communicator!"

A security guard aims his laser at me. Zadoc drops him. I proceed to sound the cables. Damn, it was taking too long! It seemed like an eternity.

Ashley and Roland are looking at me horrified. I finally found the spurious main cable and cut it. Sparks showered all over. I connect a jumper cable. The grounding of the false wire connectors worked. Suddenly the control monitors showed the true situation. Our space station had been captured and our satellites were being decimated. The Serpentine control has been transferred to the Space Station.

The feel of death hangs like a pall in our room. Many good people will die today. I tell Zadoc to ready the three best fighter-killer craft that he has in his inventory immediately.

I tell him that we must prepare an anti-invasion force and that I will put Isaac in charge. He knows what to do. He already knows the basic plan. I say, "Admiral, tell him if you have any changes." He looks at me in a daze.

I say, "We have no time to get you oriented. Make me Executive Officer NOW!" He looks stunned. He deputizes me. As number two I have the authority to organize the defense.

The three fighter-killers are being readied. Isaac will organize the anti-invasion forces. My six core people arrive. The magnetic communicator got through the communications blackout that the Serpentines had placed on our system.

Pete had received my message. I look at them and say, "I will fly a point. The formation will be delta." Zadoc looks at me. His mouth drops. He says, "Achilles, this is suicide. Nobody lives through a point flight."

I look at him and say, "Admiral, we have no choice. Pete and Hector will fly with me." We had flown this equilateral triangle formation together before.

I put Isaac in charge of coordinating the counterattack. I say, "Admiral, there may be more Serpentines in the room. Let no one make a transmission but Isaac." Zadoc understands.

Meanwhile Sharon has joined Ashley and Roland. They are terrified. Ashley is crying.

I call Isaac and the Admiral over to listen to our plan. I told the group that I would gamble on the Serpentines being enamored with the pincer concept.

It is vital that the Serpentines do not know what we are thinking. I tell them that the scout ships tipped their hand when they used these tactics to try to annihilate the limousine. Secondly, I remember reading the Serpentine scripture. "The angels of death will lift up the Four Corners of the Earth and their winds will destroy the unbelievers."

I say, "Arkite's attackers came in from the East. I will assume that they will also attack from the West." Both chairmen are now in the control room. Both agree to join their forces to blunt this Serpentine attack.

Isaac is a very good coordinator. He has nerves of steel. However, our whole plan and its success totally depend upon my assumptions.

I look at Pete and Hector and say, "You don't have to fly with me. It's your call." Pete says, "Are you nuts? Who else is crazy enough to fly with you with your cockamamie plans?" I laugh. We join hands. Then Zadoc put his hand on ours and says, "Good Luck. May the Creator and the Force be with you!"

I kneel, give the sign of the Pyramid, look up and say, "Your will and power will prevail. Our lives are in your hands." This is not much of a prayer but it is the best I can do.

Ashley and Sharon run over and hug us. They say, "Please don't go." Tears are flooding down their cheeks. I whisper, "We must go. There is nothing else to do." I then look around the room and say, "Have you ever, ever seen a sorrier group of so-called warriors? Look at us. I still smell of marsh muck. Pete is in his shorts and Hector is in his running suit. Yet, has it not been said by the Creator that the mighty and haughty will be embarrassed by the lowly?"

I say, "We must make it so!" Isaac says, "May God be with you." I take Isaac aside and say, "Note those who are most upset by our discovery of the deception. They will be the Serpentines."

Pete, Hector and I leave the room. Red alerts were sounding all over the city. Our space suits are ready. Our craft are ready. I think to myself, "Three craft are about to take on a fifty-six killer-craft armada. Each craft is superior to mine. This is idiocy."

They are waiting at the space station and will soon spear-head the invasion forces headed by fifty-six battleships! We have one advantage. The craft we are flying are armed with comet killer missiles. We have far more destructive power than anything Arkite can muster.

I know that Pete and Hector will follow me blindly. My heart is sad and glad at the same time. I am sure that the Serpentines will laugh when they see this mighty armada attacking them. Their arrogance might well turn the tide. I was taught never to underestimate an enemy.

The first thing I must do is to taunt the attacking group. I remember reading about Arkite who claims he speaks directly to God. I find this very interesting. The beast speaks to God. They all purport to tell you what God told them. My question is simple, Do they really listen to God?

Egocentric people never listen to anything but themselves. They twist truth, put their spin on truth and lie.

My feeling is that this group is from the same stem. They have a shibboleth that states, "Arrogant infidels must be destroyed by those who believe as we do. All who kill our enemies will have an everlasting life of bliss. The more infidels our people kill the greater is their bliss. This edict was given to us by the Great Creator Himself." Ugh!

My first transmission must have shock value. I start by calling Arkite, the leader of the attacking group, and identify myself. Then I proceed to call him an infidel and an abomination from hell who worships the god of greed. I could hear Arkite laugh and tell his Admiral, "Kill that madman, son-of-a-bitch, Achilles. I want him dead! I will promote the killer and reward him handsomely. We will see which killer commander is superior! You all have an equal chance to be my Operations Commander." I knew that whole group would attack us like mad hornets. I hear Pete say, "Thanks a lot, Achilles!"

I had better remember the coordinates of our ancient satellite system, created to destroy asteroids and comets that threaten to hit Earth, correctly. We are streaking at high speed toward our destination. I can see nothing. My blood runs cold. I suppress panic. Suddenly, off to my left, I see the cluster. Now we must fly over it before the mad hornets get here. We maneuver precisely and enter the system correctly.

Laser fire and missiles fill the sky around our pathetic three. Our simultaneous movements have worked well so far.

As we pass the cluster perimeter I thank God that I had become very interested in it months ago. I found out that there is an interesting thing about this ancient asteroid suppression system. It is very effective. I recently activated it. I thought that it would be a great platform for the deep space probe missiles. All of the missiles that were in the system are fully armed and ready with live heads. We had not removed them because we were studying the activation mechanism and needed to understand them.

This system is arranged like a plate that is curved to match the curvature of the Earth. My problem was to find out how the Ancestors were able to move all around and within the curvature of this structure without being attacked themselves.

I finally found out how to do this by covering our working craft with a frequency shield. My Delta Craft have the program built into them. I know the code to activate the whole array. The trick is to pass the perimeter of the structure far enough ahead of the hornets behind us so that the missiles will not attack us but will attack them. We barely pass the perimeter when I hit the activation code. Three killer craft that were behind us explode. We are shaken but unharmed. A marvelous havoc ensues behind us.

One big mass of exploding machines! I was tempted to streak toward the space station but thought the better of it. There would be survivors, but how many? Maybe we could, in the confusion, destroy the left-over craft before they destroy us.

What I did not know is that Arkite had dispatched his finest command ship to view the slaughter of my pathetic Delta Force. The ship came too close and was also destroyed by the ancient asteroid defense system.

Damn! There are five survivors. Our triangle swooped over a sick one and finished the job. Our combined firepower destroyed another. Our triangle tactics are working well. The remaining pilots are bright, or they wouldn't have survived. We do not want them to escape and give any details to the Space Station. We are now having a one-on-one battle.

We split, each taking one of the survivors. They are better armed than we are and the pilots are well trained.

Eric, the son-of-a bitch, is, indeed, the First Lieutenant of Arkite. I had heard him talking in the background during the communications we were receiving while taunting Arkite.

A laser shot grazes my ship. I escape one missile and a second that explodes close by. It did some damage.

This dogfight has lasted for an hour. I am tired. I can never get the bastard in my sights! He is clever. I look up and see Hector's ship hit at its midsection. I am horrified and saddened. His opponent comes in for the kill. Suddenly Hector's ship comes alive and rams his opponent. Both of them go up in a huge explosion.

Pete and I were having an equally rough time. While we maneuver around our enemies, we worked our way toward the space station. I was not sure that we would get there or what we would do if we did.

Pete's ship was hit! It was now a lifeless hulk, and an easy target. I communicate to Pete to get out and float in space. I will pick him up.

He bails out just as an opponent blew his hulk to pieces. I did a double turn evading my dogged enemy. I have seconds to do what I must do. I can see the temptation to blast the free floating body is too great for my opponent. As he closes in, I hit him broadside. I fire a missile. He is consumed in a ball of fire. I race alongside Pete, open my cockpit hatch and scoop him into my craft. He seems to be unconscious but I can hear him breathing. He is getting oxygen.

My opponent is crazed. Good! He knows that he has me in a hopeless position and is coming straight at me. Fortunately, he does not fire as soon as he should have. He is assuring himself of the kill. I have time to go into an outside loop. Nobody does an outside loop. It is a risky maneuver.

I catch my opponent by complete surprise. I blast his underbelly and he blows into a million pieces. Some of the debris hit my craft. I have drifted too close to the Space Station! I am being attacked by it!

Laser and cannon fire is all around me. I fly directly toward the Station. I am looking right down its throat. Their doors are open to disgorge the invasion ships. I let go of every asteroid killer missile left in my arsenal. They go right into the throat of the giant beast as if being guided. A chain reaction of explosions inside assures me that the space station is not now a threat. I am now tumbling in space out of control.

My machine is a wreck. There are holes all over it. I have been on backpack oxygen for some time and oxygen is running out. My space suit electrical system has been running on battery. I feel the pain of wounds that I have sustained. I am ready to go into a coma.

It is a battle to stay awake. I'm not going to make it! I think of Ashley. I must go on. I am going to try. My communication with control central had been wiped out long ago. I cannot get any landing instructions and cannot ride the homing beam.

I know from my emergency receiver that another battle is going on. Isaac is doing his job. I must try to get back. Pete is in bad shape.

Where is the remainder of the Serpentine invasion force? I had obliterated one pincer. Isaac is taking care of the other. I can only hope that his feeling about its whereabouts is correct!

I am aware of being in the Vortex but I also feel the gentle soothing zephyr. I am traveling upward. I am in the presence of The Light. There is an interminable silence. I see myself in another time and another place. I feel light radiating into me. Many souls around me are refreshing me. I am at peace and at one with The Light. Then I remember meeting Lucifer.

I remember listening to him. The Dark Force is very strong. I began to listen to his promises and do his bidding.

It began to occur to me that I was not doing things for others but doing things for him. I wanted to please him and rise in his ranks. Often this hurt others and in so doing I lost light and there was no replacement!

Why am I remembering this!

I awaken and I am hovering over what is left of my body in Atlantis. What is happening?

Meanwhile, inside the Control Center three remaining Serpentine supporters had to make a move. Isaac is planning to destroy their other pincer. A warning must be given to the Serpentine force to back off from the pincer strategy.

They drew their lasers from their holders with the aim of killing all in Control Central and destroying the displays. Zadoc using Nebo's laser dropped one before he himself was hit. Isaac was grazed alongside of his head by laser and lay unconscious on the floor. Displays were being shattered. The Security Head drops a second Serpentine before being killed by another traitor. Everybody else runs for cover. The last Serpentine must be stopped.

Ashley picks up the security guard's laser. She fires at the Serpentine agent. He is wounded but he is not dead. He fires at Ashley and misses, grazing her head. She falls back stunned.

Isaac awakes just as the Serpentine was about to send his message to the space station. Isaac kills him before he can activate the alarm key to alert Arkite. No message went out. Isaac wonders, "Does Arkite have some kind of feeling that all is not well?"

All the people in the room are dazed and dejected. *Is our world lost?* Isaac checks the record of transmissions. No transmission left Command Control. Neither the Space Station, bent on my destruction, nor the second pincer armada had any idea what was happening on the ground. Our armada was assembling in the laser-proof shelters that were scattered around Atlantis. The moment I destroyed the Space Station our armada was launched to fight the second pincer. Isaac had located them. They were hidden in the caves one hundred miles beyond the marshland that I had just left after escaping the scouting party. No wonder scouts were in the sky. It wasn't a mole. I had stumbled into the pincer launch site!

The ensuing battle is very bloody but our spacecraft are magnificent! We defeat the attackers but three-quarters of our craft are destroyed. All of the Serpentine craft including the troop ships are blown to bits.

Isaac has dispatched a sky ambulance to search for me. He watches the rescue mission with a heavy heart. He knows that Hector is dead. Am I and Pete also dead?

The medical ship detects a weak emergency signal from my craft. My batteries must have had a dying spark before they died. The emergency crew goes immediately to the signal spot. My craft is a hulk.

The first reports are grim. Pete might live. They report that I am alive but they do not think that I have a chance of survival. A team of expert surgeons and doctors await the return of our rescue craft. My torn body needs to be repaired.

The operation takes hours. Surgeons are gluing skin, using nanotechnology and using medical tissue to put me and Pete together again. I am being kept alive by machinery.

I lay in the critical recovery room. I am one big bandage. Only Ashley is allowed to see me because the doctors did not want me disturbed in any way. Hours pass while I hover between life and death. Then the hospital room alarms ring. My life signs are failing rapidly. A team of doctors and nurses gather around me. All of their efforts seemed futile. The moment of truth is rapidly approaching.

If they do not start to remove my organs very soon they cannot be used as transplants. All of us are pledged to donate our organs before the remains are cremated. Purification of the body by fire and burial of the ashes is the law.

They are about to begin. Ashley rocks with sobbing and anguish, trying to convince them to wait and try once more. They have sent out for the transplant team.

It strikes me that I am watching all of this action from above the bed. I move down toward Ashley to touch her and tell her that I am all right. My hand goes through her body. I am floating in air. I run out to tell the transplant team that I am all right. I go through doors and walls. Nobody hears my pleas.

I rush back to my room and look at my body. It is slack-jawed and has a pale, pallid look. Ashley is sobbing uncontrollably. I have to help her. How? I am suddenly aware that an Angel is beside me. He asks, "Do you want to live and if so, why?"

I answer, "I want to live and complete the mission that God has given me to do. I want to help God's chosen people to see The Light." He answers, "Really! You had that chance eons ago. Ashley already knows the right way and the path. It is you that worries us."

I answer, "I repent. I have sinned. I was wrong. Maybe in some small way I can help souls to see The Light." The Angel answers, "I do not know why you are being given this chance and I do not know why I like you." He is gone. He didn't say anything to me but I have a feeling that we were close in the past.

Suddenly, I can feel great physical pain. It is unbearable! The pain consumes my mind. Ashley is holding my hand. She is alone. With all of my energy I move my hand and stroke her hair very gently. I can't muster any more from my body.

She stops sobbing. She kisses me but I can't respond. She grabs my hand and I imperceptibly squeeze back. There is a long silence. Ashley looks at my chart on the end of the bed. It reads, "Died of multiple wounds." But he machines begin to beep and churn. My life signs are returning. I am fully aware of what is happening but I still cannot move.

Ashley grabs my hand again just as the transplant people arrive. She is magnificent. She stops them cold and makes them look carefully at the monitors. They are all surprised but tell her that I will be a human vegetable and will never move again. It would be better to let me donate. They should never have said that.

I do not know what she is saying but it hits them like a blowtorch. Soon the bandaged Zadoc and Roland are in the room. The emergency team returns. They understand that if they did not fix me they, themselves, might be fixed.

Zadoc says, "I have just lost some very close friends in this battle and I am not about to lose this warrior. He WILL be saved!"

They go to work on me again. My regeneration had nothing to do with the doctors. I know that there is an outside force that is allowing me to recover. We know so very little about the forces that truly run the Universe. My pain is still unbelievably intense.

One of the nurses, obviously very nervous, puts an injector holding painkillers onto my arm and pulls the trigger. She misses my artery. I open my eyes and say, "Young lady, you are nervous and trying too hard! You are supposed to kill the pain not add to it."

She drops all of her equipment and stands frozen. I look at Ashley and say, "Honey, I am sorry that I had put you through all of this torment." She screams and starts kissing me gently all over my bandaged face.

I then look at the doctor and say, "I am hungry." He replies, "You will not be eating for a long, long time."

Zadoc says, "If Achilles says he is hungry he is hungry. Feed him!" Food arrives in the room within minutes. I eat voraciously, even though it does not taste all that great. Hospital food, ugh!

Total healing will take some time but all of my vital organs seem to be functioning normally. I even belch. Ashley informs me that belching like I just did was not polite. We laugh.

Ashley informs the hospital that she will spend the night with me. They refuse. Zadoc says yes. They lost.

I ask the medical team to assemble. They look at Zadoc. He nods. I say, "You are all real heroes. Today you were overwhelmed and yet you were all very professional. I am very grateful to all of you. I understand that you saved Ashley's life after she was wounded. Your group was ubiquitous."

I continue, "If I could I would give all of you medals for superior performance!"

The Admiral says, "Achilles is correct and you will be so recommended. Achilles, go to bed now. That is an order." I reply, "Sir, I am in bed." He replies to Ashley, "Take care of this smart-ass."

The last thing I remember is Zadoc telling Ashley that he will see both of us early tomorrow. Later that night Ashley gives me some good news. She says, "Honey, I found another organ that works just fine." I sleep soundly.

Zadoc comes in early as promised. He orders me out of bed and says, "Achilles, I have a group assembled in the main dining room. I want you there."

The medical staff attaches the walking assistance equipment to me. This is routine. Patients are encouraged to walk only hours after an operation. They change Ashley's bandage. She is all upset. They had to cut her gorgeous blonde hair. The surgeons did a beautiful job. The scar will be barely visible. The wig looks natural.

The Chief Surgeon says, "You are a very lucky young lady. The laser grazed your skull but did not damage the brain. The transplant bone is doing fine. Admiral, you have been issuing lots of commands and now I have one for you. Take off your jacket and shirt. I want to look at your wounds. Do it right now!"

Zadoc does as instructed. The Chief Surgeon says, "Your rib cage was damaged but the bones will heal. Report to surgery now!"

"I will see all of you in five days except you, Achilles. You will report to rehabilitation tomorrow and, if your feisty lady will promise to make you follow our procedures, I will let you spend your nights at home. You look like a single living bandage. I do not know why you are alive. Your Guardian Angel must have had something to do with it." I say, "Amen! He did."

Five days later, as we proceed to the dining room, Ashley looks stunning. I don't know how she does it. I am shuffling along in my hospital pajamas. I am hurting but determined to move and get my body back into shape. Zadoc is alongside me. He is smiling.

Ashley takes her seat. I am maneuvering into mine. The pain is still unbearable. The painkillers are not working as well as I would like them to work. Ashley is ordered to approach the makeshift podium. Zadoc places the Medal of Valor around her neck and reads the citation concerning her actions in Central Control. He kisses her on both cheeks and she returns to her seat. Zadoc proceeds to give these same medals to Pete and Isaac.

Madeline receives the Medal of Honor for Hector. She is crying uncontrollably. He loved his family very much and they love him. The horror of war is manifest to all as Madeline accepts his posthumous medal and officially takes Hector's place in the Group of Seven.

Isaac is made Operations Officer and Pete is made Security Officer. Zadoc then says, "Will the living bandage please approach the podium?" I have a hard time getting up but nobody helps me because that is part of the therapy.

Zadoc looks at me and says, "Executive Officer, your official orders are in this packet. They are written to Commander First Class, Achilles. Congratulations!" He then proceeds to take the Medal of Honor from its case and put it around my neck. The citation was beautifully written and signed by both Chairmen. Both Nebo and Odysseus and all Ministers are at the table.

Nebo arises. He says, "Odysseus and I flipped a coin to decide who would speak first. I won. There is to be no inference of importance to our order of speaking. We have and still are trying to forge a Federation of our two nations to establish a World Government. The Rebels want the World Government to be a dictatorial government and they will attempt to establish it by force and bloodshed. Odysseus and our close advisors, including Admiral Zadoc, have met and here is our decree. The Revolution will not prevail." We all clap our hands in approval.

Nebo continues, "Now another matter must be discussed. The race results have been reviewed by the Race Committee. The false reports that were sent to the Race Committee originally were proven to be wrong both by eyewitnesses and material evidence."

He adds, "Achilles' craft had been sabotaged and Eric's craft contained an extra fuel cell. Roland's staff was involved in this fraudulent act. The evidence now gets cloudy. Some of his people say that he was not directly involved. Some people say he was definitely involved. In any case, he was derelict in his duties by not immediately investigating this matter with the Judicial Board.

"The Race Committee's approval of the following actions are now being followed:

1. Eric's craft is hereby declared to be ineligible. Eric is no longer with the Defense Department and his medal is not valid. He will be arrested and tried for his crimes.
2. Craft 333 retains its standing and all other drivers will move up one slot. Achilles will retain all aspects of his present winner's status.
3. Roland, you will be given a letter of strong reprimand from the Chairmen of Gogania and Magogania. Nevertheless you will, for the time being, retain your status as Minister of Defense.
4. Admiral Zadoc will approve all correspondence from Roland's office."

Nebo continues, "I wanted it noted here that if it were not for Achilles, who passionately pointed out that even though you, Roland, have displayed serious flaws in your judgment you have truly been loyal."

He further explains, "Furthermore, Achilles pointed out that facing public disgrace and public repudiation at this critical juncture in our attempt to win a war is not wise. This rupture will not have a good effect upon the joint venture of cooperation through the Space Command."

He continues, "We must show solidarity at this critical time. We are going to face enough problems winning this Civil War. Roland, you damn near lost this conflict all by yourself. You damn near destroyed your daughter's life. Achilles, you will be in effect the head of the Space Command. Odysseus, it is now your turn."

Odysseus rises and says, "Achilles, our nations love you. You are their hero and they will follow you into the

Vortex to Hell, your term, if you desire. They want you to run things."

He explains, "You are a field warrior and the best I have ever known. Avatar, also one of our advisors, claims that you were born with this instinct and that you fought alongside Michael, the Warrior Angel, before falling into the spell of Lucifer. Maybe this fable is so. I don't know and I do not care! I know who you are now!"

He continues "I live in the present. I know that you will never send a fellow warrior into battle doing something that you won't do. You do not have anything to prove. You have been there and have done that. Look at you! A flaming, walking bandage! Your job is to lead, plan and execute."

He says, "If you had gone to the Military Academy instead of the academic world you would never have known about the weaponry needed to win wars! You are not just a warrior but you understand that superior weaponry is the key to success! You have the knowledge and the skill and now it is your job to be our leader!"

He admonishes, "I have one piece of advice about leadership. There will come a time when you must teach your followers how to become the leaders in the field. You must let go, guide your people, let your lieutenants learn and do the strategies that you envision! A dead leader is rather useless. I don't know of anybody who can better convince you about that lesson than Ashley and Admiral Zadoc and I am sure that they will!"

He clarifies, "Zadoc is one of the brightest leaders I have ever known and nobody in this world could have spoken to you as Ashley did after the Race and lived. She has guts and has proven to be a worthy warrior herself!"

I reply, "Mr. Chairmen, I accept your challenge and am humbly grateful for your support. I will take your admonitions to heart. However, I would like to point out that knowledge itself is power and without its proper use there will be no victory and peace. Leaders must not be drawn into power lust for if they do there is no effective government."

Odysseus smiles and says, "Okay, Achilles, you are one smart warrior. I agree with your analysis. However, how are you going to translate your knowledge into usage if you are dead?"

I say, "I agree with you. My job is to destroy the enemy's soldiers by making them die for their country. My job is to keep our warriors alive while leading them so they can fight again for their country. The more of the enemy that are dead the better I like it."

We all have a round of champagne. Roland rises and says, "I apologize to all about my judgments. I am afraid that Eric duped me into believing 'exitus acta probat' (the event justifies the deed). I especially apologize to you, Achilles, you saved my life in all ways."

He says, "I appreciate it and I will never forget it. I humbly accept your admonishment Chairman Nebo and Chairman Odysseus and I will always be loyal to you." I say, "Dad, I also accept your apology." The room is silent.

Odysseus breaks the silence and says, "It is my turn. I want to confirm to you that Madeline has proved to be very capable of replacing Hector in your Group of Seven. However, I do have some questions to ask you, Achilles. How did the Serpentines ever amass such a fleet without us knowing about it? Where did the raw materials come from? Where are the assembly plants? Who are these people? Did we destroy them for good?"

He continues, "Now that I have asked these important questions I have one more. How did you ever come up with that stupid plan to save Ashley's life? Before you defeated the Serpentines your life was in grave danger! We figured that you were connected to the Serpentines. If Admiral Zadoc had not taken Chairman Nebo's laser and killed the traitorous Executive Officer with it you would have been a dead man."

I say, "I thank you Admiral Zadoc for saving my life! Mr. Chairman, I will now attempt to answer the questions."

I explain, "I knew that Ashley was the key to all of our destinies. I do not know why I knew. I just did! Perhaps it was in my parietal lobe as I meditated. I started to meditate seriously after I lost Elaine."

I further explain, "I was told, during a meditation, to meet Ashley and quickly! I knew that meeting her was my job!"

I replied to my inner voice, "I have no idea of how to accomplish such a task That did not seem to bother my inner voice at all!" It repeated, "I told you to meet her!"

I further describe my actions, "As you all know, I formed the Group of Seven to attempt to have some influence in the events that were happening in our countries. We all worked on this problem. We wanted to make changes to make our countries' citizens experience more freedom instead of being under an Oligarchy. I do not know exactly how we were going to accomplish this but I knew Ashley would be at the core. I do not have an answer for that either but I knew through deep thought that she was part of my destiny and probably the destiny of all of us."

I continue, "I ask all of you to remember the Asian Indian fable about water being delivered from the valley well to the City of Light on the hill above. It was done by designated water carriers. Each carrier had two jugs hung on wooden poles that hung over their shoulders. Over a period of time it was noted that the path to the city became more pleasant because shrubs, wild flowers and grass sprung up along the side of the path but nobody knew why."

I proceed, "One day one of the men on the path noted that his colleague was carrying a cracked jug that was watering the pathway. Instead of discarding the jug all decided to let it continue watering the pathway so all travelers could be comforted by the birds and animals that greeted them on their way."

I continue, "However, one person reported it to the City Officials because he said that the jug carrier of the cracked jug had a lighter load. There was a great discussion and the King who cared about his people said, 'I will not let the beautiful pathway be disrupted by one person with a grudge.' It was decided that the errant jug carrier would be banned from the City of Light and sent to the City of Darkness. Then he declared that all carriers would have their turn and be given the privilege of carrying the cracked jug. This way all carriers would participate in keeping the pathway watered."

I now say, "I am the jug and Ashley is the precious water. Ashley helped to save Central Control and was the one to arrange a picnic, place me exactly where I had to be to uncover the revolution and stop the Serpentine attack. My being at the exit site of one of the Serpentine pincer source locations was meant to be! The rebellion, to take control of our two nations, was in progress!"

I explain, "Ashley and I will deeply appreciate your accepting us as your burden to carry on your shoulders as we all travel our joint path toward living at peace together." Silence follows. People were looking at each other wondering what that was all about. So was I!

Finally, Roland says, "What a story! You call this an explanation? Are all of your schemes and strategies like that?" I answer, "All of my planning and thoughts follow the same pattern with surprise as a key element."

Suddenly, another voice is heard as Vera says, "Great God in Heaven! You mean to tell us that we all have agreed to carry a cracked pot around filled with water that spills its contents all over our path of life for the rest of our lives! You must be out of your ever-loving mad mind!"

The whole room is filled with roaring laughter. I laugh also. I was praying for some humor! Vera is a gem!

The laughter dies down and I continue to answer the other questions, "Who are the Serpentines? They are the rebel splinter group, headed by Arkite, who broke away from the Pyramid. They consider my father, Avatar, to be the leader of the infidels."

I say, "We all know my father as the leader of the true faith. As I see it, Eric is Arkite's First Lieutenant. He was assigned to direct all rebel activity through our traitors in

Control Central. Both pincer fleet Admirals were under his command. We did not kill Eric. I am told that he and Arkite were in a Serpentine fighter that left before I attacked the Space Station and blew it apart."

I warn, "There were many soldiers in the latest attack but there are many more soldiers, workers, factories and equipment still viable. Where? In caves scattered all over the globe. The location of the second pincer force proves the point. It came out of caves and this location was so secret that none of us knew where it was! Why? Our detection system has been compromised! Our first and immediate task is to fix this problem!"

I resume, "Our present job is to find these caves as quickly as possible. They use the Earth's raw materials to manufacture the spacecraft. Some caves are mining shafts while others are assembly plants. All plants are nanotechnology-run plants."

I observe, "The workers are the progeny of the people that our forefathers were to help and flourish under a flag of individual freedom. They are not free. The Serpentines practice Baal and worship the Beast. Their signs are the serpent, the scorpion and the number 666. Why are these symbols marks of the Beast? They define Satan. He wants to replace God."

I say, "Satan will promote six things: sin, corruption, misery, damnation, lies and false teachings. These six things will be repeated over and over and over. He will come to Earth with seven names and each time he will say that he represents the will of God. He will appeal to many people and as time goes on he will take on a total of 666 names all standing for God and appealing to more and more people. We must not let our people be drawn into the worship of Satan!"

I explain, "The serpent is the deceiver of people and the scorpion is the assassinator of people. This combination of enticement, deceit, and the threat of harm is the modus operandi of Satan. Today, Arkite is his priest and leader of the rebellion. He is smart enough to realize that he needs a tough power-hungry warrior to lead his fighters to success. Eric is hungry for power and he does not mind killing for it. He follows the dark side. This is exactly what Arkite wants."

I continue, "You wonder how Arkite remains undetected? I suspect that they have defense systems that blank out our search equipment. How else could they have blanked out our defense sensors so effectively? I could activate the asteroid destruction array and make it work because I installed a new security and operation system just a few months ago. It is not in the Serpentine system. Obviously their programs did not have my modifications because they are not in the database."

I further explain, "Who designed their sophisticated equipment for them? I don't know but I will find out. Our immediate mission is to develop probes that can do the job of uncovering the enemy. I believe that our probe technology will, indeed, uncover their locations."

I say, "Because technology detection is my forte we can move along smartly. I will develop the equipment and strategy while I am still a walking bandage as Admiral Zadoc has appropriately dubbed me."

I suggest, "Our unsuccessful assassins were fed their information from within. We have some Baal worshipers amongst us. Pete, you have a hell of a job. Someone in a very high place is a mole. We did not kill them all." Pete says, "Thanks, boss!" I smile.

Roland says, "Achilles, Zadoc and I want you to report directly to us concerning this mission of seek and destroy. We will brief Nebo and Odysseus daily and we desire that this mission be completed yesterday."

I say, "Gentlemen, someday I just might be in the super high position of issuing orders such as these, then retiring to the bar, reveling in relaxation while my insane orders are carried out!" All laugh.

Odysseus says, "Achilles, at times you just cannot help but being a smartass!" There is laughter again. He continues,

"This meeting is adjourned. Congratulations to all of you loyal warriors. This includes you, Ashley, and the rest of the faithful wives. Madeline, please stay for a few moments. Your house will be blessed and remembered for the rest of time by our grateful nations. Ashley, we want you to remain also." I do not know what was said at that meeting. I will probably never know.

Each morning I must report to therapy. I figure that I can recover without all of these people poking me, moving my limbs all around and forcing me into hot tubs, exercise rooms and lifting machines but, alas, it is not so. Treadmill work and calisthenics are part of the routine. I grumble but I do what I am told to do.

Pregnant mothers also have to attend therapy to have their muscles prepared for birth. All births are natural without anesthesia. Pain is controlled by nerve blocks. The newborn is taken from the womb straight into an incubator that maintains body temperature so that the transition from mother to world is not a shock. If the young baby has any respiratory trouble a mask is placed over its nose and mouth instantly to start normal breathing. The human brain must be fed the proper oxygen at all times. Birth is made as pleasant as possible for mother and child. Fathers, as always, do not do very much but watch and some faint.

Ashley is in amazingly good shape. They allow her to dance during therapy but they also demand other exercises that are good for her muscle tone.

Ashley and I are allowed to work out together. Interestingly enough it is taking me about seven and a half months of therapy to get my muscles and cardiovascular system in shape. All of this from one battle! Ashley delivers Athena the same week I am released. I am fit for the world again and I proudly strut around carrying our new daughter, Athena, everywhere. Ashley glows. She is at peace.

During therapy, of course, I have been working in the Probe Laboratory and it is now time to test our detector probes. They are self-contained and need nothing from the environs. Each probe will detect noise, vibrations and heat. Each probe will transmit to the mother ship its findings such as intensity of sound and estimated distance of the source. Simple triangulation will pinpoint the location of the originator.

We have separated the world into sectors. We will probe each sector piece by piece. The probe burrows itself into the ground it will silently destruct after reaching its life limit or is touched. The possibility of a Serpentine capture of one of these machines is nonexistent, I think.

The plan is ready and I give it to Zadoc who agrees with it. He and Roland give it to Nebo and Odysseus. They give their approval. Our schedule is tight because it is imperative we keep the Serpentines reacting to us rather than us responding to them. I do not like relating by reflex.

During our preparation for attacking the Serpentines I have made an effort to keep regular hours and be at home during dinner. Also, during this time, Ashley, who has always been interested in the arts, has opened her ballet company and has had several very successful presentations. Athena has her own spot in the office area and is surrounded by toys. Mommy is always close by her.

Today Ashley comes to me and says that we must discuss a problem. I listen. It seemed that Orion has become one of the school stars in Ball and Target. It is a game that is a cross between Rugby and Lacrosse but requires more physical contact. It is rough. He is good at it and has become the team captain. He has also become very popular with the girls.

Ashley asks, "Achilles, have you ever had discussion with Orion about the facts of life? Puberty has happened, Nature has filled him with hormones and you have more than your share! He must have plenty of them. Why do you encourage him to play Ball and Target? If you want him to grow into a strong young man Ball and Target is not the way! Look at him! He is all bandaged and battered!"

I retort, "Sports is good for him. He can work the energy he has to release tension and at the same time do body building! That is bad?" She replies, "You are incorrigible! I suppose the next thing I will find out is that you will think that you will fight again. You know what the doctor told you. You are half bionic now!"

I return to the first topic. I say, "What lessons about life is he learning?" She says, "Combat, always combat! Sometimes I wonder what Dad and you really learned on the playing field. Men! I will never understand them! I want you and Orion to have a serious discussion about life and its meaning!"

I knew from the tone of her voice during this request that this was not an optional entreaty!

I go to Orion's room and say, "Son, it is time that we have a talk about life. This will be a father and son affair." He says, "Dad, I would love to but I have a ton of homework to do. Can't this wait?"

I answer, "No, Son, this cannot wait. I will be out in the field starting tomorrow so I would like to have our talk now. We will discuss some of the facts of life."

He answers, "Gee, Dad, is there something that you would like to know?" I say, "Smartass! You are beginning to sound just like me!" He laughs. I laugh. We go to the garden.

I put my arm over his shoulder and say, "Look up into the sky, son. What do you see?" He says, "Dad, I see the moon and the evening stars. I see you amongst them in battle again. Does Mom know?" I reply, "I told Mom that I would be leaving to test the probes. She knows that I am trying to uncover the Serpentines."

Orion says, "So that is why Granddad and Grandmother are coming over for dinner tomorrow. You will not be here. You better not desert Athena, Mom and me. We love you and we need you! All children need a dad and a mom. We don't need a memory. We need both parents. That is the way our Creator wants it to be!"

I say, "You are wise beyond your years, Orion. This is truth. Through prayer I believe that I have been given a protective shield. I will return. Do not interpret this as arrogance because this shield can be removed at any instant should I not understand that fact and not do His will."

Orion is quick to point out that Granddad Avatar had not seen me pray very much as a youth. I say, "Son, this was a grave, youthful mistake. I have found that through prayer we are forced to remember that we are a part of creation. Glory belongs to the Creator not to us. We must learn humility, loyalty, family values, reverence and repentance."

Orion says, "Dad, you always said that we are to be strong and stand on our own."

I say, "Son, that thought is not wrong. You must do what you feel is right despite criticism. That is what you learn on the playing field. You do not win unless you have the will to do so. You must stand up for yourself and your ideas, but you cannot win without the cooperation of others."

"Stoic stubbornness is not useful. Not listening to others and their counsel is egocentric. Be very careful not to succumb to a desire for control and power. This is not the reason you are here nor is it the key to success on the playing field of life. You cannot stand alone."

I admonish, "You become a leader because others willingly want to follow you. Your strength comes from the Creator. Give some of it to your followers. Do not ever forget it. We depend upon His strength. He has given us a will and an ability to make our own choices. The consequence of wrong choice is horrendous and affects all around us."

Continuing, "Still, it is ours to make. We are responsible for what we do. No one else is responsible. We are. It is not Mom, Dad, the World circumstances or anything else."

I inform, "Your new mother loves you with all of her great heart, just as she does Athena and me." Orion looks at me with a puzzled stare and says, "I know that, Dad!"

I say, "Your mother is an Angel and she chose to love us. I don't know why. It is a great gift she has given to us freely. She will always want what is good for us. This is what a family is all about."

I say, "This brings me to the second topic, Orion. Sex! Don't ever destroy a girl for your momentary satisfaction. When you have sex you are committed to her whether you want to be or not. You have committed an act of communion. If you break this communion you have broken the faith. This is something you will face when you are with The Light. It is not cool to have illicit sex. Dating is natural and fun. I expect you to date but I want you to respect women."

I continue, "We will direct, guide and love you always, Orion." I hug him. He hugs back and says simply, "Thanks, Dad. Please try to come back to us in one piece! Good Luck!"

He returns to his studies. I return to Ashley who says, "What did you tell him, Honey?" I say, "Sweetheart, I told him what was in my heart. I was in way over my head. We have a smart kid. I don't think that we have to worry about him." She replies, "Wonderful! Great! Congratulations! Now I have three kids on my hands." I smile.

The time has come to start stamping out the Serpentine. Ashley knows. She cries as I leave for the mission. She says, "Come back to me! You must remember there are four of us depending upon you." She kisses me passionately and I can feel her body pressing on me.

She is pregnant! There is a tear in my eye as I say, "God is being good to us! I will never desert any of you. I love you with all of my heart and will forever!" She says, "Never forget that we are totally dependent on you. You must not fail us! Come back!"

We arrive at our selected search site. My ship is clearly marked. Our destination is Central America. The pilot of my craft looks real to me but it is a robot! I am in Peter's craft. I have practiced guiding the lead craft from Peter's ship for hours. Peter's absence is undetected. He is now doing his own security work and looking for moles.

We arrive at our destination. All transmissions are being sent via the decoy. We pick a spot and assume that the target is there. The probes are launched. We hear nothing. We do this for hours at different locations. This should have covered every spot in Central America! I cannot believe it! I am about to abort the mission when two of the probes signal. Using the distance and direction data we calculate a center. We launch four more probes. There is silence. Then we catch more weak sounds. Good! These manufacturing caves are much deeper than I had thought! The damn entrance could be miles from the activity cavern. We must guess correctly.

We hover over our assumed spot. We cannot see a thing. I am sure the entrance is camouflaged beautifully. Since stationary and hovering craft are superb targets we activate on our defense shields. I direct the decoy craft into ever-widening circles around the spot that was triangulated. We watch for a laser or missile. The entrance door is probably made of a metallic composite. If so, it will reflect a different pattern than the surrounding land. I activate the infrared and spectrographic detection systems. We pinpoint the difference in heat and radiation.

I have the sudden impulse to put the decoy into an instant upward thrust. This violent maneuver will render a pilot unconscious but the automated system will take charge. The sudden craft movement triggers the cave mouth defense system. It fires a missile that misses the decoy by less than a meter but its proximity fuse automatically activates. The explosion rocks the decoy but does not disable it. We locate the source of the missile.

I fire two missiles from the decoy. One hits the missile site and the other one hits the door. The door is obliterated and the site destroyed. My probe force enters the cave for some spelunking. I stop two ships after a short penetration and send the decoy with all of its sensors activated ahead. We can all see the results on our screen. All the weapons systems on the decoy are activated and set for automatic response.

The decoy works its way deeper into the cave. Suddenly, the decoy's laser fires. A piece of the wall falls away, revealing a laser gun that the decoy has destroyed. We are getting close to the central chamber. Suddenly, the decoy is engulfed in a mass of laser and missile attacks. I activate its self-destruct switch and Isaac and I back out of the cave quickly, damn quickly! The self-destruct system activates causing an ensuing explosion from the decoy's insides that is horrendous. The cave's interior labyrinth system is aflame. We can tell by the flames that are shooting out of the air vents that we never detected.

Our high circling craft detect several aircraft escaping from an alternate door. They are all destroyed. I assign five craft to follow me and Isaac into the burned out cave. All weapons are activated. I know that there are some survivors. We will try to capture as many as possible. I hear a transmission describing my death. I identify who is sending it and to whom. Isaac is detached. He knows what to do.

The ensuing battle at their Control Center is not easy. There are more survivors than we expected. Our group makes fast work of destroying all remaining weapons and soldiers. We find one survivor that has been knocked unconscious. We tie his hands and feet. We give him a dose of truth serum and we attach an electronic relaxing piece to his head. This makes one feel that he has been released to the peace of eternity. He talks freely.

We are correct in our assumption that there are many cave factories. They are in South America, Africa, Madagascar, Europe and the South Pole.

We will keep our survivor harmless until we can get him to our Control Central where experts will further interrogate him. My plan is to get the complete layout of this particular factory. Amazingly, we find its Main Control Office in fair shape. We are able to deactivate all self-destruct circuits and remaining booby traps. I am surprised by the number there are!

I communicate, over the secure circuits, to Zadoc. News of my demise is rampant but Ashley was immediately notified that I am safe and not wounded. I tell Zadoc that I will stay longer in the field. There was much we can do to learn about the workings of the factories. We must destroy as many as we can before the word is out that we know how to attack the factories. They already know we can, but how is their question.

I tell Roland that I am worried about security leaks. Pete has already found three moles in very high places.

I have destroyed three massive cave factories that exist no longer but how many more of them are there? How many and how high in rank are the moles? We must plug these breeches or we will face another invasion force very soon.

Where are the raw materials used for construction stored? Who supplies them? What kind of transportation system do they have? Where do the workmen live? How do they get to work without our knowledge?

The answers come slowly as we start to explore. Exploitation and slavery of the undeveloped denizens is the key. Mines are hewn out of veins deep in the ground. Fuel, in the form of raw petroleum pools, is abundant. Denizen human beings are being used to push the right buttons at the right time. The rogue Pyramid priests control them.

Human sacrifice on the top of the Pyramid of Prayer is common. These pyramids are a mutation from those in Atlantis. Their purpose is different. Pyramids were originally erected to guide space travelers as well as being worship centers.

This explains why we are being attacked by the natives of these lands. The Serpentines are controlling them and teaching them that God is a fearsome god of vengeance and they better do as the priests say they must do or they will be killed and go to Hell. They are in Hell!

My former friend, Lucifer, who chooses hate and anger, is at work. This force can easily take over a soul if it does not follow the code of living.

Although we are all given a free spirit and it can choose its course, it is impossible to choose right when errant priests have already spawned mythology that will dog, delight and attract the people on Earth for centuries and will also punish, maim and kill those who do not obey the priests.

Those souls who would truly have wanted to do right will receive life again on the spiral of life! They will be given new talents and karmas and a chance to take the path upward.

We attack and destroy more caves and the Serpentine manufacturing plants. Refineries are being built underneath these rogue pyramids. Sexual atrocities are rampant. My bet is that Ashley's schoolmate attacker was a Serpentine.

Innocent babies are sacrificed to Baal. Serpentines crack the babies' skulls and eat the brain. How sick can evil humanism sink? My stomach churns!

I stay in Central and South America for several months. Zadoc finally sends relief crews to finish cleansing these areas and orders me to come home. I do not resist. I have seen too much.

When I arrive home Athena squeals with delight as I pick her up, kiss her, and hold her over my head. She is a happy child. Ashley and I feed Athena and put her down for the night. Orion is with Avatar learning about pyramids. Ashley makes me strip so she can be sure all of me works. We go to the hot tub. It is a wonderful episode. I fall asleep in the tub. This is not smart. Ashley has to shake me thoroughly to awaken me. I stumble into bed. I sleep soundly.

The morning light is streaming into the room when Ashley and Athena awaken me so that I can get to work. I am drawn, tired and depressed. We have so much to do! I go into Zadoc's office. He looks at me and says, "You look terrible. I am ordering you to take a vacation starting next Monday!"

He continues, "Meanwhile, let's look at your plan for the systematic destruction of the Serpentines." I say philosophically, "We will face Armageddon before this thing is over and it will come from the Federation." He nods and says, "Achilles, it is our job to do the best we can." I reply, "You have been talking to Vera again!" He smiles.

We finish my analysis of the cave factory system and how to destroy it. We set the plan. Roland is a great ally and offers some suggestions that, if not incorporated, might have led to defeat. We now need to get permission from Nebo and Odysseus.

It is Sunday night and this process has taken a full week. After the meeting Roland says, "I agree with Zadoc, Achilles, you still look terrible. We will see you in a fortnight. Get out of here and take a rest."

I don't object. I feel rotten. I find out that all of my loyal friends are taking vacations also. They are all ordered to do so. For a moment, I wonder if this was a move for a power grab. But one look at Zadoc leads me to dismiss the notion. We all know that my group is burned out.

Roland says, "Ashley is very worried about you. We will see you this evening for dinner. Ashley is planning a catered delight for us." I say, "Antion the Restaurateur and Caterer is making dinner of course! What a surprise!" He says, "Look, you incessant smartass! You need a surprise and a good relaxing dinner! Ashley and Vera thought that it would be a nice way to start your vacation. You will soon get a call on your communicator asking you to pick up a dessert on your way home."

I say, "You wouldn't know what time, would you?" He says, "It is at seven sharp. Be there!" I reply, "Thanks." He laughs.

I go to my office and finish writing my memoranda and directions. The communicator sounds. I answer, "Hello! Sweetheart, is there something that you want to tell me?" She says, "Two things I want to tell you, Honey. First, your forthcoming son is doing exceptionally well and secondly, I want you to pick up dessert for tonight at Antion's. He forgot to bring it."

I say, "Where is Antion's restaurant?" She says, "Don't be a smartass, now go!" I say, "I think that I am going change my name to smartass. It is my families' favorite nickname." She laughs.

When I arrive home Ashley's drinks and hors d'oeuvres are ready. Roland and Vera arrive within minutes after I do. We all congratulate Ashley. Vera asks about the cave factories.

I say, "Vera, while in Peru I inspected one of the ancient runways that the giant mother ship used to supply the colonists with their needs while exploring the Earth. It was very clever to have the mother ship use winged shuttles to bring goods to the ground. They use minimum fuel and they are easy to maneuver."

I explain, "These landing fields are made from cut stones placed so well that no mortar was required. They will last forever! The pyramid control tower and the old supply depot buildings are now places of worship for the locals."

I illustrate my point. "The Serpentines were using this as a cover for a deep cave manufacturing plant. We destroyed the plant but left the runways and the pyramid. I would like to study them later. I saw one landing beacon obelisk made of a ferric ceramic combination. It is fascinating. We sent it to the laboratory. There is one in India. I wonder what became of the rest of these navigational pieces."

Vera says, "Can you destroy all caves before the Serpentines have enough craft to mount an attack?" I reply, "No, but if we can keep their fleet down to a minimum we can make the final battle a cleanup affair." She says, "Achilles, you have much to do. You and Ashley need a rest. We will watch over the children. You be sure to watch over us."

We all retire early. Soon it is morning and Ashley awakens me from a sound sleep. She suggests that we start the vacation at Antion's place. I say, "I like that idea . . .!"

We call for Mercury. As we are getting ready Ashley asks, "Honey, who is the Third Force that you seem to want to contact?" I reply, "I don't know. It could be the Federation who destroyed Eden. God, the infinite Creator, communicates with us through prophets. Perhaps it is Noah that is sent to us as a prophet. His people have something very special. I must talk to him. I have a strange feeling about this man." There is a knock at the door. Mercury is ready.

Mercury is working for Ashley at the Pyramid where she volunteers as an assistant Priestess. Ashley asks about his wife and children. He says, "They are all very well, and with my promotion to Space Commander Chauffeur, we will fare even better. Thank you for your loyalty to me. I shall always be loyal to you."

As we are driving to Antion's I note that it has grown to be very popular. He suggests that we eat on the outer balcony where the view of the sea is spectacular. Ashley tells me neither she nor Mercury identified us by name but used his name for the reservations so that we could really be together without interruption.

Ashley looks at me and says, "Darling, you look so pensive. I love you, and I will always love you. Relax!" We kiss. Mercury is standing at the open door waiting for us to enter the limousine. Ashley grabs my hand as we go into the restaurant. My palms are sweaty. She looks at me and says, "Why are you so upset?" I squeeze her hand and say, "I have seen too much evil that humanism spawns when its leaders have no morals. We must defeat them!"

Antion approaches us with a sly smile and does not identify me. I tell him that I would like to be seated on the balcony. He smiles and leads us to a table with a magnificent view. We order drinks and a light lunch. We toast to our future. I say, "Ashley, you always take my breath away because you are so beautiful." She looks at me and smiles. I hold her hand, look at her in the eyes and say softly, "I love you more than anything in creation." She says, "I can feel it." We talk as lovers should.

As we complete dessert, I look at her and say, "Please dance with me lovely lady." She looks surprised. The background music seems just right to me. I say, "Can't you hear the music? They are playing our wedding dance." We dance. She swirls and whirls as if a soft breeze was guiding her. The music stops; we embrace and kiss. There is applause from the other side of the balcony. We had attracted the attention of many other patrons. Antion and many others rush over to shake our hands. He says, "You are hired. I will have this restaurant filled every night. What a unique way to audition!" I look at him in a stupor and say, "What the hell are you talking about?"

Ashley is smiling. He continues, "Obviously you are the Mercury couple that has been scheduled to audition this afternoon on the balcony, are you not?" By this time the crowd in the restaurant is surrounding us. They are clapping in approval! They are saying, "Hire them, hire them!" I am speechless. Ashley bursts out in a hearty laugh and says, "Fame, my hero, is very ephemeral. Remember this as you conquer the world!"

Suddenly, Antion winks at Ashley. Then he says, "I knew right away that you wanted to be alone together. I am honored that you would start your vacation by coming to my humble restaurant! I could not help but throw in a bit of humor!"

He continues, "I am very pleased and honored that you would come here to start your vacation." He looks at Ashley and says, "I never miss one of your performances and you and your husband really do dance beautifully together! Commander, have you ever thought of changing professions?" I guess that my look of disbelief was still priceless.

I say, "Of all restaurants in the world that I could have picked I must pick one with a comedian owner. I think that I will keep my day job."

Not everybody in the restaurant crowd understands what is happening but good humor and vibrations are catching and everybody starts to talk among themselves with animation. I overhear someone say, "No, he cannot be Achilles because he is part of the oligarchy!" I muse, "My God! I am fighting to give them freedom, not mob rule!" I pray that I have not failed my mission before it is really started.

I take Antion's hand, shake it and say, "You have paid us a great compliment. You have also given me a good lesson in humility. You have a quick wit."

He replies, "Mrs. Ashley and I have conversed and made many plans before by telecommunications. When you visited me before I knew when you were coming and what you were going to take home." I nod and say, "You will be seeing much more of us in the future."

It is time to go because suddenly a crowd has surrounded us and blocked our way. We shake hands, sign autograph books and papers and wave as we move toward the limousine.

Mercury says, "Mrs. Ashley, you dance like an Angel. People love to see you dance. They always have. Your talent must be shared with the people. Commander, you really were very good yourself." He smiles. I smile and say, "Thank you, Mercury, but I really will keep my day job."

We eat dinner at our resort. I say, "Sweetheart, you are more than a superb dancer. Your grace radiates and fills the room with an aura of light when you dance."

She smiles and I ask, "You have great talent and people feel power in your dancing. They do not want you to stop. Yet, I can tell that sometimes you lose that radiation because of the awful demon that clouds your mind. Maybe, if you talk about it, this awful demon can be exorcised. Let me share your hurt. Let's cast this thing out of you together."

We leave the dining room and go to our room. Ashley pours us after dinner drinks. We sit together looking out the picture window at the night sky filled with glowing stars. She puts her head on my shoulder.

She says, "I want to expunge my demon!" She begins her horrid story. "It was after our final rehearsal. I had agreed to go with Damon for a late dinner at a local restaurant after we locked the doors and secured the set. All of the rest of the cast had gone home and I was checking the windows. It was then that the trouble started."

She continues, "He put his arms around me and grabbed both breasts. I pulled away. I was shocked. I didn't need nor want this untoward advance. He told me that he was sorry and would not do that again. I had just checked the last window when he grabbed me again and tied my hands behind me with a cord he had found. He then slapped me and pulled up my skirt. I screamed but nobody could hear me."

She recounts, "He secured a piece of tape over my mouth and ripped off my clothing with his knife. I was naked and exposed. He put the knife to my throat and told me that I was a stuck-up bitch and that he was going to kill me if I moved. He raped me.

"It was a nightmare! I managed to pull loose and ran out into the street. I worked my hands free, pulled off the tape and screamed. Nobody seemed to pay attention. He grabbed me and raped me again and then he stabbed me. The knife slid along my rib cage and sunk into the ground. He was in a frenzy. He had gone completely mad. He then stuck the knife into my vagina."

She relates, "People were finally coming. He withdrew the knife and said, 'You will never have a child!' He then stood up, shouted that we would be in hell together and slit his own throat. He fell onto me. I do not remember anything else until I awakened in the hospital."

I gently hug her and kiss her and hug her again. My tears are flowing. She is looking at me and wipes them with her hand. I rock her as she sobs and wretches.

I say gently, "It's over; the beast is gone. He no longer is within you. It is over forever."

She says, "I feel dirty and ashamed." I say, "You feel dirty and ashamed? Your soul is clean and it shines!"

"We have one beautiful child and we are having another. There is no way that I could keep my sanity if this had happened to me. You are a beautiful woman. You have grace and strength beyond human understanding. You are beautiful and your soul has not been destroyed. It has now been strengthened because you have exposed the demon from hell and we are going to throw him out of your mind! It is over!"

"Your attacker was out to destroy you but instead of collapsing you prevailed and his soul has been destroyed." She asks, "How do I know? Father says it was my fault!"

I reply, "Say three times out loud 'I forgive him. God, have mercy on his soul and cleanse me from his hate.'" She does. I say, "Forgiveness of an offender and a request for God to cleanse your mind of this dark cloud has been given to you!"

I request, "Now close your eyes, breathe deeply, relax, and tell me what you see." She replies, "I see a beautiful soft white light. I see no cloud of doubt. It is over."

I say, "Roland has been wrong. He seems to have a penchant for it. From this night and forevermore the demon is gone. He is no longer part of you."

She lies sobbing softly on my chest for a long time and says, "I feel free! Thank you, Achilles, my lover and my life." She falls into a deep sleep. I carry her to bed and she puts her head on my chest. I put my arms around her.

I feared that she might awaken during the night and need me. I want to be there for her. She does wake up once. I am there. I hold her tightly and kiss her gently. I stroke her cheek. I say, "It is over, all over, Darling. It is behind you. God again has confirmed that forgiveness is a very powerful cleansing force. There is no cloud in the light that floods around you." She looks at me and again falls into a very deep sleep.

Before we realize it the vacation is over and the pace of the Insurrection picks up. I finally drive the Serpentine out of Europe and North America and I am down to the southern end of Africa and South America. There have been several attacks mounted and each time I have defeated Eric but I have not caught him.

I can feel a crescendo building. They have been clever in their attacks and they damn near broke through during their last attempt. This thing should have been over long ago. I'm getting older and the children are growing up in front of me. The European campaign has taken its toll. I'm very tired again! The body just does not work like it used to work. Why am I am feeling older? The answer is very simple. I am getting older and I do not want to accept it!

When I arrive in the office Zadoc takes one look at me and calls Ashley. He says, "Get this wreck out of here! He looks like a walking Zombie again."

When I get home I go straight to the hot tub and soak. Ashley comes in and brings fresh clothing. I get dressed, go downstairs and find that Ashley and Vera have arranged a small surprise bon voyage party. We have hors d'oeuvres and head to the dining room. Who is serving the food? We know the answer. Antion, of course, with his catering, his sense of humor and talent intact.

After I have answered a series of questions concerning the war Vera looks at me in the eye and says, "Achilles, you know all about the Great Rebellion and what happened over a thousand years ago. Still, you seem to want me to tell you more."

She observes, "Something is bothering you. Why? Is it your karma? Let me refresh you. The Earth was visited by an alien planet belonging to the Federation of Planets. Their mission was to assist our people to develop faster the rules of ethics and etiquette required by the Code of Living."

She explains, "We must follow the code if we are to pro-ceed upward in the spiral path that entwines all of us to-gether. The missionaries proceeded to build a large modern city with pyramids, flying cars, public parks and plush liv-ing quarters. Adam, the leader of the mission, knew that before the knowledge to build all of this was given to the people by the knowledge cube, known as the Tree of Knowl-edge, they must learn how to live together."

She continues, "Eve broke the law and began to use the cube. She liked it. In other words, she ate the fruit from the Tree of Power and loved it. She convinced Adam to lead a revolt, build war machines, and take rule over the people on Earth. The Mother Ship found out what was happening, defeated Adam, destroyed Eden and cast out the people. Adam and the whole mission was exiled to Earth. The city was totally destroyed but two cubes of knowledge were spirited out of Eden and hidden. Our patrons left the Earth. Where are the cubes?"

She clarifies, "Tubal-Cain, seventh from Adam, was a product of Cain who killed his younger brother, Abel, in a power struggle. He founded Gogania and he had a knowledge cube. Jared, who founded Magogania, had the other."

She says, "Adam's third son, Seth, guided by the group of priests, broke away from the rebellious group and went into the wilderness to live with the locals. He had the power to connect with God. Through Seth and the ninth from Adam came Lamech, who was a prophet. He gave Noah his father's secrets about the pyramid priests and their ability to connect with God. In turn the words of God were spread to the local people by Noah."

She continues, "Because Noah is a mortal person and wants to commune with God and follow His Laws of Nature, he has been chosen to lead the new Chosen Tribe."

More, "This tribe will show the New World what happens when we disobey God (punishment and cleansing) and what happens when we obey God (grace with peace that surpasses all understanding). Noah's job is to obey God and pass His lessons about life's Living Code to his seed."

She says, "Yes, Achilles, you must help Noah survive the big flood of punishment. Your job is to help him to finish his boat of gopher wood, sealed with pitch so he can be the father of the chosen. Further, you will deliver the Pyramid scriptures that I will give to you to Tibet before the flood." I say, "Where am I supposed to be during this bloody flood?"

She replies, "Achilles, stop being obstreperous and listen to me now!" I do. She continues, "The Ark is 450 feet long, 75 feet wide and 45 feet high. It has a complete roof and a side door that has gangways to the three deck levels. Noah cannot do his job without your help. He is building a boat for a number of years but has made no virtual progress.

He calculates that it must be finished within a few precious years."

She admits, "The Ark is a disaster as of now. You must make it seaworthy and be able to withstand tremendous forces." We all stare at her. I reply, "Gopher wood can do the trick. That stuff can withstand tremendous forces but it is an extruded product. It is a mixture of cypress and wormwood extract with hydrocarbons laced with carbon fibers and is an extruded product. It is perfect for the job. It is strong and pliable. We developed this stuff a few years ago. Does he know about the reinforcement pitch that is pliable and compatible with gopher wood?" Vera answers, "What a stupid question! Of course he does not nor do I!"

She continues, "Achilles, you are supposed to be the smart one! Use your head! It is not just a hat rack. Get it to Noah and now!" I am about to say something when she interrupts my thought." "Do not even think about saying some smart-aleck remark!" I say, "I think that I will change my name to Smartass." She just looks at me.

I continue, "There is no sail? How is he going to get anywhere? That is a small vessel. What is he going to put into it and how long does he expect to float aimlessly about? I can build his boat in about ten days."

Vera states, "You boast, Achilles, and ask a lot of questions. Noah is having a hard time! He will carry animals and food. They expect to stay on board between seven and a half months to one year and ten days." I reply, "How many people will be on board?"

She replies, "Noah and his three sons along with their wives and grandsons will be on board." I say, "This is madness. Who put this cockamamie notion into his head?" Vera replies, "The world is mad but he meditates and listens!"

She admonishes, "We have turned our Pyramid of worship and learning into a trash heap of selfishness. Achilles, you must help him build his boat! He needs an advisor. Oh, yes, there is another small matter that needs your attention. He is to bring two males and two females of many living things into the ark so they can replenish them. This means birds, animals, and other things according to their kinds. Also, while you are at it, give him every sort of necessary food and store it up for them."

I look at Vera and say, "Store food, water, seeds, grain, get a male and female of every type of animal on board and have a sanitation system on a flaming rowboat! Are you sure that you haven't forgotten something?"

She smiles and replies, "I don't think so." I laugh.

I say, "This is insane. Vera, perhaps it is you that needs a vacation. Are you sure you are all right?" She replies, "I have never felt better." I look at Roland and ask, "I suppose that this fits into our plans for cave extinction." He replies, "It doesn't." I am about to summarily dismiss the whole thing as nonsense but stop short.

Orion had come in during the time Vera was telling her story. It is hard for me to realize that my kid is in his first year at the University of Atlantis! He says, "Dad, this would be a perfect time for you to assign me this project. I can use it as part of my paper concerning the use of an alternate lumber as a building material."

He continues, "Let me combine it with the ancient metal obelisk study using the one you found in Peru and the obelisk found in India. We will study to see how they were made and see if we can use them to build complex buildings."

He offers, "I will be Noah's consultant. Maybe I can learn something about their ability to communicate with space. I am a student and I will be no threat to him."

I reply, "Done! Be sure to get embryo male and female from all the living creatures that will be useful to him that we have frozen in the laboratory. Be sure that Noah knows how to defrost them and how to feed them once they are born. He will have to have enough food to feed the live animals. He can get milk from the goats. He must have a good supply of fresh water."

I instruct, "Design a cistern catching system for him instead of trying desalination systems. Since it is going to rain he must be able to catch it. I will design the roof so that the wind will be guided into the Ark to ventilate the lower decks without violating the ship's integrity. Be sure that he will have the flora and fauna seeds that will form a closed ecological system. He will need all of this after he lands on solid ground. The ship will look like a floating block. I will give you a ballasting plan."

Vera says, "Bravo, Achilles, you were toying around with this vital project and now you cleverly delegated it. However, this instant delegation of duty does not relieve you of your responsibilities! You will complete this karma with Orion's help."

I reply, "If you keep this up I won't have time. I will be too busy helping this interesting prophet! How did you meet him?" She replies, "I have not had the pleasure." I say, "Wonderful! Vera, now that I have been introduced into this weird world of hallucination, you must finish the story."

She replies, "Achilles, all of this comes from the writings of the Pyramids. If you had paid attention in school or to your father, Avatar, you would have been well versed concerning these writings. I repeat. Jared, fifth from Adam through Seth, founded Magogania. He had the second knowledge cube. Jared was also the rebel who broke away from the command of Enos, the son of Seth, that prohibited intermarriages with the Cain's progeny."

She continues, "We have found by our studies that the denizen people in this region of the world are blessed with long life. Perhaps, the length of their lives is long because of the anti-aging gene medicine, material medico, given to them by our forefathers."

She explains, "The medicine is injected directly into the bones of baby boys. All of these little ones are circumcised for identification purposes. The progeny of these babies will all have long lives. There is only so much of this material left so soon their life spans will markedly diminish. As you know, we do not have it and have not figured out how to make it."

Vera warns, "Soon all of this will not matter for our world as we know it will cease to exist and all knowledge cubes will be destroyed. I am afraid that our civilization will decay and we will have given the locals mythology instead of education. How sad this is. However, we will have left the world the Scriptures and a knowledge cube. They will be the cornerstone of the moral code for those on Earth to follow."

I look at Roland and Ashley and say, "Is Vera often like this?" Ashley answers, "Sweetheart, she knows the writings and the predictions." Vera's conversation disturbs and intrigues me. Noah is predicting a great flood that will inundate the entire world. It will rain for forty days and for forty nights. I reply, "So what! There will not be enough water in the skies to accomplish a worldwide flood! It would require several tsunamis of immense sizes to do that kind of damage and also fill the Earth with rain clouds!"

I warn, "Indeed, Noah's ship better be flexible, strong and well-balanced if it is going to be hit with these kinds of forces and survive! Orion, this is your task." I hear a voice in the background, "Thanks, Dad! Great!"

I say, "Vera, this is the dumbest plan I have ever been drawn into executing! It is a good thing that I love you." She replies, "Achilles, it is a good thing that I love you! Now get out of here, do your man-thing and rid us of the Serpentines."

Dinner is over. We were all tired. Before retiring to bed Roland says, "Achilles, come back rested. We have much to do when you return." I say, "I know I do and I know that I will need your help. This war is taking too long for comfort. Our people are being killed so we can win and survive as a people. We must try to give them a true democracy and live in peace. I feel that they are becoming restive and tired. The damn war is dragging on and on. They must continue to believe in us or we are all lost!"

I request, "Take care of the family while I am gone, Dad."

After Roland and Vera leave we clean the apartment and go to bed. Ashley and I snuggle, make love and fall into a deep sleep. I awake in the morning and find that Ashley is not beside me.

I manage to take a shower and go downstairs. She has packed, since that seems to be one of the chores that I simply can't master, and is waiting for Mercury who has arranged for a complete picnic lunch, with wine, to be ready upon our arrival at the resort.

Ashley says, "What would you do without me?" I reply, "I can't do without you. Don't get any ideas. These ballet dancers are very handsome." She smiles and says, "You are jealous!" I smile and kiss her and say, "You are damn right I am! You are MY woman and MY wife and MY bond with God!" She looks quizzically at me and says, "Do not forget it!"

She is particularly bright and glowing today. It shows in her sparkling eyes. Athena seems to enjoy our kissing as long as she is included. Too much time has passed and much too quickly. Apollo Hector, our second miracle, was growing up quickly right in front of our eyes. I had promised Hector's family that if Ashley and I had a son Hector would be one of his names. He is indeed a combination of compassion and caring as well as being brave and gracious.

We arrive at the resort. We check into our suite, unpack and shift into beach clothing. Our last beach outing was still fresh in my memory. Ashley grabs my hand and we shuttle to the beach. The security guards smile as they greet us. One says "Commander, have a very pleasant vacation. There will be no trouble." Another looked at Ashley and says, "I have not missed a single one of your dancing practices that have been open to the public. You mesmerize people when you dance." We begin to feel better. Ashley's grip has not lessened. I look at her and say, "I love you very much. Perhaps more than you will ever know." She puts her head on my shoulder.

Soon we lay on the white sandy beach. The day is perfect. I was looking forward to an exciting, relaxing time and that is what happened. We relaxed and swam in the warm waters. Lunch is perfect. We return to the resort for dinner. After dinner we go to our room. We snuggle and make love.

The rest of the week is just as delightful. It is a whirl of swimming, scuba diving, lawn ball (she beats me), net ball (I beat her), and dancing.

I arrive home to find that I will be on the move again. Roland and Zadoc have set my schedule. I attack another critical cave. The battle is, as usual, fierce.

There are more battles and I have become very weary again. Ashley always soothes my soul. Two people bonded in fidelity and love is what life is all about.

Perverted sex leads to no joy and is very destructive to a marriage. Lust alone always leads to a destructive path. Our civilization is falling into this mold. Divorce and lack of commitment is destroying us. It saddens me.

Torture and mishandling other human beings by so-called masters must be stopped! That is my goal. We have crushed one Serpentine cave after another and we are getting close to having a final confrontation at the South Pole. Is Armageddon close at hand?

Suddenly, another thought enters my mind. I have, in effect, consolidated power into the Space Command. We are running the Joint Venture. This worries Vera. Ashley warns me that I am not immortal. Too many people are telling me that I am their real hero! The fate of our nations lies in my hands!

If it were not for Ashley I might start to believe it. She keeps me in line by example. She is a renowned ballet idol but is always humble and gracious.

One night as we were having supper Ashley informs Athena, Apollo and me that Orion will be marrying Alcestis. She says, "They are inseparable. I like her parents, who are religious, and I like Alcestis very much."

I say, "How do you know this? Has Orion said anything to you?" Ashley says, "No, he has not, but he does not have to say anything. Men are so transparent. They are out doing their man-thing and fail to see what is obvious."

Athena says, "Mom is right. This is no surprise! Alcestis and I have had several conversations. She is a terrific girl." I look at Apollo and he looks at me. We don't need to say a word to one another because our communication is instant.

Athena is a beautiful, headstrong and very religious woman. She is an able administrator even at her young age. She is the planner. All of her friends depend upon her to arrange the social events. She is a very popular person at school except for those who are basically jealous.

I manage to say, "You will make a great lawyer, Athena." She smiles. Athena, like her mother had done previously, is studying to become a lawyer but she is deft at playing musical instruments and sings beautifully. She sings like the most beautiful bird ever created. Somehow, I believe I know that she will soon follow Ashley into the world of arts.

Young Apollo is a duplicate of me. He needs lots of attention and love. He has not rebelled as I did. He is stubborn and hardheaded, but he has the pliability to bend because of the strength of having a strong faith and a morality base.

Orion's influence is profound and universal. He is guided by Angels.

I end the conversation by announcing that I will be off to Africa for some more cave factory cleanup and that I shouldn't be gone over a week or so. My family just looks at me knowing damn well that it will be an extended time before I am back. They learned to live with my habits albeit they still worry about me.

While we are attacking a factory and defense base along the Nile near Luxor, a call comes in from Ashley that the Dean of Students at the University of Atlantis wanted to see us on an urgent matter. Orion is completing his graduate studies this year.

Why would the Dean want to see us? We asked our friends and drew a blank.

There are twelve universities in Magogania and seven in Gogania. Atlantis is the premier university. The Dean told Ashley that he obviously could not talk to me over the communicator but that Ashley and I should meet with him at ten in the morning Friday. It is now Tuesday.

The Dean said that Ashley and I are not, under any circumstances, to contact Orion. He is now finishing the verbal part of his dissertation. The rest of his doctoral work is complete. He asked that we bring our whole family.

Orion's undergraduate degrees were in Astrophysics, Interstellar Metallurgy and mathematics. His doctorate degree is in Homeostasis. This is an extremely difficult degree and includes the studies of philosophy, history, biology, chemistry, physics, ecology and theology.

I turn the command of the battle of Egypt over to Isaac and he comments, "Thanks, Achilles. This mess is all your idea, we are now up to our eyeballs in muck and now you want me to take over!" I reply, "Yes because you are the only one that can make it happen!" He mumbles about contagious insanity as I leave on my way to see the Dean.

I meet with Zadoc on the way home to debrief him on the situation and I say, "Isaac will have to stay a while longer before we can secure the area. There better be a good reason for calling me off the battlefield! The message to me was that the Dean of the University wants us to be at his office the morning of graduation day!"

Orion, although he will have completed his work, is not scheduled to graduate this year. He will be in next year's class. "What is happening?" Zadoc answers, "Do as the Dean asks, Achilles." I wonder about that answer. Zadoc and I are very close. He never withholds anything from me but he is being coy about this.

I managed to find out that Orion was presenting the oral part of his dissertation at a dinner meeting at the Dean's dining room. I find that strange because dissertations are not run that way.

Athena and Apollo are delighted to see me and inform me that they received individual invitations to graduation and to the meeting with the Dean before the ceremonies begin. I ask, "What is going on?" They give me that look that tells me that they know but they are not going to tell me. Why?

The morning after my arrival I am surprised by the chaos. Athena bolts down her breakfast and goes off to find her belt. Apollo grabs a chunk of fruit and rushes off to change a bandage that he got yesterday at Ball and Target. Ashley just smiles and says, "Welcome to our usual calm and quiet breakfast!"

We prepare to meet the Dean. Ashley looks stunning as usual. We arrive. Nobody is there to greet us and I think that is strange. We make our way to the Dean's conference room. It is filled with professors and University dignitaries. I look at Ashley. Her eyes sparkle. I am puzzled. She squeezes my hand. The signal from her is positive. The Dean asks us to sit at the right side of the table. The end seat is empty.

Orion comes rushing in wearing the garb of a doctorate degree candidate and suddenly stops. He obviously doesn't know what was going on either. The room is silent. It seems like an eternity of silence. The expression on Orion's face is surprise.

The Dean of Students gets up and points to the seat at the end of the table. Orion sits down. The University President begins to read. His words are slow and deliberate. Orion has achieved all requirements for his degree a year early and has done it with the highest grade ever achieved by any student in the history of the University.

His academic achievements are matched by his extracurricular achievements such as captain of the best Ball and Target team ever assembled and he has held the position as president of the student body for the third time. There is a room filled with applause.

The President looks at us and says, "I wanted you, Orion, and your parents to be first to hear about this award and hear our accolades before it is made public at the Graduation Ceremony."

Ashley's eyes are now tearing. Ashley and I hug Orion. It is a great day! Maybe this is a glimpse of paradise. I am glad that we can't see into the future. It would spoil moments such as these. We all adjourn and attend the graduation.

After graduation we all have lunch with the President of the University. Orion has an open invitation to become full professor at any time that he wishes.

After lunch we all adjourn for a huge reception that Vera, Roland and the inevitable Antion have arranged at The Great Hall.

I looked to see if there was any tinge of jealousy in Athena and Apollo. I detect none. I ask, "You kids do not seem to have any envy at all but have, instead, pride!"

Athena knows that I do not fully understand.

She articulates their position well, "Daddy, first of all we are not kids! We feel the love and confidence that you and Mom have given to each one of us. We do not doubt ourselves. Orion has given us all of the support and love that a sister and brother could possibly want. There is no reason for jealousy."

I reply, "But you fight a lot." Athena laughs and says, "Dad! We may disagree with one another and it is you who told us to openly discuss our feelings. Don't mistake sibling discussions as a lack of respect or love for one another. I would die for Orion if I had to do so to save him. He would do the same for me." I look at Ashley and tears are streaming down her face.

During the dinner with us my father says, "I want to see you before you go off to fight again, son. It is of grave importance."

I go to his study in the Pyramid early the next day. He comes over and kisses me. He has never done that in my entire life. We hug.

We sit in silence for a while and then Dad speaks. I listen. He says, "I will be seeing your Mother soon. I have missed her terribly since her passing away so many years ago. My time has come."

I am about to say something but he moves his hand telling me that he wants me to listen. He says, "As you know, the Pyramid shape is no accident. It is a navigational structure as well as a place of worship. I have learned much in the Inner Sanctum of this Pyramid. I have also learned that you must complete your karma."

He continues his instructions, "You are to deliver the scriptures to a place in Tibet that Vera will identify. The Creator desires this because there will be a book of life that will be written from them. It will survive the ages and it will describe how planet dwellers should live. The Earth is only one of many planets but for some reason it has proven to be a very difficult one to educate. The planet dweller's ultimate destiny is to assist the Creator to create. Our people on Earth are always fighting and thirst for power! This impedes progress!"

He continues, "The scriptures will serve as the source material for many religious leaders as well as the source material for the ensuing book of life."

I say, "Dad, I don't understand." He replies, "You will. Keep your faith! The Destructor will try to worm his way into your soul by using temptation. Take care!"

He warns me, "Orion will be racing in the forthcoming Olympic Car Races." I shout, "No!" He calmly continues, "You were protected by the Creator's shield when you raced and so will Orion. The Creator wishes that you take all of your craft design and computer programming skill and use it to design Orion's car."

He warns, "If you persist in not letting Orion race he will listen to you, lose his destiny and be killed. Is that what you want?" I reply, "Of course not, Dad! I love my son with all of my heart." He says, "Then show it by fulfilling God's wish! Do it well!"

I say, "How will I ever convince Ashley? She will never allow it!" He replies, "Yes, she will. Vera has spoken to Ashley as I have spoken to you. She will comply. She must! She is almost ready to advance to the higher levels and one of her requirements is that she must support you and Orion. She loves both of you beyond your comprehension."

During the rest of the conversation he recalls our lives together before and after my current position in life. He recalls the lessons of the Great Rebellion and we both wonder if our people on Earth will ever learn to obey the Laws of Nature!

As is our custom Dad says that he wants to be cremated and he wishes that his ashes be buried in the Pyramid of our homeland in Gogania. He says, "There will be resistance to this request for I have become loved and respected here but you can prevail, I know. Please do this for me, son."

Tears stream down my face. I say, "I will follow your instructions." Then I ask him why he must leave us now. He looks at me squarely and smiles. He tells me frankly that he does not know. He just knows that it is meant to be.

He says, "I will fight to live until the very end. I will not leave easily! Our God knows and I know I will be at peace as my life ends and that I will feel His great love for me."

I leave the study deeply disturbed and saddened. I will miss him terribly. My thoughts return to The Great Rebellion. It is so easy to fall into sin if one forgets the Rules of Behavior!

Rebellion against the Creator has its consequences!

Mercury can tell that I am troubled. He says that he knew that my father is not feeling well even though the doctors can find nothing wrong. I tell him that I will need his support in the coming days more than ever.

When I arrive home I am a nervous man again. I do not like it. My whole life has been based on belief, self-reliance and self-assurance. The fact is that I am really, totally dependent upon God, many people and especially Ashley.

She knows how I feel about Dad and urges me to go to bed and contemplate. Think about Avatar's life and his lessons about life and love. I comply. I begin to feel the peace that comes as I share my feelings with God even though He already knows what they are. Ashley and I sleep soundly together.

It is late in the afternoon when we awake from our deep, restful sleep. The visit to the University has given us a five-day respite. It has been a relaxing time.

My faithful Isaac has done a spectacular job of fighting and has finished the destruction of the cave factory in Egypt.

Fortunately, we have about two hours to get ready to attend an important dinner meeting. Very discretely the phone rings about half an hour later to remind us that the dinner will be in the exclusive dining room of the new Government Building. We will be dining with our fellow Space Commanders and their wives.

We arrive on time. The Space Command consists of the Commander, Admiral Zadoc, and twelve assistants often called the twelve apostles. They are the Executive Officer, Operations Officer, Financial Officer, Technical Officer (Head of Research), Space Station Control Officer, Logistics Officer, Navigation Officer, Intelligence Officer, Security Officer, Communications Officer, Facilities Officer and Legal Officer.

We are in charge of The Space Fleet, space stations, probes and all else in space! All of us are married; all have children, and all are University graduates.

The women of this group have blended together extremely well. All of them know each other and are good friends. We are all enjoying pre-dinner cocktails and chatting about our destiny.

Dinner is announced. We all go to a large circular table in the center of the very tastefully decorated circular room. Only one light is shining at the center. We all say our allegiance and we all sip wine from a common cup to signify our being one family.

The lights go on and we break into various conversations about kids, school, weather, various experiences that we have had and what we think our future will be. We are truly an unbroken circle of trusted friends and we are comrades with a common goal.

Dinner is served and Zadoc wastes no time getting down to business. He says, "We are all targets for assassination. How intertwined are they within our ruling group. What is your assessment of this group of stealth assassins, Achilles?"

I say, "Today, the rider of the Second Horseman of the Apocalypse (War) is Arkite. He is no longer stealth. We know that Eric is part of the Serpentine movement. There is someone else guiding the whole rebellion. We are following several moles amongst us but The Beast and perpetrator has remained unidentified and has allies in our midst."

I continue, "The Space Command is our only hope of defeating the rebellion and the Rebels know it. They tried to dismantle us. Eric would have directed the Serpentine attack from our own Headquarters and would have if he had won the race. Some people in power were in our midst and some were killed but not all!

"Who was behind the blanking out of our defense system? It just did not happen by itself! Ladies and gentlemen, I believe that our mole is quite obvious and that we have a very serious problem."

Zadoc says, "I know that you are hesitant to tell me the name of your mole suspect because you know that he has been a good friend of mine for many, many years. He has changed. I am talking about Nebo. Am I correct?"

I answer, "Yes, Admiral. You are correct and I know you knew it when you removed the laser pistol from Nebo's holster and used it to secure Main Control." This act was the key to removing Nebo himself from being able to take control of the situation! The rest is history. The room is dead quiet.

Zadoc nods. He says, "We have problems but they can and will be resolved. Achilles, you are the Executive Operations Officer and I expect a plan of action that has been hatched, by this group, delineating our plans to continue the defeat of the rebellion! Have it on my desk by the end of next week."

He continues, "I want all of you in this room to stay a close knit and coordinated group because you are the well-spring of our survival."

He directs me, "Upgrade our spaceships and make them meet the standards of your racing machine, Achilles; I watched your maneuvers during the race in disbelief. Your control systems and detection equipment must be a mandatory addition to our craft!"

He warns, "Ladies and gentlemen, you are sworn to secrecy. Your lives as well as your families' lives are at stake. I brought these matters up tonight because Achilles and his band of seven, that some of you worry about, can probably be of more help in uncovering Nebo and the other moles infecting us than our own security will be."

He instructs, "All of our lives are at stake. We must believe in one another and support one another. I want all of you to know that we are in danger and tight lips are mandatory if we are to survive."

His final consideration is issued. "Achilles, you will be reporting directly to me and to no other person. If I am away, Roland is your contact. I want this sacred group to take the weekend off. It will be your last rest for a long, long time."

We sing our hymn. The dinner meeting is ended.

We all know that dangerous days are ahead and Ashley has tears in her eyes as we go home. It takes me a long, long time to get her to sleep. It takes a lot of cuddling. She is frightened and so am I because I know that there are fearsome battles ahead of us.

CHAPTER 4

Closing the Circle

I am contemplating and worrying about Orion's future as I continue in the field to slowly dismantle the Serpentine forces. No matter what I do or how much planning we have done there always is a fierce battle. The Battle of the Cape of Good Hope and Antarctica is a good example. There is something else that bothers me. The Massif formations in Madagascar are a puzzle. Something is happening there that is very significant.

Even though we have stopped the Serpentine flair-up in Europe, finally crippled their African campaign and secured South America, the Serpentine forces are getting close to a critical mass.

The Australian Campaign is next. We will attack Antarctica from New Zealand and the tip of South America.

I feel that we have managed to secure most of our victories because we have monitored the information that Nebo has relayed to Arkite and we have altered his information.

However, lately, there have been some oddities in Nebo's transmissions. I believe that Zadoc believes that he has "smelled a rat" so to speak.

I have been forced to make some abrupt last-minute changes in the field because the filtered and faulty information we have given him has been changed and some very valuable information has been given to the Serpentines. How? When Nebo asks me about the changes in the field that I have suddenly made I have simply said that the on-site situation developments required it.

Nebo is very deductive. I think he has analyzed what is happening. Things will change. The pressure is intense and there are some very fierce battles on the horizon that we must win!

Along with this situation I am faced with the unbelievable task of building a winning but safe racing craft for Orion.

I put myself on duty at Headquarters and temporarily placed Isaac in charge of the field operations. Zadoc is pleased and says, "Achilles, you are finally learning to let others do the tasks while you do the thinking."

He continues, "The trick is to pick loyal competent followers. The most dangerous followers are the loyal incompetents. The rest of the dangerous ones, in order of their danger, are the disloyal competent and the disloyal incompetent."

I smile because he is doing a good didactic job. He proceeds and says, "Because you are learning leadership I might be able to retire soon. I am too old for this incessant high tension job." I reply, "No way will I let you do that! Your influence is why I am able to do what I do. You are the kingpin of our whole operation! Scrub that loathsome thought!"

He responds, "Ashley expects you home early tonight." He smiles and says, "Achilles, don't say what you are thinking!" I say, "So what is new? I am sorry, Zadoc, it just flew out of my mouth." He laughs.

The minute that I walk into our house Ashley looks at me and knows that I am troubled. She can read me like an open book.

We both are aware that Avatar and Vera warn us that Orion must race! I tell her that I am thinking about not letting Orion do so.

Ashley shakes her head and says, "It is a very dangerous thought. I know what it is like to be a spectator and deeply love a person in that race. Think very carefully before you act. What would life be like if you had not been allowed to race? Remember that I almost succeeded in stopping you."

I know very well what she means. I do not say anything for a long time. I just stare into space. I finally turn to her and say, "I am sorry I put you through that torment but I knew inside that I had to race and win. It was a karma that I had to accomplish."

I hug her and kiss her. She says, "Long ago I gave my soul and body to you." The magnitude of her sacrifice finally penetrates my thick skull. She smiles at me and wipes the tear from my eye. She says, "Help him win by building the perfect machine for the job, Achilles. That is your task. Use all of your powers of design and your programming skills like Avatar requested! Keep the faith."

Ashley says, "Orion and Alcestis will be coming to see us tonight." I pour drinks and we sit together, watching the bright moonlight and holding hands. A full hour goes by without either of us uttering a word. We finally hear the footsteps that we expected. Nobody told us but we know what will happen.

Two young people burst into the room. Alcestis and Orion are holding hands and they are breathless. They tell us all about the University's Ball for all people graduating with new degrees. They both will receive their rings with emblems designating their majors and degrees. They tell us all of the exciting things that happened but save the best until last.

Alcestis shows us her betrothal ring. Ashley hugs Alcestis and they both have tears in their eyes. I hug both Orion and Alcestis and give them my congratulations.

Orion had asked Abaris and Minerva, Alcestis' parents, for her hand a few days ago and they both had given their blessing. We were the first to see the ring on her finger.

I say, "Orion, it would have been nice if you had told your mother and me a bit earlier about your love for Alcestis but the fact that you told Alcestis first and asked her parents' blessings first shows us that she is your first love. I am proud of you because that is the way it should be! You are a team together. We accept that and we are thrilled that you two are so deeply in love."

Minerva asks that Antion and Ashley help her arrange the festivities that are to come.

We all know that they will go overboard in arranging the engagement party. The World will be invited. It will be a huge success. All state dignitaries will be in attendance and all will dance and celebrate. The wedding date is set. The engaged couple is the perfect example of young people in love.

Along with this and all too quickly, the wedding reception plans have been effectively completed. It will follow Minerva's and Alcestis' specific instructions. It will be held in the Main Pyramid in front of the altar and Avatar will officiate at the wedding itself. A reception will include hundreds of people who run the countries of Gogania and Magogania.

I now am part of the Oligarchy! I wonder if I am still acting for the people or have I been caught up in the powerful net of power thirst? This bothers me.

I know that there is a cloud for Orion in these clear skies of euphoria! There always is. I have reviewed and approved the Olympic Race applications. I wait.

Before I realize what is happening I am at the engagement party. While I dance with Ashley she reminds me that I must dance with Minerva, our son's mother-in-law. I do. She is beautiful. She is five-foot-nine with an hourglass figure. She has brown eyes and golden blonde hair and a vivacious personality. I enjoy the dance very much. The latest rhythmical prance is very sexy and is a copy of a

South American tribal step. Ashley, of course, had taught me the proper gambol.

The wonderful evening is about to come to an end when Orion comes to me and asks if Ashley and I would come to the library. I look at Ashley and her eyes tell me that she knows what is coming. Alcestis is in tears. Orion looks devastated.

He has told Alcestis that he had signed up for the air car races. This event is set in concrete. It will happen. This race with its carnage is a clear sign that we have not advanced very far as a civilization. This saddens me.

I ask the youngsters to sit down so we can talk together. Alcestis is very upset but does what I ask. I summon Alcestis' parents, Abaris and Minerva. I have no idea of what to say but I better think of something and damn fast!

All eyes are riveted upon me, including Ashley's. It is up to me to speak. My palms are sweaty. I look straight at Alcestis and Orion and say, "I knew what you were going to do, son, before you put in your application because Avatar told me and my reaction, Alcestis, was to say, 'No way, never!' Orion has so much talent to offer the world that we simply cannot expose him to such danger and in such a brutal way!"

I continue, "However, Avatar convinced me that there is more to life than is apparent to all of us. I am here to help and not hinder Orion achieve his karma. Son, I knew that you spent a lot of time with your grandfather while you were growing up. He would put you on his lap when you were very young and put his arm around your shoulder as you two would discuss life. Later you would have long talks together while sipping tea. He loves you as much as Mom and I do. He also knows how you think and he knows your karma."

I discuss the situation, "You went to him and talked about the race. He gave you the facts as he saw them. The decision is yours to make. Alcestis and Orion, the first thing that you must understand is that we parents love both of you with all of our hearts and souls. We do not want to see you hurt. Anything that hurts you hurts us even more deeply."

I continue, "Even though we think of you as terribly young you are not! You are adults and you are making adult decisions. We parents have reared you, nurtured you and loved you. We still do love you but we must also let you go into the world and live your own lives. If we try to interfere or jam our decisions down your throat we are making a big mistake. We will advise you and we will always help you. You will never be out of our thoughts nor will you ever be away from our love.

"I am going to answer your basic question. You have asked us for our advice and so we will give it to you. My personal opinion is that the races are an uncivilized part of our culture. I truly hope that this is the last one but I cannot stop them. This particular race will happen. I delayed the Olympics as long as I could. The decision to participate is yours. Son, I gave your application my approval. I agree with Avatar. I think that it is part of your karma and destiny. Vera also agrees."

I continue, "To say that your Mom and I are worried about this is an extreme understatement but we have faith in you and your judgments. Abaris and Minerva are extremely upset and it is well that they should be." I look at Minerva and see in her eyes a complete trust in me. I wonder if I deserve it.

I complete my thoughts, "If you want to race, son, you and I will design a safe and winning air car. We will design a program and its computers so that you will have the maximum time to think while the machine is carrying out the basic plan. We will update all sensors and have all new safety equipment installed. Fuel cells will not explode as they once did. Leaks in the fuel system are protected by a self-sealing sensor system."

More talk, "With all of this updated equipment there is still danger but life is filled with challenge and danger. Fear is a deadly enemy. It causes us to do nothing. Evil will then follow. I feel we were created to develop the unique talents that each one of us has been given and to use them to make the world a better place. We can bury them but the scriptures say that this will disappoint our Creator."

I look at Alcestis and say, "You can stop Orion from racing, but if you do, this action will also stop you both from reaching your full potential and accomplishing your mutual karmas together. Mankind was meant to climb mountains and reach the peaks for there is where the Creator resides. If we fall trying, he has promised to catch us, pick us up, and help us to continue to climb. If we quit half way up the mountain He will be disappointed. He can't help us if we are not willing to help ourselves."

I warn, "We are all meant to be active participators in the events that surround us. How we participate is our decision. We must choose between being constructors, the most difficult path, or being destructors, the easy path. Marriage is the answer. Man and woman were created to join together and help one another and their children climb their highest mountains. This is the right path! The burden is easier when all are sharing the load and all are benefiting."

Finally, I add, "We parents, I think, should return to the party and leave you two alone. When you want us to return we will come."

I pause and say, "The first thing I would like for you to do when we are gone is to profess your love for one another. This must be done! Then, and only then, you are ready to talk! If you both decide to race and, believe me, it will be both of you, you will know deep inside that you are inseparable and can achieve anything you want to achieve when working together as a team and you are a team! Talk about it."

Abaris, Ashley, Minerva and I depart. We all look at each other with trepidation. We go to a fireplace and all have a strong drink together. The dancing fires, surrounded by

easy chairs in the Ball Room, give us solace. We philosophize together about life and its meaning.

About one hour passes and finally Alcestis and Orion
come to us. We are invited to come to the library. It is obvious by the smudged makeup that Alcestis had been crying.
They are now smiling and holding hands. I can see that
they are more deeply in love than ever before. I know now
that they will race together. I thank God! Alcestis kisses me
on the cheek and calls me Dad. I love it.

Working on the air car is good therapy for me. The flexible outer covering will enable the craft to present a different hull form as the craft changes its speed mode. The
skin shielding is a new design. I am proud of this nascent
machine. Orion, Pete and I work night and day on her.

Although Orion has completed degree work at the University they are extremely interested in doing more research concerning some of his doctoral assignments and
he has agreed to do them. He leaves often to follow up the
results of several of these post-graduation postulations.

One postulation is to confirm that solid mass can change
to energy, travel through space at unbelievable speeds and
turn back to solid mass at a designated destination. We
think we know that it does happen. How?

I always go to the office each morning, review the battle
plans and then go to the laboratory where we are con-
structing Orion's craft. Sharon, Alcestis and Ashley usually
bring a basket of food and wine for dinner and force us to
take a delightful break from our work.

Several months go by before the machine has turned
into a sleek beautiful air car. Orion wants to fly it. I ask him
to let me test fly it first to be sure all is working well. He
very reluctantly agrees. I want to combine testing with my
newly designated duty of checking the course a final time
before the race.

Security guards are at each obstacle to assure that no
tampering or damage is done to them. All participants
have the right to fly the course once after I have declared

it is safe to do so. All craft are watched and monitored to assure that no damage is done nor any change is made to any obstacle while the participants make their runs. Nobody else is allowed near the course.

We work feverishly so that we can let Orion fly his craft and become bonded with it well before the race. I make light of the test but Pete knows that this is the most difficult part of the creation process. Pete and Orion will follow me as I put the machine through its paces.

We must test the machine to its limits and assure ourselves that we have properly defined the flying envelope. We finish all of the robot-guided runs, air tunnel testing, quality control checks and visual inspections. She is ready. Orion names her Alcestis.

I say, "She will give her life for you. If you remember the mythical story that even though Alcestis does offer her life as a substitute for her husband's life who had been condemned to death she does not die but does go to Hades. Persephone, who at this particular time, was queen of Hades admired Alcestis who was willing to sacrifice her life as a substitute for her husband's life. She loved him that much. Persephone granted her a reprieve."

Orion says, "Dad, why is it that you remember this mythology story at this time?" I say, "Orion, I suspect there is something that my subconscious mind is telling me to do!" There is something that I must do to assure reprieve! Maybe Alcestis does not die! I will figure it out!

I have a persistent uneasiness about what mischief Nebo, Eric and Arkite can do. Their philosophy of self-indulgence without a sense of commitment, loyalty, responsibility and lack of love to others will eventually destroy their souls but they can do much harm to others before that happens.

Eric is estranged from his wife and they lost one son to hallucinogens. His daughters will not speak to him. He is always surrounded by a bevy of adoring women. I know that he hates me with all of his soul. He wants me and my family dead.

I know that someday I must fight him hand to hand. Will I win? Nebo wants power and he will do anything to get it. What better way to destroy me than to destroy Orion? He will try. Can I blunt this sword? What price do I have to pay?

I call Isaac. I will need all of his intelligence and skill. When is a good time to sabotage Alcestis? I think that it will be just prior to the flight when we are making the final preparations. We have to be totally aware of all that is happening. I am racking my brain trying to think of what they can do to Orion's ship.

Pete, Orion and Ashley think that I am overreacting to a non-problem. Maybe I am. I look at Isaac who knows our test flight plans. He says, "We do this same scenario every time. Maybe someday, our antagonists will figure out what our plans are and how to thwart them."

I say, "Isaac, you are right and we must insert surprise. This is possible. You know for instance, Nebo is beginning to change his secret transmissions to Arkite. I think that he may well believe that Orion will fly the test flight because the pilot always flies the test run." Isaac nods. I continue, "I will fly it."

The super-secret word is put out that Orion is going to take the craft on the maiden journey and that Pete and I will monitor from following crafts. Only Ashley and Alcestis know the real plan. If trouble is to occur, this is the perfect time. The first flight is always considered to be dangerous. An accident could be blamed on bad design and leave saboteurs undetected. Isaac takes this threat seriously and so do I. We will do all that is humanly possible to prevent this problem.

I say, "Orion, I realize why I remembered the mythological story of Alcestis!" Only Pete, Orion and I know that, just in case of foul play, we are making two identical racing crafts, Alcestis I and Alcestis II.

The test day for Alcestis I is a beauty with clear skies and a warm breeze. Mercury takes us to the hangar. Isaac had accomplished his work. All people involved in any way are under surveillance. The three craft await us inside the hangar, ready to go, Alcestis I and two follow craft. All personnel are evacuated. We put on our space suits. The self-contained flying evacuation packets and self-contained breathing devices are placed in our seats.

Mercury has done what I requested and supplied us with the new mighty mite hand lasers and three cannons. We strap lasers onto the outer part of our suits and mount the cannons. We enter our aircraft. All of us appear identical. Nobody can tell who is in each aircraft. I activate the door control and we ease out of the hangar slowly. Our course is pre-set in the computers. We hover for a few moments to follow each step of an extensive check-off list. All is in order. We salute in military style and roar into the skies.

We complete the preliminary tests without incident. The "Alcestis" operates better than I thought that she would. As she flies close to the ground her contour changes as it should to reduce drag. The fuel consumption remains remarkably low. We rush toward the caves. I activate the appropriate program and zoom into the mouth of the first dark cavern. Pete and Orion hover above the site. I could detect the outline of the cave on the sensors. It took almost more nerve than I could master to let the machine fly through.

The structures zoom past my canopy. It is frightening. We test the craft in each of the caves and then head toward the forest. We land on the lake beach together for a lunch break. Our backup craft, AII, is automatically being fed all of the data given out by AI and has loaded it into her systems. She is following all of the movements of the primary craft.

Our sandwiches and water provided a great banquet but I am tired. Age has a terrible habit of wrecking our temporal body. This is something that Dad told me. I didn't appreciate what he was saying until now.

I tell Orion that once the testing is done he will be flying this machine until he is exhausted and he has to fly it until it becomes part of him. I say, "You and 'Alcestis' must be one being and know what each is doing at all times. It is like being truly married to your machine."

Orion says, "Dad, things do not think." I reply, "Son, Nature thinks and responds. If you have enough faith and love for Nature you can command the mountains to move and they will respond." Pete says, "Achilles, sometimes you scare me." I smile.

It is time for some high-speed runs to the North Pole and then roar into orbit. All seems well but I have a nagging feeling that something is wrong. I contact Isaac over the secure line. I alert him about my feelings. If there is a Serpentine lurking in our group he will find him.

As I look over the surface, I examine every piece of the craft with the visual sensor system. I mentally lock these pictures into my mind. My mind works well with images. Memory of words and names are not my strong suit but retaining images is. This saved my neck in college because I could recall all of the formulas and the holographic presentations given.

The new high-energy superconductor goes into full power as we thrust toward the sky. Our new thrusters are magnificent if I say so myself. The rise into orbit is spectacular!

The follow craft mimic my course but they are much slower. I have to wait for them. While I am cruising around I can hear a voice telling me to pay attention to the local space around me. I can see nothing but a barely noticeable signal that looks like inconsequential static is showing itself in my sensors. This makes me curious.

I hover around the spot. I still cannot see or detect anything positive. I edge closer and closer to this small signal until I touch something invisible to all detectors. It is solid!

My hull scrapes around it. It is a cylinder! Suddenly, I am pushed away with a nondestructive force field. I fight to recover my equilibrium. It takes several minutes and takes me miles away from the object I had found! Pete shouts, "Achilles, what the hell do you think that you are doing?

Stop playing around!" I answer, "Pete and Orion, you are not going to believe what just happened."

I continue, "I have discovered a probe from the Inter-planetary Federation my Dad told me about. It exists! It is made out of prisms that direct light power and any other signal coming to it to go around it so that one would think that it is not there! The damn thing is invisible to our senses!" Pete laughs and says, "Yea, right. Now stop clowning around and let's get on with the testing."

I am about to reply when I see something in the front part of my canopy that bothers me. I detect two unnatural lumps. Are they pressure gauges? What the hell is going on and who put them there? I am sure that they have been there the whole time but they are so tiny that they are hard to see. Being in orbit helps!

Suddenly, black smoke begins to fill the cockpit. Orion screams, "Evacuate!"

Before activating the self-contained breathing system I get a good whiff of the smoky smell. I know that it is not the stench that would come from any of the equipment failing. It is acrid. Its smell, density and volume would cause a prudent pilot to evacuate.

The two lumps near the cockpit tell me that evacuation is not the prudent course of action. I suspect that if I move the canopy it will explode. This may be a dual-controlled bomb system. I know that another trigger is involved but there is very little time to figure out what action to take. Oh, damn! Now what do I do? Over the secure circuit, I tell Pete, Orion and Isaac what is going on and what I suspect.

I am proud of the tilted nozzle system perfected by our design team. Now I will see if it will save my neck.

I must figure out a window to Earth entry and damn fast! Feverishly, the computers and I ask each other several questions. I whisper, "Alcestis, I love you and for us to continue to exist we must take action quickly."

Somehow, I feel a creating power pervading the atmosphere. A possible solution appears on the monitor screen.

I do not bother to check it out. I hit the execute button. As usual, I see admonition flashing on the screen, "Are you sure that you want to execute?" I hit the yes button. I now pray. I must trust the system to make the landing.

I cannot see a damn thing! I cannot even see the monitor anymore. I can tell from the feel of my glove that the acid smoke is beginning to eat through my space suit. I must act quickly or the ship will suffer severe damage!

The ship lands! I fumble around my belt area to find the laser gun. Will it work? I do not know but it is my one and only hope. I cut a hole in the top of the canopy so that I will not activate something while I am wiggling out. Somehow, I have a feeling that there may be a bomb in my safety pack! I may be a walking bomb! I suspect that my movement broke the sensor beam and now a timer is operating. I remove my headpiece and run as fast as I can while unfastening the space suit. Pete and Orion are still trying to come out of orbit. I trip and fall but manage to get out of the suit. I see a pile of rocks and throw the suit with all of my might.

Just as the suit and safety pack fly over the crest of the formation a tremendous explosion occurs. Chunks of rocks are flying all over the place. Fortunately, I am close to the rock formation and none of the debris hits me.

Small pieces hit "Alcestis." I rush back and cut a hole in the bottom and the sides of "Alcestis." A good wind is blowing so that the smoke is being blown out of her. I climb back into "Alcestis" and I tell Isaac over the secure circuit what happened. I tell Isaac to spread the word in the hangar that an explosion has ripped through the air car and that Orion has been killed by the blast.

He is to have the security circuits record every person's reaction. See who would attempt to get word to Arkite and to Nebo. There is more than one Serpentine involved. We must find them and quickly! Isaac tells Ashley and Alcestis the truth over our private communicator system.

I climb out of "Alcestis" again. My skin is red from the smoke reaction. She is being destroyed. Pete and Orion are pale as they run over to see me. I feel dumb standing on the meadow in my undershirt and shorts. Pete and Orion hug me and their bodies are shaking as if they were cold!

The wind has purged Alcestis of the erosive smoke. Pete and Orion work feverishly to clean all parts possible by air and vacuum before any more damage is done. We need all of the clues we can find.

Good and faithful Isaac! A craft appears armed with security guards and mechanics. They have portable blowers, vacuums and other cleaning equipment. They brought portable repair equipment and a bank of testing equipment. We also get the bomb fragments to see what it was made of and see if we can figure out who made it.

The first damage reports are not encouraging. The residue from the smoke and acid has caused major damage. It cannot be fixed in a matter of days. The holes that I cut did no harm. I thought that I had picked the proper spots. The bomb squad is sifting through every shred of evidence. They will remove the trigger mechanism from the canopy after "Alcestis" is returned to the hangar. Isaac tells me that he has nailed four Serpentines and all but one (too much pressure on the neck needle) have supplied him with valuable information. Another Serpentine was killed while he was trying to send a message to the Serpentine headquarters. Isaac had all satellites listening for the expected broadcast.

I know it but I cannot swallow the fact that one of my Seven is a Serpentine. There is no other way that so much damage could have been inflicted on "Alcestis"!

A sky crane comes to pick up the "Alcestis." We report that we would repair her and have her ready for Orion to fly but not until I take her on another fast test run.

However, the facts are that Alcestis I died.

The evening news features a story that Orion was killed while testing his race car, "Alcestis."

After we secure "Alcestis" in her hangar we let the technicians take over. They know exactly what to do. They found out that, indeed, acid ate the vital insides of the beautiful machine, Alcestis I! Alcestis II will be the race car.

Orion looks at me and says, "Dad, how much air did you have in your self-contained safety pack when you took off the space suit?" I say, "The red zero air light had been on for several minutes; obviously there was a leak or the amount of original air was low. I was beginning to feel dizzy."

I explain, "I took off the helmet to breathe good fresh air again but I was weak and fell as I was running toward the rocks. Fortunately, I got out of the suit just in time to fling it over the rocks before I fell again. The rest of the story you know."

He says, "How did you remain so calm during the whole thing?" I say, "Long ago I found that panic is probably one of mankind's worst curses. In times of crisis it's better to use that flood of mental energy that comes with danger to think your way out of the problem rather than to dissipate the energy by panic. Panic leads to nonsensical decisions and always brings defeat. Rational thinking is the route to victory."

We are all silent for a while. Finally Orion, who never drinks, says, "Dad, when we get home and after a shower let us have a tall drink." I nod.

As we arrive home we are welcomed to a test flight party. Antion has accomplished a perfect performance again. Isaac and Pete are ushered to the guestrooms. Our dinner clothing is ready for us. Our wives and Alcestis are already enjoying the hors d'oeuvres out on the lawn. We are told to be ready as soon as possible.

Zadoc takes me aside and says, "Achilles, we have to talk. Nebo is becoming more recalcitrant but it is too early for us to take an overt action. We do not have the evidence yet that is needed to convict him in court."

He warns, "We are treading on dangerous ground. We must discuss our countermove actions." We go to the library with our drinks and hors d'oeuvres in hand and I tell him what I think. I say, "Nebo will obviously learn that Orion and I are well and he will try and kill me and Orion during the air race. I do not know how but he will."

I apprise Zadoc, "Do not even give him a hint that we are suspicious. We must secure every scrap of information that we can gather. Since you have been the closest of friends for years he will not be as guarded around you. He might even try to influence you to do an apparently innocuous thing for him. You can be sure that it will be a deadly thing."

Zadoc replies, "If he succeeds, Achilles, I am a dead man." I nod in agreement. We return to the dinner party.

As we emerge from the room, Pallas, Zadoc's wife and Vera's very good friend says, "Where have you two been?" I say, "In the library discussing my task of performing the final test run for the Olympic Air Car race."

She looks at Zadoc, turns to me and says, "Achilles, you are transparent. There is something else happening!"

She adds, "I love you, Achilles, because you have given my husband a zest and purpose for living. You have given us a Space Command (World Federation) that is worthy to save. Because of this, you have touched the hearts of the people and they love you. Take care." I reply, "I hope that the people trust me. We desperately need each one of them."

She continues, "Whatever it is that you have to face, may The Holy Paraclete be with you." She kisses me and then she says, "Achilles, you have not told Sharon about the test run plans, have you?" I am puzzled. Ashley knows. She is not pleased but understands.

I say, "Hasn't Pete told Sharon? We all know that Argus, their son, would have been in the car race itself if he had been one year older. He was very disappointed but excited being a participant in Orion's check team! Argus and he are very close friends. Orion wanted Argus to get the feel of the course so he can start to prepare for the next race."

I continue, "I agreed to have the Quality Assurance Certifying Team to be Pete, Argus and me." I go over to Sharon.

She kisses me and says, "You and his dad are my son's models. I am pleased that he is not going to race but I am not pleased that you approved his involvement in your checking of the course!"

She admonishes me, "He is not experienced enough to react to an emergency. You and Pete are experienced and seasoned warriors. Why did you agree to do this?"

I reply, "I realize what I have done appears stupid and I apologize. My thoughts were to give Argus confidence in his abilities and let him be able to see firsthand what the course is all about. This should be an uneventful event and I thought the experience would give him a lift. He wants to be part of our team and we want him to feel that he is worthwhile and useful. This flight will fulfill his desires."

I add, "If you really do not want him to go I will change the plans. The call is yours. I love you far too much to ever go against your desires. We are souls on the same journey." She replies, "Achilles, I will think about it but nothing you ever do is uneventful! You are like a huge trouble magnet. I am surprised Pete agreed with you and I know that he does not know why he follows you! You are always in trouble!" She smiles at me and says, "Achilles, you truly, truly are a piece of work!"

Mothers have an innate instinct about things. I had a long conversation with Ashley. She says, "Honey, I have a feeling of danger about this innocuous certification. You have a great responsibility. Take care and be sure that all of you return to us without harm and I mean all of you!"

I install a special alert communicator in the testing cars that we are flying. I cannot arm our machines because they must act like and look like a race inspector's car.

However, what I can do is to have the Course Security Vehicles replaced by the new craft that Isaac and I designed. They have not completed their testing but Isaac and I have faith in them.

No one will know that they are armed so nobody will be upset when they see these new machines. It will look as if the old machines are being temporarily replaced by some proposed new machines and are being tested at this time to save money.

The chief of the guard force has been told and agrees that the old machines could use some updating. If the new machine features are far more useful than the old ones they will be replaced on a routine basis. Operating these new features is very simple. Damn! I need this stress like a hole in the head!

The first part of the check goes without a hitch. The security guards are all in place. I note that the new machines are there. Since nobody mentions training for the new craft, I know that they are unaware of any significant difference.

All is going beautifully. The trip to the North Magnetic Pole and our rise into orbit at the North Geometric Pole was beautiful. I took a few moments to scan the skies.

Sure enough the probe is there! It flings me away after my nose touches it. This time, unlike before, Pete and Argus are believers.

We return to earth and head for the caves. I recognize the Security Group. All checks and modifications are being made right on schedule until we reached the forest. I noted the new security craft are in place but there is something that I do not like. Something is different. I cannot put my finger on it. After our late lunch break we signal Security that we are starting our check runs of the forest.

I take the left run that is the most difficult but the shortest route. Argus takes the middle and safest route. It is the longest. Pete takes the right route that is between the other two in length and difficulty.

I confidently roar through the course and head for the end of the grove. I know where I am going and I know what to do. Damn! Something about those trees is not right! I swear that the bloody thing moved! As I approach it is obvious that there is a complete barrier without a slot for egress anywhere, except a tiny slot where there was none before. I have seconds to figure out what to do. I will aim for the slot and have my finger on the emergency nozzle power mechanism. When the tree moves to cover the slot I will shift the nozzles and go where the tree was seconds ago. Meanwhile, I have hit the red alert button!

The tree shifts and I slide through the hole before it can react to close it. I can hear the machinery move and branches scrape along my hull. As I head straight upward I hear a muffled sound. One of us is down! I break free of the forest and see Pete. Over the secure circuit I tell him to get to Argus' machine that glanced off a tree and is damaged but not crushed.

We are in a hell of a mess! I head straight for the Security Craft. As I expected after this incident occurred, the Serpentines are scrambling to their fighters! I know how to get into the Security Craft and within seconds I am over Pete and Argus who has an injured back!

Pete has him on the stabilizer so that Argus' body cannot move. We get Argus into the Security Craft and take off just as the fighters attack us.

They know that we are sitting ducks just waiting to be shot. They want us to suffer so they are a bit careless. I activate the forward laser cannons and Pete mans the rear stinger cannon. Just before the lead fighter pulls his trigger he is in oblivion.

Another fighter comes up behind us and Pete sends him to hell where he belongs. There are three more of them and I suspect more backup close by.

The ensuing dogfight is fierce. One is left when I see a Serpentine reinforcement squadron approaching. I am now low on charge and so is Pete. Our fighters, alerted because of my red alert signal, better be in the right place. They are! The Serpentines do not see our craft because they are totally focused on killing us. Our squadron is approaching from the sun. The glare gives our men time to fire first. Within minutes there are no Serpentines.

Time is vital. Argus is paralyzed. His neck and his back are broken. We are on the way to the hospital! I talk to

Dr. Abaris, obviously a close friend, at the University. He is the expert in the field of nanotechnology medicine. He will be at the hospital waiting with nanotechnology mesh nets.

Time is the key. Abaris must clean and align the broken neck and spine, wrap the netting around the broken nerves, slide the neck bone and spine over the wounded nerves, fuse the broken bones around the nerves so there can be no movement at the wound centers and start to pray that the nerve pieces will use the nano-net as scaffolding.

If too much time elapses the body will switch from an acute state reaction to a chronic mode state and the cells will not react as they should. Doctor Abaris is the only one who has perfected a method of inserting the nanotechnology netting so that the nerves will indeed climb this net like a staging and reconnect the nerves at the break points. The alignment of the two pieces of damaged cord is critical.

When this is accomplished no movement of that section of the neck or of the backbone can be tolerated. He has never had to repair two pieces simultaneously. Alignment is painstaking and tedious. It seems to be taking forever! We, with a load of medical students, are watching Dr. Abaris from the operating room balcony.

Were these nets introduced on time? Dr. Abaris is finally done and the local areas are perfectly aligned and restrained so that no movement is possible. He passes the portable magnetic resonator over the damaged areas. He studies the images on the screen. Apparently it looks good. Now Abaris must perform the final test. Has the netting material closed all gaps so that there is continuity from the brain to the toes? The signal generator is hooked to the base of the spinal cord in his neck to a receiver in his right toe.

This will tell us if the netting is working and the healing process will happen. It is a very delicate test and the signals are incredibly small. The sensing signals are given. There is no reaction from the toe. Dr. Abaris is not about to give up! He tries one more time.

We could not see the toe screen and Dr. Abaris is a non-emotional man but this time he looked up at us and lifts his right arm into the air! We can hear the words, "YES! YES! All is well!" Within hours Argus will be in therapy.

We all cheer. It is a miracle! This is what we human beings are put on this Earth to do. We must learn that helping others is the Creator's wish. It does not matter what we do as a profession. Statesmen can keep us secure, business people make the markets that supply us with our needs, actors give us good thoughts, etc. If all goals are aimed toward cooperating with one another to make life better for all of us we are doing God's work!

Why do greed, gluttony, pride, envy, anger, lust and sloth drive so many people? These things lead to destruction!

Argus is doing well in therapy and the nerves are taking their due time to grow. After healing he will have no restrictions. He will walk, move his limbs without trouble and run normally.

Now Sharon is very concerned about Argus because he wants to be with us when we complete our race course certification. She says, "Argus wants to be with his dad during the process." Dr. Abaris has no problem with this request but does not want Argus to think that he can fly a machine just yet. His full coordination is still several weeks away.

Pete thinks that it will do him good to overcome the fear of the forest. "What do you think?" I say, "Sharon, if Dr. Abaris has no problem I see no problem with the plan."

I explain, "We can compensate Peter's craft for Argus' weight. It is your call." She says, "Thanks a lot! You are putting me through hell again! I do not know why I trust you. Argus was almost killed."

She continues to berate me, "You are a trouble magnet! Argus was almost a quadriplegic! The whole lot of us must be insane to believe you but I will let him go. Thanks to you, I will never hear the last of it if I refuse!"

I wondered what would have happened if the operation had been unsuccessful? I shudder, give thanks to our

Creator and drop the thought. Pete, Argus, Isaac and I finish the certification of the racecourse.

Orion is frustrating Alcestis. He is always piloting, tinkering and fine-tuning his race car. We are making modifications and adjustments to Alcestis II due to knowledge we gained from Alcestis I. We make an analysis of all flights we make every day. It is late at night and we are just finishing a modification when I overhear Alcestis say, "Honey, why don't you marry that damn machine! You love her more than me!" That phrase does have a familiar ring. I smile to myself.

We have a pre-race party and as usual Ashley and Antion go berserk again. It is elegant! Tents are all over the place. The garden is beautiful and the food is great!

Orion and I come in late and in need of a change of clothing. Ashley and Alcestis scold us and send us to our rooms. Orion says, "Dad, Alcestis acts like a clone of Mom." I smile. We bathe and dress.

The last guest departs. Ashley and I go upstairs to prepare for bed. We are both very, very tired and look forward to cuddling. I tell Ashley that I am still worried about Orion.

I say, "The race will be fierce, just as all of them have been through history. Emotions are high and the excitement is great. I am worried about security although I think that I have done all that is possible to do. Somehow I know that some of the participants will be Serpentines. Nebo will see to that. There will be suicides. This is an ugly act. How are we going to control their actions?"

I ask, "How is Alcestis handling all of this stress?" Ashley just smiles and says, "We are descendants of the Viziers of the original Federation Settlement Council. We learned how to handle stress and it is now an innate part of our psyche." She kisses me, snuggles closer and falls asleep.

I muse, "What on Earth is this all about? Why is it that I feel as if I am in a river in a canoe that is roaring down a canyon? Am I, in reality, a passenger riding in a boat that is controlled by the currents around me? Why is Ashley remembering her past life? Is it to help her cope with stress? There is so much more than we realize around us that will help us to accomplish our karma if we will just believe and ask for help."

I think, "I suspect that I should not be fighting the currents but should be listening to them. My job is to keep my canoe in mid-stream instead of worrying about things I cannot control. Maybe that is the job of each one of us."

In the twilight of consciousness and before I finally fall asleep I remember the story about The City of Eden that was filled with light before the rebellion. I again muse, "The Denizens were able to talk to God. The circuit was wide open. Maybe it still is."

I continue to muse, "It is up to us to listen. Adam, who was the leader, followed the advice of Eve, his wife, and tasted the fruit of power."

"They rebelled against our Creator because they felt that they could run things better themselves and did not need Him. They convinced the rest of the citizens to follow them because they felt that the other citizens were not capable of running Eden. The citizens believed them! Why?"

My last thoughts were, "Adam and Eve and all the citizens who tasted power lost communication with Nature. The result is obvious. The rebellious actions of the citizens resulted in the destruction of Eden. They were all driven out.

"However, the scriptures, the Holy Word, stayed to guide the faithful. Where are the faithful? Is Noah the chosen prophet and are his followers really the chosen Tribe? Who is the Federation? Why have they sent the probe satellite to Earth!

"God has given us rules to follow. Why do we ignore them? Why are there two voices in our heads, one of light and the other of darkness? I cannot answer these questions but I certainly can try to listen to God!"

As I lay in this state of in-between I pray. I think about my son and what I can do to help him. I decide that the best thing I can do is to show him confidence, give him advice when he asks and assure the physical condition of his racing car is at its peak. I must assure that the course is as it should be and that it has no unexpected traps! I must also show supreme confidence to the entire family. I must be their example. I must not fail. Being a fit Dad is hard business, for those who care, but the rewards are immeasurable. I finally fall into deep sleep.

THE SECOND RACE

Finally, the day of the race is here. There is great excitement in the air. We have stationed all observers and security people in strategic locations. The course is clear. All holographic and broadcast equipment is in place. Ashley takes her place in the stands with Sharon. Athena is surrounded by a flock of admirers and Apollo is in the hangar pits with his brother. I am down with the official committee at the race car assembly area.

My only real concern for Orion is the possibility of suicides. Somehow I know that Nebo will field at least one. The suicide's family will be promised treasures. Stupid! A soul is lost for what?

The Committee inspects all craft. There will be no craft allowed to race that does not meet the published criteria. All craft are all thoroughly profiled by a combination of super rays and resonance imagery. Two of the racing crafts are disqualified.

Orion is keenly aware of the suicide strategies. He has gone over and over the way a victim is targeted. We saw all available recorded cubes. It is a shame that he has to think about that as well as how to win the race but he knows the course better than I do and he is mindful of the possibilities of foul play. He knows what he must do.

Alcestis has scolded him for spending exorbitant training time. He must train intensively because this makes vital reaction time shorter. She feels neglected but she is, nonetheless, totally supportive. That is good! Orion has her ribbon flying from the top of his space helmet. We could not find a rule about that so we let him wear it. I know Ashley would have trounced upon me if I had not approved.

As Orion enters his craft we exchange the space salute, right hand closed over the heart (love of family and country) and then opened to the sky (love of God). This will be the last time I will be able to talk with Orion until after the race. The very last thing he did was to kiss Alcestis. It was lingering, and he was almost late for the lineup.

Orion's postposition is mediocre. The draw has favored some of the best of the contenders. Orion and I had worked out several plans concerning the overcoming of a poor starting position. I am worried and I will not feel good until this race is over!

The starting signal is activated. I have a shock reaction to the sound and almost jump out of my skin. I go to the commission's seats and sit next to Ashley. She gives me a curious look. I must look terrible.

She kisses my cheek and squeezes my hand. I am now helpless. Letting go is the most difficult part of being a parent but letting go is vital. The young must soar by themselves.

Isaac comes alongside of me and gives me the look that assured me all was well, so far. Ashley looks over curiously. Isaac reports, "Achilles, Apollo and I thought that you were being paranoid about this whole thing. I apologize. You were not."

He explains, "When we took out Orion's superconductor upon your orders, and replaced it with the one you used at the bench for the final check, we found that the end bells had been replaced by plastic explosives. This unit lies in the bomb disposal vault."

He continues, "Not only that but when we replaced Orion's computer and cubes, as you instructed, with the ones you used for the final check we found that the cubes are not right. There is something about them that is wrong."

He says, "There is something else that I did not like. The cube controller for the thruster and the attached manifold was not right. I replaced all of them and put all of them in bomb disposal vaults." I thank and hug Isaac. I say, "Only you know and no other in our group knows." Isaac replies, "Yes, Achilles, no one else knows." I say, "I wish we knew who in our group is a Serpentine." He nods. Ashley turns pale. Alcestis did not overhear the conversation.

The same newscaster that I hated with a passion, and had tried to fire, is announcing a description of the race. The Race Commission did not approve my appeal to remove him. He is doing the same thing to Orion as he did to me. He is praising all other pilots and downgrading Orion.

Suddenly, there was a burst of excitement. The announcer is beside himself. Apparently, Orion has been the target of a suicide. He is happily stating that Orion's craft has disappeared in a massive explosion along with the suicide craft that was close behind him.

The suicide had explosives! One of our vaults where we put our discarded parts erupts with an explosion. How did they get the explosive onboard? Of course, it was part of the structure of the craft, like the end pieces of the superconductor.

What was the activating mechanism? I look at Isaac. He knows and does not seem worried. The announcer comes back but this time he is much less jubilant. He explains, "Orion must have tipped his craft so that the heat shield took the heat of the blast. He has ridden on the crest of the blast wave and he is now ahead of the pack!"

The announcer now says that Orion is apparently having trouble with his computer. I look at Isaac. He knows what I am thinking. Orion is having computer problems? How would the announcer possibly know? The trigger for the bombs is, of course, the announcer's sound waves being relayed to the cubes! Sure enough a tremendous explosion is contained by another bomb disposal vault. What an overkill! I know that we will have no more explosions from the bomb vaults.

This problem and scheme will be uncovered and resolved! The culprits will go to jail! Isaac had alerted the security and gave them the frequencies that would trigger the bombs. They were in the announcer's station. The announcer is immediately arrested but before he can say or do anything he was shot with the sedative and truth serum.

I tell Ashley, who is now terrified, to sit calmly and assure the others that all was well. She looks at me and says, "Why are evil people filled with so much hate?" I reply, "I do not know but they are all defeated in the end." The standby announcer takes over announcing so smoothly that nobody is really aware of a problem.

Isaac interrogates the announcer as only Isaac can. He also offers a deal that the announcer cannot refuse. The announcer tells us about the plot. We make the appropriate instant arrests, the same way we arrested the announcer.

Who of my Seven is a Serpentine? I think that I know. Nebo knows for sure. I know that we have another suicide attempt that cannot be solved by frequencies. The solution comes into my mind! A cave attack! Of course!

I tell Isaac to get the water cannon lift craft ready and dispatch them, under heavy secrecy, to the mouth of each cave.

The arrested announcer told Isaac the plot. Isaac and I realize that he is telling us the truth because the truth serum seldom fails and the plot is a perfect way to kill Orion, sabotage the entire race and throw panic into the crowd.

The plot is to destroy the end of a cave just after all or most of the craft have entered it. Which cave? The announcer does not know. I suspect the first one. It has a thin exit mouth! A disaster here will kill the most pilots. The race course will be ruined and the race will be a fiasco. The Race Committee will be blamed! Odysseus will be called a traitor and Nebo can rise up and call himself the Emperor of the Union of the Nations.

I get up to leave. The chairman's eyes meet mine in a steady gaze for a moment. I could see surprise. I indicate that I must go to the restroom.

Isaac and I leave and go toward the Race Committee's restroom. Nebo seems to believe me and smiles. He is relieved because he knows that the destruction of the cave will happen while I am answering a call of nature. As Isaac and I approach the restroom, Isaac asks, "Can we really thwart the suicide?" I say, "Are the water cannons in place?" He nods. I say, "They will solve this problem! These things have become very handy. It just happens that two of them sit outside cave number one where we used it to clean up the rock structures."

I call the Captain in charge of the cannon and tell him that many lives depend on his actions. He immediately stations the cannon at the cave exit. We go out the back door of the restroom where Mercury is waiting.

The two water cannons that were on-site are placed inside the cave near the end where the observation stations are located.

The cannons will not interfere with the race cars. We know that the saboteur will have to get himself in first place to accomplish his mission. I am more convinced than ever that the strike will be at Cave One. The saboteur will use all of his fuel for a spectacular burst of speed right after coming out of orbit. This will assure him of the first position. The observers will wonder about the strategy. However, there will be nothing illegal about the maneuver.

The water cannons are ready. The one shot of water from each cannon must be simultaneous and be perfectly timed so that only one racing craft will be affected. Security realizes the stakes. Nobody but security, Isaac and I know what is happening.

Isaac has his finest and trusted operators on the machines. I look at Isaac and say, "This cockamamie plan better work!" He answers, "Pray, Achilles, because we are in the hands of the Force. There is no other power that will make it work." I do pray. The palms of my hands are sopping wet.

Isaac and I are in the observation station and are relieved to see the saboteur make his move. He is roaring ahead of the pack and overtakes Orion who was first. One of Orion's best friends is in the second craft. They were just ahead of a solid pack. The lead craft must be comfortably ahead of Orion if he is going to destroy him. The race is already extremely close and exciting.

I can hear, over my private circuit, the cannon leader's voice as he says, "Steady, steady craft #18 is the target (The sum of 666). He is your target. He is accelerating well. Oops, he shifted, steady, steady." My heart is pounding against my chest. I feel like I will have a heart attack!

The Captain of the water cannons continues, "Number 18 is in the critical spot, steady, steady, fire!" All is silent for a split second and then there is a tremendous explosion. I stood frozen. The Water Gun Captain continues, "Congratulations, gentlemen. What an explosion! It could have destroyed the cave mouth, most racing craft in the pack, and the race itself. You saved the day and the Union!"

I tell the Water Cannon Captain that I will see that he receives the medals and honors that he deserves! He says, "Commander, it was my pleasure to serve our country, you, and save many lives!"

Suddenly, the race announcer says, "A quick rerun of the incident at the caves shows clearly that another suicide attempt to sabotage the race, kill all lead pilots and destroy the end of Cave One has been made. The timing mechanism was probably adjusted to speed so that the explosion would occur when the craft was several yards inside the cave exit. The suicide pilot was in a perfect position to completely destroy the second craft, piloted by Orion.

"For some reason the suicide craft suddenly shot ahead and veered off course enough before exploding so that the explosion had little effect on the cave end and no serious effect on any other racecar. We are trying to locate newly appointed Admiral Achilles to get his reaction." I thank God and I award the Water Gun Captain on the spot.

As we return to the stadium I say, "Isaac, what the hell is the announcer talking about? I am not an Admiral! I hold a Minister's position in both Magogania and Gogania with all of the privileges and pay and also am the Commanding Officer of the Space Command. I am the senior Captain of all Armed Forces. Everybody calls me Commander!" Isaac says nothing and that surprises me.

"What if Orion and I are killed? Odysseus is discredited and Zadoc, Admiral of the Armed Forces, is forced to retire. Nebo takes control as Emperor, the Space Command is disbanded and Eric fills the job as Admiral of the Armed Forces." Isaac is smiling.

I say, "Now, Isaac, would you like an analysis of what would happen should we have failed?" He looks at me and asks, "What else could happen?"

I tell him, "Nebo would have sumptuous parties and celebrations and feel all powerful. Arkite would be his advisor. Arkite would suggest that Nebo and Eric go on a good will mission to calm the people." Isaac just looks at me.

I relate, "Of course, Nebo would agree. Arkite would assure Nebo that he and Eric would be well guarded at all times! Fighters would surround Nebo's aircraft! However, suddenly Nebo's ship explodes and is totally shattered. Arkite takes over the Emperorship. Nobody can trust a turncoat and most people despise traitors. This is the end of the story." Isaac says, "Touché!"

We return to the stadium the way we left it. Ashley and Alcestis are furious! Ashley says, "What were you doing in the restroom at a time like this? That was an unnecessary move. Your timing was awful! There was a critical situation at the caves and Orion could have been killed! That is our son in that god-awful race! Don't you understand?"

I reply, "I have not been in the restroom." Suddenly her countenance changes as she says, "You were at the cave!"

I nod. Ashley gives Alcestis' hand a squeeze. They have communicated.

While Isaac and I were returning to the stadium, Orion and the other leaders had their problems. The explosion required Orion to run a computer program fault check and I am sure that some adjustments had to be made. It cost Orion time. There were two other caves to be negotiated. One of them, the dark one, requires total dependence on the computer and the external sensors. I am sure that it took all of Orion's courage to let the computer guide him through. He is only seconds ahead of the second and third craft. It is a stomach tightening and highly emotional race!

As the announcer is making his observations I look directly at Nebo. His face is transparent to me. I can tell by his jaw muscles and inflections that he is extremely upset. He turns to one of his aides and issues a command of some kind.

I tell Isaac to have that man tailed. The intensity of the effort to kill Orion is unsettling. I feel the circle of pressure around me.

Something else has been planned. I must find out where and when. That bastard Lucifer is a clever manipulator of people who worship self and power. The Chairman becomes aware that I am looking at him. His face changes abruptly. He smiles and gives me the Space Command salute. I return it. I know that means there is trouble ahead.

My palms become sopping wet as the race proceeds. Ashley kisses me, squeezes my hand and whispers. "Achilles, the race will be won by our son." I know that there is more to come. How is the Force going to help us?

Zadoc comes over to us, kisses Ashley and sits down beside me. He says in a very low voice, "Achilles, in your locker in the Chairman's rest area there is a new titanium ceramic vest that will blunt a direct discharge from a CLIP. The vest is top secret and it is vital that you wear it."

"The first place car will run low on fuel because he will take the middle route through the forest. Orion will use the short route. This will place Orion ahead. The former first car will gamble that he did not overuse his fuel to take first place. This will be a fatal error. I believe that the key tree on the short route will have been shifted but I know that you and Isaac have covered this possibility in the computer programming. Orion will win the race."

He continues, "Be at the finish line and go straightway to his craft upon landing because there is a plot to assassinate Orion. Nebo is behind it. Achilles, you must not fail! We are all doomed if you do!"

Ashley looks at me and squeezes my sweaty hand. Zadoc continues, "If you fail this mission we will lose to the Serpentines. You are the only hope left to avoid disaster." He looks at Vera and there is an instant communication. He leaves. Now I understand why Nebo gave me the Space Command salute! I am not surprised.

The announcer states that Orion will probably take the dangerous leg through the forest because he is in second place and this is a chance to pull ahead.

The announcer adds that the short path through the forest is extremely difficult because it is almost impossible for a pilot to stay within the course boundary. The view screen shifts to Orion's craft. I am a totally helpless parent watching his youngster travail.

Orion is too close to the edge! Is he overriding the computer? The announcer states that the key cross tree was shifted slightly for some reason from its pre-race location. Who authorized that? I am a wreck! Orion is through but did he violate the border? There is an explosion. The pilot behind Orion did not make it through the tree obstacle.

The replay shows Orion is legally through the forest and ahead by several car lengths. I know that he has fuel enough to complete the course. The car that was in first place guns his thrusters and overtakes Orion. He will run short of fuel just as Zadoc has predicted.

I must move quickly without drawing attention. I will have to use the same old restroom trick. Nebo is riveted to the screen and does not notice that I have left my seat. I watch the monitors as I go to the locker room.

I can see the air cars approaching the final run. It will take true discipline and faith for Orion to use the computer program to complete the course. Every movement of the air car will have an effect. The lead car will force Orion's mind to think override. He must not do that. I can see that Orion is holding to the program. Good! I am checking the screens as I rush to the finish line area. Security smiles and lets me through as I shout, "I want to be at the finish line when my son crosses it!"

Orion is second as he approaches the high barrier with its streamers hanging down. Swoosh! Both first and second craft are climbing. Just as they approach the top the first craft sputters. This is the sign of low fuel. Orion zooms past him as do the third and fourth craft. Orion is first! Orion roars past the stands; completes his turns; enters the finish line tube. He crosses the finish line first but runs out of fuel as he approaches the landing area. He glides to a stop. I am running at full speed! I wipe my brow with Ashley's handkerchief. Where did that come from? I can smell the sweet perfume of Victory. It is sweet!

An official announcement is made that my track record still stands. It had not been broken. I am surprised. Orion is emerging from the cockpit. Out of the corner of my eye I see a beaming security guard drawing his CLIP (short for Coordinated Light and Power Pistol)! He is not a guard because guards do not carry CLIPs. He is going to fire it at Orion! Without thinking I leap in front of Orion. The full power beam hits my vest. I feel searing pain as I fire my CLIP at the security guard's head because if he has a CLIP he also has a Vulcan's vest. I note at the last minute that the guard is Judas! My suspicions are confirmed! His head disappears. My head bashes into Orion's racing craft. I can hear him shouting.

I can feel Orion trying to give me CPR. I sink into semi-consciousness.

I instinctually know that I am not dead but I have a sur-real feeling. I am in the next world. I am surrounded by light and comfort. I think, "This is not so bad. What comes next?"

Suddenly, I stand in a city so beautiful that I can't de-scribe it. It is a city made out of solidified energy. Each building glows with a vivid soft light that seems natural, peaceful and beautiful. It is the City of the Light of the Shepherd! I suspect that each sector of infinite creation has one! It boggles my mind.

Our Shepherd says, "You are part of my flock. My Father, the Alpha and Omega of all creation, desires that I shep-herd this sector. Come!"

The City shows the Glory of God. Its brilliance is like that of a most precious jewel, somewhat like a yellow jasper but it is perfect and pure. There are twelve gates guarded by twelve angels. He leads me to the Great Hall. In it there is a judgment area with twenty-four seats. I see a seat for Avatar and Ashley Anne. All seats are empty at this time. Behind these seats is the Throne of Judgment.

The Shepherd continues, "Each person entering the City will be judged by what he has done. If a soul has rejected God's energy and the laws of Nature it does not drink from the pool of the waters of life and its name will not be found in the Book of Life. If love for others is not in this soul its name will not be found in the Book of Life."

He continues, "The soul that is self-separated from God by its own choice will use its energy trying to steal en-ergy from others; it will suffer greatly. It will enter the bot-tomless pit and self-destruct. This is its second and final death. That soul no longer exists."

He catechizes, "Achilles, in simple terms, a soul must not follow the dark path. The Beasts of the Earth follow Satan and will try to destroy believers one way or another. Keep the faith and they will not be able to do so!"

He further explains, "Arkite's light will fade away and he will suffer the second death."

I feel a great peace being with The Shepherd. He knows all about me and accepts me for what I am. He wants to help me grow. He loves me and he loves us all. He speaks with the authority of the Universal Source. I know that I am not yet part of the Holy City and this makes me sad. Nonetheless, the fact that I am visiting and accepted by the Shepherd means that I am trying.

He continues, "Achilles, please try not to stray! You are not making my job very easy!"

He then instructs, "Your job on Earth is to lead and instruct because Earthlings must be shown the way. This has been a most difficult planet to educate. Your job is to save and abide by the scripture lessons. You can do it. Deliver those Holy Scriptures that Vera has hidden in a protected spot to the Himalayan Mountains before the flood. The scriptures are vital and will serve those who will believe, follow and obey the Holy Ordinances contained inside. Those who do will live in the Holy City." The city fades away.

I am awake, in pain but breathing.

The paramedics push Orion inside the rescue craft and slap a mask onto my face. The mask is a vacuum pump and is taking air away from me! They throw me into the rescue craft. Fortunately, in their haste, a solid mask fit is not achieved. I stab the attendant in his esophagus and penetrate the spinal cord in his neck with my trusty acupuncture needle. Instantly, he is paralyzed. It works every time!

While I am ripping off my mask and attacking the second attendant Orion is battling the other attendant and the pilot who had put the craft into automatic.

I grab my remaining attendant's testicles. He screams and his grip on his star knife loosened enough for me to take it away. It cut deeply into my right hand but I plunge it into his throat. His CLIP is still in his holster and I grab it. Both pilot and last attendant are dead within seconds. I look at Orion and smile. He smiles back.

I say, "How complicated can an emergency rescue craft be? Most of the stuff here is for treating people in deep trouble. Do you know how to operate this thing?" Orion says, "No, Dad, but let us figure this thing out together." We both look at the array of displays. Orion says, "Dad, I think I have it. This row of switches appears to be the flight control group."

I agree. We disconnect the automatic pilot. There is something very interesting about the settings. They are not directing the craft toward the hospital. We are on a great circle headed for the South Pole. After a few jerky movements we get the craft under control. I act as co-pilot and engineer. We make a wide turn and head back to the finish line area.

I am using the bandages and equipment in the craft to control the bleeding of my right hand. I say, "Orion, I have the bleeding under control but after the ceremonies I will need the good doctor to properly treat my hand." He looks at me and says, "I am sorry, Dad." I smile at him, ruffle his hair with my left hand and say, "We probably ought to see if we can operate the communicator, Champion."

I say, "Tell the Race Chairman that all is well and that we will be landing on the finish line tarmac." He does and lands the craft right in front of his racing car. The whole place is silent. Isaac has so many security guards around that it looks like a convention.

It has not occurred to us that nobody knows what has happened in the medical vehicle. We step out of the craft and wave. The crowd gives us a thunderous applause.

I look at myself and see that I am a bloody mess. Alcestis runs over, sees that we both are okay and throws her arms around Orion. After a kiss they move to their places for the award ceremony. She is a very, very shaken woman and I cannot blame her.

Meanwhile, Ashley hugs and kisses me and has blood on her dress as a result. She is shaking and buries her head in my shoulder. I hold her tightly. I can feel the energy flowing between us. She says, "We have battled so hard against evil. Will this incessant pressure ever end?" I reply,

"Paradise cannot be achieved without struggle. Achievement requires that we use the strength that has been given to us by our Creator to accomplish our goals. The freedom given to us requires good choices."

I instruct, "People may serve God and others or they can turn toward serving themselves. Souls who served themselves are miserable and jealous. Being able to trust one another is the first step toward Paradise."

She just looks at me and says, "Honey, your tutorial may be correct but have you ever thought about our need for some peace and quiet! I am dying of anxiety and all I get from you is a damn lecture. Give me a break!" She then says, "Even so, I still love you!"

Vera comes over and says, "Achilles, I still say that Ashley was a rational and level-headed girl before she met you. Now all she does is worry about you. Damn, can't you ever stay out of trouble? Both of you look like a mess! Come over to our house. Dr. Abaris is there and he can work on your hand! You sure did make a mess of it!"

I am about to ask why Abaris is at her house but this thought is interrupted as she says, "You have damn little time to clean up and be ready for the awards and parade. Tonight will truly be a gala affair!"

I say, "I am not feeling so well." She says, "So what is new? If you could learn how to stay out of trouble you could save us all from dying from heart attacks! Feeling bad is no excuse for missing these coming events!"

I look at her and say, "Thanks for the sympathy! This is the third time in the past passage of events that I have been given this great advice!" She says, "Then you should get the idea! You are entirely welcome!"

She continues, "Abaris will fix your hand and ease your pain. That is better than sympathy!"

Abaris gives me some painkiller and says, "Achilles, not again!" I immediately think, "I hope that this is not another damn lecture." He finishes by saying, "I can see that you are extremely distressed and I can understand why. Join me in drinking a smooth and exhilarating jigger of cour-voisier!" We had two! I feel much, much better!

We barely make it to the Chairman's box for the viewing of the ceremonies. We sit next to Zadoc. We are the typical proud parents. Isaac comes over and whispers to Zadoc and me saying that a full report concerning the breech in security, the identification of all false medical attendants and the depth of the Serpentine penetration would be on our desks within a week.

I whisper to Zadoc, "What is all this crap about retire-ment! No way! I am NOT going to take over an administra-tion riddled with intrigue and deception without you at the helm. This whole thing can and will explode in our face anytime. You can't walk out of this challenge! Accept it! You are vital!"

I continue, "Who is going to train Orion to take control? You are the diplomat! I am a warrior and a damn good one but there is more to leadership than fighting. Orion needs training in both skills." Zadoc looks me in the eye and says, "Achilles, you are growing up late but fast!"

He continues, "I will be your mentor as well as Orion's." I smile at him. I feel better and I can tell that my faith in his judgment has given him strength. The visit with the Shepherd has had a profound effect on me. I now have a mission and it has nothing to do with power.

The Shepherd did not command me. He simply asked me to help Him. I think about what has happened to me and wonder why it took Vera, Avatar, and the Shepherd to make me see what my mission is really all about.

The Race Committee announces that all machines that competed in the race were checked for violation of the rules. All were clean. Eight excellent young men survived the race and all will receive recognition. I start to reflect, "Only eight out of forty-eight finished the race! This is unacceptable!"

I still believe that this Olympic race is barbaric for sup-posedly advanced people. When will we ever learn? Are we supposed to be civilized! Yet, despite all this thinking, I have to admit to myself that the race was damn exciting! These young pilots are unbelievably good!

Suddenly, I am aware that Nebo is in a deep discussion with Ashley who is charming and smiling as usual. She listens intently and comments very appropriately. She makes each person feel that they are part of her world and that they are very special.

I look into his eyes and I see lust. I shiver because I feel evil. I also have the chilling feeling that Eric is in the crowd. Of course!

If the assassination had been successful Nebo would be blaming Odysseus and would have assigned temporary positions of power to replace Orion, Zadoc and me.

He would have awarded the assassinators, dismantled the Space Command and melded us into a Union. It would not have taken Arkite long to have assumed the position of Emperor. The coup de grace of democracy as shaky and eroded as it is would have been completed before anybody could stop it.

Nebo looks over at me and asks, "Why do you seem to be so intent and lost in thought?" I say, "I was thinking about the things that the medical personnel can do. After landing I watched Abaris while he put my right hand together again. I can already move all of my fingers. It still hurts a little but it is amazing what a pain block and painkillers can do! I can open and close my hand."

Nebo laughs and says, "Nice answer, Achilles. I notice that Orion is helping an unknown religious fanatic build a boat on dry land without a clue about how and where this thing will be launched."

I must not let Nebo know that I do not want him near Noah! He is an important part of our future and needs to survive the flood! If Nebo gets an inkling of how Noah fits into the overall picture he will have him killed! I smile and answer, "This project was part of Orion's dissertation. It is intriguing to follow the genealogical path that leads to this fanatic. You should read it." His reply is, "Achilles, I have enough to do without filling my head with unrelated stuff about a nut cake."

I say, "Mr. Chairman, I know that your mind is filled with thoughts about the Union and so is mine. I am reminded that we leaders must be held accountable for our actions."

I admonish, "Throughout history it has been shown that when power becomes concentrated, accountability for actions are no longer required. The dehumanization of human beings starts as belief in God is squelched, the state laws replace Nature's Laws and therefore advancement is stopped. We must be sure to prevent this from happening.

"Our Union must work and accountability for government actions must stay in place! I know that you agree." I know that he does not agree but undistorted history proves this to be so.

I suggest, "We should go to the VIP viewing stand before the formal announcement of the race results and the award ceremony." He smiles. It is not a pleasant smile.

Odysseus, who joined our conversation, says, "Nebo, since nothing can happen until we arrive we had better do as Achilles suggests."

I say, "Chairman Odysseus, if you will escort my family I will do as the medics ask and make a quick check in at the Medical Center. I will meet you in the stands."

Nebo says, "I also have one quick errand that I must accomplish before going to the stands."

I say to Orion, "Son, you know that Noah is real. I think that we will have a flood but the question is how? I know that only an asteroid or comet could cause such a horrendous flood. Maybe it would take two asteroids with one hitting the Pacific and one hitting the Atlantic." Orion says, "Dad, we have already seen the comet that could cause that type of damage." I reply, "How long do we have?" He replies, "We have enough time to prepare the ark."

I continue, "When the flood does happen we must be prepared. I want you to help me be the guardian of the scriptures. They present the prescription for living a life that the Creator wants us to live. They will become the source of much earthly philosophy concerning life and our relationship with one another."

Orion says simply, "Okay, Dad, we will talk more about this later. There are more pressing matters for us to take care of at this moment." I know it. I know what Orion is thinking. He had spent a tremendous amount of time in his dissertation about Noah and the Mediterranean people for his post-doctorate work. He knows that Noah is real. Give him a break!

On the way back from the Medical Center I take a short cut through the secret hallways that only the top executives know about. Isaac had discovered this route long ago while doing his job of surveillance. He told me about it and we have kept it to ourselves. I am about to make a right angle turn in the tunnel when I become aware of talking ahead of me. I stop short of making the turn and listen.

Nebo is talking with several of his top aides and his top lieutenant. He says, "I would give up my Chairmanship for just one night with that bitch, Ashley Anne. She is the sexiest and most beautiful woman I have ever seen. I know deep inside that she loves me because when we talk she looks me in the eyes and I know she is looking into my soul."

He continues, "Her dancing excites me to the point of thinking rape. I will give anything to make love to her. I will make her queen of the Union." His lieutenant says, "Not so if we do not kill Achilles! He will be in charge if we cannot succeed in killing him!" All agree.

All make similar remarks about Ashley's sexy beauty and grace. The Chairman continues, "Just think, that bastard, Achilles, gets to sleep with her every night! That son-of-a-bitch renegade is going to replace Zadoc. He seems to have limitless lives.

"Maybe we had better keep Zadoc in office. Do not assassinate him yet. Speaking of assassinations, all of your assassination attempts to eliminate Achilles have failed. You cocky bastards told me that killing Achilles was a piece of cake. He has outwitted and outfought the whole bunch of you. You better be successful the next time or you will not be around long. Do you understand?"

He continues, "Maybe our champion Eric can reverse Achilles' apparent good luck. Tell Eric that I want to see him right after the ceremonies. One more thing, gentlemen, you will see to it that I sit next to Ashley Anne. Sitting at dinner with her will drive me crazy and I will savor every moment." Their reply is simple, "Yes, Sir!"

They continue to walk down the corridor. I wait until they go through the exit and then move quickly. My heart is heavy. My country is riddled with Serpentines. Suddenly, I feel an evil fog envelop me. I hear a cold and icy laugh that I have heard before. It is Lucifer! There is no mirth in his sound, only hate. I turn around and see his evil ephemeral face!

He revolted and now he is the Lord of Death and he will die the second death eventually. Fine, but right now how do I fight this dark power?

I return to the VP viewing box. Family and friends surround me and it is good to be among friends. My fears subside and I enjoy a brief cocktail before the Olympic Parade and Presentations.

Each major merchant has a highly decorated float that moves gracefully along a predetermined parade path and each one is decorated with flowers, shrubs and icons. Each has a queen representing each one of the racing participants whether they completed the race or not.

Power is never a problem for our nations because fuel cells, mini-nuclear generators (spent core disposal problem is solved by reverse manufacturing into non-radiating atoms or simply by sending radiation-laden debris to the sun). Some super fuel (such as constituted Sunflower Oil), and superconductors are used. Racing fuel (constituted fossil fuel) tanks are used because the dangers of explosion are minimal and the fuel requirement may be measured easily.

All racing Olympians who completed the race are in the leading float. The Space Command flag is in front of the float and it is flanked by the Magogania and Gogania flags. The host nation flag is at the right side and the other nation's flag is at the left side of the float.

For the moment, all of the people in attendance are focusing on them. The crowd cheers wildly and the Olympian float passes by the stands. The official band plays stirring music until the last float passes by. The Olympians fly from their float to their places on the winner's platform by using the escape packets attached to their backs. The speeches are brief but effective.

I cannot help but reflect back to when I stood in the same spot as Orion. The Chairman of the host nation gives out the medals. Orion receives a hug from Odysseus after he gave him the winner's medal and sportsman medal. This is only done if the winner had absolutely no sportsman infractions assigned during the race. Ashley and I are sitting on the left side of the Chairman as proud parents of Orion and Alcestis on his right. Orion had earned his additional award. There are no incidents to mar this occasion.

All of the people in attendance are focusing on the winning Olympians. They cheer and throw confetti. The official band plays stirring March music. The speeches are brief and effective.

All eight who finished the race are beautiful people. I had managed to make the course much harder but not safer than it was before. I never really realized it or subconsciously had I really ignored it? This bothers me.

I am not ignoring the fact that there were too many things that happened such as movement of trees at the last minute and other things that caused severe harm to the participants. A post-race inspection of the course will prove very little.

The sabotage people will have obliterated the evidence. Perhaps our skill in computer programming saved the day. I know that Orion had shared our technical knowledge with each of the eight who completed the race. This is more than a coincidence.

Nebo had requested that Ashley and Alcestis join him on the winner's platform as Orion received his medal. Nebo, the son-of-a-bitch, is making his first move toward seduction. It won't work. Ashley is no fool. However, I must admit that it was a tearful and poignant moment when the two most important women in Orion's life were sharing his glory. It was also crowd-pleasing! There were no incidents to mar the occasion because Nebo did not want any.

After the ceremonies we all leave to prepare for the evening events. My families go to Roland's house where our clothing is ready for us. I have a little difficulty in the shower because I have to cover my hand with a plastic glove to keep water away from the wound. It felt good to be in clean clothing and well shaven. I am glad that I do not have to drive. Faithful Mercury is waiting with a limousine that will fit the whole group.

While all of this is happening Isaac is unraveling the mystery of the fake paramedics. As we suspected they were all Serpentines. The hospital people all denied any knowledge of the group. The emergency vehicle did not belong to the hospital.

Somebody knew and arranged to have that ambulance craft on scene just as the assassin struck. The perfect timing of the attack reeked of Eric. He had obviously planned the whole thing.

I say to Isaac, after I tell him about the encounter in the secret tunnel, "I am going to trust Ashley's life to you. We are up against a time limit for soon the charade of a peaceful coexistence will disappear. Nebo will make his move to take over the Union." Isaac replies, "I am honored that you entrust Ashley's life to me. I will be dead before anything untoward happens to her or to your family." No wonder I love this guy.

We arrive at the Great Hall and are ushered into the special pre-event reception room. I am beginning to relax but so is the painkiller. My hand throbs so I have a stiff drink. This is not wise. However, the reception conversation is lively. Nebo is gushing all over Ashley.

While getting ready for the ceremonies I had told Ashley all that I had heard. She turns ashen and makes me hold her tight for a long time. She says, "Apathy and greed for power will undo us."

I say, "Darling, all we can do is try to preserve freedom and peace." She cries. I finally console her by saying, "Nebo is a braggart and a big mouth. He said these things to impress his henchmen. Considering all things you are handling Nebo very well."

Soon it is time to go to the main dining room. All VIP guests line up in the foyer and prepare to walk into the dining room as their name is announced.

After we are seated, the Master of Ceremonies pounds his staff on the floor. The staff is called the kerykeion (Caduceus). It is the instrument signifying power and authority. This tradition comes to us from our ancestors. The staff with a hook on top represents the power of the shepherds as they tend and protect the flocks.

My beautiful Ashley is seated next to Nebo with a copy of Orion's medal attached to a solid gold chain around her neck. Alcestis has an identical medal.

The M.C. starts the ceremony by introducing Orion and Alcestis. Orion gives a short but meaningful speech about cooperation, loyalty and family values.

After the applause that lasted for some time, the M.C. says, "Admiral, I always thought you were a stickler for proper military uniforms." I wonder why he used the term Admiral. He seems to be looking at me.

He continues, "Apparently you have not properly trained your young son." I smile, but Alcestis seems puzzled. The M.C. continues, "Maybe we can resolve this problem but we will need your assistance, Alcestis."

She beams, and proceeds to the podium. The M.C. and Alcestis have a conversation with the transmitter turned off. The room is silent. The M.C. motions to Odysseus who comes over to the podium. There is more conversation. We are all looking at one another.

I look at Orion and shrug my shoulders. Ashley is smiling. She knows! Finally, the M.C. turns on the transmitter. "We have a protocol problem," he says, "but Chairman Odysseus has come up with a solution." He continues, "Alcestis will pin on Orion's rank as Commander First Class. He has been accepted in the Space Command. Ashley Anne will hand him the signed acceptance papers. This promotion and the acceptance papers were approved by Chairman Nebo and Chairman Odysseus as recommended by Admiral of the Fleet Zadoc moments ago."

The crowd gives him a thunderous applause. He is a popular hero and well-liked by his peers. He has a solid faith in God, a great feeling of empathy for others and is a very wise and intelligent person. People follow him because they believe in him and want to follow him. I lead because people have faith that I know what I am doing, appear confident, exude courage, seem calm and seem to have some kind of connection with the Great Force. This difference is significant.

The M.C. continues, "Space Commander Orion, each Chairman will bestow upon you a cluster, the first time ever, added to your medal as winner of the Olympic air car race."

He explains, "You will have two clusters. As you know each pilot is allowed three semi-serious infractions and five minor infractions. Never in the history of the race has anyone finished first without any infractions, whatsoever, not even your father."

He continues, "This is phenomenal and must be recognized. Further, never in the history of the race has any pilot been so free with advice, counsel and helpfulness to his competitors. Seven pilots listened to you, changed their program and changed the design of their craft. They finished the race. There isn't one pilot who does not admire and respect you. This must be publicly recognized."

Each Chairman steps forward and attaches a cluster to the medal. The M.C. reads the award, "In recognition of Orion's steadfast dedication to his fellow pilots and to the advancement of the Olympics. . . ." I didn't hear the rest.

The crowd is wildly cheering and applauding. Orion kisses Ashley on the cheek. He comes over to me. We hug and I pat his back. Orion returns to his seat next to Alcestis, but the crowd wouldn't let him sit down. He waves again and looks down. I think he was praying a prayer of thanks to the Creator. He looks up and waves again. Finally, the applause subsides as the M.C. sounds the staff.

All is silent. The M.C. looks at me and says, "Achilles, you should be a very proud man this evening. You and your family are serving the new Union forged by the Space Command well." I smile.

He continues, "Why, Achilles, is it that you are so temperamental when Ashley Anne, the artist, is so even tempered?" I smile and shrug my shoulders. There isn't much else I can do. He continues, "You are also a stickler for detail but this evening you, sir, are out of uniform." I look at Ashley. She demurely smiles at me. She knows what is going to happen.

The M.C. continues, "Ashley Anne, will you and the Chairmen come to the podium." They do. The communicator is shut again. There was another conversation. Ashley and the Chairmen are talking and smiling at one another. They agree on the procedure.

"Achilles," the M.C. finally said, "will you have your beautiful daughter remove your rank of Senior Commander of the Space Command insignia." Athena smiles at me, kisses me on the cheek and removes the insignia.

I notice that Zadoc goes to the podium and motions for me to approach. I am puzzled. I approach the podium. The M.C. says, "This evening seems to be the appropriate time to make a special announcement. Admiral Zadoc, will you do the honors?" Zadoc says, "Achilles, because of your un-ceasing urgings I have agreed to remain as Admiral of the Fleet and continue to get ulcers every time you come out with some new cockamamie plan."

He continues, "Fortunately, we have a new Operations Officer in the Space Command, Orion, who is a bit more rational than you are. This will give me some peace of mind although I have a new problem because I will be report-ing to an unpredictable new boss, the Admiral serving the Union of the Nations. It seems that the Chairmen have come to the agreement that the Space Command is now its own entity as a unit of the Union of the Nations and its Headquarters will be here."

He admonishes, "You have been selected as their first Admiral. It will take all of the skill that we have to keep you in check. Admiral, step forward please." The room explodes with applause and I am speechless. Ashley Anne pins on the insignia, Odysseus places the sash over my shoulder and Nebo buckles on my sword. It is done. The crowd again erupts with applause.

Why am I having reservations? All of a sudden the wis-dom of Isaac's remarks that I had barely heard invaded my mind. He had said, after our chat about my thoughts, "Achilles, be wary of Nebo. He has ostensibly supported your promotion to achieve his ends."

The plan becomes apparent. If Orion and I are assassi-nated then Zadoc will be forced to retire. Nebo will arrange a peace agreement with the Serpentines that will include Eric as Admiral of the Fleet and Arkite the number two man in the world under Nebo as the Chairman of the new Union! I continue to stare into space. Ashley kisses me and gently reminds me that the M.C. with many raps of the staff has achieved silence. One could hear a pin drop on the floor. All eyes are upon me.

I have not the slightest idea what to say. I sweep the crowd with my eyes making many eye-to-eye contacts. I think, *Wonderful, Achilles! Now say something!*

I start my talk by stating a cliché very slowly. "There will be peace in our time." I think, *This is a brilliant statement, Achilles! Absolutely brilliant! Now just what is it you will do to make it happen?*

I really do not know but I continue, "We will achieve this goal of peace not by appeasement and accommodation, as many have suggested, but by resolutely defeating the Serpentine scourge, their immorality, lack of family values and their worship of Baal."

I continue, "This defeat must be unconditional and complete. We will at the same time establish a civilized governing structure based upon the Laws of Nature that Nature's God, our Creator, has dictated."

I say, "I will talk about these in order. Without a moral code of living we are no better than the most savage beast ever conceived. Our civilization will die in the chaos of no trust and no cooperation. Greed, gluttony, pride, envy, anger, lust and sloth are the tools of the Beast. These temptations are dangerous and destructive when followed during our daily life activities."

I define, "Family values require a family! This family is started by marriage. Marriage is a commitment between a man and his woman. They are to be ever faithful to one another and their offspring. This is the glue of civilization and a basic law of life."

I instruct, "The Creator granted us inalienable rights such as life itself, freedom to cultivate our talents and pursue the pleasure and reward of sharing these talents with others."

I say, "We must worship only our Creator and talk with Him. He is always available!"

I verbalize, "Governments are instituted by the human race and they get their powers by the consent of the governed. When a government is destructive of their inalienable rights the people must abolish it no matter how big it is or how powerful it seems. God will help!"

I finish by saying, "The Union will prevail because we believe in our people!"

I continue, "I am a damn good soldier and I believe. I believe in Ashley and our beloved children and our Union. I will fight for their preservation and to bring to us the peace that passes human understanding because our Creator will be involved in our daily lives."

I again sweep the room with my eyes. There is a long silence. This has been a mercifully short address.

Suddenly everybody is standing and cheering. Ashley's eyes are flooded with tears. I wonder if all in the room agreed with my philosophy.

Dancing starts immediately. Nebo and Odysseus with their wives are first on the dance floor. Orion and Alcestis follow them. The dancing is now open.

Nebo is watching closely as I dance with Evelyn. She obviously likes me and I enjoy her company. After we dance for a short while she guides me to the balcony where we can talk without being interrupted or overheard. She says, "Achilles, I am not going to ask you about the space probe and the infinities of space." I smile and say, "Why not?"

She smiles and says, "You already explained the infinite system in which we live and you are uncomfortable talking with me because Elaine was my niece."

She continues, "You suspect that I blame you for her death. This is not true." I say, "Evelyn, I will always feel guilty. I should have helped her more. I was not a good husband. I never made her feel good about herself. Like so many men, and women for that matter, before our marriage I made her feel like a million dollars. I then wanted her to be something that she was not."

I continue, "She was a wonderful being herself, but I decided unconsciously to make her better. I was never satisfied with myself so I was not satisfied with her. She tried to please me and in the process she lost her essence. I did not let her use the talents that God gave to her and so she could not fulfill her karma. I did not accept her as the gift that she was. She gave until there was nothing else to give. I had devoured her soul."

I look at Evelyn and say, "Why? Was it because I listened to the great tempter? I took a vow that I would be the best Dad that I could be for Orion who was devastated by the loss of his mother. I know that I will never progress higher on the Spiral of Life until I right that wrong."

She is taken by surprise. She just looks at me and says nothing. Finally, she says, "Achilles, I do not condemn you. Your burden is with God and not with me. I forgive you. You should forgive yourself. What is done is done. God will tell you what penance you must do but this is not the time. You have a karma to fulfill! Do it!"

She continues, "Get on with your life!" I stare at her. I am surprised. She persists by saying, "You need to see Elaine in a different light, Achilles. Let me refresh your memory. She was an aspiring dancer just as Ashley Anne was and is. Elaine was several classes ahead of Ashley and was doing well. Abadon and Baalah, her mother and father did not want her to dance in front of all the people. It was not dignified in their eyes and, as you know, they were powerful and had very strong wills."

Evelyn continues, "Elaine changed her major to please her parents and majored in music instead. She began to sing and was superb. She had a leading part in an opera. She graduated with honors in Liberal Arts but Abadon and Baalah again interfered and would not let her continue her path. She was placed in a job working with Chairman Nebo. If, you recall, she was working for Nebo when you met her."

I am listening intently as she says, "She was sexy, wild and beautiful and she had her eyes on you because you were a dashing, handsome and scarred athlete with a rebellious spirit. She saw you as her tool to help her to accomplish her rebellious desires but you did not bend to her will. Avatar did not like her and Abadon despises you today for no reason, really. You did not cause her problems and if you had bent to her will you would have destroyed your own soul."

She continues, "Despite the red warning lights you two married and procreated Orion. He is a beautiful person.

Be proud of that fact. Avatar and I knew that you and Elaine were not for each other. You were never synergistic together. She did not want what you wanted. She was an apparent rebel without a cause except to rebel against Abadon."

Evelyn comments, "A rebel without goals and achievements is a human disaster. Your harnessed your drive and this brought you to the top of the Military Satellite System Command. This was the antithesis of her desire. She wanted to show people her antisocial stance and expected that they would accept her unusual actions."

She continues to explain, "She was so wrapped up in herself that she forgot about etiquette and cooperation. She did not love others and she did not like herself. She saw no alternative but to go to hallucinating and mind bending. She was never a Serpentine but Baal had a tremendous influence upon her. In her way, Achilles, she was trying to find herself by using strong potions. It killed her. You were not her bête noire."

She instructs, "Achilles, you may not realize it but your father and I were very close friends. We had many very intimate conversations together. If he had not met your mother, Venus, we would have married. Nebo knows this and knows that he was not my first love. I believe that he convinced Arkite to abduct Venus and sacrifice her on the Alter of Baal to punish Avatar and the Pyramid priesthood for not making Arkite the Chief Priest. This can never be proven."

I reply very slowly, "Thank you, Evelyn, for your counsel. You have greatly comforted me. Dad never talked about Mom. I thought that he didn't love her but now I can see that it hurt him too much to even remember the horror of her death."

Evelyn's eyes meet mine as she says, "It is a shame that we human beings cannot open our souls to one another because we feel that others will use this knowledge to hurt us rather than to help us. How sad this is. If we on Earth do not learn to worship God, trust one another and cooperate we will not climb upward in the Spiral of Life."

Evelyn gives me another warning by saying, "Achilles, there will be another attempt to assassinate you during your installation recognition parade as Admiral of the Union. We have very little time so listen carefully. This assassination will come from two sources. One of the aircraft in the fly over will have a loaded laser gun. He will not only shoot at you but he will also attempt to crash right into your viewing section. His job is to kill you and your family. If this should fail there will be a security guard with a modernized CLIP. He will shoot you first and if there is time he will shoot Orion."

I say, "How did you find out about this, Evelyn?" She says, "Vera and I were in the Great Pyramid last night. We did not tell anybody that we were meeting there. Being Priestesses we could do our devotionals and have a girl talk chat without being noticed. We often share with each other our feelings and discuss our problems."

She warns, "Nebo has changed and he is scaring me. I wanted to talk about it. I decided to tell Vera during our devotionals in the Inner Sanctum. Nebo, Eric and a few others came in. We hid. We heard them hatching this plot. You could not find Eric because Nebo had him in our house. He is gone now. Your security cannot enter our diplomatic property, as you well know. Nebo is a traitor to your cause."

Evelyn continues, "Vera and I have watched you develop with interest. You apparently are one of the few fallen ones who escaped the Dark City. Since you were part of Saint Michael's force before you rebelled you are still intrigued by combat. You must eventually develop other talents."

I reply, "Evelyn, you and Vera puzzle me. You both act as if I am a relic of the past." She laughs and replies, "You are, Achilles. It is intriguing for Vera and me to talk with an ancient soul and be part of your training, especially because you are such a stubborn one!"

Evelyn instructs, "You could advance much faster and much farther if you were not so stubborn. It is difficult for the Creator to help you because you are always veering away from the path of life! However, with all of our help it can keep you on track."

She further admonishes me, "Your job now from this day forward is to preserve the scriptures that will save good souls. Punishment and destruction of this civilization is not your job. You are no longer with Michael! If you try to meddle in this dismantling process you will have disobeyed the Creator's wishes. The consequences are grave. Listen!"

I ask, "How many souls are assigned to square me away?" She replies, "Too damn many!" We both laugh.

Suddenly, Evelyn looks up. Nebo is approaching quickly and says, "Achilles, you have taken too much of Evelyn's time. People wonder where you are and they miss you!"

He continues, "You should be out on the dance floor schmoozing! The Union Board will meet in the conference room at nine o'clock tomorrow, Admiral. We have a job for you to accomplish. The meeting will be over just prior to your inauguration."

Evelyn whispers, "I might not see you again, Achilles. You take care of yourself and family, do your karma and I will see you in the City of Light." Nebo takes her by the hand and they return to the dance floor. I follow.

The dance music is superb. I manage to dance with all of the dignitaries' wives. They are really all beautiful women.

Ashley is surrounded by a host of men as she discusses her last dancing performance. Athena sings a beautiful and rich aria and I am in awe. It is one of the most beautiful pieces that I have ever heard. I was not aware that she was going to sing. When she finishes the crowd explodes with applause.

Three encores later she leaves the stage. We would have kept her singing all night! Pete comes over and says, "Achilles, Nebo is getting very paranoid. He thinks that Noah is dangerous. He intends to kill him and destroy his ark."

I reply, "Pete, our plate is overflowing and now we must add Noah to the mix and save him also!"

He replies, "Yes! It is part of your karma!"

I tell him about Evelyn's conversation and my fear that her warning would result in her death. We set our evasive plan. Isaac is the centerpiece. What would we ever do without him?

Dancing resumes. The farewell anthem will be sung in exactly one hour. Ashley and I manage to get in a dance in edgewise. She says, "Sweetheart, something is the matter with Athena. I notice that she is in the garden alone. She is not happy. She needs you and she needs you now!"

I go into the garden and sit down beside Athena. I put my arm around her and we stare out to the sea without saying a word. Finally, I say, "Athena, you sang beautifully tonight. You sounded like an Angel from Heaven! Tell me what is going on within you. I recognize the symptom because I have internal battles all of the time. There is more to this episode than is apparent." She smiles and snuggles close to me.

We continue to sit on the wall looking out to sea. It was serene and beautiful. There isn't a cloud in the sky. The moon is full.

She asks, "Daddy, how far does space go?" I muse for a while before answering, "Honey, you know that a sphere has an infinite number of points." She nods. I continue, "I can pick up a ball and look at it because it has a finite radius. Take this ball and extend any one of its radiuses to infinity. Each point is extending forever. Visualize in your mind that while each point is expanding it will pass through stars, galaxies and universes forever. Your sphere now encompasses infinity. This is the size of space. This is the size of Creation."

She looks at me for a while and says, "If we are such a small piece of such a huge whole why would the Creator care about us?" I say, "Because this is the essence of our Creator. He is a God of love, wisdom, knowledge and power! He loves each one of us equally because He has infinite love."

I continue, "Heaven (Infinity) and Earth are filled with his Grace and Glory! The beauty of this is that He can love and talk to each of us separately at any time because He is infinite. He loves His creation and each one of us equally because He does, indeed, have infinite love."

I continue the catechism, "His being infinite allows Him to have a personal relationship with each one of us. He wants us to love him as much as He loves us. He is ubiquitous and He allows us to talk to Him anytime from anywhere. He is there waiting!"

She replies, "What if we don't love ourselves?" I reply, "Athena, God made you and He wants you to love yourself because He loves you. He has given you talents and has a job for you because you are very special in His eyes. We all are. When you think about this and understand it what follows is obvious. God will love you forever and He wants you to love Him and His creation."

Athena is crying. She says, "Daddy, Please don't get killed. We love you so very much." I kiss her on the forehead and hug her. I say, "I will be around for a while longer. I have a job to do and taking care of my family is part of my job." She smiles.

I say, "Now tell me what is bothering you." She says, "At the University the crowd is always fawning all over Chairman Nebo's daughter, Medea, and giving me a rough time. She and the others in her crowd tell me that they don't have to perform in front of others. They are the children of the real leaders of the Union. Only I, who am not sure of myself, need to make a public spectacle of myself."

She is crying as she says, "They tell me that my voice is awful. They say that the only reason I am allowed to sing is because I am the daughter of a braggart and a pretender who will not be around very long. Daddy, maybe my voice is not good. Maybe I can't sing."

She continues, "I refused to sing in the University Opera. It is Othniel and I love it so very much! I am hiding behind you and telling people that you will not let me sing." She burst into tears. I hold her very closely. I rock her gently.

I finally say, "You sang beautifully tonight." She says, "Daddy, I did it for you. I can't sing anymore. I am drained of energy."

I reply, "You must understand that the evil can only exist by stealing other people's energy because evil has rejected God's energy. You are learning about the brutality of the self-centered cynics. Remember that most people who criticize have not used their own talents. They are insecure and want desperately to infect you with the same poison."

I say, "You must counteract this with a strong belief in yourself. Your talents came from the Creator. He expects you to use them. He will refresh you if you ask Him. Tell Him that you want to use your talent to make others feel good by enjoying music from Heaven. You will feel warmth inside after you tell him. Try it! Now!"

She looks at me as I continue, "The Destructor will use anything and any trick to take your talents away from you. Honey, look inside of yourself. Pray for strength and then strike out and go for it. You and you alone are responsible for what you do. You will always have the deep love and support of God, your mother and me. You also have the support of your brothers! You sing like the birds of Heaven. If this were not true I would have told you."

I admonish, "You have fallen into a snare and a trap. Beware! You have let the dark side take your energy. Do not get bitter for it will smolder into chronic anger. This kind of thing leads to hate, envy and desire to harm others. It uses up all of your energy and accomplishes nothing. These are the elements of soul destruction."

I continue, "You are now destructing yourself. You think you can't sing. You can sing but you have let your mind be consumed with other things that are not good."

She replies, "Daddy, they are so cruel! I hate them!"

I say, "I am going to give you the key to success and fullness of life. It will be hard for you but you will be fulfilled if you try and believe in the power of God! Do not harbor hatred toward your adversaries."

I urge, "Defeat your enemies by being successful at what you do. Tell your adversaries that if all they can think about is to tear others down then you are sorry for them. Then I want you to kindle friendship with those that have pure hearts. Sometimes you will be betrayed. Be smart. Do not let them succeed in hurting you. Learn to live with failures on your road to success and overcome those who mock you because of these stumbles!"

I repeat, "Avoid their traps! Please! Ask God to renew your energy for your intentions are good and He will. Then use this energy to sing the closing anthem for me and then march over to the Dean of Music and tell him that you will sing Othniel and do it right now!"

I get a big hug and kiss on the cheek as she says, "I will, Dad, I will." She still has tears in her eyes.

I immediately communicate with the Music Director for this evening's official celebration and say, "Neal, Athena has agreed to sing the closing anthem as an encore." He says, "Achilles, tell her to run like the wind. She has two minutes!"

Athena stares at me. I say, "Go, girl, go!" She laughs and runs like the wind. I chase after her. I am panting. Damn this age stuff!

Ashley looks at me and says, "That must have been some talk! Why are you chasing after Athena? You are all out of breath!"

I reply, "Listen to your daughter! We had a great talk!" Ashley smiles and asks, "Sweetheart, why do I love you?" I answer, "Because I am me!"

Athena is singing, indeed, like an Angel form Heaven!

The crowd bursts into an ovation. Alcestis and Ashley kiss her. I leave her chatting with her friends. She didn't need me anymore. I feel good all over.

Ashley and I go outside for some fresh air. Neither one of us says anything. We walk along the seashore. It is beautiful. We hold hands and cuddle on the beach and continue to make love after we get home.

I have the feeling that, though impossible, Ashley might become pregnant. I do not know why. I also know that Athena will survive the flood and that she is destined to be a priestess in the temples of Egypt. The chants and songs that she will sing will be part of her gift to the future generations.

Will my efforts to save the Union fail? Maybe, but my people will be able to survive and they will have the freedom to choose their path without the oppression of a dictatorial government! I will make that fact be true!

The Union Board meeting is serious and brief. This quarter Odysseus is the Chairman of the Board and he brings the meeting to order. He says, "Gentlemen, Admiral Zadoc has the report and I want to welcome Achilles to the Union Board as our newest member."

There is enthusiastic applause. I say, "Thank you gentlemen for giving me this tremendous honor and privilege." Odysseus says, "As you probably realize, Achilles, we all have our assignments and duties. You first duty and trust will be to immediately depart on a very secret and important mission that will require you to use your secure detection equipment and your obvious ability to deal with the native denizens."

He continues, "We have reason to believe that the Serpentines have managed to infiltrate back into Africa. We don't know how many locations nor do we know the extent. We expect an in-depth report of the situation at our next meeting exactly one month from today."

I reply, "I thought that I might have arisen to the lofty position of issuing rather than receiving orders!" Odysseus nods and says, "At this moment in time we must have you in the field! Your ability to give orders will be tested and needed! Total success depends upon your success!" I smile.

Zadoc continues, "Our battle plan includes an attack of the Serpentine's final stronghold in Antarctica. It is significant that four of the sons of our original seven warrior heroes will lead the forces that will do so.

"Orion will lead the Argentinean Force, Hector, the son, will lead the Tasmanian Force, Argus will lead the South African Force and Ishod, Isaac's son, will lead the New Zealand Force. All of these young gentlemen have proven themselves worthy in the field.

"As you know, they are all graduates of the elite Military Strike Force and well trained both in Gogania and Magogania. The battle plan has been drawn. Only Achilles and I know the plan in its entirety. We have moles and we simply cannot let the battle information get to Arkite."

I know that Zadoc will work feverishly after the official closing of the Olympics Air Show. We must be ready and poised to strike when the time is right.

Nebo says, "The battle plans will not happen until we know the exact details and the risk factors. I demand a recess." Odysseus says, "There will be no recess and we will now have a vote by secret ballot. A yes vote says that we execute Zadoc's plan. He has the entire plan and all of the details. The entire plan must be kept secret. He will control all movements and attacks! The timing will be his decision."

The Board consists of the Chairman, the Minister of State, the Minister of Defense, the Speaker of the Senate, the President of the Council of Universities, the President of the Council of Worship and the Chairman of the Supreme Court of the Union. The vote is four yes and three no.

Nebo is a non-voting member because he and Odysseus change every two years, as do Bacchus and Roland. The Speaker of the Senate changes every two years also. The Admirals do not vote. Nebo demands a poll be made of the Board. Odysseus refuses. The meeting is over.

We adjourn to take our place in the Boards Box in the stands. Our families and special invited guests are already in their seats.

The conversation is light and everyone is in good spirits. I can remember that Apollo is particularly excited about the air show. He loves precision flying. Athena is chatting with some of her new friends. She is beaming like her mother does when she feels good inside.

Athena was asked and agreed to sing the Space Command Hymn during the opening ceremonies. I know that she will be spectacular.

Orion is leading the air show. What the crowd does not know is that all of them will land, do a quick refueling and be combat ready within two hours after performing.

Ashley and Alcestis know. They will need each other's support in the days ahead.

There are refreshments at the official box office building. Antion and Ashley made the arrangements.

Ashley, as usual, is a perfect hostess. She makes all around her feel comfortable because she has the ability to get people to talk about their interesting and exciting experiences. I always find these conversations extremely fascinating. Ashley is genuinely interested in people. She is always willing to listen, give advice and help those around her.

Athena goes to the main podium where the M.C. will announce the events and sings the opening song. He has the Master of Arms ready with the staff. Each phase of the air show will be broadcast so that all in the stadium will know what is happening as they watch.

Both Chairmen and families are sitting with us but as I suspected Nebo will have a call of nature and will retire to the washroom. I muse, *Won't it be something spectacular if all of the heads of state were eliminated leaving only the one Chairman and his carefully selected group to take over power? This will, indeed, be instant and total control. This is some ugly plan. Nebo hatched it and it is a very clever one!*

It is time! The air show begins. The M.C. announces that Athena will sing the Space Command Hymn. All become silent. The stadium is bathed in the most mesmerizing voice I have ever experienced. While Athena is singing I hear a voice within my head telling me, "Fallen one, you have been given much. We expect much from you! Do your assignment!"

The hymn is over. The stadium is in stark silence. I stand up and clap. I can't help myself. I shout "Bravo." The whole stadium erupts in applause and shouts of bravo. She has been given a great gift and she must share it with the world. We have all been given special gifts that we are to share with the world. God has given us talents and expects us to give the fruits of our talents to others in return.

The M.C. announces that air show event #1 is beginning. He describes the maneuvers as they occur, giving the background of the exercise and the names of the pilots. A distinctive color smoke is coming from each craft. The intertwining of motions of each aircraft can be seen and the smoke becomes an artistic pattern in the sky. I look at Zadoc and say, "You have masterminded a magnificent show. Thank you." Zadoc says, "Achilles, Orion has trained the pilots. The rest was easy."

Several of the celebrities surrounding us remark that it is significant to have two obelisks in the field. One is to commemorate the past Olympics and the other is to welcome the future Olympics. I agree but somehow I know that there will never be another race.

My eyes scan the stadium to see if the trusted security guards are in place. They are. Isaac looks at me from his seat and then looks at a spot to my right. The ultra-beam has detected the shooters. The security guards have neutralized them with the neck device without anybody realizing what has happened. Three unauthorized CLIP-armed men have been located. There was likely to be another one standing elsewhere. Security is alert.

The M.C. announces that the spectacular finale would soon occur. Suddenly, as I suspected, Nebo arises and whispers to me "Achilles, I have an urgent call. I will return as fast as I can because I must not miss this last sequence." I nod, and think, "You transparent bastard! You would sacrifice Evelyn and your children!" He quickly departs.

The Master of Ceremonies is announcing the aircraft maneuvers as they occur in the air He is obviously very excited about the air show. His voice shows it. He is lauding the spectacular display in the sky.

He is describing a maneuver when he suddenly stops. It is obvious that something not in the script is happening. He, being a superb M.C., recovers and describes the red smoking aircraft maneuvers as impressive but they are unscheduled. They are spectacular solo stunts. Suddenly, the craft heads directly toward the stadium. Ashley is horrified as I stand up so the pilot can clearly see me. I want him to concentrate on me so that he will not see the water cannon.

I, obviously, am his focus. Ashley tugs at my arms. His CLIP cannon whines. Nothing comes out. Good! Faithful and true Isaac has performed again! He has spiked them well! I know that he has spiked all aircraft cannons for we didn't know who the traitor would be. We did know what the traitor would do next!

Ashley is frozen in place, as is all of the rest of the official party. The water cannon fires precisely as programmed. My water cannon expert Captain did it again! He will receive another substantial reward.

The aircraft is deflected upward and flies over our heads trailing a beautiful red smoke pattern. The security aircraft are giving chase. I can hear their guns firing. There is the sound of a crippled craft. Good! We might get the pilot alive but I doubt it. I am sure that he will commit suicide.

All eyes are on me. I applaud and the stadium goes wild! The M.C. says, "Our new Admiral of the Union has surprised us with a spectacular conclusion. Ladies and Gentlemen, this is not on my program. The pilot missed the VIP viewing boxes by a few scant feet! I noted that the Admiral was standing as a beacon so that the pilot could fly directly over him!"

The M.C. continues, "That takes guts and trust. Bravo to all involved!" My standing up is viewed as one of my usual macho actions to show fearlessness. Frankly, I was petrified. I noted the returning Chairman grimacing and clapping with a slow clap. He manages to smile and say, "I am very, very sorry, Achilles to miss the finale." I know what he means.

Ashley is astounded! I can tell by her countenance. She looks at me and I look at her. She says, "You are pale. Your palms are sweaty. I have never seen you look this bad since your last brush with death." I reply quietly, "I feel a terrible stress." She asks, "Is it over?" I reply, "No, you are about to see the rest of the story. There will be other attempts to assassinate me." I sit down.

The stadium becomes quiet as the ceremonies close. The M.C. sounds the staff. His flowery talk was a bit boring but he ends by saying, "This has been the most spectacular air show in history. Let us have a round of applause for all participants and contributors."

The stadium erupts in cheers. The staff is sounded again. All is silent as the two National Anthems are played. There is another spontaneous round of applause and cheers. We begin to file out of the stadium to go to the celebrations and parties that will last until dawn tomorrow. I tell Ashley to follow me out. I look over at Isaac. He is fidgety and nervous. I know why.

I tell the family to fall back and away from me as they follow me out of the stadium. The crowds are pressing in from every side. Suddenly, I feel pressure on my back. Simultaneously, I feel another arm thrust at my chest. Both are long needles that were meant to penetrate my skin but hit my titanium vest and an attached woven sleeve.

My quick thrust breaks the frontal attacker's arm. I spin around and hit my other assailant in the throat with such force that his esophagus is destroyed. Blood gushes from his mouth. Security removes him before anybody realizes what has happened.

Isaac is next to me. I scoop the loaded syringes onto a cloth very carefully and put the whole bundle into the canister that Isaac is carrying. We must find out what poison or biological agent is in them. We are at war with a very clever enemy, Arkite.

My family is petrified. I look at Ashley and say quietly, "It's over." She will not let go of my hand. She walks with me staying very close without saying a word.

We both look at Evelyn leaving with Nebo. Her look tells us both that we might not see her again during our lifetime. I say, "Ashley, she saved our lives and I don't know how to save hers. We are trying to get her into the Pyramid ostensibly to say prayers and then give her refuge from Nebo's wrath. I think this might work. I pray so!" Tears are in Ashley's eyes as she says, "I pray also."

After a pause I say to my family, "Very significant events happen quickly. It is the preparation that counts. Life itself is all about preparing for the future. Nonetheless, we are to enjoy life as it unfolds before us. Each day we must aim to achieve the goals set for us so that we can be part of the Heavenly Family. Otherwise we will die without enjoying the life that has been given to us."

I say, "The scriptures predict that two great cities will fall in the future because their people will reject the Laws of Nature and God. One will be known as Tyre, the rock of commercial activity located along the central coast of Phoenicia and the other is Babylon known for its hanging gardens and being the capital of the Babylonian empire. I know nothing about these cities but I know that there will be woe after woe after woe, three woes in all, that will befall those civilizations who do not follow the Code but rather follow the Destructor's philosophies.

"Destructors will convince civilizations to become a blend of false religions and, therefore, become ruled by political power-mongers. The results are an uncontrollable swirling of desires, passions and cruelties. The web of institutions that benefit the powerful and oppress the weak will grow like grass. Illicit commerce will be the king. Scripture presents this system as the third horseman.

"The scriptures say an Angel throws boulders into the sea and destroys two civilizations that have ignored God. Great tsunamis will flood the earth as Noah predicts. The flood is the first woe. If we do not learn by studying history then we are doomed to repeat our errors with the same result. It appears that we will repeat this destruction two more times after the flood. This will complete the series of three woes."

Ashley smiles at me and puts her arm around my waist. She says, "Achilles, for a man who does not study the scriptures you seem to have covered a lot of ground. If you do not watch out you might become a philosopher!"

I answer, "I am not sure what I will become." She laughs and says, "You will be my enigma forever and probably God's also."

When we awaken the next morning, the battle to encircle the Serpentines and push them into Antarctica, where we expect to crush and defeat them, has begun. It is being transmitted to me by secure line. I go to Headquarters. Zadoc says, "Achilles, all is going as planned. We are ahead of schedule." I say, "It is strange to receive battle reports and not be in command."

He observes me very closely and says, "It is interesting that our progeny have learned from us and it seems that they can do as well if not better than we can do. It is tough to admit, isn't it?" I smile and say, "Yes, Zadoc, but I am proud about what we taught them. They did listen to us!"

I add, "I have told Ishod, son of Issac, to watch for a rear end strike from Tuamotu, Africa, and I have told Argus to watch for another strike from Madagascar."

Zadoc says, "Achilles, you are transparent. Your trip to Africa will not start in Northern Africa to see Noah! I suspected as much. You are going to Madagascar first, aren't you?"

I nod, smile and say, "The boat builder will have nothing to do with the Serpentines. This is why Arkite wants him eliminated and has sent his spies to that area to stir up unrest as a precursor to having Noah assaulted and killed."

I continue, "We have Noah protected and I will eventually visit him to be sure all ark building is on schedule and to be sure that he is well and guarded."

CHAPTER 5

The Counterattack

Zadoc says, "I agree that your mission is to blunt a possible counterattack from Madagascar and only you and Ashley know this. The natural caves and natural water supply systems on that island are intricate and vast. They make perfect places for a fleet of Serpentine fighters to ready themselves for an attack against us. We, as of this moment, cannot do anything about Tuamotu, Africa, without alerting Nebo. We need him as an ostensible ally. It is a good thing that we created a reserve force in place and waiting."

I say, "When I come back next month I will have a report." Zadoc smiles and says, "Achilles, as usual you make life difficult for me. I will do my best to cover your mission. I assume that you are aware that this mission to crush a possible attack from Madagascar is truly insane!"

"I have told Odysseus that you will report only to me by secure circuit. I hope that the new secure circuits you built will hold for a few weeks. We need that much secured time."

That evening I am off to Africa. One part of my reserve attack group will be in central Africa. They will make reports as if Pete and I were there.

Pete and I will try to enter the hornet's nest in Madagascar and destroy their main control station. This is easier to say than to do. This island is an island of a thousand caves; it is mysterious and beautiful.

My mission is impossible unless I can attack the heart of the Serpentine control system. My first move is to capture a Goganian ship posing as a cargo ship of trade but which is actually a military supply ship.

We must do this without alerting anybody. This is no small order. We will use a subduing gas that Vulcan developed in the University laboratories. It will instantly put large groups of people to sleep. The ship must look normal to all observers.

The timing of the takeover is to occur near the end of a supply cycle after most of the ships' missions are completed and when their crews are having a night out for relaxation.

Our target ship's crew will be joining their buddies' reveries but this ship is at the end of the scheduled delivery line and is still scheduled to deliver its load of ammunition and technical equipment to Madagascar.

Vulcan has prepared us well. As the crew returns to their ship we capture them by putting them to sleep. The crew will not awaken until we are on the way. They will be in holding cells that are as secure as we can make them.

We learned that this ship's real job is to set up control stations and replenishment centers for Serpentine fighters and bombers to use. We now know all of this because it is stored in the ship's official log book. The key codes are used by Arkite to receive the locations of all stations. The locations of the stations are also transferred to the control center in Madagascar. This plan and the codes used are an assurance to Arkite that no communication leaks would foil his plans.

We found out how to communicate with the Madagascar Control Center. It was fun. The process of interrogation involved administration of drugs. This made the crew think that they were in this Nirvana and were being rewarded for their service on earth. They spoke freely about their activities with pride and codes. This is a very interesting phenomenon. The crew of our stolen ship is scheduled to brief the Serpentine Control Center concerning its mission and its success. The information gained from this, along with the ship's log, prepared us with the exact locations, codes, and weapon inventory of each control site that they serviced. Now we are under way! We are asked by the Madagascar Control Center to give our ships code confirmation. We give it to them.

We are in the crew's uniforms and know all of the code words that will get us past the alert system of the hornet's nest. I have the gnawing feeling that it has gone too smoothly. This is interesting and I feel that it is a miracle that we have not been obliterated by the Serpentine observation system while on our way to Madagascar.

Our first stop is in Zanzibar where we are to confirm that all codes, equipment and ininstructions have been off-loaded as requested into this Southern station. All craft are to check into the system through an obelisk. Perhaps our ruse is working.

Our satellite laboratory has developed a program that we can use on this mission. It translates our speech into the language of the local tribes that we will visit.

As we speak into it, this machine will talk to our hosts in their own tongue. This is very slick indeed! Our eventual goal is to teach the denizens the fundamentals of philosophy, theology, science, math, history, health and morality.

However, the mission today is to blunt the effect of the hornet's nest and to find out where the Serpentine warships are hiding. Our language system is a hit in Zanzibar. The Chief is delighted to talk with the white flying devils directly. He accepts our gifts and allows us to remain in his domain overnight.

As we adjust our computer to talk with the tribe in Antsiranana I say to Pete, "Have you ever thought that perhaps our every thought, our every emotion, every action and every sight we see is part of our immortal soul?"

Pete looks at me strangely. I continue, "I am sure that after we leave this body and go into a new body, our previous experiences become part of us. This integration makes us a soul that is capable of accomplishing more things in the future to assist in the process of creation."

Pete is still staring at me. I continue, "I think that we must live several lives and each life is designed to teach us one great lesson. If we have not learned the lessons of the Laws of Nature in our present life we must come back to Earth and try again. If each time our soul becomes darker instead of enlightened and we follow the Destructor we will fail the school of life. The final failure dumps us into the Dark City, Hell, if you prefer, that contains the bottomless pit. In other words, we destroy ourselves. It will be as if we never existed."

Pete shakes his head, offers me another brandy and says, "Achilles, what must we learn and what is the basic structure of creation?"

I reply, "We study the Laws of Nature that have been written in the Scriptures for knowledge. The basic structure of creation is pure energy."

In other words, "The Creator creates; He has a Son and a Holy Spirit. Each of these three carries gifts for us. The Creator gives us a place to live, our life and His everlasting love. The Son teaches us how to live, express our appreciation for life, give love to others and to love the Creator with all our heart, mind, soul and being. The Son also saves us from our sins by being our advocate in the courts of Heaven. The Holy Spirit is our conscience. He teaches us to forgive others, have respect for our forefathers, persist in advising us to achieve our karmas, and to never, ever engage in sloth. He gives us wisdom, understanding, counsel, courage, knowledge, piety and fear of our Creator just as we should fear our parents when we do not achieve our karmas. We all know deep inside when we have failed. It is locked onto our brain. We must listen and learn and do better!"

Pete says, "It is as simple as that?" I say, "Believe me when I say that is not simple!"

Pete says, "Sometimes you scare me. We ought to get a good night's sleep. We are going to need sleep to be in good shape with all of our faculties in order to accomplish another one of your cockamamie plans! I don't know how you convince me to follow you. It is beyond my comprehension." I smile at him.

We complete our work on the obelisk, thank the locals and head toward Madagascar. We stay on a holding pattern for some time and finally are directed to a holding area on the beach near Tulear where we will camp for the evening.

As we move toward Antankarana we will not have time to probe each cave with our mechanical moles because there are too many of them, about 270. We will launch a few that hopefully will not be detected.

However, our job is to disable the Central Control of the fleet of Serpentine ships located there. Hopefully, our satellite detectors will see where the fighting ships exit the ground.

We will make our mandatory landing at the Control Center. The native denizens living there will greet us because we have goodies for them and they know it. We will go to the local center of worship because this is also their center of government. Of course, all who arrive are checked out by the Serpentine Security Unit.

In the middle of our final preparations Pete asks, "What do you think Heaven is all about?" I reply, "The Creator, it seems to me, demands that we be totally trustworthy, faithful, loyal to Him and follow the principles of creativity at all times. We show our allegiance on Earth by being active participants in learning, performing tasks of service to others while working in harmony and effectively together. Heaven is where this type of mutual fellowship really exists."

Pete shakes his head again. I say, "When we have lived our allotted time here at *school* and we have done an acceptable job we will join with other souls in accomplishing greater tasks. This is what Heaven is all about." Pete says, "You think working with others is necessary?" I reply to Pete by saying, "Yes. Work is necessary. Sloth is boring. Sloth wastes the talents given to us by the Creator. Wasting our talents by neglect will cost a soul dearly. A slothful soul is self-destructive. Heaven takes a dim view of sloth."

Pete gives me that quizzical look again. He says, "Achilles, you have always said that we must think for ourselves, analyze the facts, use our knowledge and trust our instincts. You always say that power results from knowledge and that people like to follow a confident leader. How does all of this fit?"

I reply, "The Creator is infinite so that we should not try to analyze Him. He is energy and His mind encompasses everything. We were not given that kind of mentality."

I continue, "He has given us a mind and talents and He expects us to use them to help others and achieve. When we do people will follow us." He says, "Achilles, sometimes you sound like a politician." I smile. We go to our bunks and get sleep. We must be rested when we execute our next moves.

The next morning we finish our preparations and fly to the local center of worship at Tananarive, a Hova tribal village. It is over 8,000 feet high and I am sure that Serpentine sensors are close to this location. On the way to Hova I do launch some of our mole probes. They confirm that a major part of the Serpentine fleet is in the midst of the Ankarana Reserve. I get word to Argus to have his fleet of fighters ready to scramble. The only way to defeat a bunch of hornets is to destroy them as they try to come out of the caves. If we can plug the cave mouths the Serpentine Fleet will be bottled up!

Apparently our arrival at Control Center is routine. Our required waiting is mandatory because all ships are double checked before they are allowed to proceed. Our identification code reflecting that we are a Serpentine spy and supply ship must be working. We have come this far without a problem. I wonder.

As another Serpentine precaution, we are told that only the Captain and executive officer will be allowed into the ziggurat.

The denizen leader tells us that he will lead us to the assembly room in the ziggurat so we tell him to tell the crowd outside to sit down behind the rock formation that was close by. He says, "Why?"

I say, "We may be inside for a long time and the Big Chief wants the crowd to relax and be comfortable!"

Just before we go into the ziggurat carrying our "load of gifts" for the locals I note that there is a line of smaller steps along its face. People can walk up the staircase (Jacob's dream about a ladder with Angels ascending and descending from Heaven must have come from the configuration of a ziggurat) to the flattened top. In this case the top is filled with electronic detectors and communications equipment surrounded by a facade that looked like an altar.

The Chief distributes our offerings such as clothing, delectable food, and footwear to the people who are sitting behind the rocks. He then leads us into the Pyramid's holy room.

We walk into this room that is just below the Control Center debriefing room carrying our other sizeable gift bags. Pete and I did not give anybody a chance to ask us to drop the bags or do anything.

We know that all visitors except the Communication Command are immediately inspected at this spot. We know that we must move quickly. The instant we are in the room I throw smoke bombs. Pete cuts a hole in the ceiling that also serves Command Control and fires Vulcan's super bombs into it.

We also fire a super shock bomb into the hole. We blast the door of the prayer room open and use our rocket packs to get out of there as fast as possible.

We get to the rock crevice just in time to see the shock waves wipe out most of the ziggurat. Our ship is operable but battered. It is obvious to our crew why I told them to move the ship into a rock crevice as soon as they saw Pete and I enter the Pyramid.

I remember the bizarre rock formation that has hidden our ship. These formations are surrounded by forests, canyons, and rivers that flow into giant cave mouths.

Some of these caves are considered sacred to the Anakaranian people who bury their kings there.

We see two Serpentine soldiers attacking our ship and I kill them by using my super-CLIP pistol before they could do any damage. All hell is breaking lose!

We had just reached our ship when we heard the captain of the Serpentine group yell over their communications system, "Those bastards Achilles and Pete were supposed to be captured! Eric wanted Achilles and his filthy brood to suffer a horrible death by piecemeal dismemberment and broadcast it to the world!"

He continues, "All of us are under the threat of death if we fail to kill them but the rewards are great if we do kill them. Eric wants their bodies on display!"

How did they know who we were? We are in a lot of trouble! We jump into our spy ship and we work our way up the ravine. Pete says, "You told me that this stupid caper was a piece of cake! This is the last time I am ever, and I mean ever, going with you on another one of your cockamamie plans again!"

He continues, "They knew all about our stupid plan except our idea of instant destruction of the ziggurat." I reply, "Pete, how else could we get into the middle of an enemy's nest and shut down their major control center? Our sons are out there in one hell of a lot of danger. It is our job as parents to help and protect them!" He just looks at me with that look of total disbelief.

I have never seen such mayhem. The Serpentine commander has sent out their fighters to destroy us and they are very desperate people. So are we.

Fortunately, I had studied the topography of the area. My goal is to get into the First or Second River Cave.

Fortunately, by using my racing experience and flying sideways through crevices and trees we manage to stay alive and shoot down the first fighter attacks with the puny weapons we have. We enter the cave and plunge into the waters of the cave and total darkness. My adrenalin is high and my heart is pounding.

I order, "Retract the wings, set the guidance planes, put a man in the airlocks with one of those new Vulcan bombs that will stick to the top of the cave and pray."

Our infrared detectors have enabled us to miss stalagmites and rocks. Sonar reports, "Sir, a Serpentine underwater craft is following us at high speed." I am sure that the fighters are looking for us and it will not be long until they figure out where we will exit into the Mozambique Channel."

I thank God that the multi-capable cargo ship was minimally damaged. The underwater functions work! My problem is that I do not know how deep the river is. One boulder jutting upward could spell doom!

The Serpentines are following me and the current is strong. What do they know that I do not? They have an advantage! I know from the current that we will emerge underwater from this cave. I stop the ship. Pete shouts, "Good God! What the hell are you doing?"

I order the diver out and tell him that he has thirty seconds to set the bomb on the roof of the cave. He answers, "I can't set it in thirty seconds and get back!" I reply, "Our life depends upon your skill. Do it!" He sets it and returns in forty-five seconds.

The Serpentine craft is closing fast. He will soon be in torpedo range. We have two problems. I must activate the bomb at just the right time or the torpedo will be launched and the space ahead is a very, very tight fit. We must slow down or rip the ship apart on the rocks I detect ahead.

The crew is petrified. So am I but I remember my own advice, "Panic will destroy you every time. Have faith." There is dead silence in the ship as I wait for the sonar man to tell me when the Serpentine craft is below the bomb. Will this bomb go off in time? The report comes, "Sir, they are opening the torpedo tube." I wait. He says, "Now!" I activate the bomb and the Serpentine is destroyed. Sonar reports, "Sir, the torpedo was launched." This is not good news. Have I waited too long!

I reply, "Follow it!" He says it is hot and running well. Wait! "Sir, it is erratic. The power system seems to have been damaged by the explosion! It is stopping and dropping to the cave floor."

A cheer is heard from the crew. I slowly thread our way through the openings ahead. We hear scraping noises as we inch forward. Again there is total silence. The sensors help guide us.

Twice we had to reverse our motion. Just as we got through rock formations and resumed full speed, sonar reports, "There is an underwater craft coming at full speed! He is small and will not have a problem getting through the restrictions!"

I reply, "I think that they have a problem. In their haste the Serpentines did not consider that there might be an armed torpedo sitting on the bottom. The proximity fuse will set it off."

Suddenly, a terrific explosion rocks the cave. I hear a cheer! Now all we have to do is avoid a swarm of Serpentines under the threat of death after we emerge from the cave. What could be simpler?

Pete says, "You must, indeed, have the shield of God with you! Do not lose it! I am trying to contact Argus. He better be on scene! Achilles, you have just added fifty years into this poor body's age. Congratulations!" I smile.

We come out of the cave and into the Indian Ocean. We surface and look up into the sky. There is a fierce battle over the skies of Madagascar. The skies are filled with damaged and burning Serpentine battle craft.

The rescue group from Argus' battle group had obviously caught the Serpentine ships as they were coming out of their caves. We shift to flying mode and skim over the water.

I send a signal to Argus to alert him that we were all right and that we are leaving the area to execute the second phase. I then go silent.

I set the course north by west and speed over the surface as fast as my craft will take me. There is no way that we can take on a fighter or anything else. This ship is meant to carry cargo in the skies or underwater. The second ability saved our lives!

Pete asks, "Achilles, where are we going now and why?" I say, "Remember? We are going to visit Noah. We have done all that we can do for our battle captains. They do not need to start worrying about where we are. My guess is that Arkite has a lot more to worry about than finding us at this time."

I can hear a sigh of relief from the crew because this is out of my character not to engage in some damnable impossible fight.

We enter the Red Sea and stay on the surface of the water until it is time to skip over to the Mediterranean Sea. Soon we are over the Holy Lands. I spot the location of Noah's ark. There isn't any navigable water around. His ship is near the ancient city of Harran along the Raikh River that feeds into the Euphrates River (Turkey).

Noah and I converse by using the electronic speakers that translate our language into his language, and his language into mine. He says, "Achilles, your son was sent from Heaven to help me finish the Ark that God has commanded that I build." I nod and say, "We should be proud of our young. They believe." He smiles. I say, "How much time do you have to complete the Ark?" He replies, "I had 120 years but without your son's help I would not have finished it on time. I have spent 118 years already. The time schedule will not change."

"We have the frozen animal embryos on board and your son has taught me how to defrost and raise them after the flood. We have enough frozen food, enough water, vegetables and animals in our fields to feed us on the journey."

I say, "I will request a great favor from you, Noah, just before the flood." I tell him of my karma and my desire to keep my son who will be born soon safe. We pray together and ask God for His direction. After a long pause as we watch the sun go down we see a spray of meteorites. I say, "Is that the sign you asked for?" He replies, "Yes." We shake hands.

I say, "Noah, let us take a trip to the site of the Great Garden City of Eden." He says, "Achilles, it depresses me to go there." I say, "It will be a short trip. It will last only a few hours. We will leave early in the morning and be back for lunch."

He says, "Why do you want to go there?" I reply, "I want to contemplate with you and I want you to meditate with me." He says, "You do not like what you must experience. Correct?" I nod. He says, "Achilles, neither do I like my fate." I smile. We retire for the night. I tell Pete what I am going to do. He says, "It is depressing to go to that desolate place." I say, "I know."

Early in the morning we leave in the small scout ship sent to us by Zadoc. Soon we are over the Munkhafadath Tharthar Lake (Iran) between the Tigris and Euphrates River. The lush valleys are fed from the artesian wells caused by ground water from both rivers. We look toward the North and we land.

The existence of Eden is undetectable. There are no signs of former buildings, streets or artifacts. The removal of evidence has been so complete that it staggers the mind. It is hard to realize that a thriving civilization was once centered here. All debris had been reduced into new material and scattered. Noah says, "Achilles, how could this be done?" I explain, "The debris was put into super-hot caldrons and melted. As the caldron cooled down things began to solidify depending upon their melting temperature. Dross formed on the surface of the liquid. This was drawn off the molten liquid. The resulting dross ingots were either shipped as useful material or crushed into fine powder and scattered. Precious metal ingots and other elements were probably shipped to other locations." Noah nods as if he knew what I was talking about.

I say, "Noah, obviously, we are faced with the power of the Federation again. This time it will be a flood of such magnitude as to defy our imagination. Are we really that bad?" Noah did not answer.

I continue, "It is not an accident that the first toolmakers were found to have started in Hasquna. It must be because these were city people and they farmed the land before Eden was erected. I am sure that they had a soul." Noah asks, "Achilles, when did the soul arrive?"

I say, "Maybe it became evident when mankind started to control its destiny. This period of development is quite a jump in civilization. The first transition from stone to metal tools happened in Tall Halaf and the Halafian culture was born. Figures of heads with eyes representing God were found at Tall Birak Tahtan."

I ask, "Noah, it could be that at that time the Creator gave us our soul. He might have connected it to the parietal gland of our body thereby creating the true human being." Noah just looks at me. I am not sure what he is thinking. We sit and contemplate as we look at the scene around us. We are two souls thinking about God together. We are bonding and we realize that this bonding is what God wants us to do. He wants all of us to bond and work together, respect one another and love one another.

After a long time of contemplation I say, "Noah, we have through our knowledge, been able to use the secrets of nature to enlighten our minds that enabled us to truly appreciate life and realize that we are a special part of God's creation. Was the development of the Halafian culture the time when we began to use this ability?"

He smiles and says, "Does it really matter, Achilles? I do not know but I do know that we are what we are! We are God's children!"

I continue, "Bravo! You have chosen to follow God and His Code of Living. I am trying to do the same thing. We both have oligarchy and corruption surrounding us. The result of following this path is that it has resulted in our deterioration and our drifting from God and His Code of Living."

Noah says, "We are not evil, Achilles, but our people have come under the spell of hedonism. They have become Satan's playthings. Much like Adam and Eve we have angered God!" There is silence between us.

Noah says, "Continue your thoughts." I say, "Orion has told you that during his studies he and his professors have seen a comet approaching the Earth! It will strike Earth! Your flood will happen!"

I state, "Not only do I know when but I know how the Great Flood will happen. A few months ago I sent our most powerful quark membranes loaded with bosons as bombs (so secret that only the Head of the University Weapons Laboratory, Professor Thor, knows about them) to destroy the comet. All the bomb did was to split the comet into two pieces!"

He replies, "I also know when the flood will happen! God does not lie!" I nod and smile. I say, "Although, I thought that the explosion would alter the comet's course it did not! Perhaps this is what our Creator wanted. The size of the whole comet might have damaged the basic Earth structure. Each piece will hit the Earth in a different sector. Actually, the comet will succeed in destroying both Gogania and Magogania. Our capital cities, Atlantis and Sitnalta will be no more just as Eden is no more." Noah says, "Tell me more."

I do. "One piece will destroy Magogania by hitting just north of the Gambia Abyssal Plain several miles northward and southeast of the Oceanographer Fracture Zone. Gogania will be destroyed by the other comet part hitting in between the east end of the Agassiz Fracture Zone and the east end of the Marquesas Fracture Zone. This will cause tsunamis in both oceans so enormous that the whole world will be affected by flooding." Noah says, "I have no idea where these things are but continue!"

I do. "My job now is to keep as many of my people alive as possible and to deliver the scriptures to Tibet. Unlike you, Noah, I must keep this awful thing a secret as long as possible because I have enough rebellion already. I will tell my people about mini-escape ship plans when I am ready."

Noah nods again and I continue, "What good is it for your people to know about the flood? You are a joke to them but your little ark will survive. You had better because, from you, a new generation of God's chosen will survive."

Noah says, "Achilles, you know that I do not understand a thing about your explanation or, really, what happened here in Eden. I do not know about such things as fracture zones but I do know that neither one of us can possibly know the mind of God."

He explains, "What we do know is that we have the scriptures to tell us how to behave and we know that each one of us is loved equally by God."

He lectures, "He expects us to love one another as we do ourselves. It is our job as parents to teach our children that since we parents are the children of God so are our children the children of God. All of our lives are something very precious to Him! We must understand this fact. Then what follows is obvious. We must treat others as very precious also. Disaster follows when we forget these basic Laws of Nature."

Noah continues, "Greed and self-aggrandizement without helping others makes us an anathema to God. Achilles, where are your people going?" I answer, "Apparently, too many have chosen disobedience to Him or have rejected His love and will go to Perdition in a hand basket." He laughs and says, "How did you ever come up with that phrase!"

I say, "It just popped into my head." I muse, "Each organ and limb within man's erect body and the placement of his eyes, ears and nose allows him to sense his environment. His brain parts allow him to use the body parts and senses to interact and live with nature. However, he has other brain parts that help him delve into the workings of creation. All of this is no accident."

Noah looks at me quizzically. I continue, "Many professors looking at life on Earth as an evolution event say that the human body is the result of evolution. This may be so but this does not answer the question of a soul. When did it arrive?"

Noah says, "That makes sense but it is not relevant! Continue." I do. "If people eat from Eve's forbidden fruit their reasoning stops there. A study of the Humanities that centers on humans, their values and their capacities and disregards their soul is flawed. This type of study will inevitably fall into the theme that it is the government that must be worshiped. In other words, they consider themselves as God."

I conclude, "Therefore, Perdition awaits them. For example, my enemies Arkite and Eric want to capture me and dismember me piece by piece as a public display to intimidate the public into submission to their will. Let us eschew humanism as a philosophy!"

He replies, "The big lesson is to realize that with our free will we choose our path and the results that will match our choice. We are responsible for what we do! Facing discipline is a consequence of poor choice." I reply, "That thought is correct, Noah!"

Noah continues, "This Union that you talk about is not free from discipline either. I think that your people, using your small escape ships, will be scattered all over the world and will survive! The Force of God will be with you."

Noah continues, "Do what you must do. I think that you will save many of your errant people but they too will face an Adam's decision."

I say, "I will do what I must do." He says, "So will I and my group will survive. Let us return to the Ark my friend. I am ready!" I nod. We do.

I say to Noah on the way back to his Ark, "Although the Earth's history will be uncertain, especially concerning the date of the flood for a variety of reasons, the basic 'Truth' for the flood will survive intact because you and your progeny will tell your people about it."

I lament, "When Earth is hit by these huge pieces of matter all kinds of crazy things will happen. History happens and, if mankind survives, some people will develop enough interest to be curious about it." He nods.

I continue, "There will be stories of Atlantis being destroyed by floodwaters and by explosions and they will persist. Most people will deny it. Noah, why do so many people deny some possible scenarios of truth?"

He answers, "Because they want to be part of the 'in' group and fear to delve into the broader picture of happenings or possibilities. They fear ridicule by the people of power! This type of fear will destroy many people before the fearmongers are killed. The bitter fruit from the tree of power will wreak havoc on all involved."

I say, "You are a wise man, Noah, but there is one thing that I want to warn you about and that is this green brew of yours. I notice that you like that green stuff you brew from the liquid from wormwood."

I warn, "We use wormwood extract commingled with fiberglass fibers and a touch of carbon fibers to strengthen high-density polyethylene and extrude the lumber composite you know as gopher wood. Your Ark is made with this very good blend of product. However, albeit you get a tasty and comforting drink from wormwood extract, absinthe, it will lead straight to madness."

I explain, "There is a chemical thujone in wormwood that affects the brain and will cause you to do things that God does not want you to do. It is a strong hallucinogenic drug. Take care my friend and make no decisions while under the influence of absinthe."

Noah replies, "Achilles, how is it that you know about the things that will come to pass after we have been taken to Heaven? You sound too much like a prophet!"

I answer, "My friend, I do not know. These predictions just come into my mind." He smiles and says, "Things just come into my mind also. I do like absinthe but I will be wary when I sip this relaxing elixir." The visit with Noah is over.

I make my report to Zadoc and tell him we are on our way home. I tell him how pleased I am to hear that we have crushed the Serpentine forces.

Zadoc says, "Achilles, our children know what they are doing and I know that you are proud of them!"

He continues, "Now let us talk about you. You are late because you expanded the Noah visit to include a visit to Eden's site. Why?" I say, "It seemed to me that this was a way for us to know each other better. Believe me, it was worthwhile. He will house part of my family during the flood."

Zadoc replies, "I believe you, but as all decisions do, this has had corollary effects."

He reminds me, "Achilles, remember that you must be at the reception for the heroes of the battle on time! You are the main speaker! You had better turn on full speed and get here fast! Pete's clothes and yours are ready at your house. Antion has already prepared the whole affair and Ashley Anne looks fabulous!"

I say, "Pete and I will be home within the hour!" He replies, "You are scheduled to be in the reception line in one hour and fifteen minutes!"

He continues, "Also, your daughter wishes to discuss something very important with you tomorrow and also, I want to meet with all of the attack commanders in the Space Command Chambers tomorrow and I want you there on time!"

He repeats, "I expect to see you at your house that is now turned into one gigantic entertaining area by Antion within the promised hour!"

I realize again that I am truly not in charge of very much!

I look at the skipper of the ship that Zadoc sent to retrieve us and say, "If you want to see me and Pete alive tomorrow deliver us to the house within the hour!" He smiles and says, "Admiral, no matter how far you rise in the power spectrum you will still be expected to pay attention to your home, official duties, social duties and distaff side of the house! This will always be so."

I reply, "You really mean that I must remember my duties to serve others includes remembering that I have a wife who is responsible for keeping our family in line?" He smiles and says, "I will probably do some damage to the ship by overloading the power system but I will hover over your house in time to be ready for your function. I know that your arrival will cause speculation and some remarks about showmanship because it is not normal to be flying into your bedroom window using your escape pack while many guests will be walking into your front door fully dressed for the occasion!"

I reply, "I know and I would rather be arriving another way, of course, but I will more than appreciate you delivering me so I can be ready for the reception line. You are a good pilot and a wise one also!"

We arrive as advertised. Pete and I fly into the guest room window in our Para Pack escape units. The Skipper was right. Upon our arrival at the reception line just in time we are accused of showmanship!

After dinner, Ashley Anne and Athena go to the Gala's orchestra stage to sing the most popular song in the forthcoming show. There is a male singer also approaching the stage. I know him as the new singing sensation of the Union.

The music starts. It is so powerful and the blend of instruments with human voices so spellbinding that I find myself relaxing and bathing in the flood of notes and voices that only several angels from Heaven could have made.

Why does this seem to be deja vu? I see this blending and peace is a result of great missions being accomplished through harmonious spirits working together. I am completely at ease and forget the tensions that are building in the Union. I enjoy the intermingling voices penetrating my very soul. I have a tingling sensation throughout my body. I do not want it to end.

When the last note subsides I jump up, clap and shout, "Bravo, Bravo!" Instantly the entire room explodes into applause and a standing ovation.

I must meet the amazing male singer. I know that Athena has been working with him. Maybe their relationship has gone beyond working together! He is a tall, muscular man with dark features that come from the strong sun and breezes of the Mediterranean area. His dark brown eyes are kind and yet strong. His features make him look like a very young man and I suppose, compared to me, he is.

Zadoc is next to me and says, "Achilles, each one of the Attack Force commanders did an outstanding job! They will all be decorated at a formal ceremony and Odysseus will give the awards to the recipients. Argus not only saved your tail but he bottled up the Serpentine Fleet in Madagascar and destroyed them!"

I look at him and say, "Where did the time go Zadoc! Our trainees and children are no longer learners but they are the backbone of our support and damn good at it!"

He bursts out in laughter. He says, "Yes, Achilles, they are! These men are our future. They need nurturing and stroking! We are the old guards whether we like it or not!

Our job is to impart our wisdom and knowledge to them and let them do the job!"

He continues, "I have noticed that you grunt when you get up and you are not as limber as you once were. I have even heard you say that you are getting too old for this frontline stuff."

I smile and say, "You are right, Zadoc, we become the counselors and they are the counselees. They need the medals and the recognition. They made the calls! They were successful and it is their turn."

Zadoc agrees and says, "Remember, Achilles, Athena is a grown woman." I stare at him and say, "She is in love with the singer!" He answers, "Helios is his name. You have been so busy that you did not see the remarkable change in Athena. She loves you very much and will always love you but Daddy's little girl is a woman!"

I sigh and think, "Can this be so? My little girl will always be my little girl, but God's plans dictate that they are to grow up and it is our job to help them do so." Zadoc leaves me and lets me get lost in my thoughts. He knows what is going on in my head. Thank God for people like Zadoc.

The next day Zadoc and I have a luncheon arranged at Antion's for the Commanders and their families to congratulate them for their splendid performance. Ashley and Pallas meet us there. The food is as usual superb with all kinds of seafood and rich chocolate desserts. Being a type A person has served me well and kept my weight down. All Commanders are discussing their forthcoming fortnight vacation that will follow the forthcoming awards ceremonies.

I lead Zadoc into the small quiet bar and settle into the corner where I know that we will not be heard nor bothered. Antion long ago designated this spot for me so that I could be totally alone. It is clean of any type of bug. No eavesdropping is possible.

Zadoc looks at me and says, "What is up, Achilles?" I say, "Zadoc, we have defeated the Serpentines again but there has been no surrender. This means that there are a plethora of Serpentines at the South Pole. There is more to come! We must force and root them out! Have we really routed them out from Madagascar?" Zadoc nods and says, "Maybe and maybe not but we must play our cards right or we cannot win the battle and war."

I continue, "I have another topic and it is those damn comet pieces that will hit us. I have tried to change their courses but to no avail. Nature has ruled and we, as of now, do not have the power to do anything about it. The ancient protective shield that I used to defeat the Serpentines is not big enough to have any real effect."

I say, "We cannot unite as a harmonious people to solve the problem because the Serpentines want total power at any cost! They are great propagandists! Why don't those who worship their dark side and power see what is really happening? The cost is their soul and life! Satan has double-crossed them, they do not see it and he loves it!"

I add, "We will save our people just as the Ark will save Noah's people but none of our lives will be the same after the flood."

I explain, "I have studied the entire ocean floor around the comet impact areas. The best place for us to build the submersibles is in the caves of Madagascar. The Pacific and Atlantic oceans are going to be a mess. Hydraulic pressures, although quick to dissipate, are of concern because they will rattle the ocean floor. It will shake from pressure and impact forces. Earthquakes will result. The tsunamis will rage and will damage Europe, Africa's west coast and South America's east coast and some of North America's east coast. It will affect the Pacific Rim, China, Japan and Australia's coasts." Zadoc becomes very pensive and sad as he listens.

I continue, "The Indian Ocean will not be affected too much and the Natal Basin along Madagascar's west coast is nice and deep. The submersibles can safely travel though the Somali Basin at depths of about 3,000 feet during the yearlong turmoil on the world's surface. From there they can go to the Arabian basin. Your ship can meet me at Mount Olympia and the others can go to the Arabian Peninsula to the Tigris-Euphrates Valley. What do you think?"

He replies, "It will work! It is the only thing that will work! I see your problem. We must keep our activities in the caves of Madagascar a secret from The Federation, who seem to be unfriendly, and from the Serpentines. We can manufacture all of our ships by using and augmenting the Serpentine equipment." I say, "Correct. How do we do this simple task?"

As he is thinking I say, "We have two problems. We want to draw out the South Pole Armada so we can defeat them again and we better do it damn quickly. I hope that nobody will suspect that we are also building an escape armada. We must make it look like we are using Madagascar as a strike assembly area only created to draw the Serpentines out of their South Pole fortress!"

I continue, "We want Nebo and Arkite to think that Madagascar is not a manufacturing area." Zadoc says, "First things first, Achilles."

I say, "Maybe the Serpentines will think that they do not need Madagascar. They can attack Magogania from Gogania and the South Pole. They will merely try to isolate Madagascar for later destruction. During this time we will have fortified Madagascar and started to build our armada." Zadoc agrees.

I continue, "As you know, the Serpentines are discounting the flood theory as nonsense and slandering our warnings as a ploy to maintain control of the Union through fear."

I warn, "As always, when a group of people wants to take control of a country or organization they slander its leaders. It is their weapon of choice. Besmirching the other leaders is the game because they have no original thoughts of their own. Spinning history, distorting history, lying and distorting the facts are about as far as their pseudointellect will take them."

Zadoc laughs and says, "You really do not like Nebo." I smile. He continues, "There is no other plan, Achilles. I will do all that I can to help you make it so. However, there are a few holes that I would like to discuss after I do some thinking."

After the long but very satisfying meeting Zadoc and I bid farewell to our group and wished them an enjoyable and well-earned leave.

All return and it seems that time has passed incredibly quickly. There is a small reception after the heroes and families have returned from their leave. They have enjoyed their awards and accolades and are ready for duty. I am waiting for another talk with Athena that Zadoc told me was coming.

Athena comes over with her boyfriend and they are holding hands. She says, "Daddy, I want you to meet Helios." I note that my son, Apollo, and Helios are associated with the sun gods of mythology.

Apollo has become the most knowledgeable student at the University in astrophysics. His work at the University using probe data has been lauded. He is following the comet, now two pieces, that will strike the Earth.

Maybe the comet buster weapon may enable our escape ships to fight the advanced ships of the Federation assuming that is what they are all about.

Helios is the person who is known as the singer who is like a local sun and has illuminated the stage with his penetrating music.

I stop musing as Helios says, "Sir, I am honored to meet the savior of our Union."

How do I respond? I have not saved the Union! I will soon be groveling to save my family! I know by looking at Athena's eyes that he will be part of my family so I say, "Helios, you are welcomed to our family. You will be in charge of caring for my precious daughter. You will have the job of educating the Earth in the arts and through this avenue teaching religion and morals to those living around us."

He looks surprised. I say, "The small package that you are carrying tells me that you will soon propose." He replies, "Sir, I cannot exist without Athena. She is my life."

Ashley says, "You see, Helios, Achilles is fierce in his mission of protecting the family and he knows instinctively who is good for Athena. It is your job to prove him right." My family is looking at me in a strange way and they are smiling. I know that there is more to come. I look at them silently.

The next thing I see is Apollo, my youngest son, holding hands with Veturia. Wow! What a beauty! No wonder she will later be known as a woman that could change the heart of the gods. She has golden hair that is fine as silk, a round face graced with dark blue eyes, a perfectly shaped, small nose and thick lips. She has perfectly shaped breasts that were neither too big nor too small. She has very long legs and a small waist. I remember seeing her at the Ball and Target games rooting for Apollo who was usually surrounded by women after the game.

I had not triggered to the fact that she has always been by his side during all of the functions and that he had eyes only for her.

Apollo says, "Dad, I want you to meet Veturia." I say, "I am more than delighted to meet that beautiful girl that I have seen in many of our news programs interviewing celebrities. I understand that you were at the top of your class in journalism and communications."

She replies, "Admiral, I could never get an interview with you because you shied away from interviews." I look at her and say, "That, Veturia was a big mistake!" I laugh and she does too.

I look at her ring finger and notice an engagement ring on it. Apollo says, "Dad, we are madly in love and I want to spend the rest of my life with her." I say, "You both have my blessing." There is more to come!

He continues, "Argus is marrying her sister Vergilia."

I look at the situation, Athena (Helios), Apollo (Veturia) and Argus (Vergilia), and come to the conclusion that there will be a triple wedding. Who is going to spring the news? I do not wait long to find out.

Athena says, "Dad, a triple wedding would be spectacular!" Of course! My daughter springs it! She continues, "We all wondered if Mom could get together with all of the families and coordinate one fantastic celebration! Everybody agrees!"

I say, "Has anybody bothered to tell Mom? I suppose you would like to have the ceremony right away! Nobody in their right mind would pull a stunt like that! I cannot believe it!" I hear a cough from the back of the room and see Vera looking straight at me. I note that the whole room including Ashley is looking at Vera and then at me.

The silence is deafening. It seems to last a long time. I can remember marrying Ashley and what Vera had said. I look at my shoes. I do not know what I thought that I was going to find there. My toes cannot talk.

I look at Ashley and then at Vera and smile with a big broad smile and say, "Mom is great at the impossible. I have never heard of a triple wedding done in a few days. Heaven knows, I would never impose that kind of thing on anybody! Right, Vera?"

The entire room bursts out in hardy laughter. She answers, "Achilles, you are still an unbelievable piece of work!"

Again, the whole room is laughing and is crying at the same time. This is the essence of being human. This is how God wants us to be. The room is filled with congratulations and cheer. Ashley comes over and kisses me. Our thoughts intertwine.

After we settle down I ask for Antion. I ask Isaac to secure the room so that only the families of Orion, Apollo, Helios, Argus, Peter, Zadoc and Odysseus are present. All eyes are upon me.

I first tell Antion that Ashley will be the Chairwoman of the stupendous occasion that is forthcoming. He says, "Sir, so what is new?" The room again is filled with laughter. I warn Isaac that security will be a nightmare to say the least. He says, "Achilles, so far this is following a well-known pattern!"

The room explodes with energy, conversations and good cheer. Everyone is looking to me to give the final toast before we all go to bed for a well-earned rest.

I say, "My heart is bursting with pride and thanksgiving for this is a great day! The blessed marriages will happen and God will bless each marriage for it is His desire that we marry and rear our children to also love Him and worship Him." I pause and continue, "May you, God, bless these forthcoming marriages and these families. May Your grace, guidance and shield be with them forever!" Once more the room is filled with energy and happiness.

I break the mood by saying, "Before we all adjourn I have something very serious to discuss. I feel very badly bringing the next subject up at this time and it breaks my heart to do so but it is important. The war against the terrorists, those who would destroy our Union because of their greed, envy and lust for power, is going well. I expect that the Serpentines will surrender after our next thrust into the South Pole."

I warn, "That is good. However, I do not know what Arkite is thinking and you can be sure the terms of his surrender agreement may not bode well for the Union. Make no mistake in your belief that the Serpentines will remain our enemy. My fear is that Arkite will surrender to Chairman Nebo and not to the Union."

Odysseus says, "Chairman Nebo vigorously denies this and assures me that he will not accept the surrender unless it is made to the Union." I say, "Odysseus, you are absolutely correct." There is a pause and he is confused. Suddenly, his face turns ashen. He says, "My God, Achilles, you think Nebo would go that far?" I say, "Yes. Their thrust for power must encompass this plan!" The room is filled with a shocked buzz.

I say, "Let me continue. There will be events occurring that will change the world as we know it. The people in this room will be the core of the New World. I am sure all of you want to survive these cataclysmic events and you will but only if nobody in this room reveals one word about what I am telling you. If you say anything we are all dead. I cannot be more emphatic about not disclosing anything to anybody!"

I verbalize the point, "You do not want mass assassinations. I will try to keep this kind of thing from happening. If you value your lives and those of your children and their children to come, say nothing. Do not be fooled by anybody or anything into revealing what you have heard tonight."

I emphasize my words, "Zadoc and Vera will be in contact with each one of you as time goes on so that you will know what to do and when. There will be no other communication except by mouth and this must be well guarded. I will be unable to talk with you about this and sometimes you will find my conversations puzzling. Orders will come only from Zadoc and Vera."

I further articulate, "The Union has two enemies at this moment. The Serpentines that may well include Gogania and a group I will call The Federation. As you recall, years ago The Federation built a great city called Eden. We know about the destruction of Eden and the fact that the remnants of this group formed two countries, Gogania and Magogania. Another group split and formed an agrarian group in the area that will be known as the Holy Lands from the Tigris River and Euphrates River Valley west to the Mediterranean Sea."

I declare, "I feel that The Federation will attempt to destroy us again! However, all three of the survivors from Eden will have survivors from a forthcoming flood; but the ones, according to the Pyramid teachings, that will be known as God's chosen, will come from Noah's stock."

I continue, "The truth of the prediction will depend upon those in this room and our people. Our people will escape in mini-craft and be scattered all over the globe."

I say, "In other words, we can make this happen by our actions. We can change the Pyramid prediction by bringing the light of art, science and our belief in God into the New World!"

I reiterate, "What will cause this great flood? Sometime ago Apollo found the comet, now in two pieces, that is on its way to earth. I thought I could prevent the collision by blowing apart the comet. I managed to split the comet into two pieces. I believe that this really saved the Earth from the rupture that would have occurred if the whole comet hit the Earth. I know where the two pieces will fall."

The room is totally silent. Each of our children are hugging their future mates. Ashley comes over and hugs me. We all sip our drinks in silence.

I continue, "Noah's predicted flood will occur and it will be caused by the tremendous impact that will result after we are hit by these comet pieces. The resulting tsunamis will cover the Earth with floods and rains will fall because of the water spewed into the atmosphere and the resulting meteorological disturbances."

I instruct, "There will be four ways for us to escape. They are the spaceships, Noah's Ark, submarines and the mini-craft. The mini-craft will save the bulk of our people. Our people will survive the flood and The Federation attack!"

I state, "I feel that The Federation will attack only two of the four methods of escape. They will attack any spaceships we try to use. They will ignore the Ark. They will not know about the submersibles and there will be too many of the mini-crafts for them to handle."

I observe, "Trying to obliterate all of the mini-craft will not be tolerated by The Federation. Their orders are to scatter all Goganian and Magoganian paraphernalia and destroy the cubes of knowledge but not to kill all of us."

I comment, "Furthermore, if we do not have any escape spaceships they may well think about submersibles. We will use spaceships. I will be the lead ship in the escape spaceship armada. Each submarine will have a set of the cubes of knowledge. Noah will get one but will not know what to do with his."

I make an observation, "It will only take two generations for a society to become uneducated if the cubes are not used. We must build towers of knowledge that will hold all knowledge that we have. The cubes hold this knowledge. We must dispense this knowledge to our progeny after we arrive at our post-flood locations. This is all that you need to know."

I encourage my group, "We have time for living before you must take action and prepare for your new homes, probably on Mount Olympus. The knowledge that I gave to you this evening is dangerous enough. Any more detail is deadly."

I declare, "Many people have become corrupted by the sophisticated who think there is no God and think that each one of them is the only important thing in the universe. They are undisciplined. Most of them feel unfulfilled because of the lack of belief in something bigger than themselves. They have dedicated their lives to the gods of lust, pleasure, drugs and Baal. This is the formula to destruction."

I pronounce, "All of our people, when they find out that the end is near, will demand that they be on board escape ships. Everybody will have an opportunity to be on escape ships albeit mini-ships. This is their only hope for survival. The big spaceships will be in great battles with The Federation."

I articulate, "My armada spaceship will survive. I cannot tell you why this is so but it is. The Captains of the submersibles will be Orion, Apollo, Helios, Argus, Peter and Zadoc. Orion will be the Commander of the fleet. I will contact each one of you upon my return to Earth. Isaac will ride with me and Odysseus will ride with Peter."

I instruct, "Each commander will be responsible for picking his second in command and picking the operating crew. Each person and family in this room is responsible for picking the people who will come with you and you will be assigned to a craft."

I say, "I will take one question. Odysseus, you raised your hand first. You have the floor!" He says, "Who will be in charge of the new Union?" I reply, "You will be in charge, Orion will be your Deputy and upon your retirement he will take over."

He blurts out, "What are you going to do?" I say, "I am going to retire and play with my grandkids." He blurts out again and says, "So am I, Achilles!" I reply, "Then it will be you and I that will retire but you as Chairman of the Union and I as the Deputy in charge of the Union will install Orion as Chairman. Zadoc will retire and his position will be abolished."

He continues, "What towers, having all of mankind's learning inside, have you in your mind?" I reply, "There will be twelve Deans, one from each major academic area, on board the submersibles. My feeling is that each Dean in charge of his area of learning discipline such as physics, history, language, medicine, astronomy, philosophy, music, art, mathematics, writing, archeology, economics and engineering with all their substructures will be in charge of his sector of knowledge."

I state, "We will meet after the flood and assemble on Mount Olympus. We can combine all knowledge into a central tower of knowledge for all universities to use! It is up to you, Odysseus. You are the boss."

I conclude, "That series contained more than one question. This conference is over. Let us get on with getting these youngsters married." I raise my glass and say, "To the future generations! May your paths be bright, your resolve strong and your health excellent. May your progeny be the great generation that brings our Earth peace and prosperity under the rules of God!"

In my mind I wonder if all of this will come to pass as I have stated. I am not God. Only He knows.

The next day Zadoc and I have another Antion luncheon to attend. Ashley looks like an Angel! I have never seen Pallas so happy. Vera, as usual, looks beautiful. I am puzzled considering the heavy-duty burden that I laid upon them but they are doing what I asked them to do.

They are living life now the best way they can. They are excited. After the luncheon the women of our soon-to-be married couples and their mothers are meeting to arrange for the announcements, invitations, music, food, the decor and dancing.

There will be a ton of people attending the meeting such as floral agents, architects to assure crowd-pleasing decorations, table arrangement experts, entertainment agents, wedding planners, performers, transportation experts, room assignment and room decor experts, protocol experts, sound experts and, course, the ever-present Antion.

I ask Ashley if she realizes what this will cost and she says, coyly, "Much less than all of those war machines you build and much less than those stupid racing cars you build. This affair is important!"

What I have done is unimportant? Hmm!!! I have a very quick decision to make. Do I want to sleep with her tonight or not?

I reply, "The social part of our life and welding people together have always been your domain. This is a critical part of living with one another harmoniously. My machines will save our lives. Your expertise will keep us together. I cannot wait to see how it all comes out." She says, "I knew that you would see it my way."

Antion's is now the most popular resort in the Union but he will close for business for the four-day wedding extravaganza. Only for Ashley would he close his entire business for this period of time.

As I leave the luncheon I wonder if The Federation will go over the line of their authority and in their zeal to rid the Earth of our so-called rebellious countries cause us unnecessary harm.

The Federation is a big problem. Will they join with Arkite? I do not think so. Why would they? They must know as I do that punishment is God's business and not theirs!

I am convinced that Vulcan's comet buster may prove to be my best weapon to fight the forces arrayed against me. My detectors are helping me understand the basics of The Federation satellite operations and this knowledge is helping me design counter technological equipment.

My detection and stealth equipment has been augmented and improved by Professor Besai, our expert in this field. It is critical to our survival. However, we also have the problem of Madagascar. Did we really obliterate operations there?

I say, "Zadoc, as you know, we must ensure Madagascar is under our control. The reports I get are glowing. This concerns me. I have the sickening feeling that these reports are false! Nebo and the Serpentines may have already become allies!"

I ask Zadoc, "Have our occupation forces there been defeated? Suddenly, Nebo is too happy! He acts as if he has gained control and his shenanigans against us have been undetected. I am beginning to believe that when Magogamia faces its attack it will be a joint venture by Nebo and the Serpentines."

Zadoc answers, "Your mission is to probe this theory right after the wedding celebrations are completed. You are the key to success."

I say, "I am going to use the same tactics that we used to take Madagascar before! I have developed the stealth technology beyond what we used then. The ancient comet buster array has been modified and is ready for action. We will again use the false signals and Theudas is fully prepared."

I theorize, "We will have the Serpentine forces pass the exact coordinates needed for your group to do its thing. Zadoc, you must fire at the exact time the enemy is in the target area."

I warn, "There is a small window for you to use because we might not be able to keep the invasion force holding to the false track without somebody at South Pole Center noticing the small deviation in their fleet's flight course."

Zadoc just looks at me. I say, "I know, once bitten by a dog, a person is shy about being near him again. I am counting on Nebo's ego, supported by Arkite, to let this caper slip by their notice just long enough."

Zadoc says, "Achilles, you have put a terrible burden on me as usual. If our plan does not work the battles over Atlantis will be very costly in time, lives and equipment."

I say, "I realize this fact but the effort is worth it! Now let us assume that it works. We will then be able to build our escape fleet and be able to save most of our people from perishing in the flood." Zadoc just looks at me and says, "Okay. Another cockamamie plan is at hand and I am the fish caught by your hook." He smiles.

Then Zadoc admonishes me, "During our flood escape period the detection protection and safety of our submarines is paramount. What makes you so sure that we will not be detected? How can we rebuild the factories in such a short time? How can you possibly survive in the air?"

I reply, "Our aircraft will all be top secret stealth machines based upon the information we have gathered from The Federation probes."

I continue, "The Federation will not be able to detect the submersibles at all for they will be very deep and silent. Federation equipment was not designed to detect objects in this environment."

Zadoc asks, "Why are you so sure that The Federation will fight us?"

I continue, "I do not know, but they will. Maybe they think that all of us have lost our way. In any case, if they do, they will have overstepped their authority! Our escape craft will survive because The Federation will not be able to detect what is happening at first. After they do it will be too late. There are too many mini-ships!"

I declare, "The Federation will not suspect that we will have developed this sophisticated equipment in the short time that we have. We never have flown stealth machines like these. We have updated our boson laser cannons. This surprise will give us an edge because they will not be pre-pared for us."

Zadoc says, "A surprise for ten months?"

I correct him. I say, "It will take about ten months for the waters to recede enough to expose most of the high grounds on the affected areas. Noah's Ark will release our sub that will be attached to its bottom before his vessel is caught in the mountains of Ararat."

He says, "Really, and since when have you become an expert in predictions?" I smile and say, "Because the University has calculated that this will be about right for the impact and subsequent water subsidence."

I convey my thoughts, "Of course, our initial escape armada surprise will be over very quickly but The Federation will be busy chasing us at first because they have orders to destroy us! They will stop chasing us as we fly away because they know that we must return."

I continue, "They will not worry about Noah who is not their problem. We are the problem. Submersibles will not be in their minds. The Federation will know that our armada must return to Earth at some time. I suspect that The Federation will wait for our return to take action against us."

I stop talking, think, and say, "You know, I might take two escape craft to Mars. Pete and I can do wonders together and monitor The Federation until the full escape armada returns to Earth. I will try to remain under a stealth shield and set up a listening post on Mars so that I can follow The Federation communications."

Zadoc smiles and I say, "If The Federation craft should detect us on Mars I will have fun fighting them! As you know at one time Mars had an atmosphere, oceans and rivers. While studying Mars I found some very interesting canyons located between Phoenicis Lacus, Pavonis Lacus and Melas Lacus. These canyons are configured for sideways flying and I am good at sideways flying. The winds will be fierce and dust unbelievable. Our machines are built to survive the severe dust storms. This stuff will discourage The Federation craft and they really will not want to chase us on Mars for long."

Zadoc says, "Continue!" I do. "Of course, our armada of escape craft will go in all directions after the initial escape and, as I have said, The Federation will know that we must return to Earth or perish so they will wait for the return of the ships not obliterated in the escape battle."

"I believe, after we wipe out a good portion of their ships, this is exactly what they will do. They will sit in orbit around the Earth and wait for us to return. We will return but they will not like it! We will surprise them again. They will try to wipe us out but it will cost them very heavily."

Zadoc says, "Why?" I say, "You must understand that we will build a horde of mini-craft as well as battle cruisers in the caves of Madagascar. This will make The Federation think that spaceships are our main means of surviving!"

I reply, "The mini-craft will truly be the key to our success in defeating The Federation ships as well as be our success in defeating this madness to destroy us." Zadoc says, "Just how are you going to build all of this mighty fleet in such short order?"

I answer, "Zadoc, there is one thing, among others, I learned from the Serpentines and it is how to find and burrow down to the multi-veins and pools of natural resources that exist on Earth. They used the local denizens as slaves to help refine these resources but we have learned how to do it by nanotechnology and manufacturing techniques! Caves burrowed into the Earth make a superb stealth operation possible!"

Zadoc says, "I suppose that I will be surprised by your conclusion!" I say, "Yes, you will be surprised at what happens."

Zadoc says, "I am surprised at all times by what you do! This scenario sounds like a novel and you are the author. What happens?" I smile and say, "You must read the book to find out." He says, "What book?" I reply, "The book of life."

Zadoc says, "Achilles, you do not know what will happen do you?" I smile. He says, "You exacerbate me!"

I say, "Have you ever had a dull day with me around?" He replies, "I would like to have some halcyon days, Achilles, just to be able to smell the roses. When, during all of this fun, do you intend to deliver the scriptures and who in hell will be able to read them?"

I reply, "Vera and her fellow priests have translated it into the language of those inhabiting Tibet. I will deliver the original and the translation to them before the flood."

Zadoc says, "This is astonishing, incredible and unbelievable! The weird thing is that I believe you. I think that I will visit my psychologist!"

I smile and reply, "I will contact you from my craft after the final battle. The Federation will be gone. I will bid them farewell." He says, "There are too many holes in your précis." I say, "You have a better plan?" He answers, "No."

I continue, "You are not expected to read the ending first for Heaven's Sake, Zadoc! It spoils the thrill of reading the book."

He says, "What damn book? Please do not answer. The question is rhetorical. I know what you are going to say!" We both laugh.

Zadoc looks at his timepiece and says, "We are late again, Achilles. May the forces and shield of God be with you during the coming events! We need all of the help that we can get!"

He continues, "I will call Pallas and tell her that we are on our way." The big party celebrating the Union is now!

As I arrive Ashley says, "I knew that you would need to have your formal attire ready for you and you should be ready in ten minutes! Our children are ready. Mercury's son, Hermes, will introduce each guest as they arrive and I hope that you remember what I wrote down for you to review about each guest."

I say, "That was a book and you are expecting me to remember all of the names and something personal about each one of them?"

She says, "You are leading the Union Fleet! Each one of them has a heart and soul and they want to have the dignity to be remembered." I say, "Ouch!"

She reminds me, "This special Wedding Party Reception Dinner will be spectacular and you must do your part to help make it so. Chairman Nebo and Chairman Odysseus will be present." I look at her in amazement and say, "Hermes' list better be very accurate!" Ashley smiles at me.

We leave our quarters and enter the reception hall. The Tyler taps the floor with his Caduceus and guests come into the hall from the balcony parlor where they have already been served cocktails and been entertained by a trio from the Academy of Arts.

All had to be present before they could start down the stairs and be formally introduced to the Host and Hostess.

Zadoc was the last to arrive and Pallas was not pleased. With help from Hermes and Ashley I manage to do my duty.

The Tyler announces each guest in the proper diplomatic order as they descend the steps from the balcony parlor to the reception hall. The women look smashing and the men, while appreciating the beauty of the women, wonder why they have to put up with all of this pomp and circumstance. There is something in the human race that secretly adores all of this formality. I wonder why.

Dinner is served. The background is filled by soothing music. Ashley had put Athena in charge of it. Athena will sing a final solo. She will dedicate it to her husband-to-be and to Avatar her mentor and comforter.

She spent many happy hours with her "Granddaddy." She was always terrified that I would be killed. I always told her that the Holy Spirit was with me and that I would always come home to her.

I have always assured her that I love her, Ashley, and her brothers. Avatar told her that I have a very important job to do beyond the interests of the Union and that I would accomplish it. I told her that we all have a destiny to fulfill and that we must, for the good of our soul, do what we know deep in our heart must be done.

I knew damn well that this dinner was going to be a dyspeptic one! The head table consisted of the co-hostesses consisting of the mothers of the brides and their spouses.

This would have been great except, for protocol purposes, the Chairmen and wives are included. All started well and all guests are mellow as they are bathed in the background music, enjoying the appetizers of a seven course meal and having wine appropriate to the food being consumed.

Nebo and Odysseus flank Ashley Anne. Across the rectangular table I am flanked by Evelyn (I pray that our plan to save her works), and Aphrodite, Odysseus' wife, who is indeed a beautiful woman with auburn hair, high cheekbones, a full mouth, slightly slanted green eyes with an olive complexion and an hourglass figure. She has reared two boys and two girls. All of her children are professors at the Atlantis University. Nebo is staring at Ashley with the look of lust that I detest.

Nebo says, "I noticed that you and Zadoc were very late arriving this evening even though neither of you were involved with the planning of this great and massive event."

He continues, "Two Admirals who control the military might of the Union are together all afternoon after sending our key Commanders on a short but well-deserved leave. Is there something that you are planning that we Chairmen ought to know about?" I just look at him.

He persists, "You realize that the Union Board must be informed of any actions that you two might make! I notice that you were in a complete dark-out during this period."

I say, "The Board, as you know, is already knowledge-able concerning our overall plan. We are right on schedule. The timing of some of our actions must be kept a top secret or we will lose our warriors needlessly."

Nebo replies, "If we play our cards correctly I believe that we can get Arkite to surrender to Gogania without further bloodshed. For your own safety, I suggest that you take no more overt or covert actions without clearing it with me."

He warns, "Further, I will not support your building an escape fleet to avoid a disastrous flood that will never happen."

I reply, "I find it strange that you take umbrage that I take the precaution to have some personal and confidential discussions with Admiral Zadoc. We talk about some very sensitive matters both national and personal."

He fires an immediate answer, "Everything that you do concerns me." I say, "I must remind you that the Board has approved our plan to build escape ships."

He replies, "You are being very foolish. Escape ships have no chance of survival if, as you say, some cockama-mie group such as The Federation exists at all." I reply, "I am surprised by you, Chairman Nebo, for during this con-versation you have broken all codes of ethics and law by discussing top secret information."

He says, "It is my right as Chairman." I reply, "It is not your right to jeopardize our Union!" I stare at him as does the whole table. I can see his mind working. He grabs the arms of the chair to rise and walk out in a huff but he re-laxes his grip for this is not the time for him to play out his political theatrics.

He instead says, "I agree that this is neither the time nor the occasion to discuss these matters." Aphrodite says, "I understand that Athena will sing the final solo tonight, Achilles. Is this so?" I smile at her and through our eye contact tell her that I appreciate her help.

I say, "She will sing and I believe that there will not be a dry eye in the room after her aria." The room relaxes and the remainder of the dinner progresses smoothly. Athena does sing and there is not a dry eye in the room.

The next four days are a blur of activities. The days are filled with lunches, bachelor and bachelor girl's parties, matriarch and paterfamilias get-together functions, sports events, air shows, festivals, beach parties, volley ball events matching family against family, swimming pool parties, barbeques, evening entertainment and dancing and finally the rehearsal dinner.

Isaac's security group is a frazzle and only a few incidents have occurred. It is rehearsal time! It takes all afternoon trying to get three brides to the altar simultaneously. This is proving to be very difficult but all participants are in a great cooperative mood so getting it right is finally achieved.

There are three isles leading to the central altar and each side of the triangular altar is identical. It is much like a Triangular Ziggurat. The high priest and wedding party will stand on top. Fantastic! The rehearsal dinner went beautifully and all had enough to drink and eat. The orchestra played soothing music and all involved are in good spirits.

Even Nebo is enjoying himself. He remarks to Evelyn, "We must remember this entire event as the paradigm event. I want all of this on hologram so our people will know what civilized people do. Arkite must become aware of etiquette and ethics! Eric is lost. He will never understand."

I muse, "Even the evil ones understand that two factors must be in place to retain power. Etiquette is the respect for each other and ethics is the glue that keeps people together. What an interesting dichotomy of thoughts must be running through his destructive mind. Loyalty is the key to success! Machiavellianism is not!"

All self-impressed despots feel that people must be loyal to them and obey them even though the reverse is not true. For them the end is their god. The end is absolute power! The manifesto of humanism is that all people must be subservient to the government for the good of all!

This concept is destructive beyond belief. Nebo must not realize that his conversation has exposed his plans to take control of the Union.

What a plan Nebo has. Eric is a fugitive who has been sentenced to life in prison, Arkite is obviously running things and Nebo has agreements that will make him Chief of Staff of the Union. As soon as this is so, Arkite will kill Nebo. This is how the dark side works!

The day after the rehearsal dinner is a day of preparation and rest. We all need it! All vestige of hang-over effects and fatigue must be eliminated. Tomorrow we are to witness the event that displays what God, our Creator, has in mind for all of us Earth dwellers.

The union of man and woman into a unit of one who are in charge of running a family is the essence of creation. From each union each participant is dedicated to making their children have a life that is meaningful and secure. From this root will come more families dedicated to our Creator and their fellow human beings. Woe will come to the parents that ruin their offspring. A neglected or abused child is a child living in hell.

Back to the wedding! This wedding will follow a very traditional Pyramid Ritual. The ceremony has two distinct parts: The Betrothal and the Marriage.

Each couple has their own stairway to the apex of the Ziggurat and each walk up the stairs to their space on the triangular flat top simultaneously. As they arrive they all join hands.

While facing East the Betrothal is proclaimed the beginning of the journey together. The High Priest takes the Bride's ring and places it in the Groom's palm. He takes the Groom's ring and places it in the Bride's palm. He blesses the rings. He then asks the Groom to take the blessed Bride's ring and place it on her finger and vice versa. By doing this both Bride and Groom agree to now become one and promise to love each other for the rest of their lives.

The High Priest reminds them that they are now enriched by their avowed union and both are responsible for being true to one another and to the children they produce. He stresses the importance of life.

The couples then join hands and take their first steps as a team together. They walk around the altar three times and stop at the northwest face.

Here the marriage bond is pronounced by the priest. They are reminded that they will face joy, sorrow and harmony together as a team. Their reaction to these events that happen to them will determine their path of life.

They hear the lessons about God and His infinite creation, love, wisdom and power. Their mission of making an imperfect world better is stressed.

They now go around the altar three times and face the southwest altar. Here they share drinking from a common cup to remind them that they will share one another's burdens as well as joys. They will always work together to assure that their actions are beneficial to their family and not harmful to others.

The marriage part of the ceremony ends by facing west. Here the priest reminds the brides and grooms that they will someday review their lives together. The priest tells them that these reflections will be comforting if they have kept their vows and not so comforting if they have not. He wishes them each a long, fruitful, and healthy life together with the umbrella of God protecting them.

He tells them that the reason for the requirement to circle the altar three times for each phase is to remind them that God has three faces. He is The Creator, The Redeemer and The Counselor.

They now all face the east again.

Here all are reminded that resisting the power of evil is mandatory and we all are powerless to fight temptation alone. All need God's help. Our cooperation with others and our love of our life, as that of others, is part of resisting temptation. He blesses each bride and groom.

All grooms and brides kiss and the crowd claps.

The newly married leave and head to the reception hall.

The reception party is filled with holograph experts and three-dimension digital image takers. The reception line is amazingly rapid because by now everybody knows one another and what each one does.

I think about the future. Ashley Anne will soon retire and give the world her best performance in the newly completed and expansive University Auditorium for the Arts. Symphony, opera, play, ballet, choreography, art, and religion are combined into one emotional production.

The show will start with a lunch done by Antion and his family, who will do all the catering, followed by a break for high tea, followed by a break for a formal dinner, followed by a dessert break. During all of the breaks the symphonic unit and choir will play classical and religious presentations.

All guests will be accommodated in the newly completed, lush and spacious dormitory suites. I feel that something will happen soon that will shape all of our futures. I do not think that I am going to like it!

The reception is still filled with people when the sun is rising on a new day. The newly wedded youngsters departed for their honeymoons several hours ago but nobody wanted to return to their quarters.

Somehow, I feel that all are aware that there is much trouble for our civilization ahead and everybody wanted to linger in the aurora of warmth in the surrounding atmosphere.

As Ashley and I snuggle into bed she looks into my eyes and says, "Sweetheart, you will be leaving on your mission this very afternoon. Is this the beginning of the end?"

"What fate is in store for our forthcoming son Arphaxad? I am afraid for all of us." I reply, "I am afraid also but I do know that the scriptures will be delivered, our unborn son will be safe and our family will be here to help start a new world."

She says, "Must you always return to battle the Serpentines?" I warn, "We must have the factories in Madagascar. I have a feeling that this factory has fallen out of our hands without our knowing it. We are up against very evil and very intelligent people without a moral base."

I continue, "I have this recurring dream of a dim red light shining over my head. I am afraid of losing God. You know that the light that shines over the pure is very bright with a blue hue. The energy of the evil ones loses this brightness and all they can do is to become energy stealers but no matter how much they steal light from others their light continues to decay until it is a very, very dim red glow. If there is no reformation the glow disappears and a soul enters the bottomless pit."

I look at Ashley and say, "Don't let this happen to me." She kisses me tenderly, strokes my cheek and says, "As long as I exist you will exist, Sweetheart, do what you think God wants you to do. He gave us life in this world for a reason. He will help us reach our karma."

She continues, "Our people made trouble for themselves by their decisions not to behave. We who believe must try to make the world a little better for all. Each one of us has a mission, no matter how small it is, to contribute to this goal. No matter what station in life that we have God expects us to achieve and will help us achieve."

She pronounces, "All we need to do is to ask. We can make the world around us better. Your mission is bigger than most missions. Be sure you do what you must do." We cuddle. We fall into a very deep sleep.

It is about three o'clock p.m. the next day and Ashley and I say farewell to Antion and a few guests that are leaving at the same time.

We get into our air car and head toward Atlantis. On the way we stop at the University. Soon thereafter it would appear to all that Ashley and I left for our home but I am headed for the laboratory where seven people are waiting for me. Hector died a hero in our first battle and I shot

Judas at the finish line of Orion's race. There are five very secret stealth attack craft waiting for us to man so that we can accomplish our mission.

Madeline has replaced Hector but will not fly with us. Peter, Karl, Isaac, Elemas (replacement for Judas), Theudas and I will fly the mission. Madeline will man the sole communications center between us and Zadoc. Nobody else will be able to see or communicate with us.

I pray, "May you, God, ruler of the Force of the Universe, be with us! This mission must not fail! If we do, the Serpentines will rule, we are doomed and the scriptures will not be delivered."

I can hear Pete's voice ringing in my ear as we approach Madagascar, "This caper takes the cake as the worst ever!" I love Peter for his belief in God and me. I ask much of him and he delivers!

We know that the communications system in Madagascar is connected to Arkite's main control room. We must put a communications shield over Madagascar. This plan must work! Pete says, "Again, Achilles, this is a cockamamie plan but this is not just a cockamamie plan. It is one that cannot work!"

I answer, "Yea, though I enter the Valley of the Shadow of Death I will fear no evil because Thy rod and Thy staff they comfort me." He said, "My God, you have really lost your marbles! You are playing with a half a bag! I have less sense than that because I always follow you!" I say, "Fear not for He is with us!" Pete says, "We are all a bunch of idiots!"

Still, Pete and our people follow us. Soon the time has come. I say, "Gentlemen, station the drones. The drones are stationed." I say, "Spread our communications shield totally around us and the Madagascar complex." They do. I pray. We enter the Serpentine communication projection area, shield it and place it within our communicator dish. We then start to broadcast with the synthesized voice of Arkite that says, "This is Command Central calling." I send the Serpentine top-secret code signal.

I continue, "This is the greatest day for us. I have signed a peace treaty with Chairman Nebo. We are now the Union of Nations. This is known to no one except you loyal and brave soldiers. All that is left is to destroy all Magoganian defenses this very night."

I issue more information, "The Madagascar Group will fly to Riyadh, Africa, following the 45th longitude, to the Tropic of Cancer and meet the South Pole units that will be there at the same time! Land and communicate with one another in the staging area so that we will fly as one overwhelming force! From there we will all fly the Great Circle Route to Atlantis and destroy it and take over Magogania."

His synthesized voice says, "All must fly silently and swiftly to our assembly area! I have arranged it so that you will not be detected. Do not fail! Our cause is right!" The assurance code is used and returned.

Now we wait. I hate waiting. I feel helpless. Nothing is happening! Anxiety invading my mind! Now what? I am about to give up and go home when openings are spewing forth fighters and troop ships swarm over us! They head toward Riyadh! This is a welcome sight and a repeat of our last caper.

I cannot believe it! Our stealth systems are working! They form into a gigantic formation. There are well over 1,200 craft! This is impossible! I am stunned. They are also coming out of the caves underneath us! We record the location of each of the holes.

The controls are set in our gas-spreading drones so each entrance is covered and each vein is filled with enough gas to spread to each empty hangar space. Gas must spread into the very guts of the cave systems. We cannot move until the Serpentine formation is well on its way.

I pray that Zadoc has a chance to destroy them! I am in shock. I would never have done such a thing had I known that Madagascar was again such a major Serpentine factory! My monitors tell me that the Southern Serpentine Group is also on course.

We keep the communications shield in place and proceed as planned. Although the plan follows Arkite's plans that we were given by our mole, there is a slight difference. Arkite is very sharp and will discover the imperfection soon!

So far all looks normal if our intelligence about the attack is correct. There is nothing in this world better than good intelligence! Perspiration is literally pouring out of my hands and body.

We cannot make a move of any kind until the ancient anti-meteorite system and Zadoc do their thing. I was totally wrong about Madagascar! Not only have our original holding force people been captured or killed but the damn Serpentines have been building an armada in there! We have damn little time to take command of a complex that I thought was much smaller! It is truly gigantic. How could I have been so wrong?

The Serpentines have not only retaken Madagascar but they did it without me realizing the depth of the problem! I wait as long as I dare before invading the complex! I now say, "Send our troops with gas protection breathing devices into the huge labyrinth to establish a communications link with the center in the South Pole!"

Theudas, my faithful stealth expert, is amazing. One would think that they were the true Serpentine communicators in the center. We pick up the communications without a hitch. Only a few questions are asked. There does not seem to be any Serpentine alert that something is wrong. Our communications and stealth shield that is spread over our force located outside the factory complex is working! The Serpentine Fleet appears to be following our instructions. How long? My thoughts are interrupted.

Theudas says, "Admiral, I do not know how we succeeded with this second try to fool the Serpentines but right now, if something does not happen in the next few seconds, we are done! The communications coming out of Arkite's ship tells me he is beginning to become aware that not all is right."

I say, "How long have we got?" He replies, "Admiral, it is over now!" Suddenly our screens show that a humongous display of missile explosions are decimating the Serpentines. The explosions are enormous!

Theudas says, "Admiral, the Serpentine Fleet has been virtually destroyed. Admiral Zadoc set off the trap seconds before the Serpentine Fleet was starting to change its course. Arkite has now ordered a full attack on our position here in Madagascar using his remnant ships that escaped from our trap and a full reserve force is leaving the South Pole."

I say, "Man the battle stations!" The first Serpentine wave hits us sooner than I expected. Our stealth cursers are low to the ground and form an outer ring around the main entrances. My God! I have never seen anything like it! The Serpentine fighters are again like insane hornets. There is nothing but explosions all over the sky.

They still cannot see us and are attacking their own by mistake because it looks as though some of their own Serpentine craft are shooting at them. They regroup and attack again and again. Finally, there is a lull. Obviously, Arkite is changing his tactics. I ask the question that I did not want to ask, "How long can we hold on?"

The answer is quick, "We have plenty of power because of the power barges you brought with you. Zadoc's force is on the way! Our casualties are heavy." I hear Arkite addressing us, "Surrender now because you are defeated this time, Achilles, you low-grade bastard. Take your poison pill now or you will all die by torture you cannot imagine! I know that your pathetic force is meager and we will crush it like bugs in a nest!"

I reply, "Why don't you surrender while you still have ships?" He replies, "You arrogant bastard, die!" They charge again. We are repulsing them but our force has dwindled in firepower because of severe battle damage.

Theudas from the communications center in the cave says, "Admiral, Zadoc's force is approaching quickly and I advise you to guide them. We put up a shield of fire power with what we had left of our fighting equipment around Arkite as he approaches us."

Finally, Zadoc's force engages Arkite's force. We take some more severe damage before we see that the remnant and reinforced Serpentine Fleet is being decimated. Arkite orders a retreat toward the South and leaves with his battered force. We cheer! It is over!

The Union construction and building units will soon be on their way. We will build our escape units. All of us are exhausted. All of our craft that have survived are now useless as fighting machines. The loss of life is heavy.

I look at Pete and say, "Man's greed and lust for power are man's worst enemy. We are all created with equal love and given the freedom to choose our own destiny. The dark side road is very tempting and man's ego tempts him to travel on it. Man's greatest challenge is to learn humility."

I admonish, "Total freedom brings with it total responsibility. We can cooperate with God or we can rebel. Our fate is good by following God's Spiral Code or evil if we do not." Pete looks at me and says, "Achilles, are we going to see a new beginning and a new bright dawn for humanity after the tsunamis?"

I reply, "The forces of evil are great but the pure will survive. We must fight for it! God will see to it that we win, if we fight for right."

I continue, "Appeasement is the surest thing to disaster. Evil only understands power because they lust for it as their god. True power is freely given to those who believe in God and are willing to do His will. The ultimate fate of evil is to be the ruler of nothing because nothing is what evil creates and deserves."

I say, "We were given this victory so we could complete our karmas. This is almost an exact repeat of our last victory. The odds were great! It was almost impossible that it would work again but it did! There is more to what happens around us than meets the eye. Madagascar is under our control."

We weary, exhausted battle warriors leave for home and rest and we will rest for several days.

We arrive at Roland's house and are ushered to our individual rooms. There are the usual helpers, dressing rooms, showers and the attire we were to wear at the victory celebration at the Grand Reception Hall. All of the women, as usual, look stunning in their latest-style gowns. We all enter the air limousine and we are taken to the victory reception.

I ponder, "We had heavy casualties. There is no celebration in so very many households and their pain is so very great! We will make speeches and we will see to it that the young become educated and their households will have enough money to survive but will we, as a country, really appreciate the sacrifice! Will we give the families and the young the atmosphere of being free to accomplish their karmas and pursue happiness or will we rip it away by big government which is the death knell of any society. Big government blocks freedom and is the gateway to hell."

During the cocktail hour I ask Vera where the records and scriptures are kept that describe the Great Revolution. She says that she has preserved all of the scriptural manuscripts and has them in very safe containers that are fireproof and waterproof.

I have a hunch that these will become the source material for the chosen race to follow as they search for the ultimate truths.

Ashley comes over to remind me that it is toasting time and that dinner is ready. I toast the Champion Captains and their crews for their skill and bravery, preserving the Union, and toast to all people that were involved in the myriad of details required for victory.

Dinner as usual is superb and consists of every food imaginable. Wine flows freely. The dessert is my favorite and is a chocolate variety of tasty cakes.

Ashley discusses her last dancing tour. After this she intends to spend all of her time with Athena who will continue performing and let her take control of the business of running the Dancing Academy. Sharon will remain Ashley's business partner.

Alcestis is full of personality, is able to capture the attention of her dinner mates, and captures the hearts of all the dignitaries. Orion is engaged in some deep philosophical discussions.

The next morning at breakfast I note that all the women are humming and chatting quite happily with harmony filling the air . . . so are we men!

Vera asks that Orion and I come to see her at her study in the Pyramid later in the day. She plans to have a small dinner at Granddaddy's (Roland wants our children to call him Granddaddy). Orion complies but wonders why Roland likes that title.

Orion had mentioned to me and also to Vera that Noah truly has psychic powers. This makes him different from the others and, as expected, subjected him to taunting and distrust. Noah is from a different mold from the crowd around him. He believes in the Creator and prays to Him. Noah has not been infected by the worship of idols and big government.

Orion has found by his studies that the people in Noah's region of the world were blessed with long life. The length of their lives are somewhat exaggerated but nonetheless they live very long lives. It appears that when our insurrection at Eden failed a group of workers settled in this region and commingled with the undeveloped. Their diets, exercise, cleanliness and work habits as well as genetic medicines made their impacts. I muse, "Noah means one who wanders. Maybe it is quite appropriate for him to float around in a rudderless boat."

We go into a lengthy discussion of life after the flood. Orion loves to play the "what if" game, which he has learned to execute at the University. Orion suggests that after the flood we must build our centers of learning, establish a common language and preserve the God-based Rules of Nature. He says that this must be done quickly so that our progeny will follow the right paths be to educated properly.

He also agrees that in two to three generations the level of education could dwindle to the level of the undeveloped people.

Sufficient supplies to sustain the Ark dwellers during the flood are on board. The ability of the passengers to adjust to being at sea will be critical. He calculates that sea life could stay in orbit about a year. This should allow us to land in some high regions and start growing food from seeds.

We will freeze animal and fowl embryos for growth in our laboratories after landing. We must use hearty animals that can live in high mountains.

We decide that the high mountains will be the best bet for a safe landing. I say, "If that probe we found is feeding information to The Federation they might now be plotting how to destroy the whole lot of us."

Everybody looks at me. I explain that this is not going to happen. "Stealth submarines are being built in deep and secret caves. These submarines can be hidden in the deep trenches as they wait for their journey to dry land that will appear after the tsunamis have wreaked their havoc."

I further state, "Our Space Armada, consisting of a mass of decoy battle craft, that give the impression that they are loaded with people as they leave the Earth in all directions, will be a match for The Federation."

"The Federation will have a surprising battle on their hands and, I am sure, will decide that it is prudent to let the bulk of our ships zoom into space. They know that we must come back or perish! I do not know how many Space Craft can survive the flight out but those that do will have a real problem when they return to Earth."

Vera says, "I will go along with this philosophy but you have not resolved the problem of the scriptures." I reply, "You are correct. We must deliver them to Tibet just before the Great Flood hits the Earth and do this in great secrecy." Vera nods. She then tells us not to forget the plan to pick our crew and passengers for each craft very carefully.

I say, "That is the simplest problem of all! Everybody will have a chance to survive in their own mini-craft. Passengers on the submarines and the crew on the spaceships are the tough decisions." Orion agrees and looks pensive.

Vera looks at us and says something very strange. She tells us to be sure Noah knows exactly where the scriptures are hidden. I look at Orion and tell him to make it so.

He replies, "Where are they hidden?" I reply, "I don't know." Orion answers, "Then how am I supposed to tell Noah where they are?" We both look at Vera. She says, "As soon as you know." I reply, "This is damn confusing and you know it!" She never even cracks a smile.

I tell Orion about my conversations with Noah and about my warning him not to drink absinthe because it is deadly. He watched us distill it out of wormwood while we were making additives for the lumber for the Ark. I wish that we had not done that!

However, more importantly, I tell Orion that Noah agrees that one of our submarines can be underneath the Ark with our family as we ride out the tsunami.

I say, "What made you decide on extruding gopher wood!" Orion replies, "Strength and durability were the key needs. It was easy to take high-density polyethylene, process it, mix it with wormwood extracts and other additives and extrude it into lumber. We decided to call it gopher lumber because it is not wood! It will do the job!"

Orion also tells me that Noah's name stands for rest and comfort. I say, "That is interesting. It also stands for being a wanderer. I suspect that both of these attributes are needed for him to complete his karma and I suspect that God expects us to finish the boat he needs on time." Orion says, "Dad, it is finished now except for small alterations."

I ask Orion, "How strong do you think the great boat is?" Orion replies that it is flexible so it will not stress crack and is very resistant to tremendous forces. We decide to furnish Noah with some of our biodegradable plastic sealer and caulking and some molded plastic ribs and beams that he might need. The materials will be stronger and will last for about forty years.

I say, "This deluge will happen shortly. The boat must conform to the exact dimensions Noah has seen in his vision. Orion, be sure that the submarine is secured to the Ark correctly and the connections are secure. Our stability tests on the Ark tell us that the boat will not capsize. I hope that the Noah family is not subject to mal de mer."

I continue, "Be sure you have enough food for all." Orion replies that he is taking animals, hay and dried food. He will supply Noah with dried fruit. Rickets is a tough disease so limes are part of the fare to prevent it. Orion says, "The Ark will be ready on time!"

CHAPTER 6

Storm Clouds: The Dark Side Final Attack

The battered but victorious Union Fleet Ships are all in their hangars and being repaired in our facilities in Atlantis.

We go to Command Headquarters for a meeting but before I proceed to that meeting I see my family that is waiting for me. Orion, a proud battle commander, asks, "Are you going to have an air show as part of the ceremonial festivities for Mom's retirement?"

I answer, "Yes, if Ashley Anne agrees. This is her day, not mine." Orion smiles and says, "Mom called. She saw scenes of our battle and she is upset."

He continues, "She needs a real hug, Dad! She has been through a lot of agony lately." I nod. Orion continues, "However, Dad, Mom is Mom. A hug is not the only reason she wants you home right away. You will be having guests tonight. I am sure you forgot."

I reply, "Thanks. You are correct. I had forgotten. Have Apollo and Argus give me a report about the repairs of what is left of the battle craft. Also, be sure that they don't stretch the truth too much when they tell everybody about our battles!" Athena bursts out in laughter. "Dad, you are impossible. Go to Mom!" She is in the anteroom to the Council Chambers.

Ashley greets me with a very warm, wonderful and passionate kiss. She says, "Why do you insist on giving me so much fright and tension? Even your new son wiggled." I pat her stomach, kiss her again and rush into the Council Chambers.

Ashley shouts, "I will see you tonight at dinner. Try not to be late!" I say, "Is there something that I should pick up on the way home?" Her answer is, "No, but try to be on time!"

The dinner is superb as always and Ashley was scintillating and bewitching.

After our guests had left and we were alone we cuddle in front of the fireplace. I just look at her and say, "It is like being in Heaven when you are close." She snuggles closer to me.

Before we go to sleep I say, "Honey, they want me to fly in an air show exhibition the afternoon of your retirement night. It is your day, not mine. If it will add to the excitement and festivities then I will do it, but if it will distract from the ceremonies I will not."

I continue, "What do you think?" She says, "Darling, it is our day. I will be honored if you could fly and dedicate the exhibition to me. Fly with my scarf on your helmet like you always do." I kiss her very gently and say, "Pick the scarf." She snuggles onto my shoulder again and we fall into a peaceful sleep.

The next morning I ask Professor Meter at the University if he thinks the stationary dirigible air show command center I had built will work. His answer, as some professors do when answering a question, is "One never knows, Admiral, but there is a good possibility."

My whole show depends upon this thing and he will not give me a straight answer! Wonderful!

I better do some more testing! I have the airship taken out of the hangar and put it into its stationary position above the University and have all of the circuits tested. Sure enough, there are some problems to resolve.

I continue to work on this command center until I am satisfied that it will work. It is now fully functional. I call Apollo and Argus, show them all of the instruments, and put them in charge of all air show operations.

We maneuver the dirigible into place over the stadium and lock it into position. It is now late in the afternoon and I am very tired.

I fly, using my safety backpack, over to the Performing Arts Center where Ashley will be presenting her last show as Mistress of the Arts. I am meeting with Isaac at the dressing and preparation rooms under and behind the stage area to ensure that we have everything in order. This area must be secure and safe.

I land at the Performing Arts Center main entrance area and enter but I take, as usual, the short cut route through the hallways that I thought were secure! It is a very convenient route and, assuring myself that I am undetected, I enter the secret door. I go to the corridor that leads to the performer's rooms and the preparation spaces are where actors are to prepare for their entrance on the stage.

Soon I am experiencing deja vu! Something is wrong! I have had two battles for Madagascar, a constant tense situation with Nebo (whose lust for Ashley is insatiable), an unending threat of assassination and now this! Right after entry into the main corridor and just as I am about to make a right angle turn, I am aware of talking ahead of me. I listen.

Nebo is talking with his top aides and lieutenants. He says, "I will have a night with Ashley Anne. I am going crazy for her! She is the sexiest and most beautiful woman I have ever seen. Her dancing excites me to the point of thinking about making love to her on stage! I will make love to her." All of his aides agree that he must have her.

The Chairman continues. "Just think, the bastard, Achilles, has monopolized her too long! He seems to have limitless lives! He has outwitted and outfought the whole bunch of you and your performance up to now is unacceptable."

He continues to berate, "You let our fleet fall into a second trap, similar to the last trap, over the skies in Africa. We were decimated by Zadoc and that damn ancient comet-fighting array, forced to retreat to Madagascar and find that it is under Achilles' control."

He continues "He did this by using six lousy battle cruisers! I watched our newest battle craft fleet become decimated again over Madagascar and then we damn near lost the South Pole Headquarters."

He almost shouts, "This is an unforgivable fiasco! Eric, you damn well better figure how to reverse this trend or you will be killed by him! You blew your last chance! Do not blow another to defeat Achilles!"

He adds, "One more thing, gentlemen, you will, again, see to it that I sit next to Ashley Anne during the ceremonies. You know that I get excited just thinking about her."

They continue to walk down the corridor. I wait until I think they have turned into the next corner toward the exit and then move quickly onward. My heart is again heavy. Eric is here! What dastardly deed is Nebo hatching? Isaac is waiting for me. He too had hidden from Nebo's group. We discuss security measures.

How did they get into the preparation space? We must make some changes! We will be damn sure this time that there will be only one entrance and it will be well guarded.

The night before the final show I have a restful and calm night with Ashley and family. We had a quiet family dinner but Athena is nervous! Helios is nervous! Even Apollo is nervous!

Orion and Alcestis both are superb at trying to calm all of us. I mentioned that we will have very tight security. I did not want to increase the tension by showing how nervous I really am. I say, "I am exhausted. We all need a solid night's sleep." All agree.

Ashley snuggles close to me. I kiss her gently and stroke her hair. I say, "All will go well. I know it. You will be spectacular." She looks up at me and says, "I hope so. I want my last presentation to reflect the great feelings that I have inside for the Creator and my fellow planet dwellers."

She continues, "I want my presentation to be beautiful and emotional." I tell her that it will be.

I say, "It will reflect the love that man and woman have when joined together to mutually accomplish their karmas. I could not accomplish anything without you at my side."

She whispers, "No matter what happens, no matter what travails we may have, I will always be with you and I will give you strength through my love." She falls into a very sound and deep sleep.

The next morning I am off early. Ashley will watch the air show from our box in the stadium. It would be over in plenty of time for her to get prepared for the evening performance.

The day is passing quickly. The dirigible is ready. Good! Our airmen are ready. I check the armament. We never fly unless we are ready for battle.

The Serpentines know it. I do not expect trouble but one never knows. Pete, in charge, will see to it that there are no other aircraft in the area during the show. Somehow, I can feel that there is trouble in the winds. Where will it strike?

All is ready! We enter our aircraft, give the Space Command salute and roar off to the show! We do our usual rolls and spins as we enter through the main performance gate. Then we stop and hover. A little dirigible was launched and went to its assigned space. It makes a vapor cloud. Then its holistic projector sent a holographic movie into the cloud. The loudspeakers on the ground pick up the musical transmission as moving figures are projected onto the cloud.

Our group is introduced and each of us fires a colored vapor into the air as our name is announced. I am blue, Apollo is red and Argus is green.

My image reflects me wearing Ashley's scarf. It appears to be fluttering like a flag from my neck. As I introduce each maneuver, we accomplish it. The sound system is perfect.

We swirl around a large shaft of light that the control dirigible is shining down to Earth. I love the synchronous movement we make as we swirl around the shaft of light. We move up and around each other leaving a faint colored trail behind as we keep time with Ashley's and Athena's singing.

Placing these craft close together as we move up and around to music and to Athena's singing is more difficult than doing battle maneuvers.

We create somewhat of an optical illusion as Ashley's form is dancing around the pole and us as we make our maneuvers. Ashley didn't know that I had her image recorded while she was practicing her dance routines. Our choreography was easy. We just followed the dancing as she had performed her routines.

We end in a finale that covered us with a huge fountain of blue, red and green smoke. We disappear into it. We can hear the crowd as it explodes with applause. They really seemed to enjoy our presentation.

After the air show we meet for a quick midafternoon snack at the Antion Restaurant. We do not eat much because a large post-show banquet has been arranged for us. Ashley makes a toast to us, the pilots. She says, "The show was unbelievable. I know what effort it took and I love you for it. Achilles, my scarf fluttering around your neck showed the world that you are mine. I am so proud. I love you so very much and will forever." The meal is filled with family love and love of friends.

I stand up, wine in hand, and say, "To you my wife, my crutch and my love! To the family we reared, to our new additions, to those about to be added to our family and to our circle of friends. May we have a long life filled with good health, happiness and success; may tonight's presentations be a roaring success and may we remain under the strong shield of our God and Creator."

I chat with Orion and Apollo just before we depart and say, "Don't forget to take your lasers. 'Semper Paratus' (Always be Ready). I'm always a believer in being ready for anything. Remember, this is Ashley's last performance and the place will be jammed with people."

I continue, "If the Serpentines are going to strike, it will be now. I know that we can thwart anything if we are ready."

I see Isaac and Zadoc later in the afternoon. Zadoc says, "Achilles, you are about as nervous as I've ever seen you. All will be well. We have covered all angles. Isaac and I will not be away from Ashley or Athena for even a split second. We came this far with success. We don't intend to fail now!"

I smile, for I know that Isaac will protect Ashley and Athena. Even so, I go to the shooting range to check out the new super coordinated light and power pistol, CLPP, that we developed at the University. Orion, Isaac, Zadoc and Pete have them.

This is new and its existence is secret. These laser pistols are superb and reliable but I decided to recheck them. They are dangerous if not used correctly but their laser will penetrate any present body armor.

I watched my shots shatter a dummy that was completely surrounded by body armor and shatter and blow a hole in a bolted-shut sixteen-inch-thick steel door. This weapon will certainly surprise Serpentine troops. This modified CLPP has performed perfectly. I go home, fully armed, and rest for a few minutes. There is nothing like a nap to refresh a soul, especially an aging one.

Mercury Jr. arrives and takes me and Ashley to the Performing Arts Center Theater. The crowd is immense. The 400,000-capacity theater is full and at least that number of people is in the auxiliary theater next to the Arts Theater. Extra standing room has been made. All are dressed in formal attire.

I thought, *Maybe we are in heaven. Maybe Earth could become a paradise if we followed the basic principles set forth by our Maker. Chairman Nebo isn't too happy about my popularity but he has acquiesced to public pressure or has he?*

He is to be in our box this evening. This is a public acknowledgement of his approval of my new position. The lights dim and the performance starts.

The introductory overture was a new piece never before played in public. It is astoundingly soothing. The melody itself penetrates deeply into the mind and radiates the peace of Heaven to the listener. This set the mood for the remainder of the program. There will be 180 minutes of performance with two intermissions.

The first act depicts the meeting of two young people who fall in love at first sight. They met in a lush green forest called the Magic Forest. The music, dancing and singing are all light, whimsical and appropriate. Ashley is the forest nymph that arranged for the two lovers to meet. Athena is the young girl and Helios is the young man. The dancing of the forest nymphs is beautiful and Athena's voice is astoundingly mystic and captivating as they progress from newly acquainted people to lovers.

After each act people go to the Mezzanine, to the Great Foyer for refreshments or to go to the restrooms. Upon completion of the first act all places fill with people. They are talking with animation and with accolades about Ashley and Athena.

I must admit that I was mesmerized by Ashley's singing. During the times she and Athena sang together Ashley's soprano and Athena's alto blended into a soothing and comforting sound. I didn't realize how good a dancer Athena had become. It is a delight to hear these words from the people in attendance.

The second act is the period of turmoil when the magic forest is invaded by the evil gnomes who did not want to see the young people happy. Their mischief is predictable.

They tell Athena that Helios is unfaithful and produce a young siren whom Mephistopheles introduced to Helios. She lies to others saying that Helios had sex with her. The siren is played by one of Athena's close friends and colleagues. Her voice is perfect for the part. Of course, Athena is brokenhearted and runs away. Helios is beside himself trying to convince Athena that the story is untrue.

I hear even more good words from the people during this break between acts.

The third act is the revelation to Athena that she was told an evil lie. The Forest Nymph with the help from the Light finds Athena and tells her the truth.

Athena runs back to the forest to find Helios but he is gone. She falls down on the grass beside a flowing creek in a flood of tears. The Forest Nymph then finds Helios dejected and at the edge of a cliff just looking down into the valley.

The Forest Nymph advises him to return to the forest where he will find Athena. The story is capped by a spectacular marriage where all voices and dancers blend together and the curtain drops.

There is not a sound from the audience but I can see tears in several women's eyes. I wait. Suddenly, a pandemonium of clapping and cheers explodes from the audience. Everyone is standing and cheering. They will not stop.

The curtain rises again with Ashley standing in front of the whole troop of performers, musicians, stage hands, light technicians and a host of other participants. The cheering for more continues. Finally, Ashley announces that they will repeat the wedding song. The crowd cheers because nobody wants the performance to end. They recall the cast for four encores of the final marriage song.

The next part of the program is always a delight for the crowd and me. The cast will change into black and white formal attire and return to the stage to sing the Pyramid Anthem.

The Anthem is about the final victory of light over the dark side blackness. While the group is singing its story, a holographic projection shows God giving us light and only asking that we love one another as ourselves. He has given us the freedom to choose.

Both of these elements are essential for the continuance of creation. The danger for each soul is that we do have total freedom.

The projector goes out and the singers sing in the dark to show that if a soul follows this path long enough the soul will enter the place of no light and the soul controls nothing but darkness and it ceases to exist.

The stage then relights and all are flooded with a bright blue light that is the gift of God for those who were faithful to God. This music is soothing, melodious and comforting. One can feel the total peace of God for those who love Him and obey His simple laws. One can feel the wonders and the joy of those working with God.

We are in the school of Earth to learn this lesson. Therefore, we have good and evil with us. The Anthem, of course, tells us to choose God's light!

The singing of the Anthem is over. The crowd is quiet. Suddenly, the stage lights flood the stage. Ashley announces to the crowd that this will be her last appearance.

The crowd is silent. Although everybody knows this I can see disbelief in their eyes. She continues by telling them that Athena and Helios will be taking over the stage.

She will be their consultant. She then says that she would be very busy for a while tending to her new son, who would arrive in about two and a half months. The crowd sits in silence then breaks into a thunderous applause.

Ashley disappears behind the curtain so she could meet with all of the cast and workers as they refresh themselves and prepare for the cast party. I am certainly looking forward to that function. It is the cast's night! The whole cast rightly deserves this celebration.

I am sitting and chatting to my family. Chairman Nebo is not around but I am talking with his wife Elaine. I wonder, "Where is Nebo?" The whole place is buzzing with chatter.

Suddenly, I can clearly hear Ashley's voice ringing in my head. It is a cry for help! I bolt from my seat that is, one second later, disintegrated by a triangle of focused laser beams. I shout to Orion and Apollo to take charge of the people in our box. We are under attack!

Orion and Apollo, I learned later, did a magnificent job of directing our security forces and obliterated the attacking Serpentines.

Meanwhile, I am running with all my might down to the secret tunnel. Her voice, rebounding in my head has saved my life!

As I come toward the door I find that it is bolted shut. My super CLPP obliterates the door.

As I enter the corridor I send the emergency signal to the Hospital at the University. Medical help will be here within minutes. That scream told me that trouble was at hand.

Just as I enter the corridor leading to Athena's and then to Ashley's dressing rooms I see a swarm of Serpentine warriors.

I like to attack swarms of enemy soldiers. The arrogant bastards thought they would drop me instantly.

The shock showed on their faces as I shattered their body and protector armor with my super laser. I burst around the corner and blasted ten more before they knew what hit them. The remainder started running. I kill them also.

I look on the floor in front of Athena's dressing room. There are three Serpentines over Isaac. I blow them apart. They fall. I turn ill. Isaac is lying there badly wounded.

They had tortured him by breaking each limb before they were going to kill him. They are part of another swarm. I kill them also. I see that there are now no Serpentines in the corridors. I blast Athena's closed door open and instantly kill all of the Serpentines inside. Eric's two sons are there.

One was about to enter Athena's body which he had stripped and the other was just about to stab Helios. I kill both instantly. I tell Helios to grab a laser from one of the dead sons and protect Athena.

I rush to Ashley's room, blast the door open and see the same sickening scene. I kill eight Serpentines surrounding the rape scene, laughing. None of them, obviously, were expecting me or a super laser.

They are all wearing armor and are armed. All die with a shocked look. I'm sure they thought I was dead. I see that Zadoc has been badly wounded. I suspect that the Serpentines wanted to torture him before taking his life. This is typical of the dark side.

Apparently, the Serpentines had entered the corridor through the so-called secret door into the dressing room corridor thereby bypassing our security system. Two men are preparing to rape Ashley. They all have protective armor.

I kill Eric's third son who is watching his father and Nebo preparing to rape Ashley. They have beaten her badly. I smash the end of my hand down on Eric's neck. I hear his neck break. I jerk him up and smash his throat. Blood gushes out. I know he will die.

I blow Nebo's head off and to be sure that Eric is dead I also blow his head off.

I look down at Ashley and let out a bloodcurdling scream, "Noooooo! My God! They have beaten my wife, my love, my life." I bend over her. The bottom part of her body is bloody.I hold Ashley in my arms rocking back and forth.

She looks up at me and says very weakly, "It hurts so much!

"Hold me. I'm cold. I can feel your flood of tears." I feel a hand on my shoulder. It is Dr. Abaris. He says, "Listen to me! Please listen! We don't have much time! Ashley is alive and I detect that your unborn son is alive. Time is of essence! Do exactly what I tell you to do and do it now! Do you understand?"

I nod. He continues, "Cradle her head in your lap." I do. He says, "Do you see the syringes in the black bag?" I nod but I notice that he has never looked at me. He is very busy saving the life of Arphaxad. He says, "Give Ashley a shot with the red syringe in the right arm. I need to keep her heart beating."

Dr. Zethus is now on scene. He is not only an endocrinologist but a cardiologist. He repeats, "Give Ashley the shot now!" I give Ashley the shot. Abaris says, "We will not be able to move Ashley for several days."

"Ashley needs a network of nanotechnology nets. Give me the black syringe. It contains the nanotechnology netting material." I do.

He says, "Zethus, I need a heart assist machine to ensure her blood pressure remains normal." He now says, "Achilles, you better be damn sure that this place is secure. Your new son is going to be fine."

I reply, "Abaris and Zethus, I have already set up a complete mini-hospital in the submarine that we secretly placed under Noah's Ark. You know a flood is going to happen."

"You and your staff will be on board and be safe there. Let me know when we can make the move." They nod and they know.

Abaris says, "It will be about 10 days before we can even think about moving Ashley from intensive care. We must give her 24-hour attention. We must keep her body in the acute stage of reaction and this is not easy to do. If the body shifts to chronic reaction we are in trouble."

He continues, "She must have rest and lots of it but I do not want to induce a coma. This will be too dangerous at this stage. I want her to be awake for brief periods throughout each day."

Ashley suddenly opens her eyes again and says, "Where is Arphaxad?" I answer, "He is right next to you soundly sleeping. He is in an incubator to help him breathe but he will not need it for long. His lungs are all right but they will need a little assistance for about a week." Ashley smiles and says, "You must promise me that you will protect us and deliver the scriptures. It is your destiny. Promise me." I say, "I will protect you and deliver the scriptures, Sweetheart. Do not worry about that right now."

She says, "Remember that you are now a protector for our people and you must deliver the scriptures so they will be safe! Keep your focus!"

Orion says, "Dad, security is very tight. It appears that there will be no other incidents. You should get some sleep!" I look at both doctors and say, with tears in my eyes, "To thank you is not enough but I thank you both with all of my heart!"

Abaris says, "Stop crying, Achilles, we know what to do. We accept your thanks and we are grateful that we could save Ashley and your son." Zethus nods and adds, "Minerva and our family are grateful that we are being delivered from tyranny."

Abaris continues, "Can you imagine what pressure you have put on us? Please, please try to stay out of trouble! One more session like this and Zethus and I will have dual heart attacks! If that happens, you will not have us around to pull you out of trouble! Now go home, get out of here and get some sleep!"

He orders, "Orion, get this wreck out of here and put him to bed!" Orion puts his hand over my shoulder and says, "Dad, that was a command!" I am on my way but I ask Orion, "What happened to the guests?" He answers, "They proceeded to go to their parties and most of them did not know what had happened. There were rumors that an incident happened at the cast party but nobody knows the details. Most guests are celebrating at the huge reception." I go to bed.

It is late the next day when I feel some kind of consciousness. I see a nurse scurrying around and discover that I have a bunch of wounds. My head is bandaged, my arms are bandaged and my leg wound is killing me with pain.

Soon my children come in. Tears of joy begin to flood and I thank God for helping us survive this horrendous attack. I noted that each child had medical treatment because there are a bunch of bandages on them. They also had experienced fear and pain during the attack.

I say, "Orion and Apollo, I don't know how you handled the situation after I bolted out of the box but you did it effectively and well. The security and medical people were organized and the equipment was there for the doctors. We all have just undergone an abominable experience together."

I say further, "I love all of you, and I thank you and I thank God that it appears that we will all recover. Mom has had the worst of it! What are the latest reports?"

Orion gives the report that all of us will survive without permanent damage. Zadoc, who is now a solid bandage, wants me to report to him as soon as I awaken because our final counterattack must be arranged immediately.

I get up and kiss each of my children and hug all of them. My eyes are flooded with tears. I say, "What time is it?" Athena answers, "It is three-thirty in the afternoon, Daddy."

I say, "You extraordinary children. You have had no rest but, as shaken as you were, you did what had to be done. Thank you."

Athena says, "Dad! That is what a family is all about." I then ask, "Zadoc, how are you and how is Isaac's family?" Zadoc answers, "Beat up but all are here."

Then I ask Apollo, "Son, I know that you took charge of the mopping-up details. I saw you take the Chief Security Manager aside just as I was losing consciousness. Did you get all of the damn assassins?" He answered, "Yes, Dad, and all are dead except three who are willing to give us some very interesting information. The truth serum is working and their information is correct. Nebo signed a treaty with Arkite the night before he came to the final opera presentation. Arkite has assumed control of Gogania!"

He continues, "There was to be a big victory celebration following your assassination and the arrest of your family. We were to be publicly executed!"

He continues, "Zadoc alerted our fleet and a waiting Serpentine occupation fleet was defeated. They were not expecting any resistance."

I say, "Thank you all for your alertness and instant reaction! I thought Nebo would have been more discreet in his actions. The enemy's overconfidence has been our ally. Now we must retake Gogania and the South Pole complex immediately before they regain their full strength."

I take a long shower. It helps me think about our next move. The thought crosses my mind that perhaps The Federation Group may be infected with a dark side virus! Their actions are leading me to think that there may be renegades within The Federation and perhaps the renegades are now part of our enemy's forces!

I have just finished my shower and I am headed for the kitchen. As I enter the door, I see Vera. She has been waiting for me. She looks straight into my eyes and says, "Achilles, I love you as much as I love Ashley Anne and that is with my whole heart but you must stop scaring me to death!"

She continues, "You are going to damn well kill me by heart attack! Why is it that you draw trouble like a magnet? You almost got Ashley and my new grandson killed!" I look at her, hug her, kiss her and say, "Vera, I will try but we are in an awful war. Keep your heart in shape. You are the rock of support we all must have. I love you also with all of my heart and always will."

Vera says, "Why is it, whenever I am about to give up on you, you turn me into mush? I truly must be insane to love you!" I smile and say, "Vera, I seem to do that to lots of people. Thank God!"

I remind Vera, "The end days are coming and we have a task to do together. Stay strong and focused! As you know the high counsel will be meeting tomorrow morning."

I say, "Our agenda includes a strike to wipe out the now combined Goganian and Serpentine forces before they attempt to take total power. We will defeat this unholy union, take charge of our Union and place Odysseus in charge."

I command, "Roland must come out of retirement and assist Odysseus. In order to save the complete collapse of our people, Zadoc and I will present to them the escape plan."

I remind Vera, "We will have a mini-craft capable of space operations for every household in both countries. We will have seven space battleships plus a host of about three thousand drone battleships that will keep The Federation crafts very busy. We will have seven submarines in very safe locations deep inside the deepest trenches in the oceans and one underneath the Ark."

I say, "Hopefully, we will have a large number of our people alive after the comets cause the great floods. This has been top secret. I hope you can see why it was so important to be successful in retaking Madagascar. The caves have hidden our activity. I have reason to believe that The Federation is delighted with our war with Gogania and the Serpentines."

She looks at me as I say, "They believe that we will completely destroy ourselves by civil war. I have made it appear that the caves are radioactive. Professor Metor, as you know, is an expert in particle technology and he has discovered how to do that. Very soon I must announce the fact that we will be hit by comet pieces and assure all of the people that each family will have an escape craft."

I further explain, "The craft will be issued to each family in order by lottery but every family will have their own craft before the floods come. Each family will be issued a destination chart showing the safe areas of the Earth to land to escape the ravages of the tsunamis. I cannot think of a better way. We must have a steady stream of escape craft issued to our citizens in an orderly fashion. We must avoid the chaos that could come rapidly if those waiting get nervous."

Vera says, "Achilles, can we really make this sizeable armada in time? I cannot think of anything better for our people, but you must make fast work of defeating the Gogania/Serpentine Axis by retaking Gogania and defeating Arkite."

I reply, "I think that we can. We have already started several months ago in other captured caves. I very well realize that the plan can go awry at any time. This is why I told Noah that he and our medical group must take care of Arphaxad and Ashley Anne."

I say, "You must be on board with your family also. No one must know. Ashley and I see no alternative. Dr. Abaris will be in charge of the medical knowledge."

I continue, "Noah needs this submarine to assist his Ark to stay upright to survive. Noah said that he will treat Arphaxad as a family member. If necessary Arphaxad will be called one of Shem's six children to keep him from harm. You can see how dangerous this is for all concerned. I am worried about Ashley. Arkite may well try to kidnap her and torture her to death." Vera asks why. I reply, "Because they must think that she knows where the real scriptures are located!"

We present our escape plan to all leaders of the cities, burgs and districts. None of them had a better plan but they all said that I better be successful and damn fast!

This, I find, is very interesting. I really do not know how this war will end. We must have faith in our Creator.

The factories have been going full blast. The time has come for me to attack the Gogania/Serpentine Complex because they are strengthening their positions. They will be unbeatable soon!

Before I realize it, the time has come. It is now the morning of the attack.

As we finish our breakfast and the rest of our family and friends are busy with their new units of family and friends, I look at Ashley and say, "I had the strangest dream last night. As you know, I don't remember dreams usually."

She looks at me with a worried look on her face. I continue, "As you might guess, we have found out that the Serpentines have bribed several of the Pyramid priests to cooperate with them and they have convinced several of our statesmen to do so. We know who they are and we have quietly arrested them. I think we can stop the moles for a while but not for long!"

I continue, "The assassins that we have caught have revealed a lot of very valuable information. They have been very helpful because they are in protective custody and they want a mini-craft for their families!"

I wonder, *Have I been too late for a final strike? I could not do it sooner!*

I say, "My dream revealed how I should attack and use the mini-craft to achieve victory! I know deep inside that it is dangerous and dubious but I have faith that it is the right thing to do. The Counselor, through my subconscious mind, must have triggered this scheme."

She says, "Follow your dream!" She looks at Arphaxad who has been fed and is asleep. She says, "Vera and I will take care of Arphaxad while you are gone. Do not worry."

I continue, "The dream is not over. I am sitting at the Control Center in the lead ship of the strike, filled with anticipation and eagerness. I can hear a cold, heartless laugh like the one I had heard while I was trying to save you from rape. There was someone or something behind me." Ashley asks me, "What did he look like?"

I reply, "He is totally black. I can see as a shadow in a background of dim light. He is completely devoid of light." Ashley says one word, "Lucifer!"

Then she says, "Lead your people out of this cataclysmic mess into a post-flood world with new hope and a new way of life that believes in a loving Creator! This is your destiny! Lucifer is merely trying to frighten you away from your destiny. Do not fail us!"

Her eyes flood with tears. She says, "Go with God! He will be with you."

She continues, "God let you hear the laugh as an omen, Achilles, it was not a dream. Lucifer and the dark side are real! They take pleasure from torment and torture."

"Your destiny is to lead us to the land where we will have a future. Now, go do what you must do! Remember that I will never desert you, never!"

She orders, "Hold me tight but not too tight, please. I still hurt. Do not let evil hurt us again!" I hold her a long, long time. I promise to wear her scarf during the battle.

We attack as planned. My initial movements lead Arkite to assume that I will be using the tried and, until now, successful maneuvers. He thinks that I will engage his craft normally and attempt to stop them from using their air power to defeat our battle craft as we try to free Gogania.

I realize that Arkite has suddenly doubled his air force. He has hidden them from our detection. There must be a huge factory in the South Pole! I can tell from the chatter he is already popping the champagne bottles. He has done that before!

Instead of cloistering my forces to concentrate fire power I split them so that I am amongst his whole fleet. This is suicide! Attacking them individually is suicide! We do not have that many aircraft! Serpentine chatter is jubilant. Arkite has his cannons ready to fire.

They are waiting before firing at us. They want us to be in a totally untenable position! They are visualizing our total demolishment! I have made a very risky and tricky decision!

It is time! I open all of my battle craft ports and each one of these ports spew forth thousands of the individual mini-craft (subsequently, they will eventually be used to save our people) that fly toward each of the Serpentine battleships.

They are like a swarm of angry wasps and the Serpentines are not equipped to destroy them. They clang as they hit the monsters and bore into the hulls. There is mass confusion in Arkite's fleet. Their cannons do not fire at me on time to do serious damage.

Each pilot of the mini-craft has a target. Some drill into the control center rooms, some drill into the power systems rooms, some drill into the combat control systems room, communication center systems room, etc. All vital systems are blown apart by them. Then our battle craft will bore its way out before the Serpentine crews can do anything about it. Our losses are minimal. We blow the remaining and now crippled Serpentine crafts to bits.

Meanwhile, on the ground, the Serpentine defense soldiers are faring no better. Mother ships have spewed about 100,000 angry mini-craft all over the Capital City.

They bore into all of the Serpentine control centers. They relay a signal for all occupation troops to surrender by the order of General Arkite.

Odysseus then comes onto the visual and sound systems throughout all Gogania and announces that he has assumed control of the Union and accepts the Serpentine surrender.

Another false signal using Arkite's voice simulator is sent ordering all Serpentines to report to their local armories. The citizens gladly accept this transmission and start arresting all Serpentines.

They herd them into the armories where our troops are located and disarm them. This battle is over.

Upon landing I am summoned to attend a huge meeting. All leaders and statesmen are in attendance. Odysseus introduces me. There is a thunderous applause. I am still in my flight suit. I approach the podium and ask Odysseus what it is that I am to talk about. He replies, "Achilles, you are our leader. We do not care about the topic. We just want to hear your thoughts and plans in general!"

I look at this mass of leaders and wonder what I should talk about. In my mind I ask God to help me. Silence seems interminable but I suddenly know what to say.

I greet them, "Ladies and gentlemen, our society has just experienced a great victory over terrorists. How did we do this? We did it together! We did it because we battled the enemy with a coordinated plan. Each of our battleships opened our newly installed ports simultaneously and we spewed out our mini-craft that hit the heart of each enemy battle cruiser. They were taken by surprise and they were destroyed.

"We captured the enemy control centers in Gogania by drilling into them. We were a coordinated, smooth-running mass! There is no way we could have manned our mini-craft so effectively without your exceptional efforts."

I continue my speech, "The leaders of our countries long ago instituted a method of successfully living together. It is an unbeatable formula for success. The first ingredient centers on the family as the base of our civilization. There is a mother and a father. We honor our parents and our families. We cooperate with one another and we were willing to fight for our system."

More, "The Creator has given us this baseline. It does not matter if we are rich or poor; all of us are given the opportunity of having a lifetime mate to whom we are devoted. It then becomes our privilege to rear children and be willing to die for them. This is our first responsibility. The universal formula is to rear and educate our children as best we can."

I say, "Secondly, once our progeny pass through the preliminary schools and advanced schools where they learn language, culture, science, mathematics, history, religion and the moral code they will be better fit to face life. The schooling regimen allows youth regardless of sex or social standing to grow and learn about ethics, etiquette, and serving with one another for a common purpose. They will always be free persons in our society who can pursue their talents and enrich others by doing so."

More, "They mature and mix with others, learn discipline and respect for our leaders, and how to work with others to achieve goals. They have been given time to learn to fly, so to speak, by being with others for a common cause."

Still more, "The indoctrination also has other parental requirements. The young must get the boot in the derriere when they are disobedient."

I continue, "I did not like discipline but when I think back I learned self-respect by learning to respect the positions of others."

I say, "Serving your fellow citizens while being educated can be to serve in the military, in fire and rescue units, in medical units, in conservation units, in construction units, in national guard units, in public health units, in disaster control units, in hospital units, in supply units, in logistic units, in transportation units and, of course, in the Space Command units. This does not mean as a life job or permanently. Deciding to make one of these a permanent job or deciding to enter into the world of free markets and industry where the gross product of a nation is determined is their decision."

I caution, "In all cases, we must remember we are to serve our fellow citizens and not the government. Government must serve us, the citizens, or the citizens must throw them out of the government! The government, if not controlled, will always demand that the citizens serve them! They become gods and not servants! We must not allow this to happen!"

I speak more, "All of our reserve units have assisted us in building the mini-craft machines. I thank all of you! Never forget that a dose of faith in our Creator is not only very, very helpful but it is mandatory. It is vital." At this point there is applause. I wait for it to subside.

I say, "This battle should have been the last one for us but it is not. There is a Federation Force that is hell-bent to destroy us. I believe that this group thinks that its job is to disburse us thoroughly so that we will not be able to come together and develop our talents after the catastrophic events that will happen after the comet pieces hit the Earth."

I continue, "I think that they have completely misinterpreted their mission. As far as I am concerned they are a renegade and Serpentine unit."

I verbalize further. "Ladies and gentlemen, we will prevail despite their efforts. Our mini-craft will be all over the globe and they will not be able to find all of us and kill us. As I speak, our factory is completing the manufacturing of enough escape craft for each family. You will have one in time to evade the flood that will be caused by the tremendous tsunamis the comet pieces will cause. We can then decide to come back together and form a nation or not!"

I say, "As you probably know we already have over half of our mini-craft in operation. They won the battle for us. These along with the others coming will be distributed to you."

I continue, "We are distributing the craft by lottery but there will be no family left out. Each one of you will have maps telling you of the relatively safe areas to go to. We will not be in touch with you as the storms rage on Earth but you will have flood-free ground if you go to one of the designated spots." Again, there is applause. I wait.

I am asked a question by a man on the floor. He says, "I am Goganian just as you are. Are we included in the distribution?" I reply, "We did not fight Goganian people. We fought terrorists that took over Gogania and the leaders who joined the terrorists. All citizens of our two nations have now joined together as a Union. We will all have a mini-craft on time to escape the cataclysmic floods."

The meeting is over.

I am drained of energy and I cannot wait to get home and see Ashley. I need to be cuddled! This has been an exhausting but very successful mission.

I stop and talk to dozens of people on my way to the exit where Mercury II is waiting for me. He tells me that the people understand what is happening and are grateful that their leaders are concerned about each one of them. There will be no panic. Mercury II's conversations with all of the other limo drivers confirm it.

Immediately upon entering the limo Mercury tells me that Vera has called me on the communicator. Mercury tells me that the message is extremely important. I call Vera. She says, "Ashley is gone!" I say, "Where?" She says, "Kidnapped!"

Mercury takes me to the Pyramid. I rush to Vera's room in the Pyramid and I am greeted with the report that a Serpentine group had, indeed, kidnapped her.

I shout, "How long ago? Which way did they go? How will we ever find her! They will rape her and kill her! Where is Arphaxad?"

Vera looks at me calmly and says, "Achilles, please stop talking and listen!" I do.

Vera says, "Achilles! Arphaxad is safe! Orion has a rescue craft readied and he is having it modified for battle."

She continues, "The Serpentine craft is being tracked. There is more to this than meets the eye. The Serpentines will not kill Ashley immediately because their main goal is to torture her until she tells them what they want to know about the scriptures and their whereabouts. After she tells them they will then kill her."

Vera continues, "We must rescue her before this happens but there is more for you to know! The Serpentines think that Ashley knows where the scriptures are hidden but she does not know!"

More is coming. "Apollo will fly with you. The rescue craft is equipped to fly in space and reenter the Earth precisely where you want it to. You must listen to Angelica."

I reply, "I do not have time!" Vera says, "She is here and you damn well have time! Arkite's people ordered Angelica killed just as he ordered you killed. She felt that there were awful things about to happen and escaped before the Serpentines could grab her. She went to the Pyramid and to my best friend Regemina who, as you know, is the Head Priestess of the Inner Sanctum."

Vera is not through. "She hid her in the secret room next to the scriptures. The scriptures are no longer there but a good book filled with philosophy is. I moved the scriptures sometime ago because I knew that the renegade priests had found out how to penetrate this area. I believed that they did not know about the secret room. I was wrong. They did."

I was about to say something bur Vera was not yet through. "I told Ashley to talk with Angelica. Angelica is terrified of everybody but wanted to talk to Ashley because she knew that Ashley would do nothing to harm her."

Vera explains, "That is why Ashley and Angelica were in this room together. They heard the Serpentines curse after finding that the scriptures were not there."

They say, "Arkite warned us that the scriptures might not be here and that only three people would know where they are: Vera, Achilles and the bitch, Ashley Anne. Arkite said that he would rape Ashley Anne then torture her until she talked and then he would kill her."

Vera continues, "They also said, 'Our brothers failed to kill Achilles and as a result he has caused us great harm. We must find one of these women or we are in trouble! Let us start by using the secret room that Priest Judas, before he was killed, told us about.'"

Vera has more to say, "They then blew out the door and the Captain said, 'Well, well, look at what we have here! We are all going to be promoted! Kill the bitch Angelica and bind Ashley Anne! We must return to Headquarters at the South Pole now!"

Vera explains, "The Captain hit Angelica in the face several times and threw her at the altar. She fell to the ground and a soldier fired his laser at her. He thought that she had been killed so he immediately ran and joined the rest of the Serpentines."

Vera says, "Fortunately, Angelica was wearing one of your new body armor protectors. That is why I know what happened. Achilles, you have a double-pronged mission and you better not fail! Orion is loading comet-buster bombs into the rescue ship. Your mission is to save your wife and blow the Southern Headquarters to smithereens!"

I say, "This mission is impossible! By the way, who in the hell is the Admiral here!" She responds, "I am, damn it, and you better not fail!" I say, "Well, Admiral, how in the hell do you think I am going to get into that warship? You better have a well-equipped mini-craft in the rescue ship for me to use!"

She smiles and says, "Yes, Sir!" We wait for the word from Orion that all is ready. Angelica has been in the room all of the time we were talking.

I look at Eric's widow. Our eyes meet. I say, "Angelica, you are a very brave person and you have been through hell. Yet, you want to help us. Thank you. You will be safe with Vera and she will be your mentor."

I say, "Upon completion of this mission we must talk about other things but now I need some information from you and I need it immediately. Think very carefully and try to remember what the Serpentines said about the spacecraft they are flying. Did they refer to it as their latest version of a battleship and does it have any initials tied to it such as ND-3."

Angelica thought for a minute or so. It seemed like an eternity. She says, "The kidnappers were boasting about your demise and said that the battle craft they are flying is new and highly secret. It is non-destructible and is the third issue. They may have used the initials ND-3."

I say, "Thank you, Angelica." I say to Vera, who is communicating with Orion over our latest security communication system, "Tell Orion the craft is an ND-3 design and tell him to set the coordinates of the rescue craft to the coordinates we have developed."

I continue, "We believe that these coordinates pinpoint the protective doors that guard the South Pole Supreme

Command Headquarters. I learned this from a drone during the Madagascar campaign."

I step into the elevator that will take me to the rescue craft. Its ballistic path will lead me to the rendezvous spot. The ND-3 has one blind spot and that happens to be right behind the Main Control Room. The Captain's quarters are in the blind spot.

Vera shouts, "God be with you!" I look at my watch; we have exactly three minutes to takeoff time. If I miss it all is lost. The entrance door to the rescue craft hits my derrière as I step into the craft. We are off precisely when we should be.

Apollo and Orion check the details of re-entry. I take a quick nap during our trajectory flight. Apollo, who is now a superb pilot, awakens me. "Dad, it is time to man the mini-craft." I am immediately alert and I man the craft while checking that I have all of the equipment I need.

Apollo says with excitement, "Look at that huge beast, Dad. It is exactly where we thought it would be."

I board the mini-craft and head to the battle beast staying in its blind spot. I make a very soft landing. It is amazing what a rescue craft with mini-craft can do! I proceed to head toward the skin of the battle craft. I am in the Captain's bedroom. I drill myself into the ship. I am surprised because it seems to be a separate and very lavish room.

I am delighted but shocked at what I see. Ashley is there in a bedlike contraption chained to four posts. She is spreadeagled and naked but alive! She looks at me and says, "Thank God you are here! I had almost given up but somehow, my hero, I knew that you would come!"

I get my cutter from the tool belt and within seconds I cut the chains holding her. I throw the blanket, that Vera gave to me at the last second before I left, over Ashley and put her into the mini-craft. We leave the beastly battle craft just as I had entered it.

Meanwhile, Apollo has guided our rescue craft with comet busters into position just as the massive South Pole cover doors are opening. I enter the rescue craft and I note that the South Pole doors suddenly stop opening and start to close rapidly!

However, before they can close the opening, Apollo has guided the missiles past the doors just as they slam shut, smashing the battle cruiser to bits. The comet-buster bombs do their jobs. There is the sound of huge explosions.

By this time my rescue craft is blasting its way into a ballistic orbit. Huge pieces of metal and debris are sailing past us and I am praying that one of them does not hit us.

We are knocked off course by the explosive forces that spew from the South Pole Complex. However, we will be able to set a new course. The explosion is unbelievable. The ice-covered mountain looks like a volcano belching parts of aircraft, buildings and huge rocks and other debris into the air.

Total devastation has occurred! Orion and Apollo are scrambling to adjust the ballistic orbit and get the rescue craft into a safe course. I am fiddling with the communications system and finally manage to get it to function again.

My first words to Mission Control are, "The rescue is a success. Ashley is hurting but alive! I am sure you see the results from the comet-busters' explosions."

"Ashley is semi-conscious and will be in need of Dr. Abaris as soon as we arrive." I have been cuddling Ashley and kissing her. She looks up at me and says, "Don't hug me too tightly, I hurt! Is Arphaxad safe? I love you and I will not leave you. I am going to be all right." I say, "Arphaxad is safe. We both love you and we need you!"

I described the contraption that held Ashley to Orion and he contacted Vulcan and let me talk to him directly.

He says, "Vulcan speaking, Achilles! This machine Ashley was in is a revolting, repulsive, sickening, loathsome and horrible contraption. It is a typical inhumane terrorist thing."

He continues, "I am sure that they would have repeatedly raped Ashley and tortured her beyond belief by stretching her. If she told them where the scriptures are hidden they might have given her a little quicker death. In any case, they would have torn her body into four pieces."

He instructs, "This is why terrorists everywhere and any-where must be defeated! The Dark Side is responsible for such behavior and they revel in horror! People who choose the dark path cause the spread of evil. I can only hope that Arkite was killed during your last attack."

We finally arrive home and Dr. Abaris, with all of the equipment imaginable, gently transfers Ashley onto the hospital bed on the spot. We all wait for him to run his examination. He operates. I note the syringe with the nano-net solution and one with skin glue. He works very quickly. It is over.

He looks me in the eye and says, "If you had been a few minutes later your rescue would have been fatal for Ashley. I have stopped the internal bleeding, her vital signs are good and her recovery will be complete. It will take a few weeks before she will be feeling spry again."

My eyes are filled with tears as I say, "Thank you, Abaris. You did a rescue again and without a heart attack! We will, after all, be playing with our grandkids in the post-war world! You are damn good at your profession!"

He looks at me and says, "Good grief, Achilles! You don't seem to grasp the word stop. Stop means stop! You are making things damn difficult for Ashley and me."

He continues, "Right now, it will be very helpful to her if you come to the hospital, keep her warm and cuddle gently. It is now late at night and we are all tired."

He requests, "Please, Achilles, keep out of trouble for at least a few weeks until Ashley is a little stronger!" I reply to his request, "Yes, Sir!"

I do cuddle with Ashley until she is comfortably sleeping. I fall asleep beside her. The first thing that I notice when I wake up is that I am still next to Ashley and she is snoring. The next thing I see is Abaris. The next thing I notice is that Ashley is stirring.

Nurses bring Arphaxad into the room so Ashley can see him.

Abaris asks me, "Achilles, do you know what time it is?" I reply, "No, Doctor, I have no idea what time it is but I remember that it was about ten p.m. when I fell asleep." He says, "It is two o'clock p.m. the next day. You are in tomorrow. You have been asleep for about 16 hours and the sun is shining brightly. I want both of you to follow me to the examination room."

Ashley and I do as he asks. He says, "I took complete body checks of both of you while you were asleep. Ashley, I cannot believe how resilient you are. Achilles, you have your foot bound, your rotator cup is back in position but your motions will be restricted for a while. I am ordering both of you to complete rest for a week."

He continues, "Since I cannot trust either of you to pay any attention to me and since neither of you need to stay in the hospital I have a caretaker arranged to make you obey me." I blurt out, "Caretaker! You act as if we are kids!" He replies, "Right on!" I say, "Who?" He replies, "There is only one person in the world that can and will control both of you!" I look at the door and say, "Oh, no! You didn't!"

Vera looks at me and says, "Both of you get into the limousine now!" I say, "We are not dressed!" She replies, "Now!" We both do. Why? I do not know why. On the way home Vera says, "Ashley, Angelica wants to see you both tomorrow. She feels that she almost got you killed and she feels guilty."

I say, "Vera, you know that if she had not been in that room and overheard the Serpentines describe the battle craft we might well have been defeated by the Serpentines. The ND-3 is damn near unbeatable. She identified it for us and told us where it was going."

I say, "She also told us that you were very wise to change the location of the scriptures. It seems as though the Serpentines are very fearful that those documents will be read. That is a lot of intelligence to give us. Maybe it was meant to be that we had this data before our rescue battle with the kidnappers."

Vera looks at me and says, "I think so." All the time we are talking I have my arm around Ashley. I kiss her. She falls asleep on my shoulder. Vera is holding Arphaxad.

Vera orders us to go to bed. I say, "I just got up!" She says, "So what! I will wake you when I see fit to do so!"

Both Ashley and I go to the bedroom. Just as I was about to get into bed Vera says, "Achilles, Angelica has been through a living hell. I think it would be nice if we invited her to the annual Group of Seven and Friends meeting. I want her to meet Karl."

I reflect, "Karl is perfect for Angelica. He has been loyal, full of good ideas, one of my early picks for the Gang of Seven, and a great dog trainer! His great loss because of a government-bungled raid that killed his family has made him very quiet and pensive but his heart is good! He and Angelica have a lot in common and they both have experienced family tragedies."

I say, "Vera, you are unbelievable. You are already trying to be a matchmaker!" She replies, "Angelica is a beautiful but mistreated woman. She needs a mate. Karl does too! They belong together." I mutter, "There will never ever be another Vera! The mold was broken after she was created!"

The next morning at breakfast Vera announces that she had asked Angelica to join us for lunch. Ashley and I look at each other. I ask, "Who is serving us lunch?" She says, "Antion is, of course. Who else could do it?" I say, "This is restful?" Vera says, "Of course it is! I do not ever want you to get bored. We have work to do!"

Angelica arrives on time and after our initial greetings she asks if she can see Arphaxad. He seems to be enjoying himself but it is nap-time so he is taken to the nursery.

After serving wine and hors d'oeuvres, Angelica says, "Achilles, I know that you and Ashley are people that have deep faith, care about others, and love your country." I reply, "We have always tried to follow the path that we think God wants us to take."

I continue, "Ashley and I have noted that you have had a very rough road presented to you, yet you always were gracious to those around you. I deeply regret the horror that happened after Ashley's final presentation and I know that it gave you unbelievable pain. I wish that it never happened, but it did."

She says, "I am sure that you and Ashley know that it should never have happened. As you have perceived the result of the assault left me a broken-spirited woman. I have no husband, no children and no future." Her eyes fill with tears. She continues, "Vera has offered to let me work here in the Pyramid. Do you object?" Ashley says, "No."

Angelica continues, "Achilles, you killed my family because they were trying to kill your family. You did what you had to do. I want to tell you my story about Eric and me. Maybe it will help you understand what happened.

"Eric had never been defeated in anything until you, a rebellious upstart, came into his life."

I am remembering when Angelica was the beauty queen of Gogania. She was always in love with the swashbuckling Eric, who, I thought, always treated her poorly.

Angelica continues, "I wanted him so much but he only had eyes for Ashley Anne. I wondered why. I was broken-hearted. Yet, it seemed to me that it was lust for power and not love that drove him to her." She looks at Roland and says, "You were the avenue to power for him. You are a very powerful man."

Angelica adds, "I want all of you to know that I never became a Serpentine, never. It is an ugly religion. I loved Eric because I could see his potential and I loved his smile. He was a very handsome man but he was driven by the lust for power."

She continues, "You, Achilles, defeated him. I think it was meant to be. Vera will verify this if she hasn't told you already. The Eric/Ashley engagement invitations were already at issue when you captured Ashley Anne's heart."

Angelica relates, "He began to despise you. His hate began to consume him. I didn't know he would turn to the dark side when he asked me to marry him. There was no love there. I was pretty and witty and he needed me for social reasons. I loved him so much but he never loved me."

She explains, "The Serpentines gave him an avenue to achieve power and revenge. He eagerly took that route. He made me do things with other men while he satisfied his lust with other women. I need not tell you more. My children, my young sons, were ruined by his philosophies and eagerly followed their father, obviously, into the dark side."

I say, "Angelica, you have been in a living hell for some time. I am sorry!" She says, "I began to pray and pray for deliverance and help. That is when I went to Vera as curator and custodian of the scriptures and the Inner Sanctum."

She continues, "While Eric was feeding his mind with hate and was beating me I tried to inject love. I kept my sanity. I watched him sink further into a hate for you so great that he would do anything to destroy you."

She continues, "I overheard Arkite tell Eric that I was too friendly with Ashley and Vera and that I knew too much. I must be killed. This is when I asked Vera for sanctuary in the Pyramid. I barely escaped being murdered. He sacrificed himself and his sons on the altar of hate."

She explains, "Arkite must have promised Eric great things if he would wipe out your family in the dressing rooms during Ashley's final performance. He knew that by committing these horrible acts all of you would be destroyed."

She verbalizes, "I am glad that I could be of some help to rescue Ashley. I know that Eric's soul was devoid of light as were the souls of my sons."

She then says, "I know that they are at Level Zero, the Dark City, and at the center of this city is the bottomless pit. Souls who are in this situation realize that they have achieved ultimate darkness; they crave it! They have achieved the position of being the king or queen of Darkness!"

She has tears and says, "Here they make the final decision to reject God totally, sacrifice themselves to Satan and they become nothing."

After lunch Angela hugs Vera, Ashley and me. She says, "Achilles, we all have heard about the Group of Seven. Your Group controls the world today."

That remark worries me. What have I become? I say, "They are my close friends who have made it possible for me to do what I have done. I will never forget them. We meet annually for a morning meeting and then have lunch, attend a sports event and have a formal ball at night."

Angela says, "Vera has mentioned that I should attend." I say, "Angela, friends are invited to attend. You have earned the title, friend. Without your support we would not be meeting today. I will be delighted if you will come." She kisses me on the cheek and departs.

I look at Vera and say, "I assume you will take care of introductions?" Vera smiles and says, "I will see to it that she meets Karl." I say, "I suspect that Antion, under your and Ashley's directions, will do what is required."

Vera changes the topic and says, "Achilles, you have scheduled a meeting tomorrow with the Chairman and all ministers!"

I say, "Roland, you talked!" Vera smiles and says, "That is not what Dr. Abaris told you to do. You are supposed to rest!" I reply, "I will. This will be a short meeting because I am very tired and there is so much to do in a short time frame! You and Ashley have already given me two great days of peace and rest."

I continue, "I cherish these days with you. However, the comet pieces are easy to see by telescope. We must be ready. I have heard that Arkite has told all the people that the comet pieces will miss colliding with the Earth and that my calculations are wrong. He is saying that I am using the collision ruse to gain control of the Earth."

On the way to the meeting I muse about my life and how important the Gang of Seven is to me. Karl is Minister of the Interior, Isaac is the Minister of Justice, Theudas is the Minister of Commerce, Elymas is the Minister of Education, Madeline (Hector's wife) is Minister of Transportation, I am the Admiral of the Union, and Pete is the Chief of Staff. Zadoc the Minister of State, Roland (out of retirement), the Minister of Defense, Madeline (who replaced Hector) and Elymas (recently picked to replace Judas) are now members of the Gang of Seven. We are in effect, the oligarchy rulers of the Union. I muse again about my own path, *Quo vadis?*

At the meeting with the Chairmen and ministers we review our evacuation status. We are ahead of schedule. We have one more enemy, the renegade Federation ships.

Fortunately, they appear to have withdrawn from our immediate area and are waiting for the comet pieces to hit Earth.

The Federation will, right after the comets do their thing, be waiting to attack our escape ships. They might think that the armada of battleships they see flying away from Earth contains people and not laser cannons and ammunition. We will give them a fight that they will never forget.

The Federation war craft will be chasing us and might not see, or if they do see them, they will not understand the significance of the little craft that will land all over the globe just before the comet pieces hit Earth. These mini-craft will fly to spots that will be least affected by the tsunamis.

I am positive that, even though survivors know that upon the landing in their new home and upon the grounding of the Ark all survivor leaders are invited to assemble at Mount Olympus to try to assemble a civilization on this mountain.

I feel that many group leaders will settle where they land. They want freedom! I thought that I was giving them freedom! Perhaps I was not! It is their choice. Perhaps oligarchy is not really freedom but the way to forced servitude.

The submarines will be abandoned and destroyed after the rendezvous at Mount Olympus. The plan is fixed. The time is soon. I still wonder, "Where is Arkite? Did he escape the blast? Is he in Gogania?"

However, today is the day of the annual meeting of the Gang of Seven. Vera introduces Angela to Karl and the two spend the day together. It became obvious to all of us as the day progressed that it was love at first sight. Their chemistry together was astounding!

The day has passed and we are now all dressed in our formal attire. It is time for dancing. Karl gets up from his seat, goes behind Angelica and kisses the back of her neck and says, "Pretty Lady, may I have this dance?" She is frozen but he takes her hand and she rises looking into his eyes and says, "Karl, I will be honored to dance with you." The whole room is still.

Karl says, "Maestro, play a waltz, please." Karl has been a very effective minister but a bitter loner for too long. We were all very pleasantly surprised about what we saw happening except Vera. She was elated that her plans worked!

Angelica whispers to him, "I can't dance very well and I am frightened." He smiles and says, "Follow me." She melts into his arms. She is a beautiful dancer and follows Karl's leads perfectly. I can hear the comments from many and suddenly the room is filled with solid applause!

There is an unmistakable buzzing and an expectation in the room. Everybody is talking to each other simultaneously. Karl and Angelica dance over to the microphone. Karl takes it from its stand and says, "Angelica and I would be honored to have all of you dance with us, please." We do.

Karl and Angelica dance over to us. Karl says, "Achilles, it is you we have picked to be our protector. Angelica and I do not know how much longer your battered and scarred soul can protect us but Angelica and I love each other and we thank you for whatever life that we will have on this Earth and on the path of life toward light after this life is over. We know that we will spend eternity together with love!"

My eyes tear. Fortunately, as usual, Vera comes over and says, "Congratulations, Angelica and Karl. Taking and giving love is the greatest gift we can give each other. I am extremely happy for each one of you." They smile.

Vera looks at me and says, "Achilles, you are something else again! You may stumble and get deflected but you will never waiver from the basic path toward the light. Keep your course. We will follow you even though your schemes are frightening at best." I am waiting for the next shoe to drop. I look at Vera. She smiles.

Sure enough, Antion is at the microphone and announces, "Angelica and Karl are now announcing their engagement. Champagne will be served along with the hors d'oeuvres. Dancing will continue for the next 20 minutes. At that time, there will have been an altar erected behind the head table. Karl and Angelica will have the center seats that are now being added to the head table. All guests will keep the seats that they now have. The high priest of the Pyramid, Artemas (defender of children), will perform a marriage ceremony."

Antion continues, "The couple will be brought in by the bridesmaid, Ashley, and the best man, Achilles, who will introduce the couple being married by Artemas."

He now instructs, "The ceremony will then proceed. Following the ceremony dinner will be served and this will be followed by serving a delicious white cake that signifies purity. The couple will then depart for their honeymoon."

I look at Vera and say, "This will be a day in my hopefully eternal life, that I will never, ever forget! How did you ever manage this caper?" She replies, "Never, ever underestimate your mother-in-law." I reply, "I wouldn't dare!" She says, "Good boy!"

Karl and Angelica return from their honeymoon and we are all very busy with our final plans. I ask Vera and Roland over for dinner. They come. After a tasty prime rib dinner and after we put Arphaxad to bed we enjoy after-dinner drinks.

Vera says, "Achilles, you have something in mind. What is it?" I say, "It is now time for two things. I have a strange feeling that we will start having security problems. People are restive."

I continue, "We are now supplying the mini-craft to all of our citizens. They are well supplied with enough to sustain them through the tsunamis and aftermath. If the craft land in the designated areas there will be enough water and natural growth to sustain them. Some are anxious and want to leave now."

I continue, "To do so might well trigger The Federation to return sooner than we have calculated. Loading the submarines will cause resentment because we are loading them with knowledge, books, machinery, and copies of the scriptures and the cubes of knowledge. This knowledge will allow us to understand the basic facts and laws of nature. If the concepts are understood a complicated society will be able to survive."

I lecture, "We must show them the basic truth that God exists and His code must be followed for any civilization to be successful. He loves us and tells us to follow His simple rules of living. Without these rules in place we cannot and will not live together in harmony."

I explain, "We have the knowledge to manufacture anything using nano-based factories and very soon after landing we can move forward with dignity. Will we?"

I warn, "The people on the submarines are the leaders with experience, knowledge and ability to build the infrastructure we need. Will we cooperate and make it so or will we fail? Resentment, impatience and jealousy make an explosive mixture."

I say, "It is time for me to take Ashley Anne, Arphaxad and Roland to the submarine under the Ark. Vera, it is vital that you and I remain back until we deliver the scriptures to the proper monks in the Himalayan Mountains. We will be exposed to danger and I would be a fool not to say so."

I suggest, "The renegade priests will try to stop us, kill us and destroy the scriptures. God better be with us, Vera.

Only you know where the scriptures are and the people who must receive them. We must be sure the scriptures are in the right hands."

Vera says, "Some days you show a spark of brilliance! I will set a time for you to meet me at the Pyramid." I do not reply. I pray.

We meet at the Pyramid. Vera says, "The scriptures are not hidden where I told you and Ashley they were hidden. I made a trial run with worthless writings and hid them under the stairs where I told you they would be hidden. They were taken! My belief is that the Pyramid Priests know where I am at all times."

She continues, "They know that we are here. Judas' understudy, Haradah (fear), and Arkite must be working together to destroy the scriptures. I know Haradah has been promised great rewards if he can destroy the scriptures and us at the same time."

Suddenly, the truth strikes me why it is so important for me to take a written copy of the scriptures to certain designated monks. It is because they will hold the only surviving written word of God that has been given to us by Him. The monks will be the source of His word. Have all of my efforts to save my people been for naught?

I put a safety pack on Vera's back and then my own. I check her body armor. I check my super laser. I am ready to do whatever it is that I must do. I follow Vera. She pulls my arm and says, "Achilles, move! We are in danger."

I follow. I already know we are in danger. I wonder if we can live through it. A secret door opens. Vera shows me how to work the mechanisms. We enter. It is dark. I am glad that I had put on the utility belt. We have light. We would have been lost without it.

My mind is racing. We have, in effect, moved into the submarines! My mind wanders. Since all loyal Space Command people are on the core ships and since Central Command is guarded by automated equipment, the Space Command can operate by itself. It can withstand many attacks without loss of life. I am nervous and I wonder if I have misjudged the timing of Federation attack.

My mind repeats some scripture to me. "And there will be voices, thunder, lightning, fire and hail from Heaven above. . . ."

Vera has a receiver so she can hear the broadcasts of The Federation beamed to the Pyramid Control Information Center. It is obviously manned by Haradah.

The transmission states, "The Federation will destroy all aircraft rising above the surface of the Earth." I again remember the scripture and in part it says, "A mighty mountain will be thrown down from Heaven and one third of the sea will turn red and one third of the ships and one third of the life therein will be destroyed."

Vera was impatiently motioning me to follow her. The Cannon Law forbids the removal of the scriptures from the Pyramid unless they are in grave danger of destruction! Damn it! They are in grave danger! Cannon Law is not applicable! I pray that we do not lose them!

A priest appears before Vera! I shoot over Vera's shoulder and hit him in the head. He instantly dies. Vera says, "Thank you. We must hurry!" I agree. We dropped down to the lower level. I feel trapped. Vera points to a stone. I am about to pick it up out of the floor when three men rush into the room. They had not detected me since I am stooped down over the floor. I shoot three quick blasts. They are dead.

I pick up the stone and get the scriptures. I am turning to leave when Vera jumps in front of me. A laser hits her armor. I shoot three more people. I shout, "Vera, are you all right?" She replies, "I am shaken but all right. Get the scriptures and let us get out of here and damn fast!" We do!

We use the secret door to get out into the open air. We use my power pack because Vera's was destroyed by the laser fire that hit her in the back. We fly to the roof of a building close by. Vera is clinging to my utility belt and the scriptures are hung around my neck so I could control our flight. This required me to have free arms. She says, "Achilles, you better land now!" I do.

I take a line from the utility belt, lower Vera and the scriptures to the street below. I give the emergency call to Mercury II and then fly down to her. As we are running down the alley a group of Pyramid guards followed by Haradah confront us. I waste no time! The sun is rising! I blasted the whole group before they knew what had hit them.

I take a quick look to see that they are dead and take Haradah's communicator. Vera suddenly says, "Achilles, did you put the fake stuff that looks like the scriptures back under the stone like I told you?" I reply, "Brilliant! Now you remind me!" Her face turns white. I smile and say, "Yes, Sweet One. I did."

She looks at me, laughs and says, "Where in hell did you come up with Sweet One?" Mercury lands right behind us, we jump into the limousine and speed home. I know that the modified rescue craft will be waiting.

As I rush into the room I see ashen faces. Orion says, "We heard reports were flashed from the Pyramid to The Federation that you and Vera were caught in the act of taking the scriptures. Vera, you were shot. You were seen on the floor with the scriptures in hand. They showed priests taking out the scriptures and destroying them. I look at Vera and say, "You do have allies! Thank God!"

I say, "Orion, the truth is that they have pictures of me on the floor replacing the scriptures with false ones. Vera was shot in the back. It blew her back pack apart but her body armor protected her. I believe that The Federation will not expect that a rescue craft will be flying to Tibet."

I order, "Orion, fly us to the spot that Vera alone knows in Tibet. Vera and I will sleep later." Ashley says, "You both are exhausted. You must rest!" I reply, "We fly now or forever lose our chance to deliver the scriptures! You know, the ones that you keep reminding me must be delivered?"

She gives me a wan smile, hugs me and Vera and says, "God be with the three of you." We fly towards Tibet.

Orion says, "Vera, we are headed to Tibet but Tibet is a big place. It would be nice if I knew where in Tibet." Vera says, "Orion, you act like your father. He always insists on knowing where he is going. I am working on it!"

Orion says, "You are working on it now?" We are looking at each other with quizzical expressions on our faces. We do not say a word. She finally says, "The area that you must locate in the Himalayas is Lombo Kangra. Fly over the southern part of the Caspian Sea over Kabul then southeast by east to Lombo Kangra."

She orders, "As you get closer there will be a signal that sounds somewhat like a cat meowing. Follow that sound. There are glacier fields nearby. The mountains are rugged and jaggy. You will see a small plateau that houses a stone-built monastery. This little cube holds the dialect that you must set into your voice conversion units." We set them.

I was about to open my mouth when Vera says, "Stop asking questions and pay attention." I say, "I have not asked any questions!" She replies, "Don't." Emotions are high in the monastery. One false move and our mission will be incomplete. There is silence as we approach. I do not know how we can land. I see nothing but mountain parts and boulders. Orion does a magnificent job. We land.

A monk approaches and Vera talks to him. Their greeting does not make sense to Orion or to me. The monk smiles and says, "I received your last communication and we are excited to see you arrive as expected. I see that your promise has been kept, Holy One. We have been anxiously awaiting your appearance. Will there truly be a great flood?"

Vera answers, "Yes, there will be a mighty flood and it will rend our civilization apart. Noah and his tribe, not part of our civilization, will survive to lead our people toward the understanding that we all have one God, a loving God, who will always be with us if we let Him. The Savior, as well as others before Him, will come to study these scriptures. This savior who comes to study these scriptures will be the son of God."

She lectures, "A virgin will bear His human body and give Him birth. The job of your people will be to train him to be a rabbi. Do not let these scriptures be destroyed or changed in any way!"

She orders, "Achilles, please hand the scriptures to the High Priest." He accepts the scriptures from me, looks at Vera and says, "What you have commanded I will do. Holy One, God be with you!"

He then looks at me and says, "So you are Achilles and this is your son Orion. I am honored to see you. The terms we negotiated concerning the delivery of the scriptures are that the leader of the doomed civilization is to deliver them to me himself and hand them directly to me. Are you the leader of the doomed civilization?"

I say, "I am the leader and these are authentic scriptures that I give to you. They have guided us and told us how to live together. They tell everybody how to do so. They tell us about the will of God, about His amazing grace, His love for all His people, His rules for basic morals, His admonition to have respect for one another and His reminder to love one another."

I explain, "We followed this code and became affluent. Now we do not see the values that got us peace and wealth and because of this we have failed. I am sorry that this is so but it is! Orion and I are honored to see you."

He smiles and continues, "We would be honored to have you stay with us and teach us what you know but I understand that fate has given you a short tether. May God and His Power be with you and may your remaining missions be accomplished!"

He also accepts a cube of knowledge and asks, "What do I do with this?" I answer, "Keep it in a safe place for now. Perhaps mankind will in the future attain the knowledge and the moral base to know what to do with it."

He smiles and says, "Achilles, be not so fast! Tarry just a minute for it is important to me. I want to know what you think karma really is. You have given me a cube of knowledge that I cannot use and the Code of Life that we will come to understand and will follow. However, each one of us has been given life and with it we have been given karma. How are we to know what that karma is?"

I say, "Holy One, each one of us has been given at least one special talent and some have been given several talents. As we move along the path of life we find that we can do some things better than most people can. This is the clue. Our job is to develop our talent or talents by study, contemplation, education and prayer. We must then use them, make them grow and perhaps develop other talents to help other people along our pathway of life. We must be sure that, at all times, our deeds are useful to others and that they do not violate the Code."

I continue, "For instance, some people are good at languages, some are great administrators and some are good teachers. These talents are useful to others. We must never bury a talent but we must use it and expand it. This will please God! A buried talent will not please Him! Expanding our talent or talents will lead us along our path to the accomplishment of our karma."

I now say, "I delivered to your hands the Code that will help many people to understand God and the Code. My path required that I develop many talents to enable me to do so." He ponders and says, "It is strange to talk with a warrior with such heady remarks! I understand them. Thank you, Achilles. You have done well. May God always be with you!" I reply, "May He always be with you now and forever!"

We fly away.

I say, "Vera, I think that I am missing something. You are the High Priestess?" Vera says, "Stop smiling! I made contact with the High Priest sometime ago because I was told that in Lambo Kangra the High Priest had mastered the art of deep meditation and tapping into the left parietal lobe. He calls it interconnectedness."

She explains, "These monks are part of a tribe of ancient wandering monks that settled in Tibet. They believe that the tree shows the strength of life because it has withstood all of nature's furies and lives on to protect other life, flora and fauna. It is often killed so that other life could build shelter against the fury of nature. Interesting is it not? Our Savior will die for us!"

She continues, "These monks have the core belief that a progressing soul must have pity, kindness and patience if it is to have an everlasting life. I sent a very trusted priest to find this monk and verify their ability to form his mystical connection. He did this by using our translating and decoding equipment to talk with them. I also was able to connect directly to them by using your technology, Achilles." I say, "You did not ask my permission!"

She just looks at me and says, "Do you want the rest of the story or not, Big Shot!" I knew better than to make the statement in the first place.

Vera continues, "We exchanged ideas about what we had found through our deep meditations. I told him that I was a high priestess in charge of the Inner Sanctum in the land of the Pyramids. After we had talked together for some period of time he began to call me Holy One. He had heard of the giant pyramid prayer structures built by the people who landed on Earth in craft surrounded by fire. He says that they were from the lands of the gods."

She continues. "We began to set up time periods with these monks so we could share our recent meditation experiences. We established the fact that their God is our God."

Vera says, "During this period he told me that God had told him that his monastery would be the recipient of the Scriptures of Life and that he must spread the principles to as many people as possible so that eventually the world would receive them."

Vera continues, "It is the choice of each one of us to believe or not to believe. We talked about the visit of the Son of God and His mission to spread these words of God to all peoples on the Earth." I say, "Vera, with God's help we did deliver the word!"

Vera says, "Yes, Achilles! Remember the Holy One told me that he will know that God told you to deliver these scriptures to me for safekeeping only if you are the leader of the people who built Pyramids to worship God and tell him so."

She explains, "That, Achilles, was a conundrum. Just who was that leader going to be? God knew but I did not know nor did you. Now you understand why it was so vital that you hand him the scriptures, to be used for the good of mankind, and explain that you are the leader of the Pyramid People. This was the key needed to make the mission successful."

We fly directly to Roland's house where all of my clan is staying. Apollo says, "Welcome home, Dad. We have the 3,000 fully loaded, automated and programmed robotic escape craft. Each is under a stealth umbrella. They are located near each big city. Your seven real spaceships are among them as requested. As soon as your seven craft rise from the Earth the others are triggered to rise with you and fly the course that you have set. At the same time all of our people's rescue mini-craft will fly and keep a low profile skimming along the surface of the Earth to their designated spots."

I have about three hours to sleep with Ashley and then I will not see her until I return to Mount Olympus. We both weep after cuddling. I fall asleep.

I must get to the last, albeit virtual, meeting on time because there will be no wireless or any other long distance communication after we try to escape the rogue Federation armada. They will sweep all satellites from the skies. Some mini-craft may be able to communicate, for a while, after the flood subsides with our submarines.

It is time. Ashley and I have a very tearful parting and she and Arphaxad leave for the submarine attached underneath Noah's Ark. This will be their home until after the flood subsides.

It is time for the Union's people to leave. We have our final meeting. Things will never, ever be the same. All leaders of the Union are participating in this virtual meeting.

Odysseus is following the agenda that everyone in the Union has read. This is a very intense meeting and some very revealing things are happening. Each city, burg, community and area has picked its spot to land and wants to land as a group.

They have picked areas all over the globe but the favorites are the mountainous areas of India, Central America, Northwestern South America, Iran, Afghanistan, Pakistan, Tibet and the mountains between the Caspian Sea and Turkey.

Each group will keep its present leaders such as the mayors, policemen, firemen, and organization leaders intact. The group is expecting me and my Seven Spartan Battleships to defeat Arkite who, I think, is now part of the renegade Federation Forces.

The people want me to assure them that they will not be slaughtered by The Federation. It is amazing what they expect me to do. What do I tell them?

Obviously, I assure them they need not fear The Federation for I will cripple them so heavily that they will leave all our people on Earth alone. Our people have nothing to fear. They will not be killed. I know that they believe me.

I am still surprised and puzzled why very few people said that they want to come to Mount Olympus after the flood. They do fear that the formation of a single global nation will demand obedience and enslave them. They are correct. Big government has no soul.

This feeling is being voiced by people in Atlantis (Magoganian capital) and Sitnalta (Goganian capital). They complain that politicians circulate in their own society and

cocktail circuits, think that only they are the highly sophisticated ones and that only they know what is best for the
people and will not listen to the people!

Obviously, it seems to them that the elected national
representatives have, in effect, lost touch with the people.
They fail to represent the voice of the people. It seems to
them that the elected officials think of nothing but main-
taining their power position even if it requires lying, cheating, deviating from the law and avoiding responsibility for
their actions and avoiding God.

The people see that they have become elitists with tremendous egos. The people want freedom instead of being subjected to draconian laws and taxes. It appears that
freedom is in the heart of every soul. The government, by
not recognizing this fact, not appreciating their people and
letting them benefit from their efforts, destroys the individual's feeling of self-worth.

Further, putting citizens on a welfare-entitlement program so they will be totally dependent on the government
is not the answer. A dependence mentality is dangerous for
the people. It will not help them accomplish their karma.
Big government does not solve problems. It not only
creates problems for their people but it multiplies them
exponentially!

Effective smaller-sized governments can and will moti-
vate people by rewarding them for hard work. Individuals
working together in a common cause will bond.

Eventually, any government that does not see that bonding together is the solution will truly be totalitarian.

I can see that the people's view of the seven submarines
is that these ships are captained mainly by my Original
Seven or their selected replacements and Orion who captains the sub underneath the Ark, which is favoritism and
reeks of oligarchy! Maybe they are correct.

I thought that the only way to preserve our civilization
was to have the experts and leaders available to act as a
group. However, this cannot be done without the people.

After the flood there will be no satellites of any kind around the Earth so communications, as we know it, will not exist. No factories such as the Madagascar cave system or any other system will exist. We will be starting from the basics. Without educated progeny knowledge will be lost. If we cannot keep this knowledge alive after the flood it will take millenniums for the human race to get back to the civilization we now enjoy.

I stop musing. I sound the alarm. The plan to escape is now in progress. My seven ships are manned. I fly by power pack to mine. Originally, my plan was to mingle with the 3,000 space craft, each take a direction and lock into the decoys traveling that way. Five months later when the decoys turn around we will be amongst them.

We will all meet and face, I fear, the waiting Federation Armada.

At the last minute just prior to when my seven real Space Fighters are manned I change plans. Perhaps there had been a mutiny on the Federation Mother Ship. Why else would they turn into renegades and make mockery of the scriptures. Who else? Arkite!

Any other explanation makes no sense. If we can defeat The Federation forces there may just be a chance for a counterrevolution and if that happens The Federation will leave for their homeland.

If I can set up a monitoring station on Mars and listen to The Federation broadcasts we might figure a way to do just that! I asked for a volunteer to join with me.

I know that it is very likely that we will be discovered. Knowing Arkite leads me to think that he would suspect that someone from our group would remain close by to monitor The Federation.

He is paranoid about interlopers because he, himself, is one. I do know enough about The Federation and their firm belief in God to realize that someone in this renegade unit will try to reach the homeland and tell of the mutiny if there has been one.

Pete immediately volunteers to go with me. Zadoc takes over his submarine. Pete says, "I cannot let anyone else follow such a cockamamie plan. You will get caught and we will lose a fighting machine. Just how are you going to listen to Federation conversations, let alone, a spurious one?"

I reply, "Remember, I was with Vera a few days ago in the Pyramid trying to get the scriptures out and trying to discover how Haradah was able to communicate with Arkite without any of us knowing about it?"

I relate, "In the melee, after we had the scriptures, I killed Haradah's righthand man. I took a strange looking box-like communicator from his body. I duplicated it."

I continue, "There was no doubt in my mind that the information in this gem will tell me how Arkite was able to hack into Federation communications. Obviously, this piece of equipment had been taken from the Federation Security office. The informer had integrated this into the Pyramid's communicator."

I say, "I intend to listen and not talk. However, one never knows, I might report a mutiny." I smile. Pete says, "You scare me!" I have a question, "How are you going to communicate with a system light years from us?"

I say, "Have you forgotten about tachyons? The Federation knows the secret of how to break the light barrier and travel at speeds we could never imagine. If tachyons can do it then a spaceship can do it! We found out how to get communications with our tachyon probes so, obviously, the Federation can do it."

Pete just looks at me and says, "Am I as insane as you are? I must be because I follow you!"

CHAPTER 7

The Final Battle: Birth of Mythology

The comets are in very clear view. This is a frightening thing to see. They will hit in a matter of hours.

I feel that the submarine force has escaped detection and that the submarines will stay hidden for at least one year. Orion's submarine with Ashley Anne will detach from Noah's Ark when the waters have settled enough so that the Ark will be stable floating alone. This, I believe, will be about seven or eight months after impact of the comets has caused havoc on the Earth.

Noah will run aground and Orion's submarine will go to and hide among the remains of Magogania. After a year has passed they will cautiously go to Mount Olympus.

We are on our way to battle and escape! The 3,000 space decoys are more effective than I had hoped. Each zigzagged in groups during the initial Federation attack and each had cannons and ammunition, mini-craft and a load of fake bodies. The decoys make rather violent maneuvers that would be impossible if they were filled with people.

The mini-crafts are all over The Federation ships drilling into the hulls and exploding inside. The Federation is obviously confused. I hear Arkite shouting orders over his communicators system. He is furious! Arkite! My guess about a takeover was correct.

How was a Serpentine Force able to take over a Federation Armada?

Our fighting ships had integrated themselves with the decoys that were programmed not to fire at us.

The melee between the decoys, our seven fighter craft and The Federation craft is spectacular. The Federation has lost about three quarters of their fleet! They never seemed to realize that our seven fighters are different from the decoys, therefore, mixed with the decoys, we can maneuver amongst the mixture of real and decoy. This aided us to obliterate their warships.

My amazement is why The Federation Armada would obey Arkite's orders. Was the leader of The Federation's Earth Cleansing Force a Serpentine? If so, then this would make sense. Did a mutiny take place? Is the Force riddled with moles?

I am sure that The Federation orders were to see that all Earth craft were destroyed. My decoys, on command, break off fighting and run in all directions at high speed. We must have managed to make The Federation believe that our entire group was, indeed, filled with people trying to escape.

The Federation does not have enough fleet left to chase all of my fleet so they all break away from the fighting.

Our destroyed decoys spew out fake dead bodies so that the skies are filled with destroyed Federation and Earth space craft parts, debris and bodies. Finding us well armed proved to be a puzzle to The Federation.

Arkite explains to his force that the Earth people will be returning to Earth or starve in space. He explained that when they do The Federation will destroy them as they attempt to return home.

The Federation craft are returning to the Mother Ship. I notice that The Federation Space Incinerators are on site incinerating all debris, including our fake bodies as well as their real bodies. They are sweeping the skies of all satellites. They are incredibly efficient machines and leave only a small amount of space dust disbursed behind them.

Our decoys are programmed to fly for five months into space then turn around and return to Earth. We have faced one of two danger points. The first was the initial escape that now appears to be winding down and the second and more dangerous point is the return to Earth.

I know very well that the return is far more dangerous than the initial escape. My calculation is that the Earth will be fairly well recovered from the tsunami effects after one year. I better be right. Gogania and Magogania will no longer be entities.

The final battle will determine when The Federation will leave for their homeland. They might well be around centuries after our final battle. I do not know.

The mini-craft escapees were instructed to remain hidden under their stealth covers until a year had passed. I feel that all of the mini-craft people will either escape detection by Federation troops or the Federation will not think it necessary to try and round up and kill isolated people. In any case, I believe that their basic plan was to disburse us. If this is so, the mini-craft escape has accomplished this goal for them.

Pete and I head toward Mars to set up a monitoring system. When we arrive it will appear that two vessels went to Mars because I had placed an auxiliary ship in my battle cruiser. Pete will fly it.

It seems that no Federation ships followed any of our remaining force that went to a holding spot in space. I wonder if perhaps their detection system did follow all craft to see where they were going. Any ship that held a steady course to nowhere was followed until this fact was apparent. Our ships that did change this pattern may be attacked!

The Federation might send out a search unit strong enough to detect possible Earth Union locations on the Moon or on Mars. Their mission will be to destroy us. Maybe my plan was not so bright after all. I will find out soon enough.

Mars is an interesting planet. At one time it had an abundant atmosphere and oceans. Life had begun. There was only one slight problem for the future of life on Mars. It was too small to hold its atmosphere and water.

There were canyons cut by mighty rivers that flowed throughout the planet at one time and one huge canyon that spanned about a quarter of the globe.

We would pick one of the smaller canyon areas as our hiding place. However, meteors are always pounding the surface because there is no atmosphere to burn them into fragments before they hit. I pray that one of them will not hit us.

There is another Mars problem that I believe will, indeed, prove to be helpful. Mighty dust storms rage periodically over the surface. We fly into one just before we land in the canyon that will be our home. Hopefully, this will make us hard to find.

We manage to set up our receivers and get them over the stealth surface that we laid down. Our surface stealth force nets now cover us and we activate all systems. We had picked a very creviced area but one that had a relatively flat bottom. We are sitting ducks! Our crew, although very small (ten people), is damn efficient.

We set up all listening devices above the nets and return to our ships. The devices begin to operate. We listen.

One day we are stunned. The monitor said, "This is Admiral Boanerges. I am called a Son of Thunder. Achilles, I have admired your innovation, wit and ability not only to strategize but your ability to execute the technical plan to make things work."

He warns, "Do not get a big head. I know how to defeat you. I know where you are and I know the secret of your fatal flaw. I know that you will not talk to me for obvious reasons. Therefore, I can make this statement without rebuttal!" He chuckles.

He continues, "As you have probably surmised, Achilles, Arkite is a First Lieutenant in the dark side forces and he has managed to cause a mutiny in The Federation Mother Ship. I and my loyal people are prisoners in the auxiliary ship."

He further explains, "Earth has always been a difficult school of learning. Our well-meaning but original mistake was to try to colonize you and speed up your process of soul education. Instead of educating you we have become infected with the virus of the Serpentines."

I am fascinated as he continues, "We made the arrogant assumption we could speed up the will of God. Lessons must be learned by working hard, doing the right thing and having total faith in God. The process cannot be hurried."

More lecture, "The virus of greed and lust for power destroyed the denizens of Eden. This led to their rebellion. Therefore, we drove you out of Eden but the evil virus implanted by the Dark forces have had their heyday ever since! One is that we let two of three tribes that escaped Eden form two advanced countries. Your Union comprising two of them has rejected God! Therefore you are being destroyed now."

I look at my crew as we wait for more. "The Tribe of Noah seems to have an understanding. Because of Noah's belief they will not all die. We will not kill them or spread them all over the globe."

He gives us more information. "I now know that there has been a mutiny in the Federation Forces. One of your virus strains, Arkite the Serpentine, and his people have infected some of my people also, but not for long!"

He continues, "I believe that Arkite has detected your landing on Mars but because you acted erratically and disappeared into the surface during a dust storm it could be interpreted that you were probably badly damaged and crashed into a ravine."

He conjectures, "The rebels report that perhaps two ships are involved in the Mars incident. Arkite has began to ponder about Mars. He has ordered his mutinous Federation followers to continue to monitor the surface of Mars for any signs of movement. This decision has given you some breathing room."

He warns, "However, Arkite has sent an unmanned probe to check you out. I can help you. Stay below the rim line and spread a modified stealth force shield over your craft and your auxiliary craft. You can appear to be totally destructed if you spread debris and false bodies over the landscape above. Follow my instructions completely. Make it look like the debris could well have been caused by two craft."

This trick must have worked! It is now getting close to the time when the decoys and the six fighters are to return to Earth. We have not heard a word from Admiral Boanerges. I wonder if he is still alive. Did Arkite have him killed?

Suddenly the speaker comes alive and says, "Arkite has detected that the Earth Fleet is returning. He is preparing for battle. He, for some reason, has dispatched two battle craft to go to the Mars crash site."

He continues, "Someone has convinced him that he should take no chances so they have been ordered to cleanse this crash site area."

He continues, "You must leave immediately and prepare to fight. Leave the stealth shield in place and hide nearby. As they come to the crash site to cleanse it you must attack them. Surprise is your only hope of defeating them. Good luck!" I order my crew to do what Admiral Boanerges advised.

We hide in a canyon near the site and let the battle craft go by. They stop to view the crash site. We hit them with two quick volleys of cannon fire and flooded their hulls with mini-craft before they could get their defenses ready. They are crippled but not defeated yet.

One ship takes after me and one takes after Pete who mans our auxiliary craft. I go into a narrow canyon. The Federation battle craft that follows me sees a quick kill. Fortunately, while waiting, I had explored this particular canyon because it has some unusual features.

The Federation craft follows because he thinks that there was no way my ship can fly through the narrow top gap. He will use all of his firepower at me the instant he thinks I will crash. I had measured the gap because I really had nothing else to do.

He did what I thought he would do. His cannons were ready to annihilate me as I approach the gap area but he hesitates, to be sure he will blow me to pieces. Meanwhile, I have gone through the gap sideways. He is obviously shocked! I went through the gap! He pulls up to adjust his position!

By this time I had pulled up just before he did and let a full blast go to his underbelly which happened to be his vulnerable area. He fought to get control of his craft but before he could get full control I let another full cannon blast at him. He blows into pieces and crashes.

Now, where has Pete gone? I knew that he would also try to use a canyon trick but the problem with it is that if the pursuing craft decides to fly higher and over the canyon one becomes a sitting duck waiting to be slaughtered.

I saw that The Federation craft was playing with him and poised for the kill. He was not aware that I had flown at ground level toward him and before he was aware of me I let a full load of cannon fire into his hull. I am sure he never knew what had hit him.

Pete cones out of the canyon and uses his firepower to completely destroy him.

We secure our mini-craft and leave.

The final battle that will determine the fate of the final space survivors is in full swing when Pete and I arrive.

All of our surviving decoys had returned to Earth as well as the remaining six battle craft. The battle is raging and it will be for some time.

We try all kinds of maneuvers. We cannot defeat the enemy. We are losing ships! I release our reserve mini-craft and launch them! They were like a swarm of mad hornets! They locked onto each of The Federation battle craft by flying through their space shields! I had learned how to penetrate the shields!

The Federation has decimated or crippled most of our ships but I notice that we and our mad mini-hornets had reduced The Federation Armada to a small group. They now are being totally annihilated.

However, both my ship and Pete's small craft are under attack.

I have secret weapons in my ship that I had brought on board at the last minute before our fleet raced into space. My reasoning was, and is, to destroy the huge Federation Mother Ship!

My ace in the hole is the cluster of three comet busters that I had loaded into my ship. My problem is to get at least one of these into the Federation Mother Ship.

Only a blithering idiot would try this stunt but I feel that I am getting help from God's shield. I must have faith.

This means that once again, I must encourage the remaining Federation Forces to attack my ship!

We have worked our way toward the Mother Ship. They must be relishing our supposed demise and see no danger.

I fire one comet buster at the Mother Ship at top speed. It hits the outer defense system of the Mother Ship and the explosion does what I had hoped. It has destroyed the shielding system and some of its weaponry!

Enemy alarms are all over the airways. I know that The Federation will detect the source of the launch. I move out with all of the speed that I can muster to lure The Federation fleet to follow me. They do. Pete's auxiliary ship is drifting and helpless.

They all follow me like angry wasps follow a victim that has disturbed their nest. I have seconds to fire my second comet buster so that it will explode in the midst of the swarm.

The combined heat waves of exploding ships and my missile has destroyed or seriously crippled all Federation Ships, including Arkite's ship.

Because of my interloper communications I hear him call the Mother Ship and tell them to prepare to receive his ship on board. They prepare. Meanwhile, I have covered my ship with smoke and appear to be helpless. The Federation Mother Ship is preparing to receive Arkite and send out the mop-up ships and some fresh fighters to assure that all of us are dead.

I manage to appear drifting but all the while I am getting very close to the Mother Ship. I wait for what seems like an eternity. The doors open to receive Arkite while the fresh ships are waiting to exit. I fire comet buster number three at full speed; it goes right under Arkite's ship just as it enters The Federation Ship's interior and just as the huge door is sliding closed because of the alarm that my missile set off as it entered.

This is better than I had hoped because it then closed the ship and the blast of the comet buster would be contained inside! The explosion in the Mother Ship is horrific and shock waves are everywhere!

Arkite's ship is enveloped in the tremendous explosion but my ship takes a terrible beating and so do I.

As the shock wave passes, I call Pete. He answers! He is okay but his ship is helpless. Mine will run but not much longer. I pick up Pete and his crew and we head to Mount Olympus.

My faithful ship returns me to Earth but it will never fly again. Why do I have the feeling that I might not either?

I break Admiral Boanerges' rule and call him over the listening device. He answers, "Achilles, I am rather busy now, thanks to you, cleansing this rat's nest of Serpentine rebels and my mutinous crew members."

He explains, "The Mother Ship, now useless, will be disposed of as well as the Serpentines. Our victory, Achilles, has been because of your effectiveness and, I might add, because I helped you achieve it. I salute you. Well done!"

My reply, "You are welcome! However, I am not letting you off the hook!" He replies, "How so?" I say, "Explain to me how it is that you can condemn Earth when you are the recipient of a mutiny by no other than Arkite?"

He replies, "We are subject to the same forces of evil as you are. Arkite took over Gogania very easily. The people listened to Arkite when he explained how he could easily take over the Earth if The Federation would cooperate."

He continues, "Unfortunately, my second in command and his crew were in Gogania at that time checking on your civil war. My second in command was not happy that he had not been selected to take my spot. I did not know the depth of his jealousy."

He continues, "Your people and mine listened to Arkite describe your Magoganian style of living and explain that they could easily all have this lavish lifestyle and be gods and goddesses under his rule with the Earthlings worshipping them."

He lectures. "My ship has been gone too long and many are restive. Since life on an exploratory spaceship such as ours is not easy and can be boring, my second in command convinced his people that mutiny was the way to go! He and Arkite planned the mutiny. Arkite is a very clever devil."

More to come, "All they needed to do was to mutiny and get rid of you. They did mutiny but they did not get rid of you. I never told him how to counter your mini-craft or how to fight your robot ships."

I say, "Then, how dare you destroy my people when you are infected with the same Serpentine virus as we were!"

He answers, "We did not send the comet. That is God's punishment."

I say, "That is a sleazy dodge!" He laughs and replies, "Accept it. We did not send the comet but our mission was and is to prevent your survivors from advancing to your present technical base again until you have the moral base and belief in God to use this base wisely."

He continues, "This mission has been extremely expensive to us in all ways. By the way, I did not know about your submarines until they began popping up all over the place. This scheme was very clever of you. Your mini-craft, I call them wasps, are all over the Earth. I know that you are going to dismantle the submarines and to build your home on Mount Olympus. I do not have permission to attack you again but there is one exception."

He warns, "If your progeny try to build the tower of learning, and I suspect they will, we will destroy it. It will be called the Tower of Babel."

I ask, "Why will you destroy it?" He answers, "You delivered the scriptures, as told, and you must have forgotten that in these scriptures it is written that your progeny, who will try to build a tower of knowledge, using the knowledge cube, will be able to speak one language and can communicate in any language with the entire world."

He continues, "Achilles, your people can do this with your translation machines and, because of this, there is no accomplishment that your people cannot achieve! Nothing will be impossible. The scriptures are very pointed in this respect."

He laments, "The souls on Earth have not matured enough to allow you to achieve the level of high technical advancement. Until you are ready to follow the basic Rules of Nature such as do unto others as you would have them do unto you, you will not be allowed to achieve this competence."

He says, "As written, your people are to be scattered all over the world. Thanks to your effective, and at the same time damnable mini-craft, this has happened. I am now worried about your Mount Olympus group."

He reiterates, "Your progeny will worship Baal, the storm god of sky and rain and crops. They will also worship the god of fertility from whom people think they will receive power from the breasts of goddesses that Baal furnishes to them for this purpose."

He continues, "I am afraid that the Olympus group will be joined by some of those scattered over the globe and they will assume the role of gods and goddesses of the denizens surrounding them because of the gadgets you will leave behind."

More lecture, "These gadgets will run out of power. From the vantage point of being gods and goddesses it will be easy to forget that there is one and only one loving God of all creation and He has given all of us a few basic rules to follow such as to love one another as you love yourself."

He predicts, "Therefore, the tower of knowledge that you will build will be destroyed."

He adds, "Further, for your information, Arkite is dead. I have seen his body. He is now in The Dark City, and will soon be the high and mighty ruler of nothing."

He says, "He will enter the Bottomless Pit shouting that he is the King of Destruction! He will be nothing forevermore!"

He adds a blessing, "Godspeed in the new endeavors you will be assigned."

I wonder what that means.

I say, "Before you go, Boanerges, tell me about The Federation! What is your authority to strike us? We have not attacked you and yet you attack us! We had to fight back."

He replies, "The sector of the heavens that contain many planets such as yours is shepherded by the Holy One in the City of Light. We are planet dwellers like you are but we have stronger ties with the City than you do because we have many Level III prophets."

He continues, "They receive their orders from the City of Light as do others at this level. We are known as The Federation."

More, "It is our job to see that no planet gets out of control and jeopardizes other planets. You were getting out of control because your technology had outstripped your ethics (concern for others), etiquette (respect for others), and you have violated the basic commandment to worship God and God alone."

He adds, "Noah will be the carrier of God's word and his tribe will survive. Words from the scriptures will be spread from Tibet and will permeate the entire world. God's Son, our Shepherd, will study them as He visits the Earth and He will be the spark that can save the Earth from extinction."

I say, "I am not sure that I agree with you but I can understand what you are saying. It has been intriguing to talk to someone from another planet. I am beginning to understand that we are at school here and that we souls will study here for a period of time."

I utter, "I hope that I can graduate sometime!" Boanerges laughs.

I add a thought, "Boanerges, may God be with you always. I want you to know that I would rather be fighting with you than against you but you boast when you say that you can defeat me!"

I can hear him chuckle as he replies, "Likewise, Achilles. You have been a real pain in my side! Someday, we just might be fighting together. Farewell, my friend."

I say, "May fair winds follow you too!"

I say, "I will leave you with a conundrum, Boanerges. If the next level is the Angel level and since I am no Angel and it seems to me, that neither are you, we might be wandering around for some time. When we meet will we be given the privilege of recognizing each other?"

He laughs and says, "Touché, Achilles! We are warriors this time but our assigned tasks and karmas are another matter. Who knows what our next assignments will be? I know there will come a time when we will work together, Achilles. Accept your assignments! You will recognize me."

The transmitter goes dead. I note that The Federation rescue craft is transferring the few living people left from the Mother Ship to the smaller auxiliary ship.

I am feeling terrible. The jolt that my body endured in my battle with the Mother Ship has affected my whole body. My insides do not feel right but I try to forget all of that when my family greets me. I am greeted with cheers and warmth.

I hug and kiss Ashley Anne and Arphaxad. I already know that Ashley does not feel well. I can feel it in her vibrations. I know that we both must see Doctor Abaris very soon.

During the night my pain is unbearable. I am given a strong painkiller by Abaris and I go into a deep sleep.

I remember seeing the flying escorts that brought me to Atlantis floating around me. I ask, "The Federation started a colony on Earth at Eden. Why?" They say, "To repeat ourselves, the Earth dwellers were failing to learn the Code of Life while in Earth School and the Federation thought that they could speed the process by sending Adam."

They continue, "It was thought by the Federation Elders that perhaps if they would build a paradise on Earth, teach the denizens on Earth about the Laws of Nature they could enlighten them with superior knowledge and help all to learn and prosper."

They say, "Instead, mainly because of the influence of Eve, Adam's wife, he chose to lead his people into rebellion against The Federation. They subsequently enslaved the denizens, and acted like gods and goddesses. It was a grave mistake!"

They relate, "Eden was obliterated and all buildings thoroughly scattered by the scavenger equipment machinery sent to Eden. The Federation thought that it had completed its task but they did not assure that all cubes of knowledge were also obliterated!"

They continue, "Your Eden survivors had two cubes of knowledge. They decided to split into two tribes. Each built new cities and flourished."

They say, "That is not a bad thing but again, just as Adam allowed the dark side to take over Eden, the builders of the Pyramids allowed Serpentines to take over."

They concluded, "You know the result, Achilles. The comet had to come. Your people drifted from God. The Federation's job was to assure that your people would not have the knowledge you have now for many, many generations."

They admonish me, "Because of Earth's scheme to build towers of learning with the cubes of knowledge as their centerpieces, The Federation will be forced to destroy the towers of learning (Babel)."

They explain, "The early Tower of Babel at Mount Olympus was destroyed not long after you died and the following one, a ziggurat on the plains of Shinar was destroyed a bit later."

They say, "The Federation found six of the seven cubes of knowledge. They destroyed each one of them. The one you gave to the High Priest in Tibet has never been found."

They tell me, "Today, as you battle for your life in Korea, your mission is to tell your story to your people. Maybe they will believe you and maybe not. It is their decision. You will have at least three stories to tell. Tell them!"

They continue, "Neither you nor Ashley, of course, lived to see Mount Olympus flourish as a haven for mythology. Other locations your people inhabited on Earth were havens of mythology also."

They say, "Ashley has graduated from the school of Earth. She is in Level III. She has been there for some time."

More, "You will now enter your present body in Korea. You have more to do. You will be spared death in Korea so you can do your task. DO it! You better complete your mission! It is vital to your soul that you do so."

I ask, "If Earth is Level II where is Level I?" Their answer, "Earth is the school for Level I and Level II. Those who chose to follow the Dark Side are at Level I. Do not join them! They have another chance to graduate to Level II but it is getting more difficult for them to accept light. Many will fail and fall into Level 0."

They explain, "If they do not accept light and they go to Level 0, they must make a final decision not to accept light and face the second death." This fits in with the story that

Admiral Boanerges told me. Arkite did not choose to accept light. He no longer exists.

I request, "Can I see how I died?"

One last time I wake up in the hospital at Mount Olympus and see that Ashley is lying beside me. We are holding hands and looking at each other. She says, "Achilles, I will love you forever. I cannot express how much I love you because the love is that deep."

I say, "I will forever love you and I will forever need you. I will know when you are near because I will feel your warm spirit envelop me. Be my Angel. You will be the strength that I will need to move forward. I cannot do it without you!"

As we both look at our grieving family members, I say, "We will love each one of you equally forever and will watch over you as you progress down the path of doing what God wants you to do."

Ashley adds, "We will help when we can but remember there will always be help when you ask God for it. We are all God's children. There are no grandchildren. He loves each one of us equally."

"We have now been called to do new tasks. Remember to do what God wants you to do and we will all be together doing His work forever. You will never be alone!"

I awaken in this hellhole called Korea. I have been given all of the information concerning this particular previous life that God wants me to have. I am to share it.

I see a chopper approaching! I start to run for it. The Chinese are firing at it. It picks up one of the Spooks, our term for the CIA agents, and flies away. Wonderful! I run for cover. As I do so I see the other Spook. He is dead but his pouch is intact.

Instinct tells me to grab it on the run. I do.

I hide again and wonder if I really will ever get out alive to tell my stories?

I know what is coming next and I am correct. My guides ask the question, "What did you learn James Edward?" I answer, "God's shield was taken away from me because I had finished my karma assignments. My job was to deliver the Laws of Nature for future souls to read and digest." They say, "That answer is not true and it is not satisfactory!"

I am shocked! There is silence. I think. I try again, "Perhaps, it was because I forgot about the right 'isms'? Their answer is, "You are getting closer, continue!" I say, "I was part of an Oligarchy (Gang-ism)!"

Their answer, "That was part of it. Your people were not truly free. Now give us the rest of the answer!" I think hard, "What did I really do wrong?" Suddenly I burst out, "Volunteerism!" They smile and say, "What about volunteerism? Think about the Pyramids."

I wonder, *What about the Pyramids?* I ponder and say, "I was wrong to push the idea that all citizens should be forced to serve one another! That is not freedom but it is tyranny! I was taking away the job of the parents! Rearing is their duty, responsibility and privilege! Anytime the government gets into the family business or charity or any myriad of other things an individual does by dictating what they must do each day, the government blunders horribly! It totally rips the fabric from an individual's ability to pursue their talents and karma!"

I continue, "The government sets up layer after layer of bureaucrats, wastes money, neglects to inspire an individual to be the best they can be, rips down the morale of those they say they want to help and, in effect, happily destroys them!" The Guides smile and say, "That was very emotional! You are correct."

After more pondering, I say "The Rules of the Pyramid Builders were simple. They were taught to practice temperance, prudence, fortitude, justice, faith, hope and charity. This is a winning combination. The Builders wandered away from these principals because they became a secret society to withhold knowledge to gain power! That same old lust of power rose again."

I continue, "For instance, the key to faith-based charity is desire. It requires that one who wishes to serve others must volunteer to do just that."

More, "Government should serve each denizen as an individual with their right to have life, to be free and be allowed to pursue happiness! Denizens are not globs of protoplasm to be manipulated by the elite. Many people did not want to come to Mount Olympus or any other center of power for that very reason."

I continue, "Dictators serve the dark forces. Citizens of any free government should want to help those not as fortunate as themselves by following the simple Pyramid Rules. Governments do not have a soul. People do!"

My guides disappear. I am alone. I pray and say, "God, I am here and I am flawed. I am in need of Your shield; I need You; I love You; I need Your help. I will need Your grace and Your love forever. Amen."

I hear nothing but the wind around me and I am afraid but, nonetheless, I feel a strength growing within me. I am sure that I will live to tell these stories.

Even if I do live and even if you do read these recollections they will be useless unless you consider each day what kind of waves have radiated from the stones you dropped into the pond that surrounds you!

Your actions have an effect on others each and every day. Your destiny, your fate, and your life's path are being shaped by the amount and direction of your activity.

CPSIA information can be obtained at www.ICGtesting.com
Printed in the USA
LVOW090706240512

283063LV00001B/3/P